The Adventures of
Sonny Gogo and Tobo

By

JENNIFER HASHMI

Other Works by the Same Author

The Adventures of Sonny, Gogo, and Tobo: An Epilogue

Talks With Jesus

The Ruby Ring and the Black Knight

Merriol and the Lord Hycarbox

Gleanings

Poems for the Young and Not-So-Young

Le Grand Meaulnes, an English translation

ISBN: TBA

PublishNation
www.publishnation.co.uk

CONTENTS

Introduction

Sonny, Gogo, and Tobo, and their Adventures

This book is a compilation of four books published previously, "Sonny, Gogo, Tobo, and their adventures", "Further Adventures of Sonny, Gogo, and Tobo", "Sonny and the Heroic Deeds", and "Sonny Falls into the Mystery". These books have been edited and revised to form one complete narrative.

The Sonny stories depict a civilization that lives in harmony and mutual co-operation. Disasters occur sometimes, but a little ingenuity and enterprise can overcome the problems the peoples face. The Sonny stories expose the ways in which the bad habits and attitudes of human beings can damage their own planet. They show that people have choices in the way they live. In each story there is a dilemma which the children are able to solve. The stories are meant to show that we are not just puppets. We have choices that can affect the world in which we live.

As the story of Pongoland and the other Islands in the archipelago in the sky continues to unfold, the three boys, Sonny, Gogo, and Tobo, are seen to be maturing. Their understanding of their respective worlds, our own as well as the Islands, is developing. They become more aware of the economics and social dynamics existing between the Islands of the archipelago. Their learning-curve steepens as they do their best to put wrongs to right, and solve mysteries! The stories expose economic inequalities, and a little bitterness, existing between some of the islands, and look for ways of developing the resources of poorer islands. Friendships among members of different islands are formed, and a spirit of co-operation for the mutual benefit of all is envisioned. Two stories surround the mystery of the disappearance of somebody's night-wear, and the events lying behind this strange occurence! Another is about the sort of disaster which so often accompanies efforts to solve social dilemmas. A moment's forgetfulness can result in unforeseen consequences! Each story has a disaster to resolve or a mystery to unravel. Whatever the circumstance, with their usual resourcefulness the three boys, with the help sometimes of a wise adult, find a solution. Sonny Gogo and Tobo through it all learn to develop their skills and aptitudes.

The book begins with ten short stories, followed by much longer ones as readers have come to know the characters. These are stories for children, and the world portrayed is a safe one. There is magic in the air but no-one casts spells. The magic is discreet. It is never used as an exercise of power. Madame Fulati has a herb garden from which she makes poultices, powders and syrups to heal the peoples of all the islands. Her herbs have magic properties but the magic is probably no doubt, advanced science?

As the stories advance it becomes clear, in fact Gogo explains this to Sonny, that the islands are not places to be reached or bumped into by Earth's airplanes. The words are not said, but the meaning is clear, that the islands exist on a different dimension from that of Earth. The dimension can be crossed on the back of a Pongo owl, but no physicist could devise a way to make the journey.

The society of the islands is benign. Each island is ruled by its own King. He organizes food distribution, and ordains celebrations or festivities. He dispenses justice in any simple way this is needed. He is given respect but no-one fears him. The Kings of the islands are in contact with each other and liaise with each other in all inter-island matters. The islands "go on forever". Islanders visit, usually, only those fairly close to their own. Each island has its own specialty in terms of craft, skill, or produce, and the peoples gradually learn how to share their resources when it becomes evident that the new younger generation is prepared to take matters into its own hands!

The serenity of the islands, and the good-will, in the end make Sonny sad each time he has to leave them, and anxious to return. It is a vision of society as it could be with the will to create it.

PART ONE

Sonny Goes to Pongoland

It was Sonny's birthday. His friends came to visit him and he received a lot of presents and had a cake with candles. His best present, however, came at bed-time when his Uncle arrived. He had brought a large parcel wrapped in red shiny paper. Inside it was a sort of doll. Sonny's Uncle said it was a clown. It certainly looked very jolly with a smiling face, and wearing a red beanie cap with a yellow pom-pom on it. It had blue baggy pants and a long-sleeved blue and yellow striped tunic with yellow buttons. However, it was not quite like a man because it had a pointy nose, pointed ears, and round eyes.

At night-time Sonny put it on his bed beside him with its head on his pillow. He said goodnight to it and closed his eyes. The next moment a voice said,

"I' m not a clown. I'm a Pongo." Sonny opened his eyes.

"What did you say?"

"I said I'm not clown. I'm a Pongo. My name is Gogo." The little man sat up.

"What's a Pongo?" asked Sonny.

"I'm one. I live in Pongoland. Would you like to see?"

"Oh! Yes please!" said Sonny.

"In Pongoland we are all small like me. You are big, but if you hold my hand you will be become small, and then you will be able to travel with me," said Gogo Pongo. "Take my hand."

Sonny took Gogo's hand in his, and immediately he was the same height as Gogo. They stepped on to the bedroom windowsill, and an unusually large owl appeared in the sky flying towards them from a neem tree in the garden. It alighted beside them on the sill.

"This is Goggles," said Gogo. "Climb on his back behind me. Goggles brought me from Pongoland to see what your world is like. I was sitting in that toyshop looking at the toys when your Uncle bought me by mistake! Off we go!"

3

And off they went into the night, over the treetops and under the stars. Sonny was thrilled.

After some time they saw a bright light ahead of them in the sky. It turned out to be an island, floating like a cloud, but solid. A palace with high towers could be seen at the top of a hill. Down the side of the hill Sonny could see small houses. Goggles brought them down into a green meadow at the bottom of the hill, and they slid off the owl's back.

"Please come after three hours," said Gogo to Goggles. "Now let's go and see my Mother."

He led Sonny along a path up the hillside. There were little houses on each side painted pink, yellow, green, or blue, and Gogo eventually opened a gate on the right leading to a pink-washed house. Gogo's mother appeared at the door looking anxiously at Gogo. She too wore baggy trousers but with a brown tunic.She welcomed them in, and Gogo introduced Sonny. She invited him to sit at her dining-table and gave them a lovely fruit-drink with a slice of cake each. Then she said,

"I'm very worried, Gogo." She said. "Tobo has disappeared!"

"Tobo is my younger brother," explained Gogo. "We'll go and find him Mother."

So, when they had finished their refreshments, Gogo and Sonny set off up the hill in search of Tobo. After about half an hour they reached the Palace-gates at the top of the hill where two sentries were on guard.

"Who lives in this palace?" asked Sonny.

"The King and Queen of Pongoland," said Gogo. "We aren't allowed inside, but we can walk round the outside."

They started to walk round the Palace-walls, and suddenly a little voice could be heard calling,

"Gogo!" They looked up and saw a small face at a barred window.

"Tobo! What are you doing in there?" exclaimed Gogo.

"I climbed on to a hay-cart and it brought me into the Palace. They tipped the hay into this granary, and me with it! What shall I do?" Tobo wept.

"He's always getting into a mess," said Gogo. "How on earth am I to get him out of there? No-one is allowed inside the Palace gates without permission! Tobo will be in big trouble if he is discovered."

Sonny thought for a minute.

4

"Could I go in?" suggested Sonny. "I'm a foreign visitor from another land after all. Could I ask to meet the King? And then try and get Tobo out?"

Gogo was startled at a suggestion coming from Sonny, but at the same time hopeful.

"Let's try it," said Gogo, and they went to talk to the sentries. The sentries on their part were surprised to see a small boy of strange appearance claiming a right to visit the King. One of them called a Palace servant to decide what to do. Sonny felt quite afraid, and very over-awed as he entered a large courtroom richly decorated in red and gold. At the opposite end from the door were two thrones where the King and Queen of Pongoland sat and looked at him curiously. However he walked slowly up the red carpet to the thrones, and bowed politely.

"What can we do for you?" asked the King.

"I would like to see round your beautiful Palace," said Sonny, knowing how ridiculous he sounded.

"Certainly," said the King smiling, maybe in order to find out what this strange child was up to! He asked the servant to take Sonny round. The servant was taken aback when Sonny asked specifically to see the grain stores! However he took Sonny to the passage inside the Palace wall where the carts brought their loads, and parked. There was a row of doors along the palace wall here with wooden bolts across.

"Which one do you keep the hay in?" asked Sonny.

"That one," said the servant pointing

"Please may I have a glass of water?" asked Sonny. "I'll wait here."

The servant went to fetch water and Sonny opened the door to the hay-store. Tobo was sitting on the floor still weeping, but when he saw Sonny he ran out.

"Quick!" said Sonny, and they ran to the gate and passed through. The sentries were surprised to see a little Pongo boy leaving with the foreign guest, but before they could ask questions the two had gone.

"Oh well done Sonny!" said Gogo. "Come along Tobo. Mother is very worried."

They returned to Gogo's house where his Mother ran to pick up her naughty Tobo. They didn't tell her the full story. She offered them some ice-cream to eat in the garden, and they sat laughing and joking about their adventure. Sonny even gave the other two an exaggerated re-enactment of the scene in the courtroom. Exactly three hours after they had arrived Gogo and Sonny were back in the meadow.

"Pongoland night-time starts when it's morning in your world," said Gogo. They climbed on to Goggles's back.

In no time, it seemed, they were back home and climbing in through Sonny's window. They were both very tired after their adventures and in two minutes were asleep.

In the morning Gogo said not a word, but as Sonny got up he gave a big wink.

Gogo and the Electric Train

During the days following Sonny's first trip to Pongoland, Sonny and Gogo developed a routine. Gogo made Sonny promise not to tell anyone he was not a toy. Sonny did not even want to because if grown-ups found out Gogo could walk and talk they might lock him up in a zoo. So during the day Gogo rested. He slept a bit or watched Sonny play, and Sonny gave him things to eat.

At ten o'clock every night Goggles, the owl, was waiting for Gogo in the neem tree to take him home. Sonny begged to go again to Pongoland, but Gogo said he should not go too often because he needed his sleep.

Gogo was very interested in Sonny's toys, especially the electric train. When he saw it, he could hardly wait till night-time to ask Sonny what it was. There were no trains in Pongoland, so Sonny explained about trains, and railway-stations. Gogo wanted to take it to Pongoland to show Tobo, but Sonny said firmly no. He liked Tobo, but who knew what the naughty Pongo might do? And if the train got damaged or lost in Pongoland Sonny would have a difficult time with his parents. He let Gogo play with it for a while and then went to bed.

When Sonny was asleep Gogo got up and wound up the train again. The train set off at high speed straight through the bedroom door across the passage and into Sonny's parents' room. Their light went on. Gogo leapt on to the bed and lay still. Sonny's Mother came in saying,

"Sonny what are you doing up at this time of night? You should be asleep." Sonny was asleep, but he roused and looked round.

"Go to sleep now. I will keep the train in our room." She left and the other light went off. Gogo lay still for a few a minutes and then got up again. Goggles had come. Gogo had an idea.

"Goggles tonight we will bring Tobo here," he said. "I want to show him Sonny's toy-train."

Off they flew. Within an hour they were back with Tobo behind Gogo on Goggles' back. Tobo was thrilled. His Mother had not wanted him to come, but he had begged so hard that she had agreed. Gogo brought the train for Goggles to take into the garden, and the owl placed Gogo and Tobo beside it. Gogo wound it up and set it running along a path. He explained to Tobo about trains and railway-stations.Tobo was very excited and immediately wanted to wind the train up too. Gogo let him have a try. Tobo wound it up and placed it on the grass. Off shot the train, and the next minute, splash! The train had driven straight into the garden pond. There was a sound of bubbles and it sank to the bottom.

"Oh Tobo!" groaned Gogo. "Now look what you've done! How are we to get it out? What will Sonny's parents say?"

"I'd better fetch Sonny," said Goggles.

"Oh dear, he'll be very cross," said Gogo.

Sonny *was* cross. So cross he forgot to welcome Tobo. Tobo stood penitently while Gogo and Sonny thought what to do.

If I climb into the pond my pyjamas will be wet and then what will my Mother say?' said Sonny. "We'll try and fish it out somehow. I'll get a spade."

They poked in the water in the dark, disturbing the fish and the mud at the bottom of the pond, but they couldn't raise the train.

"The clock-work will be all wet!" mourned Sonny.

"You mean it won't work?" asked Gogo dismayed.

"I don't know."

Finally Sonny had to climb into the pond, and Goggles left the wet train and the wet Sonny back in his bedroom. Then he took the dejected Pongos back to Pongoland. Sonny dried the train as best he could and changed his pyjamas and got into bed.

The next morning Gogo lay looking at Sonny. His Mother came in. Sonny was very worried. What would she say about his pyjamas? And the train? But she put out his day-clothes and said nothing. When she left to go and make breakfast Sonny turned to Gogo.

"Wait till she sees the train!" he said. He went through to his parents' bedroom to look at it, but there it was on the floor as good as new and perfectly dry! He went into the bathroom where he had left his dripping pyjamas, slimy with pondweed, and they weren't there!

He returned to his bedroom and looked in the cupboard. His pyjamas lay there clean and pressed.

Sonny turned to Gogo, in surprise, but Gogo Pongo merely winked.

That night he asked Gogo,

"What happened to my train and my pyjamas?"

"It was daytime in Pongoland," said Gogo, "and the sun was shining. After I'd left Tobo I came back here for your things. I took them to Pongoland and Mother washed your pyjamas and hung them out. We dried your train in the sun and Mother polished it and oiled it. It's as good as new. I got back only an hour ago."

"Oh…. well thanks," said Sonny.

Pelids in Pongoland

Sonny lived in a small house in a small town with his Mummy and Papa. He was a very lucky boy because he had a Pongo friend called Gogo. To everyone else Gogo Pongo looked like a toy clown with a pointed nose, and pointed ears. He wore a red pointed hat with a yellow pom-pom on it, baggy blue pants, and a long-sleeved blue and yellow striped tunic with yellow buttons. But he was not a toy. He was a visitor from Pongoland. He had been looking at toys in a toyshop when Sonny's Uncle bought him by mistake and gave him to Sonny. During the day he lay still like a toy, but at night-time he got up. Once, he had taken Sonny to Pongoland.

Now it was nearly Diwali and Sonny was very excited. He told Gogo all about Diwali and the fireworks and lights and sweets and Gogo was thrilled.

"Can I bring my little brother Tobo to see the fireworks?" he asked.

"No," said Sonny firmly.

Tobo was very loveable but who knew what mischief the naughty little Pongo would get up to with fireworks around?

That night Gogo took Sonny along with him again to Pongoland. Goggles, a large owl, waited every night in the neem tree in Sonny's garden to take Gogo home. When Gogo took Sonny's hand Sonny became Gogo's size. Goggles flew across to Sonny's window-sill and the two climbed on to the owl's back.

Away flew Goggles up over the tree-tops and under the stars. After some time they could see a light in the sky. That meant they were approaching Pongoland. When it was night-time in our world it was daytime there. The owl landed in the usual green meadow and Gogo and Sonny jumped off his back. Sonny saw the steep path leading up the hill in the distance. At the top he could see the towers of the Palace where the King and Queen of Pongoland lived. There were lots of houses on the hillside and Gogo's Mother lived in one with pink walls. Pongos were out walking and doing their shopping or visiting friends. Both men and women wore baggy trousers and tunics like Gogo's but in varying colours. Tobo was out playing and ran to meet them. His Mother was pleased to see Sonny again, and gave him a large piece of cake.

"The Pelids are here again," she said to Gogo.

"Oh dear," said Gogo. "The Pelids live on another island called Pelidoland. They are very greedy for fruit. As soon as it is ripe they eat up all their own. Then they come around, travelling on their large white birds, stealing other peoples'. We'll go and see, Mother," he said.

Gogo, Sonny and Tobo set out to find the Pelids. The fruit trees were in an orchard near the top of the hill just below the Palace. All kinds of fruit grew there and all the Pongos got their fruit from these orchards. The road wound steeply up the hill, and as they approached the orchard Sonny could see about a dozen strange-looking men. They had long thin legs and feet and thin arms with long pointed hands. Their ears were pointed and they had long noses, and below these very fat tummies. They were running out of the orchard with bags and cloth bundles full of fruits.

Gogo shouted, "Hey!" but they ran away.

In a field next to the orchard there were large white birds with long legs. The Pelids climbed on to their backs and away they flew before Gogo and Sonny could reach them. Tobo came up panting.

"They'll come again next Saturday. My friend Tilbo heard them say so," he said.

"Can't we think of a plan to stop them?" said Sonny.

"What plan?' asked Gogo. "If we stop them one day they come another."

"I have to think," said Sonny.

During the next days he thought hard. Then he had an idea.

"I kept my birthday money to buy extra fireworks," he told Gogo on Thursday night. "I'll buy them tomorrow and we'll take them to Pongoland!"

He bought as many bombs and crackers as he could, and on Friday night he went with Gogo to Pongoland. He took the fireworks and a ball of string in his school bag. He and Gogo had formed a plan. When they reached Pongoland they went straight to the orchard. It was Saturday now in Pongoland, and the Pelids were due. Gogo and Sonny tied the fireworks one by one along the string. Then they hid with the first firework behind a bush to wait for the Pelids.

Sure enough in a little while they arrived with empty bags and baskets. Sonny waited till they were near the trees. Then he lit the first firework

12

behind the bush. It flared and the flame ran along the string to set light to the next firework which went off in about ten sharp cracks. The flame ran along the string again to the next firework which was another another bomb, and on again from fire-work to firework until all the fireworks had exploded. The Pelids were terrified. They leapt and shouted, not knowing where the next explosion would occur. Then they turned and ran. In no time Sonny and Gogo saw the white birds soaring into the sky with the frightened Pelids on their backs. The Pelids had never seen a firework before. How Sonny and Gogo laughed!

"I don't think they'll be back again this year," said Sonny, "if ever!"

Sonny and the Lost Key

The day after the adventure in the orchard in Pongoland Gogo lay impatiently waiting for bedtime. When Sonny's Mummy had left the room Gogo sat up.

"Sonny!" he said. "The King of Pongoland heard all those fireworks and wanted to know what all the noise was. I went to the Palace to explain to the King and Queen. They were delighted. Sometimes they don't have enough even for jam for the year because the Pelids have stolen so much fruit. They want to thank you and they're going to give a party in your honour!"

"A party!" exclaimed Sonny.

"Yes. It will be held in the courtyard of the Palace and I have to take you there tonight. There'll be games and a feast and they will give you a present." Sonny was very excited.

"But if I put on my best clothes," he said, "they'll get dirty and creased and Mummy will wonder what I've been doing."

"The King has sent special royal clothes to our house for you to wear. Let's go."

In Gogo's house several people had gathered. Gogo introduced Rennot, a friend of his Mother, a jolly Pongo lady in a green and yellow striped tunic, Tobo's friend Tilbo, and two of his own friends, Bevet and Purdy. Laid out on Gogo's bed was a special Pongo suit for Sonny to wear with gold and silver stripes and a gold cap with a silver pom-pom on it. Just then Tobo came running in.

"Mummy!"he cried. "The Queen has lost the key of her storeroom where she has locked all the party food! Without the key there won't be any party!" Every one was dismayed.

"Let's go and see," said Gogo. He and Sonny ran up the hill to the Palace gate where two sentries were on guard as usual.

"This is Sonny," said Gogo. 'The party is for him and we have to see the King and Queen." The sentries called a servant to take them to the courtroom. Gogo and Sonny bowed to the King and Queen.

15

"Ah Sonny, the foreign visitor!" winked the King. "We are very pleased to see you. You did us a great service and we want to give a party for you."

"But I've lost the key to the store-room," said the Queen.

"When did you last see it your Majesty?" asked Sonny.

"When I put it back in the office after locking up the food," said the Queen.

"Has anyone been in the office since?" asked Gogo."

"No," said the Queen. "The door is locked."

"May we go and see?' asked Sonny.

"Please do," she said. She told the servant to take them. In the office was a desk and a cupboard and on the wall was a hook for the storeroom key, but no key was on it.

"The window is open," said Sonny.

"Yes but see out of the window," said the servant. They looked and saw that the office was high up one of the towers.

"So no one could come in through the window," said Sonny.

"Except birds," said the servant.

"Birds are used to carry messages," explained Gogo. "There are quite a lot of islands and birds carry people and letters."

"Suppose one had come from Pelidoland?" suggested Sonny. "One of those white ones."

"One did come with a message just before the Queen left the office," said the servant.

"That must be it then," said Sonny. "Could Goggles take us to Pelidoland?"

"Of course," said Gogo. They hurried down to the meadow where Goggles was waiting for his share of the party food. The journey was short and as they approached Pelidoland Sonny could see lots of Pelids with their long thin legs and round fat tummies. Gogo told Goggles to take them to the Queen's balcony. They peered through the curtain into the Queen's bedroom. She was talking to the King and holding up a key on her long Pelid finger.

"The Pongos set traps to protect their orchard," she was saying, "but they must have stored a lot of fruit. I sent my bird to steal the Pongo Queen's key. Tonight I'll send a band of Pelids to get fruit from their Palace store."

"Excellent idea," said the Pelid King. The Queen hid the key under her pillow and they left the room. In a moment Sonny and Gogo were in

16

the room. They quickly took the key and returned to the balcony. Then they climbed on to Goggle's back and flew back to Pongoland. Goggles left them in the Palace courtyard and they hurried to the courtroom. How happy the King and Queen of Pongoland were to see the key! How shocked they were to hear the Pelid's cunning plan!

"I shall hide my key in future," said the Queen.

Sonny and Gogo went back to Gogo's home to get ready for the party. Sonny looked splendid in his gold and silver suit. When they returned to the Palace tables were set in the courtyard, and Pongos were gathering. The King's servants organised games, and when the children were tired they were led to the tables for tea. What a wonderful feast it was! After tea the King called for silence. Then he asked Sonny to step forward. The King told everyone how Sonny had saved their fruit, and how he had even recovered the Queen's key from Pelidoland! Amid cheers and clapping he presented Sonny with a gold pen. The present had of course to be small in size, but this was a special pen. The King told Sonny that for the whole of his life it would never run dry no matter how much he used it.

"We have wonders in Pongoland too!" whispered Gogo to Sonny.

"Oh you have a great many wonders," said Sonny.

Gogo and Tobo Ride on A Train

Soon after the Pelidoland adventure Sonny said to Gogo Pongo,

"Next Sunday we are going to visit my grandparents and we are going in a train. I'll take you with me so that you can see the train."

Gogo was thrilled.

"Can I bring Tobo here on Sunday morning so that he can go too?" he asked.

"Yes if his Mummy will let him come. I have to take my homework so he can go in my school bag."

So the next Sunday morning Goggles brought both Gogo and Tobo from Pongoland, and Tobo lay under Sonny's blanket until Sonny woke up. Sonny was very happy to see Tobo, and told him he must keep very still and quiet the whole day. He stood Tobo carefully down the side of his school bag, and fastened it loosely so that Tobo could peep out from under the flap.

How thrilled Gogo and Tobo were to see the trains and the railway station and all the people hurrying about! Sonny sat Gogo by the window and kept his schoolbag on his knee so that both of them could see out.

When they reached Sonny's grandparents' house his Grandmother hugged him and told him to look in the kitchen. He did so and saw there was a serving of hot gulab-jamun ready for him made by Grandmother.

He popped half of one in Tobo's mouth and the other half in Gogo's. Then he went into the sitting room where Grandfather was reading the newspaper. Grandfather also hugged him and gave him a bar of chocolate. Sonny kept this to give to the two Pongos later.

His parents sat on the verandah and Sonny went into a bedroom to do his homework. There were a lot of toys kept for him, so he got these out for Gogo and Tobo to look at. Then he sat down to do his homework. After a while he looked up, and then sprang from his chair in horror. Tobo was gone!

"Oh no," groaned Sonny. He ran to Gogo.

"Where's Tobo?" he whispered.

18

"I don't know," said Gogo. "He ran off while I was looking at the toy airplane. I daren't move in case anybody came in. What shall we do?"

"You'd better keep still here. I'll go and look for him." He went through to the sitting room but his Mother called out, "Have you finished your homework dear?"

"Not yet Mummy," he said.

"Well finish it before lunch," she said.

So he had to go back to his room. During lunch he looked around anxiously for a sight of Tobo's red and purple suit, but there was no sign.

"What are you looking for darling?" asked his Grandmother, worried that he wanted something she hadn't provided.

"Nothing Grandmother thank you. This is my favorite dish, matar-paneer," he said. Suddenly his Daddy exclaimed,

"The clock's on the floor!" And sure enough, there it was on the floor near the door.

"How extraordinary!" said Grandfather. Sonny thought that perhaps it wasn't quite so extraordinary. The next minute CRASH from the kitchen. His Grandmother hurried through.

"The pile of steel glasses has been knocked over!" she cried. "I can't see a cat anywhere!"

After lunch she gave Sonny two pieces of burfi which he kept for Gogo and Tobo. Then his Mummy told him to lie down now to sleep. What was he to do? The next moment his Grandfather came into the bedroom,

"Sonny have you been playing with my spectacles?" he asked. "They're broken and I can't read without them."

"No, truly, Grandfather," he said. "I'm so sorry about that."

Oh dear, naughty Tobo, he thought to himself. As soon as his Grandfather had gone he said to Gogo,

"Gogo this is an emergency. We've got to talk. Tobo's broken Grandfather's spectacles now. What will he do next?"

"Goggles is here," whispered Gogo. "We'll send him home."

"Goggles!"

"Yes. I couldn't tell you but Mummy wouldn't let Tobo come unless Goggles came too to watch over him. He followed the train."

"Where is he now?"

"In a tree in the garden I suppose."

Just then a penitent and drooping Tobo crept out from under the bed.

"I'm sorry Sonny," he said.

"And so you should be!" said Sonny severely. "It was you who broke Grandfather's glasses wasn't it?"

"Yes. I was trying to see how things looked through them and they fell. We don't have any spectacles in Pongoland."

"'We have clocks," said Gogo.

"I know, but I liked that one."

"Well I'll call Goggles to take you home." Sonny put the two Pongos out through the window and lay down to sleep. When he woke up Gogo was back.

"Has Tobo got home?" he asked.

"Yes," said Gogo softly.

Sonny took Gogo and his school bag through to the veranda where everyone was sitting. Grandfather picked up his newspapers sadly, and then looked at it in amazement.

"I can read the paper without my glasses!" he exclaimed. "I can even read the small print!" They were all astonished.

"How can that be?" asked Grandmother. Sonny looked at Gogo and Gogo winked.

That night at home he asked,

"What happened to Grandfather's eyes?" asked Sonny.

"We have a wise woman in Pongoland called Mother Fulati, and her daughter," said Gogo. "They make ointments and plasters and medicines and treat all of us. Their family has always done it since the beginning of Pongoland. No one else knows their medicinal secrets. After I had taken Tobo home I went to her for some drops for your Grandfather's eyes. No-one in Pongoland wears spectacles because of her drops. She also has a spray to use so that we don't feel anything that might hurt. So I brought a little of that to sprinkle on Grandfather's eyes while he was asleep. Then I could put in the drops without him feeling me."

"When can I next go to Pongoland?" asked Sonny. "I must thank Mother Fulati very much and take her a gift."

"We'll go next Saturday night," said Gogo.

Sonny Visits Mother Fulati

Gogo Pongo had told Sonny that he would take him to Pongoland the next Saturday night. Sonny bought Mother Fulati a beautiful cake out of his pocket money, and borrowed his Mother's tin to take it in. As usual Goggles was waiting on the neem tree to pick them up. Away they went over the treetops and under the stars.

Goggles put them down in the meadow, and Sonny could see the big hill of Pongoland and the towers of the King's Palace at the top, but Gogo said that today they would not go up the hill. Instead they went round the foot of the hill to the right. In a few minutes they came upon a stream running down the hill-side. On the opposite bank he could see a jungle. They climbed into a boat, which was waiting, at the edge of the river and Gogo rowed them across. Sonny held the cake on his knee. Like himself it had reduced in size when Gogo took his hand.

When they reached the other side they climbed out. The jungle loomed darkly over them. They followed a path which ran steeply up through the trees and came to a clearing where there was a fairly large wooden house with a thatched roof, and a long verandah. It was surrounded by a big garden full of many strange plants. They went up some steps to the verandah, and knocked on the door.

"Mother Fulati makes her medicines from the plants in her garden and from the jungle," said Gogo quietly to Sonny.

The door was opened by a slender and beautiful lady of maybe fifty. She had long hair tied up in a bun, and wore an ankle-length dress of green and brown. She didn't look like a Pongo, thought Sonny, though her ears were slightly pointed.

"Good afternoon Mother," said Gogo. "This is Sonny."

"Hello Sonny," said Mother Fulati with a sweet smile. "Come in."

They entered her cosy kitchen, and Sonny said,

"I have come to thank you very much for the eye-drops you sent for my Grandfather, Mother Fulati. He can read without glasses now. And I've brought you a cake."

"How kind of you Sonny!" said Mother Fulati.

"Selina," she called, "Gogo has brought Sonny to meet us. Bring them some of our special fruit-juice dear. Selina is my daughter," she told Sonny.

A very pretty girl, also with long hair tied in a pony-tail, entered the room with two glasses full of a red juice. It tasted delicious.

"I've been very puzzled today Gogo," she said. 'My cat Telipas is sitting at the top of the big tree in the garden and won't come down."

"Maybe something frightened him," said Gogo. "Let's go and see."

They went into the garden to look, and sure enough there was the black cat watching them from the top of the tree in the centre of the garden. No amount of calling would persuade him to come down.

What a strange life these ladies lived, thought Sonny, all by themselves in the jungle. They must have a lot of visitors though! As he looked round he glimpsed something black and red under one of the plants. He lifted a leaf and saw it was a huge beetle!

"What's this?" he asked. The others looked at it in amazement.

"I've never seen a beetle like that before!" exclaimed Mother Fulati. She bent to pick it up but the next moment she gave a cry of pain,

"Aah! It bites!"

"Telipas won't come down because of the beetles, I suppose," said Gogo.

"Look! There are lots of them!" cried Sonny pointing. They looked and saw the red and black beetles were all over the garden.

"They're eating through the stalks of my plants!" cried Mother Fulati in dismay.

"What shall we do?" wailed Selina.

"Let's see where they are coming from," said Sonny.

They hunted round looking under all the plants, but being careful not to touch the beetles.

"Look! Here!' called Gogo. They went to see where he was pointing and saw a narrow path leading into the jungle. Along it more beetles were arriving.

"They'll eat up the whole jungle!" cried Mother Fulati.

"Quick! Let's follow the path," said Sonny.

They ran down the path till they came to a group of black birds with long yellow beaks. They were standing in twos. Each couple held a cloth between them in their beaks and out of these cloths were running the beetles.

"Oh I see!" said Mother Fulati. "These birds arc from Galipoland. Their King wanted me to tell him the secrets of my medicines and I refused. I said his people can come to me anytime for treatment but the secrets belong with my family forever. These beetles are his punishment!" Sonny had an idea.

"Mother Fulati, that stuff you use so that people won't feel pain. Do you have much of it? Suppose we sprayed it over these beetles what would happen?"

"If it went all over them they wouldn't be able to feel anything at all till the effect wore off," she said.

"Well, could we do that now?" suggested Sonny.

"Yes, if you think it would help," she said. They ran back to the house and Mother Fulati got out her sprays and the drum she kept the liquid in for pain. These they took to the garden. Then Sonny asked Mother Fulati for two bed sheets, and they spread them on the ground. Then they set to work, spraying all the beetles.

"We'll have to work fast," panted Mother Fulati. "The effect doesn't last long."

Immediately the dazed beetles stopped eating the plants. They couldn't understand what had happened to them. They couldn't feel anything. Not even the ground under their feet!

"Gogo!" called Sonny. "Help me collect up the beetles! Quick! We'll put them on the sheets."

The two of them ran round gathering up the bewildered beetles and dumping them on the sheets. Then they tied up the two sheets like washerwomen's bundles with the beetles all inside.

"Now let's take these bundles to those black birds," said Sonny.

The four of them carried the two bundles back to where the birds were still standing. Mother Fulati spoke to them.

"Please take these bundles to your King. Tell him the people of Galipoland are free to come to me for treatment. But tell him I can never tell him my secrets, and if he damages my plants the Galips as well as the Pongos will suffer."

The black birds rose into the air with their two heavy burdens.

"Away they go," said Mother Fulati. "Thank you very much Sonny. If you hadn't had the idea of using my spray Pongoland would have been without medicine for a long time. Now come along back to the house and we'll have a celebration meal."

The Princess's Coronet

One night Gogo Pongo said to Sonny,

"The King of Maridoland's daughter is to be married to Lord Lannet who is the son of Lord Tamon in Maridoland, next Sunday. That will be Saturday night, and you are invited to attend." Sonny's eyes sparkled.

"Where is Maridoland?" he asked.

"It's one of our islands and a lot of us are going including the Galipos because their King said he was sorry for sending those beetles to Mother Fulati. Your gold and silver suit is in my cupboard. You can wear that."

Sonny could hardly wait for Saturday night and he bathed very carefully before going to bed. His Mother was most surprised! Goggles was waiting for them in the neem tree as usual and away they flew over the tree tops and under the stars.

When they reached Gogo's house they found his Mother ready in a beautiful crimson tunic with a navy blue cap. Tobo was in a new suit of pink and blue. He had been made to sit in a chair and not move before they went. Gogo's suit was navy blue and silver and Sonny's gold and silver one was neatly pressed.

All the owls were waiting in the meadow and the people were gathering. Then the King and Queen arrived and they all set off together. Maridoland was a mountainous island and Sonny could see some snow-capped peaks. The Palace itself was built into a mountainside. The Maridos cheered as they arrived. They were the same height as the Pongos but had round noses and black curly hair. The courtyard was decorated and four thrones had been arranged at one end. The King and Queen of Maridoland were seated on the centre two. The King of Pongoland called Sonny to meet them and Gogo went too. The King and Queen of Maridoland greeted Sonny, but were in great distress.

"Pongo," said the King, "the princess Ahoosti and Lannet have had a quarrel! There used to be a special coronet used at the marriages of princesses but it is lost. Ahoosti decided she wanted Lannet to find it for her. He said he didn't know where to look. She started to sulk and Lannet called her a silly goose. Now she won't get ready for the wedding! She has a kind heart really. If he had at least tried to find it she would have been happy. What are we to do?"

"Sonny here has helped us out of some of our difficulties," said the King of Pongoland. "Can you think of anything Sonny?"

"I'll try your Majesty," he said, but he hadn't much hope.

When they got back to Gogo's Mother, she greeted them with,

"Tobo's run off! If he's got his suit dirty I'll be so cross!"

"We'll look for him Mother," said Gogo.

"It's one thing after another," he muttered to Sonny as they set off through the crowds. "Oh look! A balloon man! Tobo loves balloons. Have you seen Tobo?" he asked a small child carrying one.

"Yes. He let go of his balloon string and it went floating up the mountain. He ran after it up that path." The child pointed.

Gogo and Sonny raced up the path. It was narrow and twisting, and then it came to a sudden end. After that there was only a steep drop down the side of the mountain. Had Tobo, looking up at the mountain, fallen over the edge? Gogo and Sonny looked down in horror.

"Tobo! Tobo!" they yelled.

"Gogo!" came a little voice. "I'm here!"

They looked and saw a ledge some way below with bushes growing on it. On it they could see the pink and blue of Tobo's suit. The bushes must have caught him as he fell.

"I'll get Goggles!" shouted Gogo. "You wait here Sonny."

He ran down the path. In a short while Sonny saw him flying back on Goggles. They landed on the ledge. The next moment they all disappeared! Sonny was very puzzled. Where had they gone? Then he saw Goggles flying up to him. Was Tobo hurt? But Goggles told him to get on his back and down they went to the ledge. Then he saw where the others had disappeared. There was a hole in the mountainside behind a bush. He went inside and there were Gogo and Tobo very excited.

"Look!" said Gogo. He looked and there in the wall of the small cave was a hollow, and lying in the hollow was something bright and shining. Sonny looked closer. It was a little gold coronet inlaid with rubies and diamonds. This must be the hiding place of some bird, maybe a jackdaw or a raven, since only a bird could reach this hole in the mountainside.

"The lost coronet!" shouted Sonny.

"Yes!" said Tobo proudly. "I found it!"

"Oh well done Tobo!" said Sonny. "We must give it to Lannet."

"Yes but Ahoosti wanted Lannet to find it," said Gogo.

"Well let's put it where he can find it then," said Sonny. "It's got to be an easy place because there isn't much time."

"Goggles, take Tobo back to Mummy please, and then take us back to the Palace," said Gogo to the owl.

Lord Tamon's own palace was a little further down the valley but was also built on a mountainside. They could see the bridegroom's family carriage, and the wedding party already gathering by the gate. Lannet himself was getting ready in the King's Palace. Goggles set them down on part of the roof of Maridoland Palace. They took the coronet and went softly down some steps inside the Palace. They came to a long corridor where there were lots of old paintings and statues.

"There!" said Sonny. He placed the coronet on the head of a statue of a woman. "Tell Goggles to find Lannet and bring him up to the roof. Say someone wants to speak to him."

They waited in the corridor till Lannet arrived on the roof looking very puzzled. Goggles wouldn't tell him who wanted to see him, and he couldn't see anybody at all! But he could hear someone.......

"Lannet! Lannet!" a voice called from down inside the Palace. He hurried down the steps and into the corridor.

"Lannet!" the voice called again, but there was no one to be seen. He took another few steps and stopped. There on the head of a statue of Ahoosti's grandmother was the coronet! He forgot all about the mysterious voice. He took the coronet and ran off with it down the next flight of steps. Gogo and Sonny came out from behind another statue where they had been hiding.

"So that's alright!" said Sonny. "We'd better get back to your Mother. She'll think she's lost us now."

Gogo's Mother was very relieved to see them. Their clothes were still fine, and even Tobo looked all right after she had dusted him a bit.

The wedding went forward and a smiling Ahoosti received on her black curls, by the hands of a smiling Lord Lannet, a little gold coronet inlaid with rubies and diamonds.

Sonny and the Golden Locket

After the marriage ceremony of Princess Ahoosti and Lord Lannet in Maridoland there was a big feast, and Marido acrobats, magicians, and dancers showed their skills. Then it was time to go home. The Pongos returned to their owls, which had also eaten well.

Sonny saw a lot of big black birds with yellow beaks.

"Are those birds from Galipoland?" he asked Gogo.

"Yes," he answered. "See, the Galipos are coming now."

The Galipos were taller than the Pongos and had long silky brown hair. Their eyes were almond-shaped. They went to their black birds, and Sonny saw one very finely dressed gentleman.

"Is that their King?" he asked.

"Yes,"said Gogo.

The King and Queen of Galipoland got on to their birds, but as the birds rose from the ground the Queen slipped and fell. Everyone exclaimed in horror and rushed to help her up, but she was in pain.

"My leg is broken!" she cried. The King was very upset.

"Where's Mother Fulati?" someone called.

"I'll fetch her," said Gogo.

He and Sonny ran to look for her in the Pongo group. When she heard about the accident she came immediately.

"The Queen needs one of my special plasters," said Mother Fulati. "We'll take her to Pongoland."

A Marido was sent to fetch a piece of straight wood and a bandage and Mother Fulati bound up the leg for the journey. Then they flew to Mother Fulati's house in the jungle in Pongoland. Sonny wanted to see these special plasters, so he and Gogo went along too with Selina and the King.

They all helped to arrange the Queen comfortably on Mother Fulati's bed in her surgery, and Mother Fulati got out a thick green plaster. This Selina heated in front of the fire. Then Mother Fulati carefully set the broken bone and wrapped the plaster round it.

29

The next morning at home Sonny slept late and had an early night because he was tired after the festivities. At three o' clock in the morning, however, he felt someone shaking him. It was Gogo

"Wake up!" he said. "You've got to get up. Mother Fulati took off the Queen's plaster this morning and her leg is fine, but she says her gold locket is gone! She thinks Mother Fulati or Selina took it in the night! They are very angry. She must have lost it in Maridoland. We've got to go there and try to find it."

Sonny got out of his bed sleepily and went to the window. Goggles was there waiting for them and away they flew back to Maridoland Palace.

It must be here somewhere in the courtyard,' said Gogo.

Maridos were busy cleaning up and washing dishes. Gogo told them what they were looking for and when the King of Maridoland heard about the loss he sent for them.

"Sonny," he said. "We did not need your help after all to find the princess's coronet. Lannet found it himself. But now we hear the Queen of Galipoland's locket is missing! I'm sending everyone round looking for it. Please go where you want."

They thanked him and left.

"Where was the Queen sitting during the feast?" asked Sonny.

"About here," said Gogo, pointing to a chair. "I saw her."

Magicians and acrobats were sorting out their equipment and packing it into boxes. There were gaily-coloured ball and rings, silk scarves and sticks, birds and rabbits, but Sonny and Gogo couldn't find the Queen's locket. In the end they decided to return to Mother Fulati and tell her of their failure. As they were leaving a magician hurried up to them.

"Please take one of my birds to Mother Fulati. It's looking quite sick."

"Alright," said Gogo, and tucked it under his arm. Back at Mother Fulati's house they told her they hadn't found the locket and showed her the magician's bird.

The birds of the islands understood speech and could talk a little, but this one said not a word. When Mother Fulati asked it where the pain was it just opened its mouth. Thinking it must have a sore throat she peered inside. There was a flash of gold. Mother Fulati inserted her finger and drew out a gold locket. Its fine chain had been caught round the bird's tongue and the locket had got stuck at the back of its mouth behind the beak.

"Is this your locket?" she asked, showing it to the Queen of Galipoland.

"Why yes," she said. "How did it get into that bird's beak?"

"The bird belongs to a Maridoland magician."

"Oh!......of course......I forgot." The Queen went red. "A magician borrowed it for a trick. He made it vanish and then it reappeared round a bird's neck. This must be the bird."

"He told me to give it back to you but it slipped into my throat by mistake," said the bird.

"I'm very sorry Mother Fulati," said the Queen. "I should not have accused you."

"I'm sorry too," said the King. "'We've given you a lot of trouble lately. I hope in future we'll be better neighbours. Thank you too for the plaster, after I'd tried to destroy your plants with beetles! I won't do anything like that again."

"We'll take the bird back to Maridoland on our way home," said the Queen.

"It's time for us to go now Sonny," said Gogo. "You've got school tomorrow."

Murgo Pongo Sees T.V.

For some time after the marriage of Princess Ahoosti and Lord Lannet Sonny did not go to Pongoland. His Mother said he was looking very tired, so Gogo Pongo wouldn't take him. However Gogo's father, Murgo, who was in the service of the King of Pongoland, was due home soon. He had been on a mission to a far distant island, and as soon as he arrived home Gogo promised to take Sonny to meet him.

Meanwhile Sonny took Gogo around with him a lot so that Gogo could see as much of this world as possible . Gogo especially liked to see the T.V. He could not understand how it worked. He thought the people he could see on the screen must be inside the box but Sonny said no the box was full of wires.

One night Gogo said,

"Papa is home now. I'll take you to meet him tonight."

Sonny was thrilled. Soon after midnight Gogo woke him to say Goggles had arrived, and was waiting on the windowsill. He took Sonny's hand, and Sonny became the same size as Gogo. They climbed on to Goggle's back and away they flew over the treetops and under the stars.

Gogo's father was a large handsome Pongo gentleman with a wise but jolly face. He greeted Sonny kindly and Gogo and Sonny sat talking with him. Gogo told his father about T.V. and said to Sonny.

"Why don't we take Papa now to see your T.V.? We could be there and back easily before morning in your world."

Sonny said politely that he would be happy to show Gogo's father the T.V., but there weren't any good programmes during the night.

"You mean he has to see it during your day?" said Gogo dismayed.

"Yes, it's nearly all advertising in the night, but if Goggles could bring you," he said to Gogo's father, "to our garden one night at about nine, you could see something interesting through our sitting room window."

So this was arranged, and the next night Goggles brought Murgo Pongo to Sonny's garden, and placed him in the branches of a raat-ki-rani bush outside the sitting room window. The curtains were normally closed but Sonny went and opened the one by the bush and looked out into the garden. He could see Gogo's father peering in at the T.V. set, amazed.

"What are you looking at Sonny dear?" called his Mother, "Close the curtain."

"In a minute Mummy," said Sonny. "There's an owl in the neem tree."

Sonny remained at the window as long as he could, but in the end his Mummy became impatient about the curtain and came to close it. She glanced outside and gave a cry.

"There's a face in the bush outside!"

"What!" exclaimed Sonny's father getting up. He opened the wire window and they saw Gogo's father.

"Good gracious!" said Sonny's father reaching out to pick him up. It's a toy clown like the one Sonny has, only much bigger!" Gogo's father knew he must keep very still and behave like a toy.

"I wonder whose it is?" said Sonny's Mother. "Do you know Sonny?"

"No," said Sonny in great distress.

"Well it's time for supper now," she said. "Go and put it on the shelf in your room Sonny, and we'll find out whose it is tomorrow."

"Switch off the T.V. before you go Sonny," said his father. "I've got a headache. Some of these programmers are too tiring after a hard day's work."

Sonny switched off the T.V. and then picked up Murgo Pongo who in this world was much smaller than himself. He placed him on his bedroom shelf and whispered,

"You can go home with Gogo later."

Then he returned to the sitting room. Gogo was lying on the sofa looking at him anxiously. Sonny nodded to him that all was well. At bedtime he placed Gogo bedside his father on the shelf, and the next morning Murgo had gone.

Sonny's Mother was surprised to find that the big toy clown had disappeared somehow, but although she and Sonny looked everywhere they couldn't find it.

Sonny's father however had an even bigger surprise waiting for him. When he opened the door to pick up his morning newspaper he saw a finely carved wooden box, about a foot square on the veranda. A small brass ring hung on one side of it. Underneath it was a piece of paper. It was a note addressed to him. It said,

"DEAR SIR, I HOPE YOU LIKE THIS GIFT. PULL THE RING TO MAKE IT PLAY. IT SOUNDS AS GOOD DURING THE NIGHT AS IT DOES IN THE DAY!"

Sonny's father called Sonny and his Mother to see it. He pulled the ring, which drew out on a string. Immediately the most beautiful music came from the box. It was like wind in the trees, birdsong, the splashing of mountain streams, and the shush shush of waves falling on a seashore, all in one melody.

"How lovely!" exclaimed Sonny's father. "But why does the note say it plays just as well at night?"

"I think because the T.V. doesn't," said Sonny.

That night instead of watching T.V Sonny's father went to his room to listen to his musical box as he called it.

"This is so soothing," he said. "And so refreshing."

Sonny's parents never did discover who had given the box, but when Sonny went to bed he asked Gogo what it was.

"It's a windaphone," explained Gogo. "We have very clever craftsmen in Pongoland. One day I'll take you to see them at work in metals and wood and other things. Inside the box is a bag which fills with air when you pull the ring. Then the air comes out slowly inside. Beside the bag are dozens of tiny reeds and whistles of many different sizes and shapes. The air flows through them and gives that sound. It plays for half an hour at a time. Of course children don't have time to sit listening to windaphones, but it you play one to a baby it goes to sleep in no time, and grown-ups love them. My father thought that as he likes them probably your father would too."

An Unusual Picnic

One night Gogo whispered to Sonny, "Come to Pongoland tonight. We're going to have a picnic!"

Sonny was thrilled. As soon as Goggles arrived away they flew.

At Gogo's house there was a lot of excitement. Two baskets were ready full of food, and a donkey borrowed from the Palace to carry the baskets waited at the gate. Gogo's and Tobo's friends, Tilbo, Bevet, and Purdy were there, and also a strange man. He was taller than the Pongos, but thinner, and he had straight dark hair and green eyes. Gogo's father Murgo Pongo, told Sonny that this was Kilti, and that he was a Tolik from Tolikland. He was a guest in Pongoland learning metalwork from Pongo craftsmen. Later he would go back and teach Pongo arts in Tolikland. He was to accompany them on the picnic.

The party soon set off down the hill and along the path round the bottom of the hill where Sonny had been before on his visit to Mother Fulati's house. They did not cross the stream however. They continued on round the hill to the left and then across another field, and up another hill. Kilti did not want to go so far. He said he was tired and could they have their picnic in the field? Murgo said that there would be a very good view from the top of the hill, which in any case was not very high. He made Kilti ride on the donkey the rest of the way.

Near the top of the hill they set down the baskets and the grown-ups rested while the children played. Kilti was uneasy and kept looking at his watch. He said he should be back at the workshop soon.

Murgo Pongo laughed and said, "Take a holiday for once!"

After a while Gogo's parents opened the baskets and spread out pies and cheese and trifles and fruit and cakes. They all ate well and enjoyed themselves except Kilti. Sonny thought he was very rude looking at his watch all the time and wanting to go. After lunch Murgo, Sonny and Gogo stood at the top of the hill to look at the view. Sonny could see Mother Fulati's jungle across to the right, and in front below there was a meadow. Gogo said there were meadows all round the island, and beyond them all round the very edge of the island an area of thick very thorny bushes grew to stop anyone approaching the edge.

Then they saw something strange. Three grey birds with black and red markings flew in and alighted in the meadow. On their backs were three men carrying bags. They got down from their birds and started walking towards the hill. Near the foot of the hill they disappeared from sight and Murgo, Gogo and Sonny waited to see where they would reappear. However after some minutes the three men appeared again in the same place and started to walk back across the meadow. This time their bags seemed to be quite full and heavy.

"Quick !" said Murgo. "Those are Toliks. They've collected something and are going back to their birds. We must stop them!"

"Bevet and Purdy!" called Gogo. "Come with us!"

The five of them set off running down the hill. At the bottom they could see a place where there had been a lot of digging.

"Whatever the Toliks collected must have been buried there," said Sonny.

The four children ran in front across the meadow and Murgo panted along behind.

"Get the birds!" he yelled. Then the Toliks saw them and started to run too. They had heavy bags though and the children were faster. Gogo, Purdy and Bevet reached the birds first and climbed on their backs so that the Toliks couldn't fly away.

"Now," said Murgo. "Open up those bags please." The three frightened Toliks slowly opened their bags. The others gasped! The bags were full of gold ornaments!

"I see," said Murgo. "And who buried these ornaments at the foot of the hill? Kilti I suppose? He didn't come to Pongoland to learn how to make our metal-ware. He came to steal our gold. No wonder he didn't want to come to our picnic when he saw we were coming up this hill. He was afraid we'd see you!"

"Please let us go!" begged the Toliks. "We won't do it again. You've got your gold back."

"Alright you can go," said Murgo. "But Kilti will stay here at the King's Palace until our King gets an apology from the King of Tolikland. Please tell your King that."

The Toliks flew away and Murgo and the children picked up the bags and climbed up the hill again to where Gogo's Mother and Tobo and Tilbo were watching everything.

37

"Where's Kilti?" asked Murgo.

"Look." cried Sonny. 'He's running away."

Kilti had set off running down the hill back the way they had come. Gogo jumped on to the donkey and chased after him. He easily caught up with Kilti, and then he tied him by the hands with the rope used for tying the baskets to the donkey. The others joined them bringing the empty baskets and the bags of gold.

"Kilti!" said Murgo sternly. "You will go with me to the Palace and we'll see what the King has to say about all this! You will stay there till the King of Tolikland sends an apology."

Murgo climbed on to the back of the donkey and set off with Kilti trudging behind him at the end of the rope. The rest of the party followed slowly.

"What a good thing we came up this hill for the picnic!" said Sonny. "Where is Tolikland?"

"Quite a long way from here," said Gogo. "We don't know the Toliks very well. The Maridos are our best friends. The Galipos are usually friendly. The Pelids are all right except when it comes to fruit!"

'How many islands are there?' asked Sonny.

"Oh they go on and on, but we've only got birds to travel on, so mostly we just visit close neighbours. If we have to go to distant places we borrow the birds of other islands, and do the journey in stages. And now it's time for us to return to your world Sonny."

They said goodbye to Gogo's Mother, Tobo, Tilbo, Bevet and Purdy, and set off across the meadow to where Goggles waited patiently to take them home.

Sonny and Great-Uncle Parkin
Part I

Sonny was a boy who lived with his parents in a nice house which had a pleasant garden. In the garden was a pond in which goldfish swam. It was surrounded by a lawn where Sonny and his friends would play, and sometimes the ball fell into the water. Once a toy-train fell into the water, but that is another story.

Sunny was unique and different from his friends in just one way. He had a small friend called Gogo who lived in Pongoland. Once, on a trip to this world Gogo had been looking at some toys in a toy-shop when Sonny's uncle, mistaking him for a toy, bought him as a present for Sonny. The little man had the size and appearance of a toy-clown, and as he kept quite still out of fright, no-one suspected that he was a small person until he was alone with Sonny. He had a jolly smiling face with a pointy nose, and he had pointed ears. He wore blue baggy trousers with a blue and yellow and striped tunic, and on his head a red beanie cap. Sonny was delighted to have him for a friend.

The greatest wonder however was that at night he went home to Pongoland. A large owl called Goggles would alight on Sonny's bedroom window-sill. Gogo would climb on to his back, and off they would fly to his island in the sky. There, when it was night in our world it was day there, and as the sun rose on our world it set on Pongoland. Because of this Gogo slept quite a lot of his day with Sonny. That was alright because Sonny had to go to school and do his homework, and meet other friends. When he was free he and Gogo would talk, and Gogo would tell Sonny all the latest news from Pongoland.

On Saturday nights when Goggles arrived Gogo would take Sonny by the hand. As he did so Sonny would shrink to Gogo's height, and the two of them would climb on to the owl's back. Then off they would fly into the night, over the tree-tops, and under the stars. Sonny told no-one about these trips because he knew no-one would believe him. Normally he was away about four hours. On Sunday morning he was allowed to sleep late.

So this compensated for the night's outing. Occasionally when there had been an emergency he had traveled other nights too, but these extra journeys were not allowed normally by Gogo's mother.

Emergencies there had been, and Sonny's friendship with Gogo had been eventful, and sometimes even hair-raising.

As this story begins there had been a period of quiet after the day of the picnic with Gogo's family and some of his friends. A visitor to the island from Tolikland had proved to be a thief. He had come to study metal work from Pongo craftsman, but instead tried to make away with a quantity of gold. Murgo, Gogo's father, Gogo, and Sonny had seen the grey, black, and red birds from Tolikland waiting to be laden with the bags of gold, and were able to intervene, but it had been a close shave.

This Saturday night however Gogo seemed a little disturbed. He and Sonny had not been able to talk all day as Sonny's Aunt and cousins had come to visit. When Sonny retired to his bedroom at nine o'clock Gogo couldn't wait to tell him the news.

"Guess what. My Great-Uncle Parkin has arrived from Nacheetoland and says he will stay for a while".

"Isn't that nice for you?" asked Sonny.

"No it jolly well isn't. You don't know Great-Uncle Parkin. He wants to play with us children all the time. He goes with me and Tobo to our school gates in the morning, and he's there waiting for us when we come out at two o'clock. It's so embarrassing, I can't tell you. He's very big. I mean really large, so he can't bend. He talks all the time so our friends go off elsewhere. In any case if they stick around he insists on sharing our games. He can't bend down to pick up balls, so one of the children has to pick them up for him. He can't understand any rules so he throws them in the wrong direction. He can't hit a ball with a bat so someone has to keep giving him another ball to have another go. And all the time he's laughing and teasing Tobo and me in front of our friends. I know we should respect him so we don't say anything, but Tobo went home crying yesterday, and hid in the kitchen all evening. Even there he wasn't safe because Great-Uncle keeps going in to see what's in the fridge. His teasing is really insulting and these days we don't want to go to school and face all that humiliation every time."

"Oh dear," said Sonny. "That's awful. Don't your parents know?"

"I expect they do in a way, but if he wants to play with the children it's difficult to stop him."

"Where's Nacheetoland?"

"Oh it's an eight-bird journey from Pongoland. He married a woman there and stayed to live there".

"But she hasn't come with him?"

"No fear. You can imagine what a relief it must be to have him away on holiday for a while".

"And he doesn't say when he's going home?"

"No. Maybe Aunt Karaka scolds him or something. We've hardly met her, but she's said to be a bit of a tartar. So maybe Great-Uncle also likes a break."

"Well ………. couldn't you invite her, hoping she'll take control of your Great-Uncle?"

"It's eight birds away. A letter would take ages and she'd probably say no! If she's enjoying a rest, she won't want to fly to Pongoland to join him!"

"What about your Mother?"

"Oh she's worn out. She has to cook mountains of food every day."

"I'ld like to meet your Great-Uncle," said Sonny, bursting with curiosity.

"You will. Tonight. He's very rude, so be prepared. Then we have to figure out how to handle the situation. Tobo's refusing to go to school. If he's made to go he cries, and that makes Great-Uncle even worse."

They climbed on to the window-sill and Gogo took Sonny's hand in his own. Sonny became the same height as Gogo and the two of them peered out of the window. Goggles was waiting in the neem tree opposite the window, and flow across to pick them up.

Sonny and Gogo clambered on to his back and away they flew into the night, over the tree-tops and under the stars.

After some time they could see a light in the distance. This was the sun shining on Pongoland. As they approached, Sonny could see the hill on which Gogo's house stood, and the towers of the King's Palace at the top. Goggles brought them down to a green meadow at the bottom of the hill and alighted on the grass. As usual Gogo asked him to return for them in three hours.

As they started up the road which led to the village built on the hillside, Gogo said,

"Great-Uncle may just try to make you laugh at Tobo and me. He doesn't normally insult our friends. He just likes to make me and Tobo look silly."

Sonny was glad his relatives all seemed to be friendly cheerful people who brought him sweets and other small gifts, and liked to praise him. How horrid to have a Great-Uncle who humiliated you. He must be quite old, Sonny thought.

When Tobo saw them coming up the hill he ran out of the house and down the road to meet them. He flung himself into Sonny's arms. Today he was wearing red trousers with a blue and yellow striped shirt and yellow hat. He was a few years younger than Gogo, and tended to get into messes, but was very lovable, and Sonny was sad to see him so distressed. He had been crying and was now hiccupping.

"Great-Uncle Parkin is playing hide and seek with Tilbo and Pevet and Mandy," he choked. "I tried to play but he told them where I was hiding every time. He doesn't close his eyes while you hide. Then he said I was hopeless at finding good places. The others thought I was."

"Well O.K." said Sonny."Let's sit down for a bit and think. We have to find a solution to all this. He shouldn't be allowed to get away with cheating, and hurting people. Is he old?"

"No," said Gogo. "but he's fifteen years older than Papa. We can't just be rude back to him."

"No .... There's no way to get your Aunt here?"

"I don't think so," said Gogo. "Anyway Mummy and Papa would have to invite her and they've got their hands full with Great-Uncle."

"I think I've got a sort of idea," said Sonny.

"Oh Sonny have you? What?" asked Tobo hopefully.

"Well – let me meet him first. It may not be feasible."

"They continued their climb up towards Sonny's house in the little Pongo village.

The houses had different coloured walls and roofs, and Gogo's house was pink with a cream roof. As they entered the gate a vast voice shouted,

"Here they are! Come to play have you? Or try to, ha ha ha. Who's that?"

"This is our friend Sonny, Great-Uncle," said Gogo.

"Hello," said Great-Uncle Parkin. His voice boomed out of a cave-like chest. His girth was enormous. A tape-measure wouldn't meet round it, Sonny reflected. He wore yellow trousers, and a yellow and black striped shirt and black hat. Like a wasp, thought Sonny. With a similar sting.

"My, your face is flat! What happened? Trip on a banana-skin and fall on it? Ha ha ha." He guffawed at his own joke, Sonny did not smile.

"People come in different shapes, colours, and eyes, like fruit and flowers," he said.

"Oh – oh – yes. True, true," said Great-Uncle Parkin.

"So where I come from our faces are flat," continued Sunny, looking him straight in the eye, daring him to laugh.

"Ah – yes – I suppose they do." Another booming laugh.

"Is your Mummy in?" Sonny asked Tobo. The three of them went into the house leaving Great-Uncle Parkin with the other children.

"Oh well, that wasn't as bad as it could have been", said Gogo. "Sorry about   your   face".

They went through to the kitchen, to find Gogo's normally cheerful mother shedding tears into the sink.

"What's the matter Mummy?" cried Gogo, running to her.

"Oh – your Great-Uncle said my muffins were hard at breakfast and told your father what a brilliant cook his wife is, and how I ought to go and take some lessons from her."

"Well why not go. Just to get a bit of rest?" suggested Sunny.

"I can't do that. Murgo can't cook. He never learned. Gogo is learning but he's too young for all this, and Parkin is Murgo's Grand-Father's brother after all."

"Would you excuse Gogo and me please while we take a walk?" asked Sonny.

"Yes of course, off you go. Tobo love, please clear the table."

Sonny and Gogo set off up the hill. Sonny urged speed so they panted a bit as the King's Palace came into view ahead of them. There were enormous iron gates and high walls. Guards stood by the gate. On the left they passed the orchards where the Pelids used to try to steal Pongo fruit.

"Let's stop a bit here," said Sonny, sitting down on the grass verge, Gogo joined him.

"What are you plotting?" he asked Sonny, who had proved so resourceful on so many occasions.

"Well. The idea is a bit vague as yet. Your Great-Uncle wants to feel important doesn't he? He's got a large body, but inside he isn't grown up."

"That's true," said Gogo.

"Well – it's just a glimmer of a thought yet, but I wondered if we could – somehow – get him out of your house and into the Palace."

"What?" said Gogo.

"Let's go and visit the King. After all he gave a party for me once and presented me with my magic pen. I'm sure he'll see me."

"Well – alright. Yes I expect he will."

They continued to the Palace and gave the Guards the message that Sonny had come to visit the King and Queen of Pongoland. Very soon afterwards Sonny and Gogo were admitted, and escorted to the throne-room where their Majesties were holding audience for petitioners.

"Ah Sonny, how delightful to see you and Gogo," said the King. Sonny and Gogo bowed and approached the thrones.

"How are you both?" the Queen asked."I still keep the key to my store-cupboard hidden," she laughed.

"We're fine", said Sonny, and looked round at the petitioners.

"We have a tricky problem here today," said the King."One of the birds brought a very large gentleman from Maridoland on the last leg of his journey from Nacheetoland. I don't know what the fate of the other seven birds was, but the Maridoland bird is with Mother Fulati claiming its back is broken. She said it isn't. She says the bird is sulking because of having to carry such a large gentleman from Maridoland. It does have strained muscles and its wings are damaged. She says it must rest with her for a fortnight, and she will apply some of her ointments. The problem is all the birds now refuse to carry the gentleman again. This young man here," the King indicated one of the petitioners, "says the large visitor is causing disturbances in the village, and people there want me to send him home. I do have that authority, but how can I force a bird to take the risk? And several other birds too."

Birds were used as transport between the many islands in the sky, but only as far as the next nearest island. Anyone wishing to go further took a bird from that island to go on to the next, and so on.

"This must be my Great-Uncle Parkin," said Gogo gloomily. "He's causing disturbances in our house too. Both my Mother and my brother have been in tears since breakfast."

"Oh dear," said the King. "I'm sorry to discuss this embarrassment in front of you. I didn't know he was your Great-Uncle."

"That's alright. We were just discussing him ourselves," said Gogo looking at Sonny.

"I did wonder", said Sonny, hesitating how to frame his next sentence. "I sort of wondered if you might invite him here to stay at your Palace, your Majesty."

"What?" said the King, "I don't want disturbances within the palace precincts no matter whose Great-Uncle he is, and I am very fond of Gogo and Tobo,"

"No. But your residence is very large and there aren't any children here."

"No – unfortunately not."

"Great–Uncle causes trouble by trying to play with children and cheating. Also he is so big he needs helpers all the time."

"Yes, I have heard many stories. He causes the children to quarrel and that starts their parents quarrelling. It's a ridiculous situation."

"I think inside he feels like a child Sir," said Sonny. "He tries to make friends by breaking up other peoples' friendships".

"Yes, yes," said the King.

"And I am upset about Gogo and Tobo and their Mother, and the only solution I could think of at the moment was an invitation to the Palace? He could be treated like an honoured foreign visitor - as you treated me once if you remember, but actually be kept inside the palace grounds and out of harm's way".

"Yes, yes, but how do I send him home if the birds refuse to carry him? I could have a riot in my own house if he stays long."

"Well we could think of something couldn't we?" said Sonny hopefully. "Just count removing him from the village as stage one."

And so it was agreed. By lunch-time a large gold-embossed card arrived at Gogo's house requesting the honour of Mr. Parkin's presence at the royal Palace itself for a stay. Great-Uncle Parkin's eyes nearly popped out of his head and he nearly burst with excitement. The family could not pack his clothes quickly enough for him to leave for the King's Palace. How his wife would preen! How proud she would be that Parkin was the guest of a King! That would show her how important he was in the world of affairs!

A horse was found to conduct the honoured guest to his destination, and the Palace gates closed behind him. He was taken to a sumptuous room and two serving–men were appointed to look after him, give him all he asked for, and keep an eye on him!

Gogo's household settled back into its normal peaceful rhythm, and Sonny had to return home. There were some anxious whispers during the next week between Gogo and Sonny who at the moment could offer no solution to the vexed question of transport. For the moment that problem had to be left with the King and Mother Fulati.

As the week passed on Sonny found himself constantly worried about Great-Uncle Parkin. Gogo's reports weren't happy. The Queen was furious at his way of taunting the staff. The Palace cook was in a huff because of his criticisms of her dishes. The King said he could not concentrate on important political and domestic issues because of Parkin's regular attendance at his daily audience! Parkin could not be locked in his room, but his presence in the audience hall caused constant disruption. Gogo wondered how long the King would tolerate it before locking him up in a cell. This would be a big shame in his family.

Sonny felt responsible and wracked his brains for a simple solution to get Parkin back to Nacheetoland. But how? Eight birds away. On the Thursday evening he asked Gogo to draw a plan of the islands, and show exactly where Nacheetoland was.

"The islands go on forever,"said Gogo," but I can show you the ones we know." Sonny gave him a large sheet of paper and a pencil. He drew Pongoland and then Maridoland. From there be calculated the distances to Galipoland, Pelidoland and Tolikland and sketched them in. He could mark in a dozen others in their approximate locations.

"I wish I'ld concentrated on geography more at school," he said. "Well where is Nacheetoland?" asked Sonny.

"About here," said Gogo, making a dot.

"And where are these islands in relation to our world? Do you know?" Gogo scratched his head.

"It's half an hour by owl from here to Pongoland. Let's say – roughly shall we? – five hours by owl to Nacheetoland. "

"In which direction?"

"We'll have to ask Goggles."

When Goggles arrived that night they called him over from the neem tree for an urgent consultation. The island birds could understand what was said to them, and speak a little. He said more or less due north to Nacheetoland.

"My Grandparents' house is due north from here," said Sonny.

"No!" said Gogo, agog with possibilities,"but how - ?"

"I don't know but surely we can fix it. Goggles, if we can get Great-Uncle Parkin to my Grandparent's house, would you be able to carry him from there to Nacheetoland?"

Goggles thought for a long time. He didn't like Great-Uncle Parkin, and moreover all the birds were on strike from carrying him. Still, Parkin had made Tobo cry and his Mother cry and…….

"I could take him as far as Tolikland," he said. "From your grandparents' house that would be about fifteen minutes. Then one of those birds involved in the gold robbery might be persuaded, as a favour to the King of Pongoland, to do the last stage on to Nacheetoland. It wouldn't be too far."

"That's wonderful!" cried Sonny.

"Yes but how are we going to get Great-Uncle Parkin to your house first, and then on to your Grandparents house?" said Gogo.

"Why, by train of course!"

"And that means your parents have to be persuaded to take the trip," pointed out Gogo.

And this was the problem, but that is another story…

Sonny and Great-Uncle Parkin
Part II

We heard in the last story how Sonny had sketched out a plan to transport the very obese Great-Uncle Parkin back from Pongoland to his home island of Nacheetoland. This was an eight bird journey from island to island away from Pongoland, and after the bird which carried Great-Uncle from Maridoand to Pongoland had been injured as a result of carrying such a heavy weight, all the birds were refusing to carry Great-Uncle Parkin. In any case they did not like him because he grumbled and insulted them all the time he was travelling.

Sonny's scheme was somehow to get Great–Uncle Parkin to his home. Then take him by train to his Grand-parents house which was much closer to Nacheeetoland. Goggles was prepared to take him on to Tolikland. This journey would be about fifteen minutes. From there Goggles felt one of the birds involved in attempting a large gold theft from Pongoland would be willing to do the King of Pongoland a favour by carrying Great-Uncle on to Nacheeetoland. The plan was complex but workable Sonny and Gogo thought after discussion. They relied entirely on the love and loyalty of Gogo's owl, Goggles.

How the ride from Pongoland to Sonny's house was to be conducted was yet to be decided. There were no stopping places on the way, and the journey took half an hour, about the same time as the journey from Maridoland to Pongoland.Goggles wanted to carry Great-Uncle Parkin in a sheet held by himself and another owl, but Gogo did not see how they could persuade him to accept such an indignity. He did not allow he was fat for a start. Nor had he shown any wish to make the journey. He was enjoying himself.

So a good deal of diplomacy and persuasion would be needed, thought Sonny. These discussions between Gogo, Goggles and Sonny took place on the Thursday night. Sonny would travel to Pongoland on Saturday might, and the three of them agreed that they would plan out their strategy by then.

49

Sunny began by asking his parents when they would be visiting his Grand-parents again.

"Can we go this Sunday?" he asked. His parents were surprised at this sudden enthusiasm to go to his Grandparents' house. Usually he liked to sleep late and then play with his friends on Sundays. However they agreed to think about it. Sonny hoped to get Great-Uncle Parkin to his house on Saturday night. If he couldn't he would be in a mess, as he could hardly ask to go again to his Grandparents' house the following Sunday, which was his Father's only free day. In fact their plan would fall through.

By the time Goggles came for them on Saturday evening, both Gogo and Sonny were tense and nervous. Goggles warned them the King and Queen would not put up with Great-Uncle Parkin much longer. The cook was threatening to leave and he was creating chaos in inter-island relations as a result of his comments during the daily audiences.

Gogo took Sonny by the hand and as he did so Sonny shrank to the same height as Gogo. They climbed on to Goggles back, and away they flew through the night, over the tree-tops and under the stars. Soon they saw the light of Pongoland shining in the sun. They descended to their usual stopping–place in the meadow, but instead of starting straight away up the hill to Gogo's house, Sonny and Gogo stayed in the field discussing plans with Goggles.

They decided they would go up to the top of the hill first to meet the King in private. Goggles would fly there too and wait in a tree by the gate for further instructions. He had found a friend willing to carry Great-Uncle Parkin in a sheet between them as for as Sonny's house, but Great-Uncle was going to be furious and surely would not agree.

As usual at the palace gates Sonny asked the guards for permission to meet the King. The King was only too anxious to meet Sonny, and in no time he and Gogo were in a private meeting chamber with the King.

"My wife's furious," he said. "I am at my wit's end. He's got to go. Have you thought of a plan?" Sonny and Gogo outlined the scheme, but the King agreed persuading Great-Uncle Parkin would not be easy. He would look silly in a sheet, and his aim at all times was to dominate proceedings.

"You remember that stuff Mother Fulati sprayed on those beetles to keep them quiet? Would she have enough of it to keep Great-Uncle Parkin quiet?" asked Sonny.

"She'd need gallons," said the King. There was a pause as they visualized Mother Fulati spraying Great–Uncle all over.

"Well what about some potion he could drink to put him to sleep?" suggested Gogo. This sounded more feasible and might even be a good idea.

The King thought. "Yes", he said, "let's try it. I don't know what you will do with him in your house Sonny, but I am most anxious to get him out of mine."

"That's alright Sir," said Sonny uneasily. "Maybe we could keep him asleep for some hours?"

"I don't know. We'll wait for Mother Fulati", said the King, and they did. A servant brought in some delicious sweet lime-juice to drink, and they talked about old times, and heard the latest news from the islands. Sonny was like an islander himself now. He knew so many people.

In due course Goggles arrived with Mother Fulati and his owl friend, Wobbles, carrying a large sheet.

"Hello, Mother Fulati," said the King. "We need an urgent consultation with you. Let the owls remain here."

The King himself talked to Mother Fulati about the idea of putting Great-Uncle Parkin to sleep in order to transport him to Sonny's house, because he would refuse to travel in a sheet. She listened carefully but said firmly.

"Oh no. I put people to sleep in order to treat their illnesses or their wounds. I don't put anyone to sleep to prevent him being a nuisance. What an idea! Those beetles I temporarily dazed were a quite different thing, and even they had recovered within ten minutes".

The King sighed. He had suspected she would consider putting Parkin to sleep a big misuse of her skills. Sonny and Gogo listened as the grown–ups discussed the issue.

"Why don't you tempt him to your house with something?" Mother Fulati asked Sonny.

"Well I could," said Sonny, "but the birds are refusing to carry him because of his weight, and he will definitely refuse to go in a sheet."

"What about the train-journey?" asked the King.

"I think my parents are willing to visit my Grand-parents tomorrow," said Sonny.

"If not can you entertain him somehow," said Gogo, "until we can think of something else."

"He can't," said the King. "Parkin would ruin your life Sonny, and how would you ever keep him quiet?"

"He can't stay at Sonny's house," said Mother Fulati.

"Could you send him on an important mission to my world Sir?" asked Sonny.

"Like what?" asked the King. "He's no diplomat."

"To inspect our trains?" hazarded Sonny.

"In these islands we walk everywhere or ride a horse or donkey," said Mother Fulati.

"Do you know the King of Nacheetoland ?" asked Sonny.

"Yes. He's my cousin. The islands' royalty all inter-marry."

"Well could you ask Great-Uncle to take him something, and send a message to your cousin asking him as a favour to entertain Uncle for a couple of days in return for his trouble? He sets great store by looking important, and he was very excited about staying with you."

"Mmm," thought the King. "I could send him a little consignment of a new range of gold jewelry our craftsmen have come out with. If Parkin could take a few samples that would be quite helpful for us, I suppose. We rely on trade with the other islands."

"You'd have to carry it all in your school–bag Sonny," said Gogo, "and Great-Uncle Parkin isn't going to be all that small even in your world."

"No but the jewelery wouldn't take up much room. That's going to be very small."

"You've still got to get Parkin to your world in a bed-sheet," pointed out Mother Fulati.

"Well suppose I send him instead in a sheet of spun gold as a special honour," suggested the King. "It would be worth it to me, and he could keep it as a gift for his wife. I'll tell him I would prefer the gold jewellery to go that way as far as your world because of the distance."

"This sounds very workable," approved Mother Fulati.

And so it was agreed. Great-Uncle Parkins was called for a special audience with the King, and his mission explained to him. The King complimented him on his understanding of inter-island affairs. Parkin pricked up his ears when he heard the cloth would be a gift for his wife. My goodness! How pleased she would be! And the King said the King of Nacheetoland would certainly want his presence in his palace for a day a two to talk over his visit to Pongoland. He would be respected throughout the island after this.

Goggles and Wobbles waited in the meadow. The servants at the Palace had tied the four corners of the cloth of gold to the bodies of the owls and a special messenger had brought the gold jewelley wrapped in red velvet purses. Great-Uncle Parkin arrived on horse-back escorted by members of the Palace Guard. He sat on the cloth of gold with all the solemnity of a king mounting his throne. Sonny was already on his way home on the back of another owl. His heart was in his mouth as it would be no joke controlling Great–Uncle Parkin, even reduced to the size of a toy, for a whole morning, and suppose his parents decided not to go to his Grand-parents house after all! Goggles promised to wait in the neem tree to help out in case of difficulties. As soon as he heard that the trip north was to go ahead, he was to set off to the Grand-parents house and be there when Sonny arrived. He had been there before on a previous excursion, so knew the area well.

Sonny was home well before dawn, earth time, and waited in trepidation for Great-Uncle. Eventually he saw a dim shining in the sky. The cloth of gold! It came nearer until Sonny could see the two owls and a pompous–looking Uncle Parkin dangling in the cloth between them. They came closer and closer until they had their burden close to Sonny's window-sill. Sonny reached out a hand to lift Uncle Parkin into his room. Even in this world he was a solid weight. Great-Uncle looked a little confused and a little affronted. He had been told Sonny and everything else would be much bigger here, but he still felt awkward to find himself so small.

Sonny unfastened the gold cloth from the owls' bodies and put the tiny red purses on his bed. Goggles retired to the neem tree, and Wobbles returned thankfully home. Sonny folded the cloth carefully, in this world about five feet square, and put it in a paper bag. This he placed at the bottom of his school bag. Then he put the red purses in another bag and tucked it into a side pocket. In a second pocket he placed a large folded duster. Then he put his school books in the bag. Great–Uncle Parkin watched intently.

"When do we go?" he demanded. "I am to travel by crane, I believe".

"Train," corrected Sonny.

"Oh. When do we leave?"

"In about another three hours," said Sonny. "Why don't you get some sleep till it is time to go?"

Sonny lifted Great-Uncle Parkin into his toy-cupboard, and shut the door. He explained that he wouldn't be long, but that secrecy was essential on this mission, and Uncle Parkin must remain hidden at all times. Uncle Parkin looked a little confused, but agreed that discretion in important matters was essential! Sonny crept down to the kitchen, and came back with a large (for Parkin) slice of vegetable pie. He put the plate in the cupboard with Uncle Parkin, leaving the door slightly open. By the most amazing good fortune, after consuming the whole of the portion, and after all the excitement of his day, Great-Uncle Parkin lay down and fell asleep.

Sonny couldn't believe his luck. He took back the plate and washed it, and then closed the toy cupboard door quietly. Then he climbed into bed, very tired himself. He dozed for a while but was very afraid of what Great-Uncle might do. Also he had to be up when his Mother got up in order to find out what the plans for the day were. He was exhausted with all the anxiety and tension, but knew he must look ready for anything when his Mother came in. As soon as he heard her moving about he went to clean his teeth, and called to ask if they were going. His luck held. They would travel by the 9.00 a.m. train. Sonny went to his window and signaled thumbs-up to Goggles.

Sonny bathed carefully and put on the shorts and tea–shirt his Mother had put out for him. She was surprised he had eaten a bit of pie in the night, but he just looked embarrassed and said nothing. Parkin was still asleep. He was snoring, but with the cupboard door closed this was not audible outside the bedroom. As the time approached to set off by car to the station Sonny opened the cupboard door and lifted out Great-Uncle Parkin. He woke with a start and demanded to know what was happening.

"We'll be leaving soon," said Sonny, "in a car."

"Ka?" said Great-Uncle. "I thought you said a drain!"

"No. First a car. Then a train," said Sonny patiently. "I am going to put you in my school-bag, and please keep very quiet Uncle, as this is a secret journey. No-one must know."

"Oh, yes, the King of Pongoland said I should preserve absolute anonymity. However I am very hungry. Where's my breakfast?"

Sonny rushed down to the kitchen again and brought back a Pongo–sized sandwich he had prepared for the journey. He knew a large quantity of food was essential to the success of the enterprise, and had made up a little packet of food for him from his own breakfast. He placed Great-Uncle Parkin in his school-bag along with some of his school–books in such a way that the small round man could see out, as once earlier he had placed Gogo and Tobo, so that their eyes could see out from under the flap. So Parkin had a good view out of the car-window, and later out of the train- window. The food he tucked in his pocket.They were off.

However the train had been moving hardly half an hour when Parkin called out.

"I'm hungry."

"What?" said Sonny's Father. "Already? You've only just had your breakfast Sonny."

"I am not ……………phumf………………wumf……………" came from Sonny's school-bag as he squashed down the flap to shush Parkin. The next station was approaching and the train whistled so Sonny managed to divert his parents' attention. His Mother gave him a biscuit and he opened his bag a little to take out a book and to give half the biscuit and the sandwich to Parkin. That kept him quiet for the next half-hour, but Sonny could not relax for a minute. He took a walk up and down the corridor, and reminded Parkin again of the need for silence. Eventually the frightful journey came to an end. His Grand- parents' house was within walking distance of the station and Sonny walked ahead a little in case Parkin had anything to say, and to remind him again to be silent. At least they were here and Goggles must be around somewhere. He told Great-Uncle that Goggles would come for him at one o'clock to take him to Tolikland. A journey by gold cloth could not be undertaken in this world's day–time for all to see.

Sonny explained that he would place Great-Uncle Parkin on the branch of a tree for Goggles to pick him up. All the plans had been a managed carefully. Parkin was in fact very excited. He had loved the train journey, and was already rehearsing in his mind how he would describe it to his wife. How amazed she would be! And Sonny's sandwich had been most delicious. In fact he could do with a little something now. Sonny and his parents had reached the Grand-parents' house. As usual Grand-Mother had all sorts of home-made delicacies ready in the kitchen. Sunny passed half a jam tart into his school – bag for Parkin. He could not eat much himself. There was sweat on his brow from worry, and he felt slightly sick. His Grand-mother saw he looked a little pale and told him to go and lie down a bit until she called him for lunch. She said children had to work too hard at school these days. His mother looked doubtful, but she too could see he looked pale.

Sonny lifted Parkin out of his school–bag and put him in the play–cupboard in the room he always used when he came to his Grand-parents' house. Parkin was still working his way though the tart. Sonny closed the door and lay down. He missed Gogo. Usually in all these situations he had Gogo to talk to and discuss things with. It was being alone with his anxiety that was upsetting his tummy.

His Grand-mother came in and walked straight to the play-cupboard and opened the door.

"Why!" she said, "You've brought one of these clowns you have." Sonny saw Parkin's look. "Cl.." he started to exclaim. Sonny broke in,

"The jam-tarts were lovely Granny," She looked towards him and smiled and Sonny looked at Parkin who shut up. His Grandmother looked back at Parkin.

"Sonny? Did you put the tart in there? There are crumbs!"

"Yes, just for a minute. I thought I'ld eat it later."

"You're not feeling too well are you?" said his Grand-Mother anxiously.

"I'll be alright after a little rest Granny," assured Sonny."I am just a bit tired.

"Alright, well see if you can sleep a bit." She returned to the bedroom door, went out, and closed it. It was twelve forty five.

Sonny had had enough. He took the two parcels out of his school-bag, and put the paper–bag containing the cloth of gold and the bag containing the jewellery in the duster he had brought, and knotted the four corners together for Goggles to hold in his beak. He picked up Parkin and climbed out through the window. It was a short run to the beech tree. And oh glory, Goggles was perched in the branches. He flew down and Sonny placed Parkin on his back. Goggles took the corners of the duster in his beak. With a silent nod he rose into the sky. Sonny watched the bird as he disappeared with his heavy cargo.

In a flash Sonny was back in bed. By the time his Grand-mother came to peep in to tell him lunch was ready the colour was back in his cheeks, and he was ravenous. He had eaten hardly any breakfast on account of supplying Parkin, and through sheer worry had not been hungry. Now he hoped to make up for his starvation. The grown-ups were all relieved to see the colour back in his face, and the enthusiasm with which he tucked into lunch.

"There," said his Grand-mother, "I knew he was just over-tired".

"He was very keen to visit you today," said his Father. "A trip here always does him good".

"Not to mention his Grand-mother's cooking," said his Mother beaming.

Back home that night he waited for Gogo who had been left behind in Pongland to sleep. Eventually at ten o'clock he arrived on Wobbles' back.

"How did it go?" he asked anxiously.

"O.K. but I am worn out Gogo. I've got to sleep now." He told Gogo the story of the day and then his eyes closed. Gogo set off back to Pongoland to tell the King and Mother Fulati that as far as they knew Great–Uncle Parkin was back in Nacheetoland. Goggles had said he would rest for some time in Tolikland, and return after he heard news from the King of Nacheetoland that Parkin had arrived. There was also the question of the gold jewelry, and whether the King of Nacheetoland would in fact decide to place orders with the King of Pongoland.

The following week Sonny slept soundly every night at home. Gogo came and spent the days with him, sleeping in his bed till tea-time. Sonny learnt they were still waiting for Goggles. In the meantime life in the Palace had returned to normal. The cook was happy, the Queen was happy, and in the audience–chambers peace was restored.

The next Saturday might Sonny went with Gogo on Wobbles' back to Pongoland. They went first to Gogo's Mother's house. There was some concern about Goggles. Had he been injured? One or another of the family watched out for him constantly. Then as Sonny sat in Gogo's house drinking strawberry squash a message came down from the Palace to say Goggles was there. Tobo begged to be allowed to go up to the Palace too, so Sonny, Gogo and Tobo set off up the hill to the Palace. The guards admitted them at once, and a servant come to take them to the private audience room. The King and Queen were both there with Goggles. Gogo and Tobo rushed to hug Goggles, asking of he was alright and had not been hurt by carrying Great-Uncle Parkin. He promised that although all his muscles had ached for a while he was not damaged and after resting for a while had been perfectly fit to return home. He had stopped one night at Galipoland.

"And guess what!" said King. "My cousin has sent an order for fifty pieces of our new gold jewelery. Bravo Parkin!"

"That's wonderful!" said Sonny. "How was Great-Uncle Parkin, Goggles?"

"Very happy," said Goggles. "He stayed two nights at the Palace and then returned to his wife with the gold cloth and a ring the Queen sent her. He's a hero at the moment and loves it."

"Well that's fine then," said Gogo. "We'ld better go home and tell our parents."

"Wait a minute," said the Queen. "You and Sonny and Goggles deserve big rewards for all your efforts. It must have been very difficult looking after Parkin in your world Sonny".

"It was," admitted Sonny.

"I am going to ask Goggles to deliver a gift to your parents. It was they who took Parkin to your grandparents' house after all. They'll wonder where the gift came from, but that's all."

"For you Sonny and Gogo and Goggles," said the King, "there will be gold medals for exemplary service to Pongoland."

Gogo and Goggles were speechless. Those medals were rarely given and much prized by any recipient. Sonny was delighted but wondered privately where he'd keep it.

"It's alright Sonny," said Gogo, "we keep your best suit in our house. We'll keep your medal too, and you will wear it on festive occasions here."

"Oh yes of course, thanks," said Sonny.

"And as we love parties in Pongoland I will announce a big party in honour of Sonny, Gogo, and Goggles for next Saturday," said the King. "The medals will be presented by me then."

As they walked down the hill Sonny, Gogo, and Tobo discussed next week's party excitedly. Gogo and Tobo's parents were overcome when they heard the news of the medal!

"It's the first in our family," said Mongo with pride. "Well done Gogo, well done."

Sonny could not tell his parents about his medal of course, but he was deeply interested the next day to see another parcel had been left on their door-step addressed to his parents. (The first gift from Pongoland had been a windaphone for Sonny's father.) His parents took it indoors and opened it wonderingly. Inside was a large bedspread of fine spun gold, woven with blue silk thread. The design was intricate and unlike anything seen in this world, Sonny's parents gazed at it in awe.

"But who sent it?" asked his Mother. His Father looked at the card.

"It says," he read, "A free sample of our excellent hand-loom range with the compliments of Pongos Ltd. But how extraordinary!" They studied the card.

"Some sort of advertising campaign," suggested Sonny's Mother.

"It looks like it", said his Father, "What an amazingly generous thought! We seem to be very lucky."

They never could trace the company which had sent the "free sample",
but the bedspread remained a treasure in Sonny's home for the rest of
their lives……

Sonny and the Spangles Part I

When Gogo returned from Pongoland he had exciting news to impart. Sonny was getting ready for school and his school-bag was open on the floor. Gogo arrived sleepy after his long day at home, but he was not ready yet to climb into Sonny's bed.

"The Spangles are coming to Pongoland next Saturday!".

"Who are the Spangles?" asked Sonny.

"They are a musical group from Maridoland. Rosy is the lead singer. Wanda and Perry are also singers. Magda plays the tintareena and Tolly plays the bola. They are very popular in Maridoland and famous in the islands. Sometimes they do tours, and a tour is to start next weekend, starting with Pongoland. From there, on Sunday morning, they will go on to Pelidoland and so on. They'll be away quite a long time probably."

"What's a tintareena and what's a bola?"

"Well – a tintareena is a sort of tub, narrower at one end and broader at the other, a bit like half an egg. It has strings on top, and you play it with a piece of sharpened copper in your right hand, and you put the fingers of your left hand on the strings. A bola is a deep kind of drum, and you play it with two little hammers, sometimes very fast. The musicians sit at each side and the singers stand in the middle."

"What do they play?"

"Some old songs we all know. And they write their own new ones. Quite a lot of the songs we sing were written by Magda. She's very musical."

"What are the songs about?" asked Sonny.

"About the islands and the birds, and about our history. Sometimes about our politics and very funny," said Gogo.

"Shall I be able to hear them next Saturday?" asked Sonny.

"Of course! That's what's so exciting. They're setting up a stage in the meadow where the birds stay, and spreading carpets on the ground for us to sit on, and there'll be tables with cold drinks and refreshments. They'll stay overnight and leave early next morning for Pelidoland. Their concert will start at four o'clock so you will be able to hear the first part. You won't be able to stay for the rest of it as it'll go on quite late and you have to get back here."

Gogo had never explained to Sonny that he always stuffed bits of a particular Pongoland moss under his bedroom door. In this world the leaves were too small to notice, but their perfume had the effect of making a person forget what he was going to do. It someone was going to enter Sonny's room he or she would forget why, and go on somewhere else. This effect would last a few hours and would not last through till breakfast time. Sonny was usually back in his bed by dawn. On Sunday mornings he was allowed to sleep late, and could recover from his night out.

Sonny looked forward to the concert, and decided to wear his best T-Shirt. The next Saturday he had an afternoon sleep and then a bath. By ten o'clock he and Gogo were waiting on his window-sill. When Gogo took Sonny's hand to prepare to go, Sonny shrank down to Gogo's size. They peeped out of the window towards the neem tree where Goggles waited for them. When Goggles saw their faces he flew across to pick them up. Then off they flew into the night over the tree-tops and under the stars.

Maridoland was quite mountainous. Sonny had been there on more than one occasion and loved the gentle people with their dark curly hair and round heads and round noses. He had attended the marriage of the King's daughter Ahoosta to Lord Lannet. They now lived in Lord Lannet's castle on a cliff ledge overlooking a deep valley.

Pongoland was more green with meadows, rolling hills, and a jungle where Mother Fulati lived with her daughter amongst their herbs and healing plants. The King's palace was at the top of the highest hill. Lower down was the village where Gogo and his younger brother Tobo lived. As you climbed the hill you passed orchards with many sweet-tasting fruits before you reached the Palace gates.

Goggles set them down as always in the meadow which spread round the bottom of the hill. There were long and short grasses and small flowers, and insects hummed busily. Today carpets had been laid out for everyone to sit down. A low wooden stage had been erected for the musicians. There was a thick red carpet on the stage. Opposite the stage at some distance from the carpets was a long trestle table set with a white cloth. On it were large glass jugs of different coloured sherbats with ice floating in them, and there were lots of sparkling glasses for the guests.

There were plates of savoury delicacies and tiny cakes and sweets. The refreshments would be served at five o'clock. At nine o'clock there would be a dinner, but unfortunately Sonny would have to be home well before that. Sonny felt sad to think he was missing most of such a lovely evening, but knew he was very lucky indeed to be there at all.

The concert would not begin for some hours yet and Sonny was to have lunch at Gogo's house. Until then Gogo suggested they could go and look at the toy factory where all Pongoland toys were made. This meant walking round the hill to the left.

Magic lived and breathed in the air of the islands. Hardly anyone ever performed any magic, but magic things would happen. Gogo made Sonny small without effort and without comment. Medical treatments verged on the magic. A few drops of one of Mother Fulati's eye tinctures were put in Sonny's Grand-father's eyes, and he did not need reading- glasses any more.

Sonny discovered now that it was Pongoland wizards who crafted the toys. They were helped by young apprentices. They made not only toys but recreational devices for adults. The windaphone Gogo had given Sonny's Father was made in this factory. It played all the beautiful sounds of Nature and was soothing for any harassed adult.

The wizards were regular Pongo people in appearance but had special gifts. This was a hereditary craft and the qualified wizards when at work wore long gowns with symbols of the zodiac embossed on them, and tall pointed hats. There was almost no conversation in the factory as the making of the toys was accompanied by the recitation of verses or charms to endow each device with a unique power.

Sonny and Gogo wandered quietly among the craftsmen. Gogo whispered that the women of these families used their gift to make special beauty preparations, and lucky potions of all kinds. Mother Fulati sniffed at these potions and said it was all quackery, but the people of Pongoland and even from other islands put great faith in them, and there was a big inter-island trade in both the men's and the women's products.

By one o'clock they were at Gogo's house for lunch. Tobo was there playing with a set of farm animals and he got up quickly and ran to Sonny.

"Are you coming to the concert?" he said excitedly.

"Yes of course!" Sonny hugged the small boy Pongo. Gogo's Mother greeted him warmly and they sat down to lunch. Sonny always felt like one of the family in Gogo's house and his Mother treated him like her own two children.

Tobo would go down the hill with Gogo and Sonny after lunch to watch the final preparations for the concert. The King and Queen of Pongoland were to arrive on horse-back at four. Gogo's Mother said the five Maridoland musicians were already in a special tent put up for them to prepare themselves.

By three-thirty almost the entire population of Pongoland seemed to be in the meadow. The people were mostly seated on the carpets and singing old songs and clapping their hands.

At four o'clock the royal entourage arrived and everyone stood up and bowed or curtsied. The King and Queen saw Sonny amongst the guests and waved. He bowed back. Then everyone settled down for the concert.

The five young musicians filed out of their tent and ascended the stage. Gogo whispered that the first was Tolly with his bola, then Wanda and Perry, then Magda with her tintareena, and finally Rosy who was a pretty girl of about twenty. She took the central position. They received a tumultuous applause, and the music began. The first item was a song about the islands.

"The winds of the Isles
blow soft and free,
the flowers bloom
for you and me.
"If I could choose
to other worlds
to fly away
for just one day
I know I'ld see
some wondrous things.
"But 'ere that day
had slipped away
straight back I'ld fly
on all my wings
to my Maridoland,
to my Maridoland.

This song brought loud patriotic applause and cheers. The tunes were mostly composed by the Spangles, Gogo told Sonny. Only occasionally did they use old traditional tunes of the Islands. A song which brought much laughter, including to Sonny who had shared in the event, went;

64

"When Prince Lannet said no
 to Ahoosti, his bride,
when she said, "Find my coronet!"
our Princess did cry, full high and wide,
'O.K. then, I'll never marry you,
O.K. then, I'll never marry you!'
"So he sat on his bed
and bowed down his head
and mourned, 'but where shall I look?
The thing's so small,
this joint so tall,
and today we should be wed,
today we should be wed,'
"Yet he did not shun
his lady's glum
but searched the castle high.
Then he saw it spread
on her Grandma's head,
and lo the pair was wed,
and lo the pair was wed."

How the audience cheered! At five-thirty they crowded round the table for refreshments, laughing and chattering, and excited for the next part of the show. Sonny was sad to have to go but it could not be helped. Gogo wrapped a few eatables in a napkin for him to take with him. Goggles was waiting nearby so Sonny climbed on his back and away they went.

Sunday passed quietly at home. Gogo had not come but Sonny knew he was busy.He had been up most of the night, so slept through the afternoon, rising blearily at five o'clock for tea. He played outside in the evening and at bed-time.

Gogo was back in his bed. When Sonny entered his bedroom a distraught Gogo whispered,

"Sonny, the Spangels have disappeared!"

"What!" cried Sonny,"What do you mean?"

"We saw them off at seven o'clock this morning, but they haven't arrived in Pelidoland. It only takes fifteen minutes or so."

"You mean the birds had an accident," cried Sonny horrified.

"How could seven birds have seven accidents? The players had a bird each from Maridoland, and there were two birds to carry their instruments and clothes. Their own Maridoland birds are touring with them. They are scarlet and grey with black beaks. At quarter to eight someone arrived from Pelidoland to ask where they were. We said they had left three quarters of an hour ago. Since then birds have been flying to and fro searching, and everyone's frantic. I left nine to come here. It's really worrying."

"Do they fall into our world if they fall?" asked Sonny anxiously.

"No," said Gogo kindly. "You can come to our world because I take you, or Goggles takes you by himself. We don't really live in your space".

"You don't?" said Sonny amazed.

"No, I couldn't explain to you at first. After all, your airplanes would see us wouldn't they? But they don't because we are in a different space," said Gogo.

"I don't understand that", said Sonny, very confused.

"No. It doesn't matter. You can visit us with me or one of the birds, and that's all we need think about. Our islands match your countries geographically, but that doesn't mean that anyone can reach them by going upwards. We travel by thought, sort of. I think, 'Pongoland', or Goggles does. That sets the course, and we get there. Many things we do would be counted magic in your world. But the Maridoland birds can't fall down here".

"But – wait a minute,"said Sonny. "Couldn't you think 'Nacheetoland' from here? We went by train to my Grand-parents house and Goggles travelled from there."

"Yes we could think 'Nacheetoland' but the bird still has that distance to fly. The problem for the birds is always distance."

"Well where would the birds fall down?"

"We don't know. We've no idea where our space starts or finishes. Some say it goes on for ever. We've almost never had a bird accident in the air because we keep them very fit, and never send them far at one go. There's no such thing as a traffic accident like you have with all those cars and trains," said Gogo.

"And in any case seven birds can't all fall down'" agreed Sonny.

"No I wish you could come Sonny, said Gogo. "I know you must be tired but you come from a different world, and sometimes you see things we don't."

"Of course I'll come. This is more important than being tired and in any case I'm not," said Sonny.

"Another thing I haven't explained," said Gogo,"is I put bits of a Pongoland moss under your door nowadays. It's tiny here like dust. But it has a curious scent which makes people forget what they were going to do, so they do something else instead. Supposing your Mummy meant to come into your room for instance, she'd remember something else she had to do, in the kitchen for instance, and go downstairs".

"I never worried much", said Sonny."I was too keen to go with you, and in any case we set off late. She doesn't normally come in after ten because I tend to wake up if she does".

"It's one of Mother Fulati's plants she uses for medical purposes. We can't buy it in a shop. If we want some we have to go to her and explain why. If she thinks the reason is alright she'll give us some, and only a bit. She says most of her plants are dangerous if wrongly used," said Gogo.

At ten-thirty Gogo took Sonny by the hand. As he did so Sonny reduced to Gogo's height. Goggles flew across from the neem tree and away they flew into the night, over the tree tops and under the stars.

When they arrived back in the meadow a scene of confusion met their eyes. The stage was half up and half dismantled. Some of the carpets were rolled and some remained, but the trestle table was gone. Pongos big and small were standing around staring into the sky in hopes of a sign of a Maridoland bird. In the meadow there were several Maridos and their birds, flown in when they heard of the disappearance of the Spangles.

"No good waiting here," said Gogo. "Let's go up to my house and see what my parents think".

Murgo Pongo, Gogo's father, worked in the service of the King. So whatever there was to know he had usually heard, and Gogo's parents would be discussing it.

When Gogo and Sonny entered his house they found Murgo and Gogo's Mother quite distracted. Tobo was sitting unusually quiet. He had been crying. The Pongoland King had asked Murgo to enquire all round the island to discover it there had been any Pongo plot against the Spangles. The very idea seemed unthinkable. Murgo had come first to his wife as she worked part of her time in a clothing factory, and met together with many other women of the island. She too said no-one had been anything but happy about the visit of the Spangles.

"Supposing anyone wasn't happy what would he do?" asked Sonny. Murgo thought a bit.

"You see we never kill each other like you people do. We don't kill our animals or birds. Sometimes there are fights and people get hurt, but I have never heard of an islander killing anyone."

"I wish our world was like that,"said Sonny.

"Our world is much simpler than yours", said Murgo. "Heaven seems much closer here I believe, and we know we go there when we die. We don't send people off to Heaven because we are cross!"

"Well suppose someone was jealous of the Spangles, or didn't like them. What might he do if he was angry?"

"Stop the tour?" suggested Murgo. "On try to prevent it. That's the likely thing. But no-one did."

Gogo and Sonny looked at each other.

"Of course there could be all sorts of reasons, why they didn't turn up in Pelidoland", said Gogo.

"Yes. Would you mind if we went for a walk to think?" Sonny asked Gogo's parents.

"No, think all you can," said Gogo's mother. "Murgo is just going to go round the village."

"Let me come too!" cried Tobo to Gogo.

Sonny and Gogo and Tobo set off up the hill.

"Supposing someone wished them harm," said Sonny. "Do you have any musicians in Pongoland who might feel jealous?"

"We like to sing and dance but we don't have any really good talent," said Gogo.

"What are the Spangles paid?" asked Sonny.

"They aren't paid anything," said Gogo surprised. "We barter our things, like food and household things and toys, because the people who produce them have to barter for what they need. But you can't barter for music."

"The musicians also have to live," said Sonny.

"Our Kings look after us. That's their job. Artists and musicians live close to the palaces and the kings send them provisions. My father receives the same. When artists go on tour to other Islands the King of the host country makes an exchange with the King of the players. All our craftsmen send part of their produce to the palace. We don't have any banks. Everything is stored in the palace. When anyone is too old or sick to work the King sends him what he needs."

"So you don't have money?" asked Sonny.

"The King does have some coins. His head is engraved on them, and because we deal in metal Pongoland makes coins for other Islands. The same coin but with their King's head on them. They are used between the Kings as tokens of something owed. Later they are used in exchange for some produce when it comes available," said Gogo.

"So in this case no-one was jealous about money," said Sonny."Why would anyone want to harm the Spangles?"

"I don't know," said Gogo."It's a real mystery."

"So maybe they went somewhere else", said Sonny

"Like where? All the nearby Islands know the Spangles have gone missing."

"And the Spangles couldn't make their birds go a longer distance," said Sonny.

"No and they are due to sing in Pelidoland tonight. They wouldn't run off."

"So if they went somewhere else it would have to be against their will."

"Yes," said Gogo,"But the Spangles are going turn by turn to all the surrounding Islands in any case. Why kidnap them?"

"I don't know", said Sonny. Tobo had been listening carefully.

"Maybe for a ransom?" he piped in. He had read about ransoms in history books where people were forced to do something because someone had been kidnapped. Supposing a ransom was asked for the Spangles! Wow!"

"What ransom?" asked Gogo.

"Well something," said Tobo doggedly. "Something musical if they've kidnapped the Spangles."

"That's an idea!" said Sonny excitedly.

"Music isn't a thing," pointed out Gogo, "you can't be given it."

"Well what about the instruments then?" said Sonny.

"A hundred tintareenas or we won't give you back the Spangles. It's crazy Sonny," said Gogo.

"I know. But something on those lines."

"And in any case why the Spangles? You or I would do just as well," said Gogo.

They sat on the grass verge a short way below the Palace where they had often rested.

"Go and see if there are any windfalls Tobo," said Gogo, and Tobo ran off into the orchard.

"We're allowed to gather fruit which has fallen off the trees at the moment," said Gogo. "The Queen is collecting a lot for jam, but there is plenty to spare."

The Pongoland orchards were very good and covered the slopes of the hillside. Sonny was thinking.

"Gogo, supposing someone has kidnapped the Spangles, they'll have to feed them wont they, and people don't have money for five extra people and seven birds."

"No. You think they would have to steal or beg or something," said Gogo.

"They can't ask the king for provisions for their prisoners," said Sonny.

"We could look and see if anyone is gathering an unusual amount of extra fruit!" joked Gogo.

"Yes let's! At least we'll be doing something,"said Sonny.

Tobo came back with apples and pears, and they munched these for a while. The sun was bright and warm but not too hot. Bees were buzzing around and Sonny could hear the small birds of Pongoland chirruping among the trees. How he loved this place! You didn't need a T.V. if you lived here, not even one which played twenty-four hours a day, as they did now. There was too much to do, and the Spangles' concert was better than any T.V. programme.

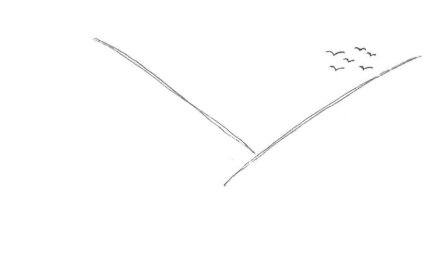

Sonny and the Spangles Part 2

After they had eaten Gogo, Sonny, and Tobo wandered into the orchard. Tobo was very excited. It was his idea which had led to this new adventure and he was going to spy around every tree for anyone carrying a lot of fruit.

Sonny and Gogo weren't so hopeful, but thought it worth-while looking at least. Sonny felt the sort of motives which could lead to the kidnapping of a pop-group in Pongoland were beyond his power to imagine in any case. He was a child like Gogo, and did not know much about island affairs. Gogo felt any reasonable idea should be followed up, to be on the safe side. His Father was always very thorough his Mother said, and he wanted to be the same, and one day enter the King's service too.

The orchards stretched quite a long way round the hill and down towards the meadows. A river round the other side of the hill, and the hills beyond became craggier. They were more difficult to climb with steep rough paths. Most of the population lived on the hill on which the palace was built, but the sheep farmers lived on the more distant hills where their sheep and goats grazed. Cows were kept in the meadow-land.

Sonny had not been round that side of Pongoland much except for once when he went on a picnic with Gogo's family. Gogo said those hills contained gold, copper, and other metals and gems used by the Pongos in their beautiful metal work. Some metals they mined. The work was done in caves hollowed into the hills.

As the children emerged from the orchard on the far side they looked across the valley to the next range of hills. They could see the sheep grazing on the slopes. Gogo said they made their warm clothes from the wool of their own sheep. They could see a brown earthen track winding up between two of the hills. Sonny asked where it led and Gogo said to the metal workers' caves.

"Should we look there do you think?" asked Sonny.

"Well I suppose we should but it's lunch-time. We're already late."

"I say let's go Gogo, because it's no search if we just stay in our own back garden,"said Sonny.

"Alright", said Gogo reluctantly. "Tobo had better go back and tell Mummy where we've gone. She won't be too pleased!" Tobo did not at all want to go home. He complained he always missed all the fun.

"It's a long way Tobo", said Sonny. " Even we are going to be tired. And we can't go unless someone goes back with a message".

Tobo gave in and went off grumbling.

Sonny and Gogo set off down the hill. They could follow the path in the valley until it met the earthen track. The weather was quite warm and they were both thirsty and hungry, but they pressed on.

"You'll enjoy seeing the metal workers in any case Sonny," said Gogo."It's really fascinating watching them. We all go from time to time to see what they are doing. They sell their wares in our market, but we can also go and barter directly with the workers if we need to. That way you often get something new, or you can order something special."

Eventually they reached the brown earth path which led up a fairly steep slope. By now they could hear the sound of hammers on metal. Some of the workers were singing. Mainly men worked in the caves. Gogo said they never closed. The precious metals and stones could not be left, so night workers came on duty as the day workers left and went home.

"So actually there's always someone on guard here,"said Sonny"You can't walk in with five people and seven birds and not be noticed."

"No you jolly well well can't," said Gogo.

"Oh well. It's worth looking around," said Sonny. "Maybe someone noticed something."

As they approached the first cave they could see a group of people wrapping up large bundles.

"They are to go to market," said Gogo.

"Hello," said Gogo to one of the men. "We're looking around to see if the Spangles came round this side of the island at all. You know they disappeared."

"Yes," said the man, "but they didn't come round here. In any case you all waved them off to Pelidoland from the meadow."

"I know," said Gogo, "but there's just the slightest chance someone brought them back to Pongoland. They didn't turn up in Pelidoland. So we thought we'ld search round a bit."

"Kidnapped them you mean?" said a woman, "Two men, three girls, and seven birds?"

"Well they aren't in these caves," said the man, pointing inwards.

"No, well we'll look further up," said Gogo, and he and Sonny set off up the hill.

"It's so awkward," said Gogo. "There are more caves."

"Are there any unused?" asked Sonny.

"Not with anything valuable in them," said Gogo, "and they are all open as you can see."

As Sonny looked up the hillside where sheep were grazing he saw a flash.

"Look! Up there Gogo! Something's flashing in the sun!"

"It'll be someone with a jug or something," said Gogo. "Oh no! Look! That man is playing it".

"Is it a trumpet?" asked Sonny.

"We don't have any trumpets. We have pipes. I can hear it now, can you?"

"Yes. It's not very musical."

"No. Usually our pipes are quite high-pitched. That's sort of hollow."

"Let's go and look," said Sonny.

They left the path and climbed up the grassy slope. As they approached they could see the man was a middle aged Pongo in brown trousers, green shirt, and brown hat. He was playing a copper instrument.

"Is that a pipe?" asked Sonny.

"No it isn't! I've never seen anything like it," said Gogo.

The man was blowing through a narrow mouth-piece, and the instrument rounded into several globes of increasing size until it opened out at the other end. Each small globe had a hole in it.

"Would you mind my asking what that instrument is?" asked Gogo.

"It's a bonka," said the man.

"A what?"

"A bonka. I invented it. I like to sit playing it sometimes while I watch the sheep,"

"Er. Yes," said Gogo and he and Sonny exchanged looks at the wierd groans coming out of the instrument.

They moved on a bit.

"He must be tone-deaf," said Sonny. "It's frightful isn't it?"

"Ghastly. He's not a metal worker so he must have designed it, and got one of the workers to make it for him,"

"Let's ask him if he heard the Spangles," said Sonny. "Maybe he would think they were off-key."

Gogo giggled. They returned.

"Excuse me Sir," said Sonny. "Did you go to the Spangles' concert last night?" The man looked put out.

"Yes I did. I don't know who could have trained them."

"You didn't like them?" asked Sonny.

"They'ld be alright with some improvements," said the man.

"Like what?" asked Gogo.

"I don't know. I'm only a musician,"said the man.

Gogo and Sonny walked away.

So there's someone with a grudge isn't there," said Sonny. "He's jealous. And angry."

"Yes," said Gogo, "but where does that lead us?"

"I don't know. Where does he live?"

"No idea. We can ask at one of the farm-houses," said Gogo.

They walked across the grass to the nearest little farm-house with pale yellow walls. It was fenced and had hens and chickens scratching near the door. There was also a large out-building for the sheep when they were brought in to be sheared.

Gogo knocked at the door and a stout lady in a blue skirt and darker blue shirt opened it.

"Hello," said Gogo. "We've just passed a man playing an instrument he calls a bonka. Does he live round here do you know?"

Toplo and his bonka!" exclaimed the woman." He lives at the top of the hill that way." She pointed. "No-one will have him play near their houses. His wife's left him because she can't stand it. The house is red. Even that's an eyesore. He's a queer chap."

"Thanks," said Gogo. "May we have a glass of water each please?"

"Of course! Come in and I'll give you some of my peach sherbat. It's turned out very well this year." They went into her kitchen where there was an appetising smell from a large round cauldron on the oven.

"Maybe you'ld like some broth?" she asked.

Sonny and Gogo could not say no. By now they were starving, as well as weary. In no time they were sitting at her scrubbed table with a bowl of broth each and a piece of home-made bread. They ate silently.

"What are you doing round this side of the island?" asked the lady. "I'm Minette."

Gogo introduced them and explained they were looking for news of the Spangles. He told her they wondered if the Spangles might have had to return to the island. The woman sat down at the table.

"That's an interesting idea," she said. "Do you mean they may have been kidnapped?"

"They might have been," said Gogo. "It's just an idea."

"And you're looking suspiciously at funny old Toplo?"

"Well –yes," said Sonny, embarrassed. The woman did not laugh as they might have expected.

"He's got a thing about that bonka," she said. "After all he loved it better than his wife. He doesn't know what real music is. Some people can't understand music. But how could he kidnap five people and seven birds? And in any case how would that help him? Unless you think he might have done it out of spite because they are popular and he isn't."

"Well we aren't actually thinking much at all yet," said Sonny. "More looking for ideas. We'll take a look at his house."

"He's a crazy man," said Minette. "He once threw a chair out because he bumped his shin on it. You go and look. If he heads up back here I'll call him in for a glass of sherbat."

"Thanks," said Gogo.

He and Sonny, much refreshed, set off up the hillside in the direction Minette had shown them. As they rounded the crest of the hill they could see the red house with its black roof on a ledge lower down. They walked down towards it. The house was bleak. There were no hens in the yards, no curtains at the windows, no sign of life.

An unhappy man. They went up to one of the windows. Toplo obviously did not take care of his home. It was dirty and untidy.

"There's no-one here," said Sonny.

"What a miserable place isn't it?" said Gogo.

"Let's look at the out-house," said Sonny.

The farm out-house was some distance from the home because of the noise and smell of sheep-shearing. This one was locked. They tried the door, and heard noises within.

"Help!" called a voice.

"Hello!" called another voice.

"Hello!" shouted Sonny and Gogo, "Who's in there?"

"We are! The Spangles! He's locked us in!"

Sonny and Gogo couldn't believe their luck!

"We've been searching for you all over the island. We wondered if someone somehow had brought you back to Pongoland," called Gogo.

A voice answered.

"He wanted to show us his instrument! He said it was a new design and it would only take a minute to show us! He waved to us from the top of the hill. We thought we'ld better come down and see what was the matter. And here we are! We looked at his instrument. It's frightful!"

"He calls it a bonka!" said another voice. "It makes a noise like the air coming out of a hole in a large balloon. Several large balloons."

"I know, we've heard it," called Sonny.

"He wanted us to get him an order for bonkas, and use them in our group to advertise them. One of the metal-workers is his brother and would make them," said the first voice.

"We said no!" called someone else. "So he locked us in here where he had put his bonka for us to see. He says we can't come out till we order the bonkas. He's a madman."

"Where's the key?" asked Gogo.

"He has keys on a ring on his belt. We've got no food and the birds are suffering dreadfully. I think mainly he wants to punish us because when we play everyone claps. Please get us out," said one of the voices.

The door was of heavy wood and the handle and lock were of iron.

"Don't worry," called Sonny. "We'll do something. We'll get you out as soon as we can. Toplo is watching his sheep on the other side of the hill, so we'll have to leave you for a moment. Don't worry."

They had to leave the poor Spangles to suffer for a while longer as they hurried back over the hill.

"Minette will help us," panted Gogo.

"Yes she's a very nice lady," said Sonny.

As soon as they reached the top of the hill they could see Minette's yellow house.

"Let's see Minette first," said Gogo, and they hurried down the hill. They could not hear the bonka. They went and knocked on Minette's door, and she opened it. Behind her they could see Toplo drinking sherbat.

"Er- Minette," gulped Gogo, and signalled with his hand up the hill and pointed at Toplo.

"What?" whispered Minette. She stepped outside and pulled the door too. "What's happened?"

"He's got the Spangles locked up in his shed," whispered Gogo. "He won't let them out till they order bonkas from him and agree to play them in public."

"What!" exclaimed Minette quietly. She closed the door and took her key from her pocket.

"Shall I lock him in here?" she suggested.

"He's got his shed key hanging on his belt," said Sonny.

"It's a risk," said Minette locking her door, "but I can ask for his key before I unlock this door. He might do damage in there though."

She went to her kitchen window.

"Hey Toplo!" she called. "You give me the key to your shed or you are a prisoner here." Sonny and Gogo looked at each other gleefully. Toplo ran to the window furious.

"What do you mean?" he shouted. "You let me out of here right now Minette".

"Not until you pass me your shed key through the window. I will then keep you prisoner for a while as a punishment. At least you won't starve or go thirsty like the Spangles at the moment."

Toplo looked at Sonny and Gogo.

"You interfering twisters!" he cried. "You had no business poking roiund my farm!"

"At least we found the Spangles," said Sonny. "You're a crook Toplo and we will tell the King. Gogo's father works for the King."

Toplo went purple.

"You can't do that," he said.

"Yes we can," said Gogo. "I can't hide a kidnapping from my father, and he will tell the King himself straight away."

"But….. but……… I'll go to prison," whispered Toplo.

"You should have thought of that," said Minette firmly. "You didn't mind imprisoning the Spangles. Now hand over that key and I'll tell the King that basically you are just a silly old man. Maybe he'll take a bit of pity on you."

Toplo was whimpering.

"I've made such a nice instrument. It just needs a bit of promotion to make it sell all round the islands."

He handed over his shed key to Minette who gave it to Gogo. The two boys set off at a run up the hill.

How joyful the Spangles were to be free! Gogo said it would be best to take them to Minette's house first. The birds were angry but thankful to be free. The Spangles and Sonny and Gogo climbed on to their backs, and in another minute they were all back outside Minette's house. She welcomed them with open arms and then unlocked her door. Toplo crept out.

"How dare you lock us up!" shouted Rosie.

"It was a small thing I wanted," said Toplo, "You're famous and you sing everywhere. No-one wants to hear me."

"No, well why not take some lessons like we did," said Magda, "but that bonka will never sell I can promise you. It can't play a tune."

"Let's put him in my shed," said Minette. Instantly they all surrounded him, and Tolly and Perry grabbed him by his wrists. They dragged him over to Minette's shed and locked him in.

"That will take care of him for a while," said Minette. "Come along in all of you. I've got broth all ready on the stove, and plenty of grain for the birds."

She gave them each a glass of sherbat first, and put grain in a trough for the birds and water in a bowl. The others were soon round the kitchen table eating Minette's fine broth and freshly-made bread.

"We must go on to Pelidoland now," said Rosy. "We're very late but we'll be in time for the concert."

"Yes you do that," said Minette. "We'll see to Toplo. Our King will discuss with your King what sort of recompense Pongoland owes you. I can only apologise on behalf of our island. Toplo has really brought shame on us."

Gogo hung his head. He could not remember when Pongoland had suffered such an embarrassment and humiliation. All because of a foolish old man like Toplo!

After lunch they trudged home, lighter in heart at least that the Spangles were on their way to Pelidoland.

Gogo's parents were very worried about their long absence. After all, if the Spangles could disappear, so could Gogo and Sonny! Tobo had spent the afternoon rushing to the gate to look out for them coming down the hill. How thankful his parents were when he could shout out that Gogo and Sonny were coming!

And how furious Murgo was when he heard about Toplo's crime! He said he must go up to the palace immediately. Palace guards were already scouring the island for news of the Spangles. Now they could go and fetch Toplo from Minette's shed. Toplo's brother would also have to be collected from the caves, although the kidnapping was only Toplo's work.

Later Minette kept her promise to give a plea to the King for some clemency for Toplo but the King refused. He said the honour of Pongoland was at stake and he must be able to show Maridoland that proper punishment had been given.

After some discussion with the Maridoland ambassador the King decided to give the Spangles a set of instruments of their own choice in the metals of their choice and embellished in finest gold. The King of Maridoland agreed that this was a fitting recompense.

Back home on Monday morning Sonny's thoughts were on the events of the night before. He was very thankful at the outcome, but very tired indeed after all the walking, and climbing at top speed. He could have only three hours' sleep before getting up to go to school but he was very happy!

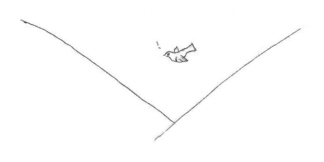

81

Sonny and the Trade Fair

Part One

One morning Sonny woke up to see Gogo's face close to his, his eyes sparkling with excitement. Sonny had not been to Pongoland for a while as he was having his school exams, and needed to be sure of good nights' sleep with no distractions until they were completed.

"What's the matter?" he asked grumpily because he was tired of missing all the fun.

"Tomorrow is our Trade Fair!" said Gogo.

"What's that?" said Sonny.

"Why once a year there's a big fair when all the islanders bring their produce to sell! Each island hopes for big orders from all the other islands. You know we specialize in gold and metal work with precious stones. We always sell a lot on Trade Fair day."

"But you've got no money!"

"We barter as always. We each stock up on supplies to last till the next year."

"I've never heard of the Fair before," said Sonny.

"I know we children never bother. The islands take it in turns to host the Fair, so it's been somewhere else in recent years, but tomorrow it is in Pongoland!"

"There will be a lot of visitors. Where do they stay?"

"All the royal families stay in the Palace. The other people stay in tents we put up in the meadows. There are lots of preparations going on. All the tents have to be put up, and we have to have a great deal of food prepared. It's set out on long tables for breakfast, lunch, and dinner. Quite often people from the nearby islands, like Maridoland, don't stay over-night, but after dinner there is always an entertainment put on by the host island."Sonny's eyes shone.

"My exams finished yesterday and it's Saturday tomorrow. Can I come tonight?"

"Of course! Mum and Dad especially asked for you to come. We'll have a lovely time."

Pongoland was one of the many islands above the clouds, but they could be visited only in the company of one of the inhabitants on the back of one of their birds. No aeroplane ever encountered one. Each island had its' own birds for transport to other islands, and Gogo always flew between Sonny's house and his own island, Pongoland, on the back of Goggles, his family's owl. Gogo was the size of a large toy clown, and had a somewhat similar appearance with baggy trousers fitting close to the ankles, and a striped shirt, and cap with a pom-pom on it. His nose curved up to a point like all the inhabitants of Pongoland, and his hair was black and curly.

No-one ever performed magic tricks in the islands, but magic was taken for granted. Things were done or happened without comment when the need or purpose was right. Sonny managed to travel because Gogo took his hand to go. He then reduced in size to Gogo's height, and they climbed on to Goggles' back together from Sonny's bedroom window-sill. Needless to say Sonny's parents knew nothing about it, or the interference would have stopped the journeys, and would have obliged Gogo to stay at home. As it was he spent the night in Pongoland where it was day. Then returned to Sonny's house in our morning. There he slept in Sonny's bed till night-time. Sonny's parents thought he was a toy because he never moved when they were in the room. He had been investigating in a toy-shop in our world when Sonny's uncle picked him up, thinking Gogo was a toy clown. He bought him as a birthday present for Sonny. The two children were soon fast friends, and Sonny had been many times to Pongoland, and had enjoyed lots of adventures there. Some of these were caused by Gogo's younger brother Tobo. Tobo was a happy little Pongo boy but apt to get into messes.

Sonny had to go to school that day. Then he planned to go to bed early to get some sleep before Goggles arrived to take Gogo and him to Pongoland. After a trip there he would have an afternoon nap.

Goggles duly arrived and waited on a neem tree not far from Sonny's bedroom window. He hooted a couple of times to let them know he was here. Sonny opened the window and the owl flew across to the window-sill. Gogo took Sonny's hand as usual and Sonny became the same height as Gogo. Gogo then went across to the bedroom door and scattered some dried moss from Pongoland underneath the door. The powder was so fine it could hardly be seen. It had the effect of making anyone intending to enter the room think of something else and go away. Then they climbed on to the window-sill and on to Goggles' back. Off they flew, over the tree-tops and under the stars.

Sonny always loved these journeys through the night sky. How lucky he was! After a while they glimpsed the sunlight in the distance shining down on Pongoland. They could see the green meadow where the travel birds collected, and where Goggles usually landed. Hills rose up from the meadow, and at the top of the highest they could see the towers of the Palace, the home of Pongoland's King. Gogo's house was half-way up the same hill.

Normally the meadow was covered with long grass and wild flowers, but today a huge space had been cleared. In the distance could be seen many tents, and trestle tables spread with white cloths, and laden with tureens and bowls of food. In the fore-ground there was a great deal of bustle. Each island was allotted a long table on which to display its' produce, and these tables were placed at the other end of the open space. Some of the products were already ticketed by customers wishing to agree later on to a barter. Some of the actual items were exchanged on the day of the Fair itself, especially to individual islanders, but in the main the products were samples for the visitors to see and make their orders accordingly. The process was already in progress, and a great deal of haggling going on, after which an agreement would be made. Gogo told Sonny that certificates of exchange passed between the two parties to avoid any confusion later, and deliveries would be made the following week.

Amongst the crowds wandering from table to table were the royal families. They had to see that the basic supplies were ordered for the coming year. Some islands needed wood, some needed metals, some wanted wool or cotton cloth. A great deal of food stocks were acquired for household requirements. These would later be displayed in the shops on the high streets of the islands. Each family could order according to its own needs. The Kings had the responsibility of assessing correctly how much would be needed of each item for the year. The Palaces maintained the stocks in huge granaries, underground cold rooms, and in warehouses within the walls of the palace. In emergency islanders could apply directly to the palace for an unexpected need.

The individual islanders stocked the pantries and cupboards of their houses with whatever caught their eye. They had to come to the Fair armed with goods they had stored ready for exchange, and they made their own agreements with the table-keepers. The large supplies were carried away in sheets or bags, and those going to other islands were carried there by four of the island's birds, one at each corner.

Goggles landed in the meadow, and would wait there until Sonny and Gogo were ready to return. In spite of all the exciting things going on they headed straight for Gogo's home first to meet his family.

They were all thrilled to see Sonny again and hugged him joyfully. As usual they had appropriate Pongo clothes ready for him to wear during his visit. Today he was to wear black and silver-coloured trousers, and a silver and yellow striped shirt with yellow cap. As soon as he had put them on they made him sit at the kitchen table and have toast and honey. Tobo was rushing round unable to contain himself with excitement.

Then after a pause Gogo's father, Murgo, who was in the service of the King, said,

"I hate to greet you with news of another problem Sonny, but unfortunately we're in a bit of a fix. It's a secret but I know you will not tell anyone."

Seeing Murgo's serious face, Sonny was a little alarmed.

"What's happened?" he asked.

"Well you know we are famous for our gold and metal work inlaid with jewels from the island's caves. It is very fine indeed, and we sell to all the islands, even those far distant from here come for our work. One Pongo necklace can be exchanged for many cheeses, so that means we are more affluent than those islands which have mainly farm produce to exchange. Last year this led to bad feeling, it seems, in Flannon."

"But Dad," said Gogo, "the King has always taken that into account. He has always given an extra third in gold to purely farming islands. There aren't many," said Gogo to Sonny, "but Flannon is one of them."

"Well as you know Flannon is far distant from Pongoland. It is a five-bird flight from here. The King knows their Royal Family naturally. Last year it was their turn to host the Trade Fair. The King and Queen and I and a few other officials went, and a few islanders, but it was too far for most people to spare the time. Also Flannon doesn't have interesting things to barter. There are almost no luxury goods. They lead simpler lives than we do in Pongoland. It seems they did not do well at the Fair."

"So what happened? Asked Sonny anxiously. Pongoland's troubles had become his troubles.

"It seems some of them blamed Pongoland for their poor returns. This morning a party of their young men arrived here out to make trouble."

"Oh gosh!" exclaimed Gogo. "Are they going to fight? What sort of trouble?"

"I don't think so," said Murgo, "they haven't said. There's a group of them standing near the tents looking pleased with themselves. The King is definitely disturbed."

"Should Gogo and I go down there and wander casually near the Flannon tent?" suggested Sonny. "We might be able to pick up what they are saying. They won't take any notice of us. We might find out what sort of trouble they are planning." Murgo thought a bit.

"Well I can't see any harm in that, but don't go too close, and don't let them see you are listening. Be careful, O.K.?"

"We'll be careful," promised Gogo.

"Let me come too!" piped up Tobo.

"No Tobo," said his Father. "If Sonny and Gogo go to the meadow Mummy needs your help."

Tobo looked disappointed and pleased at the same time, but he went through to the kitchen to help his Mother pack all the food she had prepared to take down to the meadow for the visitors. All the families contributed to the meals served on Fair day.

Sonny and Gogo set off down the road back to the meadow.

"I'll ask Goggles to help," said Gogo. "He can peck around near the tents."

They hurried across the meadow and then strolled casually in the direction of the tents. They walked along an aisle between food tables. The tables for the produce were at the other end of the field. Each of those tables had a placard in front announcing whose the table was, and behind the table stood islanders hoping for orders. All the visitors had shopping-lists, and members of the royal families had lists for their whole island to build up sufficient stocks of food provisions and other necessities for hot and cold weather for the next year.

It was a time too to renew friendships and make new friends. In the area set aside for the food tables many groups were already talking excitedly and exchanging news.

Sonny and Gogo proceeded slowly until they were close to the tents. Lots of islanders were coming in and out of their own tents, as most people stayed overnight.Since there was always an entertainment arranged for the evening when the trading was done, few wanted to miss that. Sonny and Gogo glanced towards the tent labelled Flannon. A group of young men stood conferring privately near the entrance. Sonny said,

"Gogo why don't you go closer to try and hear what they are saying? If I went they would be suspicious immediately."

Gogo wandered over slowly to the end of the food tables, and paused to study the dishes. Sonny watched from behind some women and children. He caught a glimpse of gold from behind the men at the entrance, and thought there must be someone richly dressed standing inside. Gogo edged closer and risked a glance inside the tent. He too spied someone, a young man or boy, in a gold coat. What was going on? And what were the men near the tent flap plotting? They were talking so quietly he could hardly catch a word. Then he heard the word 'prince'. What? Prince whom? Was the person in the gold coat a prince? If so why on earth was he hiding? Flannon had its' King and Queen and two daughters. They were well-known and were out there walking round with other royalty.

It was gossiped that the older daughter was ready for marriage but so far her parents had not decided on a match. Oldest sons became kings of their island, and their wives, princesses from other islands, became their queens. If the oldest child was a girl she became queen of her own island, and whichever prince she married from another island became king of her island. The parents were guided mainly by the choices of their children, but sometimes according to the interest of their island. These were the customs which the islanders had accepted as their way of doing things. The King of Flannon had no son. Neither had the King of Pongoland, or indeed any children at all. The question as to who would be next King or Queen of Pongoland always weighed on the minds of the royal family, as on the minds of the whole population.

But what was going on in the Flannon tent? Had they chosen a husband for the princess and meant to present him later as a surprise? That was a possibility, but how would that be trouble for Pongoland? No-one in Pongoland cared whom she married. After a while the young men retreated into the tent and closed the flap. Gogo went back to Sonny.

"There seems to be a richly clad young man in there," said Gogo, "I couldn't see

properly but the men at the entrance spoke of a 'prince'."

"Prince who?" asked Sonny.

"No idea. Flannon doesn't have any princes. What can they be plotting? Let's go home and tell Father."

Murgo looked perplexed.

"Anyway," he said, "it's time for us to go. We'll all of us keep our eyes and ears open." The family set off to the Fair.

It was a wonderful day. Of course the children weren't there to buy anything. The parents wanted to buy food ingredients and cloth mostly, and they went armed with gold, copper, or silver objects beautifully crafted by their artisans. These craftsmen exchanged their work for their own needs, and contributed a great deal to the King's stock to use for barter at the Fair. In addition, mostly the women of the Island wove beautiful fine cloth, often threaded with gold or silver, or indeed woven from very finely spun metal. The metal threads interwoven with red or blue cotton or wool thread produced rolls of cloth of the highest quality, much in demand by all the islands. Many of these rolls were added to the King's store in the Palace to be used at the Fair.

The King's stores also supplied the little shops of Pongoland, situated on the High Street, From these shops the islanders could ask whatever they needed with no exchange. The King's store belonged to them all.

Today Gogo and Sonny walked in the direction of the Flannon table, as did Murgo himself. He had had a private word with the King of Pongoland who was now looking seriously disturbed. Sonny approached him and greeted him.

"Sir," he asked, "is something wrong?"

"Er, well Sonny, you are a very old and valued friend of this Island, so I can admit to you privately that I am concerned about who this "prince"might be. I ask you not to mention this subject to anyone except ourselves and Murgo's family."

"No, of course not. Who do you think he might be?"

"I don't know, but they are up to mischief to get revenge on Pongoland, or maybe just to get a better deal at the Fair somehow. But," the King paused a minute, "I'm worried because I had a younger brother who disappeared twenty years ago."

"What! Gogo never told me."

"He probably doesn't know. The adults of Pongoland don't speak of it much because it is a painful subject. My brother, Anton, went off to "seek his fortune", he said. Normally he would have married a princess from another island and settled here, or if she became a Queen, he would have gone to live on her island. But Anton was restless and wanted adventure, so off he went on his owl. We had letters from time to time sent by owl courier, and one of them was indeed from Flannon. The

Flannon royal family who entertained him said he left their island, but after his visit there nothing more was heard of him."

"Oh that is really sad," exclaimed Sonny, "did you think he had had an accident?"

"Yes," said the King quietly. "That seemed to be the only explanation. If he had been alive he would have returned, or at least written to let us know what he was doing."

"So," said Sonny slowly, "you are wondering if that "prince" has something to do with your brother? But he wouldn't be hiding in their tent! It doesn't make sense!"

"No, it doesn't. I'm just uneasy that's all. Those Flannonders by the tent are way too smug. They are up to something."

"Can't you ask the King of Flannon?"

"What would I say Sonny?" asked the King.

"Is there anything Gogo or I can do?" asked Sonny.

"No Sonny thankyou. I'll handle it myself."

Sonny returned to Gogo and told him the gist of the conversation. Gogo wasn't surprised to hear about Anton because of the gossip he had heard at home.

"Let's keep an eye on that tent though Sonny. Whatever the man in the gold coat is up to he mustn't go out into the Fair without us seeing."

"No, right," agreed Sonny. So they set up a guard to keep watch. However, after some time they became very bored and went to have lunch. Three men came out of the Flannon tent to get plates of food and took them back inside the tent. Sonny and Gogo talked to Murgo, and he told them to go and enjoy themselves. He said he had arranged for the tent to be watched.

So the children ran off happily to enjoy the day. Gogo's mother was sitting talking with her friends. She had ordered cheeses and butter from one of the dairy products tables in return for a roll of silver and blue cloth. She herself was a weaver in the cloth factory. Sonny and Gogo walked on.

"What do you know of Anton?" asked Sonny.

"Not much. Maybe he thought he hadn't much future here as a younger brother. Younger princes usually join the King's service, often in the diplomatic service, but Anton seems to have wanted to do something he felt would be more exciting. I think I might in his place. So he set off to look for something. He was a bit older than my parents."

"Do you think he must have had an accident?"

"Yes, he must have had. He would definitely have sent word to his family if he were alive. That can't be Anton in that tent. Why on earth would he be hiding! It's crazy. No, something else must be going on."

"They want a bigger share of the stuff here. You can understand that, " said Sonny. "So what might they do to get it? The Flannonders should have put their heads together years ago to see what they could do or make. Everyone needs wood. They could even plant trees! Look at Mother Fulati! She's got all those plants and makes medicines. She supplies the King with a huge stock and takes orders from so many islands. Flannon shouldn't be blaming others because they haven't done something like that. But do you think their royal family knows anything about this? The princesses are playing ball with other boys and girls. They don't look one bit as if there is a plot on."

"No," agreed Gogo. "Still probably no-one would tell them. Flannon has beautiful rivers with lots of fish, and they have woods and fields. No island is actually poor. The people of Pongoland work really hard."

"Yes," said Sonny, "you showed me the mines a long time ago and the factories where the women make all that cloth and all those household things. Maybe the King of Flannon is too lazy to think! Look at our King! Busy all the time to make everything here work."

Sonny said "our King" because when he was in Pongoland he tended to forget he wasn't a Pongo.

"Some of the Flannonders write poetry and songs. The King should be organizing the people to make things, like say books?" he joked.

As the sun was setting the islanders began to pack away the produce which was to be taken home, and that which they had bought. It would be carried on sheets or in bags by the birds. Mats were spread on the ground in front of a dais on which the Pongo entertainment would be performed. Musicians arranged themselves in front of the dais to provide the music. Everyone began to gather there in readiness for the Show.

Before the performance the King of Pongoland appeared on the dais to greet all the visitors, and thank them for making the day so happy and successful. He then returned to the special area set aside for the royal families and other dignitaries. Murgo sat there, but Gogo's mother preferred to sit with the children in front of the stage .

Sonny looked round for the Flannonders, eager to see if the 'prince' would appear, but there was no sign of the young men. The Show began with a choir of teenagers singing old Flannon folk songs. These gathered together people of all ages as they reminisced about their history. Neither

Sonny nor Gogo could concentrate, as they sensed something, possibly threatening, might be about to happen. They looked across at Murgo. He too was alert, glancing across at the Flannon tent. The King was apparently relaxed and chatting with his guests but Sonny knew he was not happy.

At last as a beautiful soprano stepped on to the stage to general applause the flap of the Flannon tent was lifted. The young men came out bringing with them a teen-age boy dressed in a gold coat, tight-fitting gold trousers, and on his head a golden Pongo cap. They filed round from the tents to the front towards the dais.

"This is it," muttered Sonny. The group went up the steps on to the stage. They excused themselves to the young singer and went to stand in the middle. To give him credit the boy was blushing crimson. The leader stepped forward,

"Your Majesties, your Royal Highnesses, ladies and gentlemen, we are here to represent the people of Flannon. The royal family of Flannon sprang up, and the King of Pongoland jumped to his feet shouting,,

"What! Explain yourselves!"

"That is easy," said the leader of the group. " Your brother Anton stayed with us on Flannon for a while twenty years ago. While he with us he secretly married a Flannon girl, and they had a son. Anton set off back to Pongoland with the news, but as you know sadly he never arrived. No-one knows what happened to him but this is his, Prince Vinit."

Everyone gasped, and then believing what the man said, they began to clap and cheer. The King suspected trouble, so apart from going on to the stage and embracing the boy in the gold clothing, he said nothing.

"Now we come to the next point," said the leader. "As we know the kings of the islands have always been given a large portion of the earnings at the Fair to keep in store to supply the people through the next year. Any younger brother or sister of the king works in the service of the King and is given a portion of the earnings. Prince Anton left us to return to Pongloland, and he intended to bring his family here to live on his own island. Prince Anton did not get back here. The widow and young son of Prince Anton, Vinit here, were therefore due a pension. We calculate that Vinit and his mother are now owed twenty years arrears in pension."

The King was dumbfounded. The King of Flannon was equally aghast. Obviously the existence of this prince was news to him. Vinit was scarlet.

Eventually the King of Pongoland told the audience,

"This must be talked about later in the Palace. There are many things to be sorted out and clarified." But the leader hadn't finished.

"If you look towards the birds' landing area where the piles of goods are ready to be taken away, you will see that the Pongo goods are surrounded by men from Flannon. So if Pongoland is unwilling to pay what it owes , we will take back with us the amount due to Anton's widow."

Everyone stood up to look to where the birds waited with the piles of stock to be carried away tomorrow. The Pongoland cargo was piled ready to be taken up to the Palace, and round this a number of Flannon men stood on guard. The Pongos in the audience started to run towards the landing area, but the King shouted,

"Stop! We will not fight over this. We will talk. Vinit, you, and you," he said to the leader, "and all of you will now come with me to the Palace. I warn you that the men of Pongoland will fight if necessary to prevent what belongs to us from being stolen, but we are civilized people and prefer to talk things through."

So both the Pongo and Flannon royal families, Vinit ,and the men left to go to the Palace, while the men guarding the Pongo cargo sat down to wait.

After they left the audience had no heart to continue with the concert, so the musicians played quietly while everyone talked at once, exclaiming and contending. Murgo had gone with the King's officials to the Palace, so Sonny, Gogo, and Tobo sat with Gogo's mother. She said,

"I can't believe this, Who is that boy really? Are they trying to tell us they have met us every year at the Fair and no-one ever once thought to mention they have Anton's wife and son on their island! It's ridiculous."

"Vinit could be half Pongo though," commented Gogo.

"Well he *would* have to look half Pongo to try this on, but the Pongo half isn't Anton's," said his mother with spirit. "It's the fishiest story I ever heard!"

"Yes," said Sonny, "they do have to explain why apparently no-one knew he existed until now."

"I wish we could get a private word with Vinit," said Gogo, "He looked completely mortified."

"Why don't we go up to the Palace and see what's happening?" suggested Sonny.

"You stay here boys," said Gogo's mother. "Let the King handle it and his staff."

"You're right, but I just feel we could hang around up there a bit to see what we might find out," urged Sonny. "We'll keep away from trouble."

Seeing the eager eyes of Sonny and Gogo she relented.

"Alright then, but I am relying on your *really* good sense." Tobo was excited.

"Let me go too!" His mother was about to refuse, but Gogo said,

"Let him stand in our garden so that we can get any message to him."

"Alright, but he and I will both go and stand in our garden," said his mother firmly.

Sonny and the Trade Fair

Part Two

Sonny and Gogo set off up the hill to the Palace. Gogo had told Goggles what they were going to do, and asked him to wait for them in one of the trees near the Palace gate. This was sensible and satisfied his mother.

As they drew near to the Palace they hid in some bushes to see what was happening. The gates were wide open, but the Palace guards were there. The courtyard was full of people but the king and his staff had gone inside. Neither they nor the prince nor the Flannon leadership was in sight.

"I wish we could creep in," said Sonny.

"No chance," said Gogo.

"I wonder where that prince is," said Sonny.

"We could ask a guard," suggested Gogo. "You ask."

He said this because the Palace staff knew Sonny was much in favour with the King. He had been helpful a number of times in sorting out problems, and the King always said he had a wise head on young shoulders.

So Sonny approached one of the guards.

"Good evening," he said politely. "What's going on? Are all the leaders inside?"

"That's right Sonny," said the guard. "What are you doing here?"

"Just curious, but everyone is worried."

The guard nodded.

"I gather that those Flannonders are saying that boy is Anton's son. He's not a Pongo boy though."

"Why do you say that?" asked Sonny. " He could be half Pongo."

"His ears aren't pointed."

"How do you know? He's wearing a Pongo cap."

"Someone snatched it off him to see," said the guard. "What with rounded ears and brown hair he only has the Pongo pointed nose."

"Still the pointed nose is important," said Gogo.

"The people of Flannon have black hair like ours," said the guard. "How come his is brown?"

"Oh wow!" cried Sonny. "That is interesting."

"Too right it is!" said the guard.

"Might we come in?" asked Sonny.

"Certainly not," said the guard. "Official business is going on in there. Not for children."

"O.K." Sonny and Gogo went back to sit behind the bush. They chewed over the news.

"It looks as if he is probably half Pongo," said Gogo. "The islanders, except for the royal families, somehow hardly ever inter-marry. We don't even travel all that much. If we do it's for a job; not to stay. The birds have never liked staying away from their own habitats, so that restricts us."

"I can't help feeling that boy isn't enjoying this. Whoever he is, he seems to have been bull-dozed into this stunt. But brown hair or no, we can't be absolutely certain he isn't Anton's son."

"No," agreed Gogo, "why don't we ask Goggles to fly over into the Palace to see what's going on?"

"Good idea," agreed Sonny. And Gogo hooted to Goggles.

The owl was happy to fly into the garden. It was almost dark now, so he could go unseen.

"See if you can find out where Vinit is," said Sonny.

The boys sat back to wait for news from Goggles. He was gone for some time but came back with news.

"Vinit is in one of the bedrooms at the back," he reported, "and he is locked in!"

"So he isn't taking part in the talks?" said Sonny.

"Not at all. He is very fed up. I stood on his window-sill to talk to him. I offered to carry him out (with your permission)," he added nodding to Gogo, "but he said there would be no point. There is nowhere for him to go here. He wants to go home."

"So what's going on?" asked Gogo.

"Those Flannonders want our share of the earnings at the Fair first, or that is their bargaining point, and they hope to persuade our King that Vinit is his rightful heir, and therefore due a pension back-dated twenty years. Vinit wouldn't get it of course as he is just a pawn."

"You think he is an imposter," said Sonny.

"Yes, certainly," said Goggles.

"They have to prove somehow that Vinit is our King's nephew. Then because he has no children of his own, Vinit becomes his heir," said Gogo.

"How do they prove that? By asking his mother? But she didn't even come, and The King and Queen of Flannon don't seem to have much to say."

"Maybe this is the first they have heard of it, and they are also waiting to see the proof," said Gogo.

"What does Vinit himself say about it?" asked Sonny.

"Vinit isn't sure," said Goggles. "It's true he's been brought up by his mother who is a Flannonder, and he doesn't remember his father. It was news to him though that his father was Anton."

"Who else could his father have been?" asked Gogo. "His mother must know and she isn't commenting apparently."

" Vinit says she was persuaded to agree he was Anton," said Goggles. "For her it will be very nice if Vinit is to be King of Pongoland. She isn't arguing," said Goggles.

"So why is Vinit fed up then?" asked Sonny.

"Because they are using him to steal wealth from Pongoland, and he doesn't like those men. They boss him about and treat him like a child. He says he would never be a real king with real power. Those men would stick to him like glue telling him what to do and say, and they would use him to make themselves rich. He thinks he would go on being a prisoner just as he is now. He says most of the people of Flannon have no idea what is going on here."

"Has he had a chance to talk to the King?" asked Sonny. He meant the King of Pongoland. "He needs to talk to him."

"No fear," said Goggles. "Those men locked his bedroom door, and they won't let him near anyone else."

"We need to get him out of there," said Sonny. "We can take him somewhere to hide until those men leave the Palace."

"Good idea," agreed Gogo. "Goggles could you persuade him to come with you? Say to the orchard? From there we can take him to some hiding-place."

"The mines are a good place," said Sonny. "We can talk to him, and tell him we will try to help. Then while you take him to the mines we can sort something out this end."

Goggles flew off again.

"This is exciting isn't it," said Gogo. "I don't know what Father and Mother will say, but at the moment this seems the best thing to do."

Goggles was soon back with a distressed Vinit. He was about fifteen years old, and had brown hair. He had lost his cap. His ears were not pointed, but not as rounded as human ears. His face was like a Pongo face but not quite the same.

"What are you going to do?" he cried. "What's happening now? I want to go home."

"We thought it would be a good idea to hide you for a while," said Sonny. "Their plans can't go forward if you have disappeared. Then we have to discuss with the King whether or not you could be his nephew. That is between you and your mother and him. Those men just want to create trouble."

"Yeah – OK," said Vinit. "My mother has to tell us. We've got a farm on Flannon. I love it! I've always been told it will be mine when I'm grown up. That's what I want. How can I be a King?" Vinit shook his head unbelievingly.

Goggles flew off with him to the mines and was under strict instructions to stay with him. One of the other owls would make contact when the time came.

"Now we really have to get inside the Palace," said Sonny. "Is there any back way in?"

"Not that I know of," said Gogo. "Of course there's the old tunnel from our house."

"What!"

"Yes. Long ago it was a secret way in and out of the Palace. A senior official has always live in our house. Dad has the key to the door though, and he's with the King."

"Where does it come out in the Palace?" asked Sonny.

"The kitchens. Dad showed us once. Even supposing we could open the door at our end Dad and the King would be furious to see us walk into court!" Gogo shuddered to think of the scene.

"Yes, that wouldn't work. We should be able to think of something though if we can once get inside," said Sonny.

"Alright well let's go to my house and check on the door," said Gogo. "What are we going to say to Mum?"

"Tell her the truth. We can't come to any harm after all."

Gogo's mother listened to their story. She was relieved to feel they had got Vinit out of the hands of the Flannon men. The King would deal with the rest. Sonny and Gogo had handled so many adventures very competently, and she thought that if they could get to Gogo's father, at least, to tell him what they had done that would be the best thing. She and Tobo went down to the cellar with them. Gogo led the way to the back of a cold storage room where there was a heavy wooden door with a large key-hole.

"Your father doesn't carry that huge key around with him Gogo," she said. "He just puts it where he can find it. We hardly ever have occasion to use the tunnel after all. The walk up the hillside is much nicer, and through the gate." She looked up at the beams running across the ceiling of the cellars.

"He's probably left the key up there somewhere on a beam.

"Why don't I get the ladder so I can go up and look." He and Sonny carried the ladder between them to the cold storage room. Gogo placed it against the wall next to the tunnel door and climbed up. Sure enough it was on the beam on the other side of the door. In no time they had it in their hands. The key-hole was oiled but the lock was stiff.

"I can't remember when we last opened that door," Gogo's mother commented.

"I wish I could go too," said Tobo hopefully.

"Not today love," said his mother. "We will go and keep watch in the garden again."

The boys took the key with them as the same key opened both doors. The way was steep as it was the shortest and most direct route to the Palace. In about ten minutes they had reached the door leading into the kitchens. They paused a minute, listening at the door. Then they peeped through the key-hole but couldn't see much.

"Imagine the cooks' faces if we walk in on them," giggled Gogo. Sonny squinted through the hole for some time.

"I can't see anyone," he said. "But we're kids! We're exploring right? You're showing me the tunnel."

"O.K." agreed Gogo. The key turned in the lock and the next minute they were in the Palace kitchen. They closed the door but decided to leave it unlocked for quick exit. Gogo knew the Palace well as his father had brought him several times to see round. He led Sonny up the stairs to the ground floor. There they entered a richly carpeted well-lit corridor. They walked along past a few doors and into the main hall. Sonny looked up to see a huge dome over-head. Gogo crossed the hall confidently to an ornate arched door. Sonny recognized this part of the Palace as he had been here himself more than once. They put their ears to the door to see if they could hear what was going on. There were raised angry voices as the Flannonders tried to bully the King into agreeing to their demands.

"No manners have they?" remarked Gogo. "They could make their case much better if they spoke quietly and reasonably. " They could hear the King's responses, but not what he said.

"The trouble is we don't know if Vinit could be Prince Anton's son or not," said Sonny.

"No," said Gogo. "What do we do now?"

"Wait our chance, I think," said Sonny. "We need to catch your father, or the King, to tell them we've got Vinit safely."

"Right," said Gogo despondently. "I don't want to be unpatriotic, but I can't help worrying about the trouble we are probably in."

"I know," said Sonny. "Can't be helped. You have to do what seems best sometimes. Those men must have plans for getting Vinit out. Maybe on one of their own birds. His attitude to this whole thing wouldn't help their cause. No way are they going to let him talk to the King."

"We have to get him to our King and Queen," said Gogo, "but time is getting short for you. That's our problem. I'll have to call another owl to go to the mines and send Goggles back here. Then he can stay on guard there till Goggles gets back. Tobo can go with you." Sonny agreed there was no choice. He had to be in his own bed at home by dawn no matter what.

"You keep watch here while I go and look for an owl." Gogo's presence in the main part of the Palace was accepted. He was Murgo's son and Murgo was here. He went to a small door over-looking the gardens at the back so that the guards by the main gate didn't see him. They knew he was unauthorised! From there he could hoot for an owl. Then he returned to the hall to wait with Sonny. At that moment a footman carrying a tray crossed the hall. Sonny stepped out boldly.

"Hello. Excuse me. Please would you tell Mr. Murgo Pongo that his son is out here waiting to speak to him?" The footman studied the two boys. He knew Gogo of course and although the situation in the Court-room wasn't good he could hardly refuse to tell Murgo that his son was here.

"Wait a minute," he said.

A minute later Murgo came out looking preoccupied and a bit exasperated.

"What on earth! Sonny! What are you doing here?"

"Dad!" whispered Gogo urgently, "We've talked to Vinit! He says those men are just crooks and the people of Flannon don't know anything about what's going on here. He says he doesn't know who his father was, and his mother is frightened of those men."

"We've hidden Vinit," supplied Sonny.

"You've – you've what! Where? What are you playing at?"

"Dad they had locked him up! He was a prisoner. They don't want the King to meet him because he won't say what they want him to say," said Gogo.

"We want to bring Vinit to the King to talk to him privately, and those men have to be sent home," urged Sonny.

Murgo relaxed a bit

"You two go and sit in there ," he said, opening a door into a sitting-room, "and wait there till I come."

Murgo returned to the Court-room and requested a quiet word with the King. On learning what he had to say he called for the Palace guards. Immediately twenty guards-men entered the Court-room.

"Take these men to the lock-up while I decide what to do," he ordered. The men tried to put up a fight but were no match for the trained guards who led them away.

"Now where is Vinit?" he asked. "Who is he and what's he up to? "

Murgo went to call Sonny and Gogo into the Court-room.

"Sonny and Gogo," he sighed. "Up to your necks in one of Pongoland's predicaments as usual. So where have you put Vinit? What did he tell you?" The boys repeated the conversation with Vinit and asked to bring him to the Palace.

"By all means. That is what I keep asking for but his representatives claimed he is too young to speak for himself." He studied the boys.

"Did you think yourselves that he is really my nephew?"

"It's hard to say Sir," said Gogo. "He doesn't know himself, and while he looks as if he might be partly Pongo, the other part doesn't look to be Flannon. His hair is brown."

"How strange! And his mother has never told him what happened?"

"Up till now he thought his father was a travelling Pongo who went missing, but his mother never said he was royalty. That is a big surprise to him," said Sonny, "and he doesn't want to be a king. He wants to be a farmer. His mother has a farm."

"Alright then," said the King, "let Vinit be brought to me."

"Sir," said Gogo. "Sonny will have to go home now. It's getting late."

"Alright yes it is quite dark. Do you have a bird?"

"Goggles will be waiting in the back garden," said Gogo.

"Good. Thankyou Sonny. Will you be here tomorrow?"

"Yes, Sir," said Sonny.

So Sonny at this exciting stage of events had to go outside to Goggles. Gogo asked Goggles to drop down in his garden to tell his mother what was going on, and to ask for Tobo to escort Sonny home. Sonny was too frustrated for words to have to go, but there was no option. They stopped at Gogo's house briefly to explain the situation to Gogo's mother. Then Tobo joined him on Goggles' back and they were away. Sonny had done the journey many times but had no idea how they passed from the world of the islands to his own world. Only Gogo and his family knew that. On their arrival Tobo would take his hand and he would be back to his own size.

He thought he wouldn't sleep, but in fact he was so exhausted he slept till ten o'clock. The sun was high in the sky by the time he aroused. He rolled over and wondered for a moment why his room was so light. Then he remembered. He looked round for Gogo but he wasn't there! Oh goodness what had happened? No matter what, Gogo was always there in the morning. His mother of course would not notice that one of his "toys" was not on view.

He got up slowly and went to the bathroom. He needed a good shower. Later he went down to the dining-room for breakfast. His mother looked up smiling.

"You had a good sleep!" she remarked He grinned but knew he had not had a full night's sleep. In fact in spite of his anxiety about Gogo, he lay down on his bed again in the afternoon for a nap. This time he woke as the sun was going down and felt refreshed. He looked round hopefully for Gogo but still there was no sign, so he went down for tea. His mother had a visitor so she didn't make any comment to Sonny. He went outside to see if any of his friends were around, but really he was waiting for Gogo. Probably he had been made to go to bed in his own home. The King and Murgo would be dealing with Vinit.

Eventually he went to bed and read a book, listening eagerly for Goggles. At last he heard the owl's hoot and rushed to the window. There was Gogo on Goggles' back.

"Sorry I couldn't be back here this morning," he said. "I knew you would be worried, but there has been so much going on that Mummy made me go to bed there."

101

"Yes I guessed so. What's happened?"

Gogo reached out and took Sonny's hand. Immediately he reduced to the same height as Gogo and climbed on Goggles' back. Gogo himself went to Sonny's bedroom door. He had some of the powdered Pongoland moss which he sprinkled under the door . This would cause anyone approaching the door to change his or her mind and go elsewhere. Then he switched off Sonny's bedlight and joined Sonny on Goggles' back.

"Such an evening!" he said. "Goggles brought Vinit back to the Palace, and the King took him into the sitting-room with my father. He asked Vinit all he knew about his parents. He told them his mother had only ever said that his father was a nice man from Pongoland. She had never said he was a prince. Then those crooks told her they were going to take Vinit to the Trade Fair dressed as a prince! They said they were going to tell the King of Pongoland that he was Prince Anton's son. His mother was so scared of them that he never did learn whether or not what they said was true."

"And is his mother a proper 100% Flannonder?"

"He thinks so. He knows his brown hair is odd. His ears are alright for Flannon."

"So what's going on now?" asked Sonny.

"The King is keeping those men in custody. The King and Queen of Flannon are also perplexed. This is the first time they are hearing this story. Our King would have liked to go to Flannon himself, but he's got all the Trade Fair stuff to deal with. So he's sending my Dad. In fact Dad left last night. The King wants him to bring Vinit's mother back, if she'll come. With the men in gaol she probably will. Vinit is staying at the Palace and the King wants us to spend time with him to see what he's like and what he says."

"We'll ask him some leading questions," said Sonny, "and see if he gives any clues. Do you know of any island where the people have brown hair?"

"Yes," said Gogo, "there are all colours of hair. If we hadn't been concentrating so hard yesterday on the Flannon tent you would have noticed. There are different colours of skin too."

"Yes I did notice that," said Sonny.

Today Goggles took the boys straight up to the Palace and they alighted in the court-yard near the main door. Vinit was sitting there waiting. He was not at all pleased as he wanted to go home.

"Now that you've got those guys in the lock-up why can't I go? I can't tell you any more. If Mum comes she will tell you whatever she knows. I don't want to be King of this island! Let me go."

"The King isn't going to try and keep you here," said Sonny consolingly."And your mother will want you to be with her. I expect then you'll go back together."

"Let's go for a walk," said Gogo."We might as well show you a bit of the island while we wait." The others readily agreed.

Vinit cheered up after that. Sonny and Gogo entertained him with stories of their adventures as they went along. He said he would like to meet Toplo and he would love to see the bonka! Sonny and Gogo laughed, but they set off to the cottage where he now lived out of everyone's ear-shot. As they drew near they could hear the weird screeches and groans.

"Wow!" exclaimed Vinit, "That's awful!"

"Yes," said Sonny, "but don't say so."

"We don't tell him it's nice either," warned Gogo. "He needs to learn to face facts."

Having heard one of Toplo's pieces, Vinit excused himself saying they would have to move on or they would be late. Once away from the cottage he exploded in laughter.

"Whew," he said, "no-one could put up with that long."

They took him to the spinning and weaving factories where the Pongoland cloth was made, and finally they brought him to Gogo's house. His mother saw them coming and went out to welcome Vinit. She soon cheered him up with fruit squash and fresh muffins.

"Pongoland is very nice," said Vinit. "It's just that home is home."

"That is true," said Gogo's mother. "I suppose your father felt that after some time in Flannon. Maybe he just felt he wanted to come back here."

"If he was a Pongo," said Vinit.

"You think he might not have been?" asked Gogo's mother.

"I'm confused now. Mother has obviously been hiding something."

"What's your earliest memory?" asked Gogo's mother.

"Arriving at our farm," said Vinit. "We arrived on the backs of two black and white birds."

"Where from?"

"Across the sky. I remember the stars."

"You mean you settled in Flannon, you and your parents? But you went there from somewhere else?"

"Maybe. I have no memory of where we flew from."

"Well the island of Scafe has black and white birds," said Gogo's mother. "Flannon's birds are hawks. Scafe isn't too far from Flannon. Of course I've never been there, but we study these things in geography at school."

"What – what colour is the hair of the people of Scafe?" asked Vinit nervously.

"It's – brown dear," said Gogo's mother.

Sonny and Gogo looked at the floor and said nothing. Tobo, who was hovering behind his mother, went quietly to the kitchen to get some ice-cream, and returned with a generous serving for Vinit. Vinit, who was trying to hide tears in his eyes, accepted the plate with a smile at little Tobo. Gogo went to get ice-cream for all of them.

"Listen dear," said Gogo's mother, "until your mother arrives we can't sort this out properly. Whatever she told you she had a good reason. Mothers protect their children."

After the ice-cream the boys went out into the garden to kick a ball around a bit. Gogo whispered to his mother,

"Could Vinit stay here until Father gets back?He'ld be much happier with us."

"Yes, I think so too," she agreed. "I'll send someone to the Palace to ask the King."And so it was arranged. Sonny returned home in good time that evening, and Gogo was to stay at his own home to keep Vinit company.

It wasn't until the next Friday evening that he returned to Sonny's house.

"My father and Vinit's mother are here," he reported. "They are all at the Palace."

Sonny climbed on to Goggles' back and away they flew over the tree-tops and under the stars. They headed straight for the Palace. Vinit's mother, Mona, was in the drawing-room. She knew she would have to tell the King of Pongoland what had happened all those years ago.

"Yes, it was Anton who brought Vinit and me back to Flannon," she said, "but Anton just rescued us. He wasn't my husband. My husband was a Scafe man. I met him at the Trade Fair when it took place on Flannon, and he took me to live on Scafe. We had Vinit and lived there. The Scafe peoples' noses are a bit pointed you will remember. Then there was trouble over our farm there. Anton was travelling around the islands learning about all the different customs, so that was how he met us. There was a Scafe girl there who had expected to marry my husband, and when he came back from the Trade Fair with a Flannon bride her family was furious. They wanted my husband, Tom, to cancel his marriage to me and send me back to Flannon. They had a neighbouring farm and they wanted the two farms made into one big one. Tom didn't want to but they insisted and things would have been very difficult. But then they wanted to take Vinit from me and keep him with his father on Scafe with them!

That was where Anton came in. He heard the story and got two Scafe birds in the night. Quietly he took Vinit and me away and brought us back to Flannon. He helped us a lot, settling us in on our present farm, and he stayed long enough to see that we had all that we needed. Then he left. I understood that he was going back to Scafe to see that Tom's family wouldn't follow me. He didn't tell me what his plan was, but no-one ever came from Scafe, and I never saw Anton again. For Vinit's protection though I never told anyone on Flannon what had happened, and I never went to the Trade Fair. That I think was common sense."

"Is there any chance Anton is alive do you think?" asked the King.

"I shouldn't think so Sir," said Mona sadly. He would have contacted someone. He just disappeared."

"Well I will make discreet enquiries," said the King, "though not of course bringing you into it at all. And who are the thugs we have in the lock-up?"

"We haven't done well at the Trade Fair for a long time now so sometimes the young people get frustrated. A few of them hatched this plot to try and force Pongoland to hand over their earnings. They bullied me with threats. I suppose they may think Vinit might be Anton's son, but I certainly never suggested such a thing. Of course I live in fear of someone coming from Scafe looking for Vinit, so I have never mentioned Scafe to Vinit."

"No, I understand," said the King. "Now young man," he said, turning to Vinit, "I know you are eager to be home and are going to be a farmer. Have you learned anything from the Trade Fair?"

"Yes Sir," said Vinit."I have learned that the Flannonders need to modernize. We need industries and factories like you have here in Pongoland where people can produce things for Flannon, and for exchange at the Fair. I'm thinking cotton and flax. And I'm thinking dairy products, like say goats' cheese for one."

"Well done!" cried the King, slapping Vinit on the back. "A young man after my own heart. Let me know if I can help in any way in establishing your industries. I shall be truly delighted."

"Thankyou Sir," said Vinit.

"Anton was a fine young man, Sir," said Mona. "He was a rover, that was all. He would have sorted out Tom's family if he reached Scafe, and then moved on elsewhere. One day he might turn up here again."

"You're right Mona, thankyou," said the King . "At least you have eased my mind that he was using his life well, and behaving as a prince should."

"Well maybe I'm not a prince," said Vinit, "but he has shown me how to live like one."

Murgo and his wife and the children set off down the hill to Gogo's house as Vinit and Mona prepared for their journey back to Flannon the next day. They were to spend the night at the Palace, and the King and Queen were piling up gifts for Flannon. They said that it would be a good idea to share their bounty with their not so fortunate neighbour. The King of Flannon would be left to deal with his erring subjects.

The children sat round the kitchen table in Gogo's house that evening talking over the events of the past week.

"What have you learned?" asked Murgo.

"That life can be complicated," said Sonny.

"That it's good for the islands to help each other," said Gogo.

"That when people don't do well they sometimes blame other people, " said Tobo.

"Bravo!" said Murgo. "Three good answers! Another helping of ice-cream each, don't you think Mother?"

Sports Day in Pongoland or the Lost Pyjamas

Part One

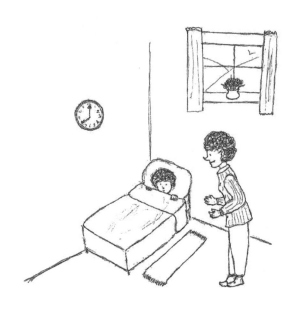

After Vinit and Mona returned to Flannon, and an escort from Flannon had taken the prisoners home, things settled down for a while in Pongoland. The Palace staff stored away the produce bought at the Trade Fair, everyone set to work at their various tasks, and the children returned to school.

Sonny did not go to Pongoland for some days, as Gogo's family too was busy storing away their own purchases in the cool cellar beneath the house, or in cupboards upstairs. Murgo had a lot to do both in the Palace and in his own house and needed Gogo at home to help. Gogo also had exams coming up, so came to Sonny's house each morning to sleep and to report on what was going on, but returned to Pongoland alone at night. Sonny had end-of-term activities at his school, including a play to which parents were invited. Sonny had a small part in this but was preoccupied with unfolding events in Pongoland.

Gogo reported each morning on a stadium being built not far from the meadow. The King had decided the children needed more exercise and also needed to develop their competitive spirit. Although the islanders co-existed in harmony most of the time, the bitterness of the young Flannonders that their island was not successful enough at the Fair had caused the King to feel his own people should have maybe a bit more ambition. Young Vinit had been inspired by the sight of all that went on in Pongoland to go home and try and get people there to start up trades and crafts which would improve the standard of living in Flannon.

"We older people like peacefulness," the King thought to himself, "but that isn't right for the children. They need more excitement, and they need to think and plan for the future of Pongoland."

Thus the next day he and others had explored the land which lay to the east of the meadow to discover where a stadium, and even a swimming-pool, might be built.

"We'll have races and cups and prizes," he said. (He had heard through Murgo what Gogo had told his parents about our world.) "There will be athletics and swimming and the children must be trained at school to do well in these sports. Then we will have a Sports Day! Everyone will be invited."

The excitement among the children was intense. Gogo was going to enter in the running and jumping events, and Tobo had decided to swim. When the pool was built he would practice to be the fastest child in his age-group. His parents encouraged him, but warned him someone else might win! He must do his best but if someone else swam faster he should not be too disappointed and must congratulate the winner.

Tobo understood this, but thought that if he practiced all his free time he *would* win! When the pool was ready he was among the first to jump in. It was really strange not having to swim against the current as one did in the river. The school-teacher stood by the pool calling advice, and the children splashed up and down the lines which had been drawn on the floor of the pool.

Sonny listened to Gogo's accounts with great interest.

"I do hope I will be able to come to the Sports Day!" he said eagerly.

"Of course," said Gogo. "Would you like to take part in something?"

"What about the high jump and long jump?" asked Sonny .

"Alright I'll put you down for those. You can borrow swimming-trunks."

Tobo's mother was worried as she felt Tobo was getting over-excited, and would be really disappointed if he didn't win anything. Murgo said,

"Well we can't succeed at everything, so if he loses he will get practice at that!" But Tobo wasn't even sleeping well. His mother fretted that he was working too hard at it. Gogo said he didn't think he was, but agreed that Tobo was a bit over-stressed.

Then one morning he heard his mother exclaiming,

"Tobo you've got nothing on! Where are your pyjamas?"Gogo went into his brother's room and saw Tobo peeping bashfully over his quilt.

"I lost my pyjamas in the night," he said.

"What? Where?"

"I don't know."

His mother was exasperated.

"Tobo your pyjamas can't just disappear! You had on your blue ones, and I tucked you in myself."

Gogo looked hard at Tobo but Tobo just looked back.

Sonny, on hearing about this, said,

"Well of course he was up to something in the night, but how could that result in his pyjamas disappearing?"

"I know," said Gogo, "he doesn't want to talk about it, so Mum and Dad aren't pushing it for the moment. He's not usually reticent about anything though! Usually he can't stop talking!"

"No," agreed Sonny.

"Well you are coming tonight so he might tell you."

When Sonny arrived at Gogo's house it was a Saturday morning, and Tobo was having his breakfast. He looked at Sonny and said,

"Hello," and then looked away. Sonny thought,

"He's got a guilty secret!" After breakfast his mother sent the children into the garden to play or walk. Sonny put his arm round Tobo's shoulders.

"Come on, Tobo," he said, "you can tell me. What have you been doing at night?" Tobo looked up scared,

"You know?"

"Know what?" asked Sonny.

"That I've been doing something at night."

"Obviously. Your pyjamas didn't evaporate. So what happened to them?"

"They just disappeared. You see - I wanted to put in extra swimming practice at night when the pool was empty. So a few nights I went down to the pool. I couldn't swim in my pyjamas so I left them on a chair. Well - when I went to pick them up on Thursday night they'ld gone!"

"Alright, so putting aside that you know you shouldn't have gone out of the house in the night, it's obvious someone took them."

"I know but all the children were in bed. Even all the grown-ups. No-one was around!"

"Let's tell Gogo," said Sonny, "we need his brains too." Gogo had busied himself with some weeding to let Sonny talk to Tobo. Now that they beckoned to him he joined them. Tears were starting to roll down Tobo's cheeks as Sonny told Gogo what he had been doing. Gogo was too concerned to be really cross.

"Honestly Tobo," he said,"but still it's weird isn't it?"

"And a bit scary," said Sonny. "No parents let their children wander about at night, but in Pongoland there isn't really much that can happen. Everyone goes to sleep. Everyone gets up in the morning. That's how Pongoland is. Of course I come here during my world's night-time but I'm with you."

"Well why don't we go down to the pool and investigate," suggested Gogo. "Before we tell Mum and Dad, that is."

So the three of them went down to the meadow where the birds were pecking about and chatting to each other. Then they went along the path which led behind the stadium to the pool. The boys went from chair to chair looking for any sign of one having been moved.

"Which chair did you put them on Tobo?" asked Gogo. Tobo went to the back row at the end, and showed them where he had left his clothes. The three boys stood looking at it, but it didn't seem to have a message for them.

"When you went to get your clothes had the chair moved at all?" asked Sonny.

"No," said Tobo.

"And you didn't notice anything at all while you were swimming?" asked Sonny.

"No, it was dark you see. There were just the stars. It was lovely!"

"It must have been great," said Gogo irritably, "but you weren't supposed to be here. And if you hadn't been you wouldn't have lost your pyjamas." Tobo looked down at his feet sadly.

"So where could whoever it was have come from?" asked Sonny. They looked round. There was woodland on the other side of the sports area, and meadow. Next to the pool was the stadium and on the other side of that the meadow. Any disturbance nesr the meadow would have caused bird calls. Tobo said he hadn't heard any. It would have been a really surprising thing to hear in the night.

Up from the meadows rose the hills, often quite high in Pongoland. Most peoples' houses were built on the hill-sides, connected by little lanes or roads. The farm-houses were built on their land. The cloth factory was not far above the swimming-pool. From the meadow where the birds stayed there was a long walk the other way round the hill, and from that path another one led upwards to the caves where the mining was done and the craft-work. On the hill-sides cows, sheep, and goats grazed. The farm-steads were higher up, and close to the Palace which stood at the top of the hill over-looking the meadow, there were orchards.

The boys stood looking to left and right for possible routes for a night wanderer to approach the pool.

"Might it have been another swimmer?" wondered Gogo. "Someone with the same idea as Tobo had, and then was put off to see someone else already there? Then maybe he took the pyjamas for a prank!"

"Yes," agreed Sonny, "that does sound a possibility."

"If so," said Tobo, "somebody took my pyjamas home! Should we put up a notice with a drawing on it of my pyjamas, saying, 'Lost, one pair pyjamas. Please apply Mr. Murgo Pongo.'"

The boys were hysterical with laughter, Tobo even rolling on the grass.

"Presumably they are in somebody's house though," said Gogo, "but they won't be much use to anyone. They are too small for most people."

"If they've gone to a home they were probably taken as a prank," said Sonny. "Why not ask around at school? If it was some kid he won't be able to keep it quiet!"

"No-one's said anything so far though," said Tobo. "I dropped hints, and did listen around at school yesterday."

The boys went slowly back home, and Tobo told his parents what he had been doing in the night. They were angry with him and told him that as a penalty he would not be allowed to go to the next school swimming practice. Tobo was downcast but not surprised. Obviously there was going to be a punishment.

They spent much of the day in the stadium practicing their running and jumping, and timing each other. Sonny watched the other children, looking for any signs of any of them looking at Tobo, and he went along to the swimming-pool to look for any clues there among the children splashing about and practicing their races. There was a lot of noise but no-one looked guilty.

On their way home for tea Sonny asked,

"Does Pongoland have cups as prizes?"

"We will have," said Gogo. "We have never had a Sports Day before so they have to be made. The men in the mines are busy now making them all. There is talk that we should practice through the Winter and invite contestants from the other islands to our Sports Day next year! There will be three cups for each event, a gold, a silver, and a bronze."

"There doesn't seem to be much time though," said Sonny. The events were to be held the next weekend.

"No," said Gogo, "but the King has made the making of the cups a priority for these two weeks."

"And there's going to be a feast afterwards!" said Tobo, his eyes sparkling.

"Yes it's going to be really nice," said Gogo happily. "Everyone will be there."

After tea Goggles and Gogo took Sonny back home. It was before dawn in this world. He lay in bed mulling over who might be responsible for taking the pyjamas and for what purpose. He couldn't help feeling that if it had been a child's prank he would have boasted about it by now. The whole purpose of a prank is to make everybody laugh. Did someone need a pair of child's pyjamas for something, or did someone want to make Tobo nervous? But now that Tobo had told his parents he wasn't one bit nervous, and he wasn't cross about his punishment because he knew he deserved it. Why would someone actually need the pyjamas? Sonny fell asleep.

The next night Sonny said to Gogo,

"I've been thinking and thinking. Normally everyone is asleep at night in Pongoland, so who might be awake?" Gogo stood looking at Sonny for a moment.

"Why the metal-workers of course. They are working over-time in shifts to get the cups made in time for the races."

"O.K. so let's just suppose that one ot the workers went over to the pool. For whatever reason." Gogo thought for a while.

"Well I can't see why one would. They are tired enough as it is without trecking half across the island to take a look at the swimming-pool."

"Yes, that's right, but let's just work it through. Have you got a podium?"

"No, but they're making one of those too, out of wood decorated with metal."

"So – just to imagine a situation – a worker came over to the pool at night to check out something. Where the podium would stand? Something to do with measurements? Then by chance he sees Tobo's pyjamas, picks them up, and takes them back to the mines?"

Gogo stared at Sonny.

"Whatever for?"

"I don't know. I'm just exploring ideas. What is the man's thinking? I'm assuming it's not likely to have been a woman in the middle of the night."

"It's not likely to have been anyone! No, so O.K. This person happens on the pyjamas, and someone in the pool, so he takes them?" said Gogo.

"Might he have thought that the swimmer is up to no good, so he removes the clothes so that whoever it is has to go home with no clothes on?"

"But they belong to a six year-old!" objected Gogo.

"Yes, so what does that suggest to the man? That some parents are not far away?"

"They'ld be sitting with the clothes," said Gogo.

"So they would. So the kid is alone. I think whoever it was thought the pyjamas would be useful for something," said Sonny.

"Well if it was someone from the mines we might find out if we go there," said Gogo.

They hooted to Goggles who was waiting for them on the neem tree, and Gogo asked him to take them straight to the mines instead of to the meadow as usual. The mines were always exciting Sonny thought. There was always so much bustle, sounds of hammering, the furnaces, tapping, and thousands of many coloured jewels piled up ready to be set into the ornaments and utensils the craftsmen were making. The mines were lit up by the furnaces and by lamps set into the walls of the caves. The workers were good-humoured, and there was always the sound of their talking in amongst the sounds of the hammering. It was warm and busy and a great deal of fun.

Sports Day in Pongoland or the Lost Pyjamas

Part Two

As requested Goggles flew straight to the Pongoland mines, and landed on the grass near the entrance to the main cave. Sonny and Gogo went inside. Now that they were there they were embarrassed about how to put their question.

"Let's just say we've come to see how the work on the cups is going on," murmered Gogo.

"I don't see how we can ever lead up to, 'did someone take Tobo's pyjamas from a chair near the pool'," objected Sonny.

"No. We'ld better just look round for clues, like a bit of blue cloth poking out from somewhere," agreed Gogo glumly. Sonny giggled.

The work was certainly very interesting. Progress seemed to be good. The boys saw a few of the cups already stored in a cabinet. It was only the atmosphere which didn't seem to be as usual. Normally the miners were contented people who enjoyed their work, but today they seemed to have had a quarrel. At any rate the contentment was disturbed. Sonny and Gogo wandered slowly round, apparently to see the making of the cups, really to discover anything suspicious.

One of the men offered them glasses of fruit squash which they accepted and sat down. Eventually Sonny coughed and remarked,

"A funny thing happened to us the other night." Gogo looked agonized. The men looked up enquiringly.

"Yes. One of us went to the swimming-pool for a practice in the night and his pyjamas disappeared from the chair where he had left them." Sonny looked round for reactions. The atmosphere was electric. Eventually one of them spoke.

"Who took them?"

"We don't know. We are trying to find out."

"Well why have you come here?" asked one of them men beligerantly.

"Only that – ," Sonny paused but went on bravely, "the only other people awake at that time were the miners, so we wondered why maybe one of them might want some child's pyjamas."

There was an angry reaction and several of the men surrounded the two boys. Sonny and Gogo became frightened. Normally these were men who were friendly and cheerful.

"What's going on?" asked Gogo fearfully.

"That's what we'ld like to know," said one of the men, "and you obviously know something or you wouldn't be here."

"Do you have the pyjamas," asked Sonny, thinking 'in-for-a-penny-in-for-a-pound.'

"Neeko here," said the man closest to him, pointing to a darker-skinned man behind them, "picked up the pyjamas from the swimming-pool on Thursday night. "He went to measure the space where the podium is to stand, and what did he see but a little kid's clothing on a chair there. Naturally he brought them back here. So where is the boy then?"

"I don't know about any other boy ," gasped Gogo. "The pyjamas were my brother's. You must have seen him in the pool."

"There was no-one in the pool when I was there," said Neeko. "The pyjamas belong to my son Pym."

"What??" Sonny and Gogo felt as if they had fallen into some other world.

"So you must stay here until we find out what your connection is with his clothes," said the earlier speaker.

"You know us – Sonny and Gogo? We've often been here to watch you work. How can you think we would be part of some crime?" cried Gogo.

"Not part of a crime. You are kids. But you are connected with whatever is going on and we have to find out what that is."

They took the boys into an alcove of the cave and sat them down. The first speaker, Lenny, told them he wanted the full story.

"We have told you!" said Sonny. "Who is Pym? Tell us about him instead."

"Pym has disappeared!" cried Neeko. "I want him back."

"Excuse me," said Gogo politely, "but I think you are not a Pongo."

"I'm from Tooliland," said Neeko grudgingly, "it's three birds away."

"So – what was Pym doing in Pongoland?" asked Sonny curiously. Neeko sighed.

"We brought him to the Fair. He was so keen to come. When we got back to Tooliland we found he was missing. There were several of us plus the stuff we were taking home. We had each thought he was on one of the other birds, but he seems to have been hiding out here."

"Why would he do that!" exclaimed Gogo.

"He was so thrilled with the metal-work he wanted to try it himself apparently," said Neeko.

"We found him hiding in the mines," said one of the workers. "We were going to take him to the King, but he begged us to let him stay here a while and see our work. We figured his father would come back for him in any case, and the King was so taken up with those crooks from Flannon, plus the Fair stuff. So we said O.K. stay with us till your Dad comes."

"He was really naughty though," said another of the men. "This is dangerous work and if you aren't careful you can get hurt. And no-one should wander in the mines who doesn't know them."

"What happened?" asked Gogo fearfully.

"The worst happened. A few days later he disappeared," said Lenny. Several of the men groaned. "When Neeko came we had lost him!"

Sonny and Gogo looked at them in horror.

"And you are thinking he may have wandered off down one of the passages?" gasped Sonny.

"We don't know what to think,"said Patsy, one of the few female metal-workers. She set fine gems in the best of the jewelry. "We've gone down the passages calling, but none of us can go too far because they wind round inside the hills. Anyone can get lost." She wrung her hands in despair, tears starting to roll down her cheeks.

Sonny and Gogo didn't know what to say. This was truly a nightmare.

"You must have looked round the island?" asked Gogo.

"We go out at night because this is such a disaster we don't want anyone to know. Both our Kings are going to be furious."

"But you have to go back and explain to your people in Tooliland," said Gogo, looking at Neeko. He started to cry.

"However can I tell his mother? I sent our bird back with a message that we are staying on here for a few days, and I'm hoping to have good news before I contact Tooliland again."

"And – the blue pyjamas?" asked Sonny.

"Oh, well, we had lent Pym a few Pongo clothes," said Lenny. "All his luggage had gone back to Tooliland. "Naturally when Neeko saw those pyjamas on a chair by the pool – well a Pongo boy couldn't have left them there in the middle of the night. He thought they must be clothes worn by Pym. Pym had been very excited about the Sports Day and had been very keen to see the stadium and the swimming-pool. So Neeko thought maybe Pym had crept off in the night for a swim! But he wasn't in the pool. He was a real handful."

"He always has been," said Neeko, shaking his head.

"Well now I'ld better tell you my story," said Gogo. "The pyjamas belonged to my brother Tobo who is six. He's taking part in the swimming events in the Sports Day. He was so keen he crept out at night to do extra practice. When he came out of the pool he found his pyjamas were gone, so he had to go back to bed without them. At first he wouldn't say where he'ld been, but yesterday he told us."

"That's the sort of thing Pym does," said his father.

"We're really sorry about Pym. Can we help at all in finding him?" asked Sonny.

"Whatever you do, don't go wandering off down those passages," ordered Lenny.

"No of course not. We know better than that," said Sonny, "but supposing one person searched along a passage holding a ball of string, and another person stood in the cave holding the end of the string? Couldn't we do that ,taking one passage at a time ?" The men looked at him in silence for a moment.

"It's not a bad idea," said Lenny, "but you two boys will sit in the cave by the end of the string."

"Yes of course," said Gogo, "I'll ask Goggle to tell Mummy and Daddy where we are."

"Don't let him tell them about Pym!" cried Neeko in anguish.

"No alright," said Gogo. He spoke to Goggles and returned to the others. Someone called Don brought some string. He attached the end of it to an anvil and set off down a tunnel. Sonny and Gogo sat down to wait. Don went further and further down the tunnel, calling, "Pym! Pym!"

Meanwhile Sonny said to Gogo,

"Supposing he didn't go down one of the passages, where else might he have gone?"

"Wherever he went people would recognize that he wasn't a Pongo boy, and very young. He would have been brought back here."

"Yes, I suppose so," said Sonny.

"He was here with all the Fair people," said Sonny, thinking aloud. "The people from his island left, but he had got separated from them, and managed to stay behind. He did that on purpose because usually a child would be frightened to be left. Then somehow he found his way to the caves and hid there. Did he really want to learn about metal-work?"

"More like he wanted to join the other children in the stadium or pool!" said Gogo. "They said he was excited about the Sports."

"But no-one would have let him go there alone," said Sonny.

"Maybe he just went off exploring and found the caves? Would he have gone down one of those tunnels by himself? That would be really scary."

"Did he meet Vinit I wonder? You remember Vinit waited in the caves for quite a long time. Then later we took Vinit round the island and he stayed with us. After his mother came from Flannon Vinit was very keen to show her round before they left. He must have taken her to see the metal-work. Did he tell Pym about Pongoland?"

"Supposing he did I doubt if Pym would want to see cloth factories," said Sonny. " And he wouldn't be interested in climbing hills. He couldn't go near the Sports areas anyway without being seen. What would Vinit talk about to entertain another foreigner?"

"The bonka!" exclaimed Gogo.

"He would definitely want to see that" said Sonny. The boys approached Lenny.

"Did Pym by any chance meet Vinit?" asked Sonny.

"Yes he did," said Lenny. "We didn't say he didn't belong to one of us of course. "

"Did Vinit come back again later with his mother?" asked Gogo.

"Yes they came for a short while. They didn't stay long as they were going home that day."

"Did Vinit mention the bonka at all?" Lenny looked cross at that.

"Piece of nonsense that is. He may have done but I was busy with my work."

Sonny and Gogo went back to sit beside the anvil.

"The idea seems a bit far-fetched, but he certainly might have wanted to see the bonga," said Sonny.

"But how would he get there?" said Gogo.

"Well he's obviously a resourceful kid! Anyway it's an idea. When Goggles gets back shall we ask him to take us to Toplo's house? There's no harm in checking. It's a very isolated place if he did go there."

119

They told the men about their idea and they agreed that the boys should at least go and see.

When Goggles returned, who should be on his back but Tobo! Gogo groaned. Tobo climbed down from the owl's back and ran into the cave. When he saw the string he was intrigued.

"What are they doing?" he asked Gogo.

"Looking for something down a tunnel and they don't want to get lost." Tobo went to the tunnel entrance and of course he heard the words,'Pym! Pym!'

"Who's Pym?" he asked Sonny and Gogo.

"Listen Tobo," said Sonny, "he's a little boy who's got lost, so they are checking to see if he went down one of the tunnels. But they don't want us to say anything to anyone! They want to find him before his mother finds out he's missing."

"O.K.," said Tobo, "well I won't tell anyone."

"No of course you won't," said Sonny. "Right now we are going to check if he went to Toplo's house to see the bonka. Do you want to come?"

"Oh wow, yes! It's ages since I've seen that!"

Gogo explained to Lenny that they had had to tell Tobo about Pym, and that he was going with them to Toplo's house.

"Alright," said Lenny. "Good luck!"

Some time later the three boys landed on the hill-side near Toplo's cottage. There was no sound, so maybe Toplo was out with the sheep. He had designed the bonka himself, and had wanted the metal-workers to make more. He had wanted to show one at the Fair and get big orders for bonkas from people from other islands. But the craftsmen wouldn't hear of it. They said he would make a laughing-stock of them. As a result he had gone off in a huff to sit with his sheep. Nowadays he did not often go to the mines.

"I do hope Toplo hasn't locked Pym up so as to demand orders for bonkas, in exchange for Pym, from Tooliland!" exclaimed Sonny.

"I wouldn't put it past him," said Gogo grimly. They climbed to the top of the hill, and there in the distance was Toplo with his sheep, and he wasn't alone. Sonny, Gogo, and Tobo set off at a run.

"Pym!" shouted Tobo. The little Tooli boy looked up.

"Oh hello," he said as they drew near, "were you looking for me?"

"Too right we were looking for you!" said Sonny sternly. "What are you doing here?"

"Oh this nice man has been teaching me to play the bonka. I said I would like one as a present for my parents! It's lovely!"

"And who is going to give what for it?" asked Gogo.

"Oh that's alright," said Pym happily, "Toplo says it will be a free sample! In return he wants me to get orders for more! Isn't it exciting!"

Sonny and Gogo collapsed on the grass, hardly knowing whether to laugh or to cry.

"Pym," said Sonny patiently, "no grown-up at all likes likes that bonka. Your parents won't be one bit pleased if you take one back to Tooliland."

Pym looked crestfallen, and Toplo was furious.

"What business have you to come here," he cried, "spoiling my agreement with Pym! He's an intelligent boy and he can see the potential for my instrument."

"Well anyway," said Sonny, "what is he doing staying up here? His father is worried sick, and the miners are scouring the tunnels for him."

"Oh has Daddy come for me?" asked Pym, looking pleased.

"Yes Daddy has come," said Sonny, "and you weren't where you were supposed to be – in the work-shops learning about metal-work? Everyone is frantic."

"Well I want to make a bonka," said Pym sulkily.

"And does Tooliland have any copper to make one from?" asked Gogo.

"No – I thought I would make it in Pongoland. I am helping Toplo advertise! I asked an owl to take me to Mr.Toplo's house because I wanted to see the bonka, which he did, and then took me back to the mines again. Then I wanted to make one as a present, but the metal-workers said I had to practice making chains first." He looked doleful, and Sonny and Gogo could hardly keep themselves from laughing. "That was hopeless so I walked back here to tell Toplo."

"In the night," said Sonny.

"Yes," said Pym guiltily.

"You know that was wrong," said Gogo.

"Yes but I thought I would just talk to Toplo, and go back to the mines in the morning. But Toplo invited me to stay here till my father came, and learn to play the bonka! Then he would have one made for me as an order, and send it on to me."

"And how was your father to know you were here?" asked Sonny. "And you, Toplo, should have had more sense! Why on earth didn't you take him back to the mines?"

"Because he likes my bonka!" cried Toplo. "It's been real fun teaching him to play it. It gets lonely up here. How was I to know his father had come back!"

Sonny sighed. A real child and a grown-up child. What could you say? Pym had a poor sense of time. He didn't understand much about bird-days and inter-island journeys. Toplo was concerned only with his obsession. He didn't bother that other people would be worried.

"Well we'll have to take you back now," said Gogo. "See, this is my brother Tobo. He's about your age. He went swimming in the night."

"Did you?" said Pym admiringly.

"And your Dad picked up my pyjamas thinking they must be clothes lent to you."

"So you were left with no clothes!" exclaimed Pym, and rolled on the grass with laughter.

"Come along Pym," said Sonny firmly. "I'll wait here while Goggles takes you three back to the mines. Your father will be there waiting for you."

"No, I'll wait Sonny. My parents aren't keen for you to be left alone anywhere in our world."

"O.K. Goggles will be back soon."

Back at the mines there was a terrific hullaballoo. Neeko shouted angrily, and then hugged Pym tightly. The men were cross about lost time looking for Pym. They still had a lot of cups to make. Sonny explained to Neeko about the bonka.

"I'ld like to see it myself now!" he laughed, "but we have to get home. Your mother is going to be so worried about our being away so long Pym."

"Can't I stay for the Sports Day?" begged Pym.

"No!" said Neeko. However when Gogo arrived he had a suggestion.

"I wondered, now that we have Pym safely back, would you be willing to let him stay at my house till next weekend so that he can take part in the Sports Day? Our house is not far from the stadium and pool, and we would take great care of him. Of course I have to ask my parents, but I know they would love to have him. Then you might like to bring his mother back next Friday to attend the Sports Day and see him perform!"

Sonny thought this an excellent idea, and so, when he thought about it, did Neeko.

"Well that's really nice of you Gogo," said Neeko, "if your parents agree. Shall we wait here while you go and ask. Incidentally how was it I didn't see Tobo in the pool when I found the pyjamas?" They all looked at Tobo.

"Oh, well I practiced swimming under-water. There's one event where you have to swim a length under-water. And there's another where you have to pick up something from the bottom of the pool. You must have missed me because of that. And there was only starlight."

"Oh, I see," said Neeko. Goggles took Gogo home to ask his parents if Pym could stay with them until Sports Day. Murgo was delighted in fact. Anything which promoted inter-island friendships was always to be encouraged, and he knew the King would welcome the idea.

"And so it was that Neeko flew home to report on the well-being of Pym, and to extend the invitation from Pongoland to his wife to attend their Sports Day next weekend.

Pym chose to enter the running events as he couldn't swim very well. Every day through the next week he practiced his running, and was entered for all the events in his age-group. And what a crowning joy to the week it was, and to his proud parents, when he did in fact win a cup for the hundred yards sprint! Sonny and Gogo did not win anything, but Tobo won a cup for the under-water length event! Everyone felt he had deserved it!

After the Sports there was the Feast promised by the King, and Pym's parents were the special guests of Tobo's parents. By now Pym and Tobo were fast friends, and there was talk of Tobo paying a visit to Tooliland later in the year.

The Feast was a joyous occasion, though Sonny, as so often, had to leave half-way through, in order to be back in his own bed before dawn. Gogo went with him but returned to Pongoland to spend the remainder of the day with the very happy Toolis.

Pym Meets Giants!

The morning after the Pongoland Sports Day Gogo sat beside Sonny's pillow, waiting for him to wake up.

"Er – Sonny," he said tentatively, "something has cropped up."

"What?" exclaimed Sonny, alarmed.

"Sonny, you see Tobo and Pym have been playing together a lot this last week, and Tobo has told Pym about you and his visits to your house. Pym is thrilled. Before he goes back to Tooliland he wants to visit you."

"What?"

"Normally we have an absolute rule. That is Mother and Father made it a strict rule, that only I will ever come to this world, and very occasionally Tobo. And once Dad came. No-one else ever. Most of the birds have no idea how to get here even. Goggles and I chanced upon it and Goggles never tells anyone."

"So why on earth do you want to break the rule for Pym of all people, prince of disasters?!" cried Sonny, horrified at the implications surrounding a visit by a young island child who was not going to understand the absolute need for silence, and keeping still most of the time.

"His parents of course came for the Sports Day and are all going home tomorrow. If I were to go now and bring him back to spend the day here until we all go to Pongoland this evening, we should be able just to show him round your house. Couldn't we manage it between us, never letting him out of our sight, and giving him something to eat?"

"But Gogo why? Can you see Pym lying quietly part of the time, and making no sound the whole of the time? This is the guy who went off all on his own for personal reasons, which turned out to be an urgent need to play the bonka! And he's six!"

"I know. We're in a bit of a bind. His parents have no idea of where Tobo meant. They think it is just another island where people like you live, and not too far away. That's what Pym thinks. Tobo of course never told the real story, but Pym was asking about your island, so he played it as if you live on your island. His parents would like Pym occupied today while they do other things, so they think it would be really nice if we take Pym off to visit you for a few hours. The Pongos do know we cross dimensions, but by now they take you for granted and think that a knowledge of this sort of travel is far too risky to even talk about. They never speak of it to other islanders."

"So you think that hopefully we can just kid on to Pym that this is an island house?"

"Yes! I thought we could make a game of it. I'll give him a special mask to wear while he's travelling which will cover most of his vision. We'll get him here and back without his ever knowing where he went. He will think for the rest of his life that he went to Sonny's island."

Sonny was intrigued in spite of himself.

"O.K. so you get him here and then you take off his mask. Then what? We must have a proper plan in which he will have a fun day, but won't see things we don't want him to see, like the fact say that people on my island are, give or take, five times taller than anywhere else, and I who am a child am around like three times taller. Whereas in Pongoland I am your height? Wow."

"I know I know," said Gogo irritably. "But I can make you my height here."

"What! And my parents downstairs!"

"I suppose there's no hope of them going out?"

"If they go out they will take me. They don't leave me alone."

"No, so say we take him out to some lonely place, and tell him he must wear his secret mask so no-one will see him," said Gogo. This made Sonny explode with laughter.

"You can't do that with six year-olds! No, we have to keep him in this house. I can ask to play in the attic. We don't want Pym to see anyone. If I play up there my parents will call up, rather than come up. We can play an expedition game. I'll ask Mum if she can give me sandwiches for my lunch up there. Then we'll all three spend the day there."

"Pym will have some weird stories to tell his parents," commented Gogo, but he was glad Sonny was thinking constructively.

"Yes!" said Sonny with a smile. "But we're on the edge here."

With this rough plan in place Gogo hooted to Goggles.

"And don't tell Tobo!" Sonny called after them as they flew away. While Gogo was gone Sonny went downstairs for breakfast, and to ask if he might have a packed lunch. His parents were not against his pretend-expedition. They had done things like that themselves when they were children and knew what fun it could be. His mother gave him sandwiches and fruit and a cold drink in a little attaché case, and wished him a safe journey. So far so good.

Not long afterwards Goggles was back, thankfully with only two. Tobo himself was growing quite sensible, and understood the difficulties this trip was going to face. In fact he was quite helpful in re-enforcing the magic mask idea for the journey. Pym put it on dubiously, and soon realized he could hardly see anything with it on, but everyone bustled him on to Goggles before his complaints became too loud.

On the way Gogo kept him entertained with stories and rhymes, so that in no time, it seemed, he was in Sonny's world, and on Sonny's window-sill. Gogo took Sonny's hand before he removed the mask, so that Pym was presented with a Gogo-sized Sonny.

Pym looked round Sonny's bedroom goggle-eyed, but Sonny and Gogo were keen to get him up to the attic straight away. Gogo took the precaution of asking Goggles to wait on the roof near the attic window in case of emergencies.

"If the worst comes to the worst," muttered Gogo, "we can just pop Pym on Goggles' back and send him home."

"Good thinking," said Sonny as Pym looked round at his toys and furniture. "Now let's hope we can get upstairs before anybody comes. I've put the expedition stuff up there already. Mum has given us a lovely lunch, so we should be able to occupy Pym. But we have to be quiet. Does Pym understand that?"

"Yes, we told him. He didn't ask why."

"Sonny," said Pym, puzzled, "the furniture is very big!"

"Yes it is, isn't it?" said Sonny, looking at Gogo. "Now we are going on an expedition. Come along. There's climbing to do first."

Somehow they got him up the stairs to the attic. Pym's credulity was stretched to the limit. He might be only six but he wasn't daft.

"This is a giants' house," he concluded. Sonny and Gogo couldn't think of any response to that, and once they were in the larger of the two attic rooms they pushed the door to. The attic was used for storage mainly, so there was no furniture. Sonny devised a story for their expedition, in which the trunks and boxes were mountains. He had scattered a few small toys around for Pym to play with, including his electric train. He had remembered how much Tobo had loved it.

This indeed proved to be a master-stroke. As soon as Pym saw it he was entranced. He didn't understand about trains any more than Tobo had at first, but he soon learnt to turn the key and make it go. Round and round it went.

Then there was a small ball, so they had a game of foot-ball with one of them as umpire. This kept him going for a while. Then they climbed up the boxes, and Gogo lifted Pym up to see out of the window. If he happened to see anyone down below the person would look small. He saw Goggles and waved to him.

After that they served lunch rather early. Sonny's parents seemed to be respecting the spirit of the expedition and weren't trying to interfere. Sonny and Gogo were beginning to feel things were going as well as could be expected.

After lunch they wondered what to do, but Sonny thought a game of hide-and-seek amongst the trunks and general junk would be a very good game. He was the first to close his eyes and count to twenty. Gogo and Pym tip-toed round and hid in different places, Pym suppressing his giggles. Sonny searched round and found Pym behind an old cupboard, and Gogo in a half-filled trunk. Pym closed his eyes, and Sonny and Gogo hid behind household paraphanalia. Then Gogo closed his eyes while Sonny and Pym hid.

Gogo found Sonny hiding under old clothes, and went on with his search for Pym. He searched high and low, but no Pym! He began to panic.

"Surely he wouldn't climb out of the window!" he cried.

"No, he can't have," said Sonny, who hadn't seen where Pym had hidden. "It's too high up."

The answer came the next moment however in a scream from downstairs. Both boys jumped, and opened their mouths in horror! It was Sonny's mother!

"Oh my goodness!" cried Sonny. "It's Pym!"

Quickley Gogo took his hand to restore him to his normal height, and he almost flew downstairs.

"Mum! What's happened?" His father had rushed up from the ground floor and his arm was round his mother's shoulders.

"Sonny - one of those clown dolls – whose is it? It isn't yours. It's smaller. I just saw it RUN INTO YOUR BEDROOM!!"

"Now Jane," said his father patiently, "you know it couldn't have. It must have been an optical illusion."

"No! I saw it quite clearly!" She went into Sonny's bedroom, and Sonny followed, looking round wildly. Pym was lying on his bed, his eyes staring glassily.

"Mum, how could it have run in here?" said Sonny weakly. He really didn't know what to say.

"I don't know, but I know what I saw, as plainly as I see you. It was running along the landing." She went to pick Pym up, but Sonny got there first and picked up Pym himself.

"Jane," said his father, "come downstairs and have a brandy. You've had a shock."

"Thanks, I think I will, but it was like that horror film where a toy doll opens its' eyes. I'll never forget it. I'll have nightmares."

She went downstairs, supported carefully by his father.

Sonny looked at Pym with blazing eyes,

"PYM, WHY DID YOU COME DOWN HERE!!" he whispered.

Pym was ready to faint. His shock was worse than Sonny's mother's. They were all GIANTS!! He was terrified and about to scream, but Sonny clamped his hand over his mouth and rushed upstairs with him.

"Gogo – the worst! Mum saw Pym run into my bedroom. She's nearly in hysterics."

"PYM!" bawled Gogo in a whisper, "we TOLD you, we WARNED you! How DARE you disobey like that. You have caused a GREAT deal of trouble."

Pym by now was weeping copious tears. Sonny wouldn't let Gogo return him to a small size because he needed to go down and comfort his mother. Gogo said to Pym,

"On this island Pym people are big. My family knows and the royal family knows, but we NEVER tell anyone. People on other islands would be frightened. Now you know. You are only six but if I ever hear you have told anyone else about this, even your parents, I, and my family, and the King and Queen of Pongoland, will be EXCEEDINGLY angry. Do you understand?" Pym was quivering.

"Yes, Gogo," he said, "I'm very sorry I disappeared. I thought Sonny's bedroom would be a good place to hide."

"That's O.K.," said Sonny, sorry now for the terrified little boy. "You just have to remember always what Gogo has told you. Will you do that?"

"Yes, Sonny, I promise," said Pym.

"Good. When you are bigger you can visit Pongoland again and talk to us about it as much as you like. Alright, well he'ld better go home," said Sonny to Gogo. "I must go and help soothe my mother."

"Yes, I'm really sorry about this Sonny," said Gogo.

"It's O.K. I should have watched where he was going. My fault. Anyway I must go downstairs. I'll see you later shall I?"

"Yes, I'll come back," promised Gogo.

Sonny's mother was persuaded to lie down for a while. His father wanted to call a doctor, but his mother said no. He would think she needed a psychiatrist. She thought she needed a psychiatrist herself, but not until she felt normal again. By now her common sense was persuading her that she must have been hallucinating. Sonny didn't say much, because whatever he said would be a kind of lie, so he patted her hand, and asked her more about what she thought she had seen. His mother was comforted by his sympathetic willingness to listen. Inwardly he was still furious with Pym.

Gogo arrived back that evening. He had been crying. His parents had been very angry indeed, talking about gross abuse of Sonny's hospitality. Pym's parents were not told, under Pym's bond of secrecy. Gogo asked Sonny how his mother was, and now Sonny cried. He had been very upset but could not let his mother see. Gogo too shed some more tears.

"Anyway, get some rest Sonny," he sniffed. "I am to take you back tonight to hear my parents' apology.

Sonny had a hot drink, said goodnight to his parents, and climbed into bed. He slept for three hours until Gogo woke him. Gogo had put extra moss-powder under Sonny's door to guard against either of his parents coming in.

Gogo's parents met him with great embarrassment, and pain about what had happened.

"How is your mother?" they asked anxiously.

"She's asleep," said Sonny. "She was beginning to think she was mistaken, but she wasn't."

"I've been to see Mother Fulati," said Murgo. "I explained the situation as best I could without saying too much, and she thinks she can give both your parents some remedy to help them forget. As we know some of her preparations affect the mind, and she is very careful to ensure that they are used only for healing purposes."

"Thankyou!" cried Sonny with a rush of hope. "It would be so good if she could do that."

"Can you eat any breakfast?" asked Gogo's mother.

"Well no, I don't think so, thankyou," said Sonny.

"Never mind, see here I have made some fresh tarts. I'm sure one of these will help. We are waiting for news from Mother Fulati."

The three children all felt they could eat one or two tarts, and were thus occupied when an owl arrived at the door. It was Mother Fulati's Monty.

"Mother Fulati invites Sonny and Gogo and Tobo to her house. She has a remedy," he said.

Everyone's hopes went up. The children climbed on to Monty's back and away he flew to the nurseries kept by Mother Fulati near the top of one of the hills close to the border of the island, looking sky-wards. The hillside was richly covered with trees and bushes of hundreds of varieties. As they entered Mother Fulati's huge garden the aroma from thousands of different plants she was cultivating met their nosstrils so powerfully they were made almost dizzy. This was her domain and she ruled over it supreme. The King himself could not dictate to her how she would use her remedies. As the boys went up the path she and her daughter Selina ran out to greet them.

"Well hello!" cried Mother Fulati, beaming. She was an elderly Pongo lady who wore a scarf round her head and, instead of the trousers worn by the other islanders, she wore a wide multi-coloured skirt with a short red blouse. It was said this was because she was not pure Pongo, and owed her skills to ancestors from a distant island. However she had lived in Pongoland all her life and had married a Pongo gentleman. By now she had been a widow for a good many years, and only the older people of the island could remember him. Selina was a dark beautiful girl already skilled in her mother's profession.

"Lovely to meet you boys again after a long time," said Mother Fulati. "You remember all those beetles frightening my cat! You really helped me that day. Come in and have a glass each of my wonderful new fruit-juice squash."

The drinks were apricot in colour and really delicious. The boys began to relax and feel cheerful again. The knot of anxiety in Sonny's stomach loosened a little.

"Now," said Mother Fulati to him, "I've got here a pad of cotton-wool into which I have sprinkled two of my flower essences. One of the essences is for happiness. The other is for release from fright. This last one I use for people who have had a nasty accident or shock. You know how when something bad happens you keep remembering it again and again? Well this essence stops it replaying itself. I've also added the tiniest drop of something I rarely use. It causes forgetfulness. It could cause your mother to be a bit hazy about yesterday as a whole, but the effect won't last into tomorrow. It won't affect anything which happens after the dose. I don't say she might not wonder occasionally if she hadn't seen one of Sonny's toys move once, but she will dismiss the idea as ridiculous."

"Oh thankyou Mother Fulati!" said Sonny with tears in his eyes.

"Now, now, she is going to be just fine. The happiness essence will mean she wakes up tomorrow feeling really good. You must go back home soon so that you can give it to your parents in the middle of the night. You hold the pad under your mother's nose for a count of ten. And then under your father's nose also for a count of ten. He had a big upset too after all. And now, the precautions! I am giving you the cotton-wool pad in a sealed air-tight bag., When you have used it you must put it back in the bag carefully, and see that it is again air-tight. These essences must not be released into your world's eco-system. Do you understand? There could be harmful repercussions. Then you bring it back to Pongoland and give it to me, or ask Goggles to bring it to me. I know I can trust you. Bring it back to Pongoland as quickly as you can."

"I understand," said Sonny. "I will bring it back tomorrow. Thankyou very much indeed Mother Fulati."

"Now," she said, "Monty will take you back to Gogo's house. Then you must go straight home to give this to your parents as soon as possible."

After profuse thanks from all the anxious boys Monty took them back to Gogo's house. Gogo's parents were also extremely grateful to Mother Fulati. Gogo and Sonny set off immediately to the meadow to meet Goggles and return to this world.

It was about two-thirty a.m. by this world's time when they arrived, and Sonny's parents were asleep. Sonny went to their room and tip-toed to their bed very quietly. Softly he held the cotton-wool pad under his mother's nose to a count of ten, and then under his father's nose in the same way. He then crept back to his own room and re-placed the cotton-wool in its' bag. Then he sealed it very carefully. After all the stresses he and Gogo were both soon fast asleep.

The next morning when they woke up the sun was shining on a bright new day. Sonny's mother peeped into Sonny's room to see if he had woken up, and then came in.

"Sonny!" she said, "it's a lovely day. Why don't we go somewhere fo a picnic? Would you like that?" She looked cheerful and brimming with energy. Sonny was delighted, and said he would love to go. There was no talk of walking clowns. Of course he himself would never refer to the incident again, lest he re-awaken any memory.

"Gogo!" he said urgently, "would you please take this little bag back to Mother Fulati straight away? I need to spend the day with my parents, but then maybe I can go back with you to Pongoland this evening to report to Mother Fulati on how things went?"

Gogo too had been very relieved to see Sonny's mother looking her normal self again, and full of happy plans. He agreed to fly straight back to Mother Fulati's house with the little bag, spend the day at home, and return to Sonny's bedroom that evening.`

Sonny then went downstairs to join his parents for breakfast. His father was reading the newspaper as was usual at that time of the day, and his mother had already started preparations for their picnic.

"Why don't we go to the sea-shore Sonny? Would you like that?" said his father. Sonny was excited as they didn't often get the chance to go on a family picnic, and that too by the sea-side.

"Yes I would. We'll take a ball, and of course a bucket and spade, and I've got some pocket-money saved. I'ld like to buy some pretty shells, and I'll treat you both to ice-cream!"

"Wonderful Sonny! Thankyou dear," said his mother.

By nine o'clock they had everything packed in their car. Sonny had taken care to put his pocket-money in his wallet. He had a private mission, and that was to buy a little collection of the prettiest shells to take as a thankyou gift to Mother Fulati tonight. He would never ever forget the last two days, and knew that in future he must be a great deal more careful in keeping his two lives separate. He was a very lucky boy indeed and he must not become careless.

PART TWO

SONNY AND
THE HEROIC DEEDS

Chapter One

Time Has Passed

Time had passed since Pym's unfortunate trip to Sonny's house, and Sonny and Gogo were about to celebrate their twelfth birthdays. Gogo's father, Murgo Pongo, planned a joint birthday party for them. Sonny's 11+ exams were behind him and he felt free to enjoy himself. Gogo's end-of-year exams also were completed, so he too was in the mood for some fun. Murgo planned to hold the party in the meadow at the bottom of their hill which the owls used as their landing and take-off ground. It was here also that the Annual Trade Fair was help when it was Pongoland's turn to be host. There was plenty of space to put up tables for food as well as a dais for a rock concert Murgo had organized. Murgo was the King of Pongoland's First Minister, so he knew all the families on the Island. Everyone was invited.

Pongoland was an Island in the sky, and one of many Islands which existed in a slightly different dimension from our own. Sonny was a human boy whom Gogo had met several years earlier on a trip he made into our world. He struck up a close friendship with Sonny, and started to take him back to Pongoland nearly every weekend. The only way for a human child to go to Pongoland was if he was taken there by one of Murgo's family. The people of the Islands were about eighteen inches tall by human measurement, so in order to go there at all Sonny had to shrink. There was a mystic knowledge of the way things work in the Islands. It was never spoken of and Sonny never asked questions, but things could be caused to happen which would be considered impossible in our world. Gogo would simply take Sonny by the hand and he would become the same height as Gogo which was about a foot tall at the beginning. Now they were sixteen inches tall according to our world's measurement. Together they would climb on to the back of Murgo's owl, Goggles, and fly away over the tree-tops and under the stars.

The mode of transport on the Islands was birds. Each Island had its' own birds to carry people back and forth between the Islands, as well as inland sometimes. The populations of the Islands differed, as did the life-styles to some extent, but each Island was governed by a King. Each Island had its' own royal family, and usually, but not always, the princes and princesses inter-married amongst themselves. This practice had built up a very close relationship between the Islands.

Sonny had visited several of the Islands close to Pongoland, but he couldn't travel far as he had to be back in his bed before morning at home. When it was night-time in Pongoland it was day-time at home, so Sonny's trips had to take place between going to bed Friday night and sunrise Saturday morning. Gogo had been bought in a toyshop by Sonny's Uncle for Sonny's birthday. Gogo had merely been looking at the toys when he was mistaken for one himself, and bought! For self-defence he had had to keep completely still, and to this day Sonny's parents thought he was a toy. If he didn't return to Pongoland after bringing Sonny home he spent the day sleeping on his bed. Sonny had developed the habit of having a long afternoon sleep on Saturday so that he could return to Pongoland Saturday night.

By now Sonny was very well-known indeed in Pongoland because of the many adventures Sonny, Gogo, and his younger brother Tobo, had been involved in. The King liked Sonny because he had so often, in times of crisis, seen solutions which did not occur to Pongo people. Sonny's imagination worked differently, but Gogo was always an eager comrade in all their adventures, and over the years Gogo and Tobo had developed some of Sonny's capacity to trace a very simple logic running through an apparent conundrum. Gogo's parents treated Sonny like their own child, and so were very keen that he should celebrate his twelfth birthday with Gogo. That was besides the celebrations organized at home by his own parents. The twelfth birthday was a mile-stone in the lives of Island children. They continued to go to school, but began also to learn a trade or craft.

In general, occupations were passed down in families from generation to generation. Thus the miners of the precious stones and minerals to be found in the Pongoland hills taught their sons to dig and to evaluate their finds. Those who worked the minerals and created beautiful jewelry and household items, taught their sons to do the same. Farmers trained their sons to care for the land and the animals. Mostly sons took over one set of skills and girls another, though there were no hard and fast rules about this. At twelve years old children needed to choose what they would do. Mostly the girls learnt the spinning and weaving of various cloths, and the art of embroidery. The women made the most wonderful silk cloth, as well as warm woollens for Winter. Sewing and tailoring were the occupations of many women on the Island, but nearly all of them also ran their households. Work in the factories therefore was for half the day only, morning or afternoon.

Pongoland was fairly wealthy because of the quality of its' produce. Some Islands were more artistic or musical. Some tended to have more writers. Each Island hoped to have its' own unique brands, and the Islands bartered their products with each other. The Kings evaluated the products and worked out the relative value of each. They regulated, so to speak, the exchange rates, for purposes of bartering. They each had copies of the fat ledgers they had created containing lists of the values of each item as against the values of the other products in the market. Ledgers were referred to however only in the case of a dispute, because the Islanders themselves had a fine sense of the worth of the things they were exchanging. A little haggling and the issue was usually resolved.

All the Islanders loved concerts and parties, and there were regular get-togethers to which the inhabitants of the neighbouring Islands were invited. The King of Pongoland had instituted an Annual Sports Day for the children of the Islands to compete in. He had learnt about Sports Days from Sonny's description of those held on Earth, and thought them an excellent opportunity for the Island children to learn skills through sports and athletics, while exercising their bodies and keeping fit.

Sonny was excited when he heard about the birthday party. Gogo told him his mother would have his party clothes ready for him when he arrived, and promised to shrink Sonny's present to him to Pongo size.

Sonny's own parents planned to take Sonny to the Zoo as a birthday treat, but that was to take place the week after the Pongoland party. That day Tobo came with Goggles to pick him up and take him back to Pongoland after his Earth bedtime. He had had his usual afternoon sleep. His parents were a little puzzled by this keenness for an afternoon nap but were used to it by now. Tobo sprinkled the usual powdered moss under his bedroom door. The moss gave off an undetectable odour which had the property of inducing forgetfulness. Thus when either of Sonny's parents meant to go into his room, as they approached the door, they forgot why they had meant to go in. The range of the vapour from so small a source was not far. It did not extend to the stairs or into another room, so was harmless.

Tobo's news today was that the King and Queen were to attend the party! Sonny was surprised. Of course Murgo was Chief Minister and close to the King, but that didn't mean usually that the King attended Murgo's children's birthday parties. Goggles greeted Sonny. All the birds of the Islands could talk to some extent and were used to taking messages as well as delivering parcels. Gogo's parents trusted Goggles also to keep an eye on the children and rescue them if need be!

Tobo took Sonny's hand and as he did so Sonny shrank to Gogo's height. The two boys climbed on to Goggles back, and away they flew over the tree-tops and under the stars.

They left our world under a night sky, but as they approached the Islands, the early morning sun was already shining. As Goggles approached Pongoland Sonny could see the green hills and the Palace. Around the other side was the forested hill where Mother Fulati and her daughter Selina lived in their cottage and prepared medicines from the plants growing in their garden. Their house and garden were surrounded by the forest so they had all the ingredients they needed for their work.

The Palace stood at the top of the nearest hill, shining in the golden rays of the dawn sun. Below the Palace were orchards which supplied fruit for the islanders. A winding path led up the hill from the lowland plain to the Palace. Murgo's house was halfway up. The meadow at the bottom of the hill where Goggles now landed was nearly ready for the party. A huge marquee had been erected and inside were a great many little tables and seats. A special large table had been set with a pale gold cloth and that seemed to be the one intended for the Royal Family.

All due respect was paid to the King and Queen as they administered the affairs of the Island. The King stored the Island's supplies of grain, wool, silk, and many other products, ready to be transported as required down to the central market place where there were the Island's shops. There was no money. The supplies belonged to the people. They had been procured in exchange for the merchandise produced by them and brought to the Trade Fair every year. The islanders did keep a certain amount of their own products in their cellars to bring, as individuals, to the Fair for small personal exchanges. For their regular household supplies they went to the market to obtain them from the appropriate shop. No-one horded. No-one cheated. The supplies were there, their own. The exceptions were the very valuble gold and jeweled items. These were of far greater value than the breads and cheeses and household items the islanders bought, and the King used them for the larger purchases for the Island as a whole.

The King also administered justice. There was very little crime, but anyone who had a complaint appeared at the Palace on Court Days. The King interviewed the accused person and decided on the merits of both sides of the argument. Anyone found guilty of harm had to repay in the form of service. On occasion both parties found themselves doing service!

Beyond the respect due to a King and Queen the islanders had a free and easy relationship with the Royal Family. The King and Queen knew them all, and they knew Sonny very well after all the adventures he had been involved in in Pongoland. They treated him as if he was Gogo's brother.

Sonny and Gogo alighted from Goggles' back and set off up the hill to Gogo's house. Its' white gate opened on to the hill path. The walls were painted cream and the roof was red. The boys entered the little garden through the gate and Sonny saw that the house had been decorated with red, yellow, and blue balloons. Mrs Murgo was bustling around adding the final touches to the food she had prepared. Each mother had made things to contribute to the Island's party, but this was her own special feast for her son and Sonny. The Palace had announced that they would contribute the Island's cake. After all it was going to have to be pretty big!

Gogo ran out to meet Sonny and Tobo. He was already dressed in a suit with a gold tunic and red silk trousers. There was also a red silk cap but he didn't have it on. The young people of Pongoland had begun to feel the traditional caps were not cool. The parents sighed and let it go.

"Come on Sonny," he called. "Come and put on you suit!"

Sonny went into the house and through the dining-room where the food was set out, and upstairs to Gogo's bedroom. His party suit was laid out on the bed. His also had a gold tunic but with blue silk trousers and blue cap. Sonny changed into the suit, observing protocol in not putting on the cap. They would take the caps to the party, but put them on only as required. Tobo appeared at the door dressed in a silver-coloured tunic with maroon trousers. As soon as Gogo was ready they went downstairs excitedly. At that moment Murgo came in looking serious. He greeted Sonny and said,

"Come along," he said, "I have brought a carriage to take us up to the Palace."

"What for!" cried Gogo, astonished.

"The King is most anxious to talk to you and Sonny," said Murgo. Sonny's heart missed a beat. Had he done something wrong? Murgo didn't normally look so grave. Oh dear! What could have happened? Tobo started to go with them to the carriage, but Murgo checked him.

"No Tobo. Not today," he said. "The King wishes to talk to Gogo and Sonny alone." Gogo looked frightened! He and Sonny exchanged glances in dismay. Something terrible must have happened!

The carriage belonged to the Palace and had been sent to pick the boys up. They climbed in and set off. It was an open carriage and drawn by two horses, so normally this would have been a wonderful ride in the sunshine, but not today. The journey took only ten minutes, and the carriage went through the gates kept open for them. Then the guards closed them. They alighted and went into the Palace. For a fleeting moment Sonny wondered if he had been taken prisoner! However his common sense reminded him he was in Pongoland to celebrate his birthday, and anyway the King was hardly likely to take a child prisoner. He almost laughed at the thought.

In fact Murgo, Sonny, and Gogo were invited into the King's personal sitting-room, and shortly afterwars the King himself arrived. He was all courtesy and friendliness, and sat down with his three visitors.

"You will be surprised to find yourselves here this morning," he smiled. "I will wish you both happy birthday later on at the party, but there is a subject I wish to discuss with you beforehand. As you know the Queen and I have no children, and you know how important it is for the royal families of the Islands to have a son or daughter to succeed. All the affairs of each Island are known and understood by the Kings and Queens. All the stores, all the account books, all the legal history, and much more are stored in the Palaces. The Kings and Queens are custodians, and they train their heirs to succeed them in the responsibilities of administration. Trade agreements are made between Kings or Queens. Purchases for the whole Island are made by the King or Queen, and as you know of course we have an old established exchange system which is monitored when necessary by the King. A great deal of work is done by the royal families and they in turn rely on the co-operation of the islanders to make sure things run smoothly. See how everyone this very day is participating in the work to make this the best birthday party ever!"

Sonny and Gogo nodded their heads trying to look wise, while wondering why on earth their King should suddenly decide to confide his problems to them! I mean….. what?

"So the point here," said the King, looking at Sonny, "is that I don't have an heir. Sonny I have known you now for four years. I know you to be well-mannered, tactful, courageous, resourceful, and a natural leader. Whatever challenges you have faced while visiting here you have been able to come up with solutions. Shall we ever forget Great-Uncle Parkin!" The boys smiled. "And you have been able to carry through an enterprise, keeping your mind on the main objective, to a successful conclusion. The qualities I see in you are the qualities I would have wished to find in my own son."

Sonny and Gogo looked beseechingly at Murgo. The King understood their dismay.

"Don't worry Sonny," he reassured him. "You will never be coerced to do anything, or pressured into doing anything which goes against your conscience or wishes. You have your own home, and your own parents, your own world. However I would like you to consider taking the role of a prince here, and of a son to my wife and me. We would train you in all the skills you will need to possess to be a King here one day, and Gogo would always be at your side. The role of Chief Minister is also inherited, and Gogo has always known that one day he will be Chief Minister."

Tears came into Sonny's eyes. King of Pongoland? Him?

"But my parents would never let me!" he cried. "They don't even know I come here! They don't know Pongoland exits!"

"I know," said the King, "and although your visits here have so far been without their knowledge, if you agree to my suggestion you will certainly need to talk to them."

Sonny felt as if the floor was shifting under his feet.

"But how?" he asked.

"We will invite them here for just one visit," said the King. "We will show them round, and let them see what we do, and meet the Islanders."

By now even Gogo was looking confused and upset.

"Your Majesty," he said, "I don't think that will work very well. You haven't met the people of Sonny's world. They haven't any real imagination. They think that what they see and feel is all there is! Once when by accident Sonny's mother saw Pym running along her landing she nearly had a nervous breakdown. And that was because she saw something she didn't believe could happen!"

"I know," said the King, "I really do Gogo. I can in any case allow only one visit. It is their right so it must be. But the dangers of contamination from Earth are real. I have allowed Sonny here because of his nature. But there is a corruption on Earth which I cannot allow here. Because of Sonny I know there must be very many people on Earth like him, but we aren't in a position to investigate all that. As Sonny so often does, we must stick to practicalities."

"So do you mean I would have to live here for ever and never go home?"

"No. You will of course visit your world, and spend time with your parents. And for the next few years you will continue to come here on the same basis, just at the weekend. You must complete your education on Earth, and grow up. Then your parents can explain to people that you have accepted a job abroad. Thousands do. There would be a condition though Sonny. I will need you to marry a Pongo girl. Or possibly, of course, a girl from one of the other Islands. All the Royal Families inter-marry."

"And if I decide not to become a Prince I will be banned from Pongoland?" he cried in horror.

"Not immediately," said the King, "but as you enter your teens you will take on adult concerns and responsibilities. In the end a choice will have to be made. The position is that you are invited to make Pongoland your home, settle here, and become King, or, for the protection of our civilization I should be forced to end the visits. The thought of that saddens me but I too have to make difficult choices."

He saw the looks of hope and horror mixing in the faces of both the boys. He looked at Murgo,

"It is difficult for them to understand," he said.

"I know," said Murgo. "And the challenges?" The King sighed.

"Yes. The challenges. Sonny if you decide to be our King, there will be three tests to be passed. Rites of passage. All princes or princesses destined to be monarch have to complete three tests set by the reigning monarch."

If it were possible Sonny looked even more alarmed.

"What!" he cried.

"Yes, three tests. Knowing you I imagine you will enjoy them, but we won't go into all that until you have made your decision. If you agree to become our King the first step will be to tell your parents about Pongoland. Then to bring them here to see for themselves. If they agree to my proposition you will start your training here at the weekends. If they do not agree, but you wish to come here eventually, we may have to suspend your visits for a while. Gogo would be with you a lot of the time and keep us posted on how things are going. When you are adult you can make your own decision, but that is a long way off."

"You can take your time, Sonny," said Murgo. "You have until your thirteenth birthday to decide."

"No. Thankyou, Murgo," said Sonny decisively, "I don't need time." He turned to the King.

"The answer is yes, of course. I am already more at home here than on Earth, and often wish I could just stay here. I will talk to my parents, somehow," he looked at Gogo, "with Gogo's advice and suggestions. Please invite them here when you are ready. If they agree I am ready to take the tests whenever you like. If they say no I will finish my education in my world and then come here."

"Well done Sonny," said the King. "We will talk again later, but now I think it is time for us to go to a party!" Sonny stood up and bowed to the King,

"I would like to thank you very much Sir for this huge honour. I will do my very best to prepare myself to serve Pongoland something approaching as well as you do."

The boys left the room. The King turned to Murgo.

"As decisive as ever, even at his age," he smiled. "Those two young men will make a fine team, as we have always been."

As the boys got back into the carriage with Murgo they were very quiet. They had a lot to think about, and they realized their twelfth birthdays would mark the end of their childhood as they had always known it. From now on they would be in training for adulthood. On the one hand this was an exhilarating prospect. On the other hand the safety and careless freedom of early childhood was nearly at an end. Both knew that from now on they would be expected to grow in maturity and wisdom.

Meanwhile preparations for the party in the meadow were nearly completed. Mrs Murgo's jellies, buns, and sandwiches had been collected and taken down to the meadow to set alongside the contributions of all the other mothers. A band had arrived from Meridoland and was already playing background music on the dais. Sonny, Gogo, and Murgo returned to Gogo's house. Mrs Murgo and Tobo were ready and putting last-minute provisions into a bag, so the whole family set off together down the hill on foot.

Sonny and Gogo's spirits lifted immediately. Never mind the cares of the future! Just now it was party day! On a table in the marquee stood the enormous cake sent by the Palace. It was tiered and iced all over in blue with trimmings of green leaves, yellow flowers with tiny orange hearts, and silver lace-work. On top were twenty-four gold candles for two boys aged twelve. Sonny and Gogo gasped, wow!

The guests arrived before the first musical item of the day. This was performed by the Meridoland group called the Spangles. The verses referred to many of the incidents of the past four years in which the boys had come to the aid of an agitated Islander! Everyone laughed and clapped good-naturedly. After that there were games and races for the children. The Queen presented a prize to each winner. The adults sat around in twos and threes on the seats brought to the meadow for the day. When the children seemed to have run off some energy everyone was invited to come into the marquee and serve themselves from the tables which were set out round three sides. The cake was to be cut later. The Meridoland band resumed the background music.

Sonny was haunted again by what the King had said and wandered off with Gogo for a few minutes.

"What do you think Gogo?" he asked anxiously.

"I agree absolutely with your decision. If you don't become King you will have to stop coming here, and that's what I care about. You'll love it!"

"Yes. I think *we* shall love it. My anxiety really is about telling my parents. I sweat to think of it. And how are we to bring them here?"

"By putting them to sleep and carrying them in a blanket? You climbed on to Goggles' back without a second thought but they won't! You will have to introduce the subject though somehow."

"Are you kidding! Tell them casually that they will need to be reduced to the size of garden gnomes to be like everybody else?"

"Yes but Sonny, if we can bring them here asleep they won't know they are the size of garden gnomes will they?"

"Well they will have travelled here by an owl," said Sonny glumly.

"No," said Gogo, "by *four* owls. They will lie on a blanket and be carried by four owls."

"Gogo you have no idea how absolutely crazy this whole thing will be to my parents. They can't think anywhere near big enough."

"No I suppose not. All this seems so normal to us. It *is* normal. We have to think of something plausible."

"And don't forget that my career choice now is to be a King. Not an architect Dad, no. A King. I'll be sitting cosily with a school counselor in no time."

"Sonny I don't think this is going to be for us to work out by ourselves. The King knows how things are, and they will come here by his invitation. Do you think he has no idea how he will get them here? Of course not. We can trust him you know."

"O.K….. Yes. I was having a moment of panic," said Sonny.

The King and Murgo had been watching the boys and noted Sonny's glum face. The King called him over.

"Sonny! Come and walk with me for a minute. You are trying to process the idea of being King here," he said kindly.

"It's not that so much Sir. It's how to tell my parents about Pongoland. I just don't know how to do that."

"We will help you with that," said the King. "The mental gap between our two worlds has to be bridged for them. You know Mother Fulati can prepare all manner of potions, not just to heal the body, but on occasion, when it is deemed necessary, to alter the mind. Gogo has been using that moss regularly for years. Another remedy of hers soothed and reassured your mother the day she saw Pym running about your house. The remedy was essential. She could never have come to terms with what she saw.'

"You mean Mother Fulati could make them something to take the edge off the Pongoland experience?"

The King laughed.

"In all my career she has never let me down," he said. "Whenever I have been faced with some apparently impossible situation she has come to my rescue. I trust her completely."

"I would be so grateful Sir. I trust her too."

"Leave it to me. Grown-up worries have to be dealt with by adults. Let's forget all that for today, and I will ask for Mother Fulati's help. The incredible must appear normal. She will devise something so don't worry."

Chapter Two

Sonny's Parents Learn the Truth

The next week went by as usual in Sonny's home. He went to school, did his homework, played with his friends, and watched TV – which by now was available all night! But his parents noticed he was preoccupied. The following Sunday they took him to the Zoo, and they had a wonderful family day out. Sonny's main present was a new bicycle and he nearly cried. His parents were so good to him! At least until he was eighteen he would carry on as before while he underwent his training in Pongoland at the weekends.

That very night Gogo arrived on Goggles carrying a green bottle and Goggles was waiting on the neem tree. However Sonny had not rested in the afternoon and had school the next day, so could not go to Pongoland.

"That's OK," said Gogo. "Let's just talk."

They sat on Sonny's bed and Gogo uncorked the green bottle for a moment, and closed it again.

"We mustn't breathe this," he said. "It's the stuff for your parents from Mother Gulati."

"So I have to hold my breath as I ask my parents to sniff it?"

"No! Just hide it somewhere. It's to let them breathe when they travel to Pongoland, so that Pongoland will look OK. We'll be outside on Goggles' back in the fresh air so it won't affect us."

"Right. Is there anything for when I have to tell them about Pongoland in the first place?"

"For that I've got some drops," said Gogo, taking a little bottle from his pocket. It became six inches long for Sonny's world. He held it sideways and showed it to Sonny. Inside was a little model ship, perfectly fashioned. Sonny exclaimed in wonder.

"Yes, it's lovely. When the liquid has evaporated they might like to put it on display. The thing is you get it out to show them when you get to the subject of Pongoland. You can tell them that this is from Pongoland, and, (having taken off the stopper), encourage them to look inside to see the workmanship close to. They will then automatically breathe in the vapour. Keep talking. Tell them you have been invited to succeed as King there. There will be in a slight opening of their consciousness. That will allow what you say to be at least partially understood. Then that same night we will take them to Pongoland."

"Alright," said Sonny dubiously. "Could it be next Saturday night then? And I will talk about Pongoland just before bed-time."

"Fine. I will go home now, but I will come back tomorrow for the week so that I can keep everyone informed there, and let them know if there are any snags," said Gogo.

Sonny laughed dolefully.

"It's all snag Gogo," he said.

Gogo returned the following morning to spend the week with Sonny. On Wednesday Sonny asked,

"Please would you take me to meet Mother Fulati tonight? I think I need to discuss with her myself the effects of the potions."

"Of course," said Gogo.

They left a little earlier than usual so that Sonny could be back in bed in fairly good time. Today they passed over the meadow and headed straight to the forests on the slope of the farther hill where Mother Fulati's house could be seen in a clearing. The house was surrounded by a very large garden in which there were tree-lined paths, and many beds for flowering plants and herbs. They landed on her lawn. The jackdaws and crows in her trees started up a ruckus and her cat disappeared round the back of the house. Mother Fulati herself came out of the kitchen on to her small patio, her arms outstretched to greet them. She hugged them and ushered them into her house. Before they could say a word she made them sit at her table and gave them each hot buttered scone. She was said to be of ancient gypsy stock, and unlike the other people of Pongoland she wore a long full skirt to her ankles with a short blouse fitted into the waist. Her hair was full length and knotted at the back of her head. Her daughter Selina smiled at them but she was up to her elbows in flour as she kneaded dough for bread. There was a large kitchen range for the many remedies and potions which had to be brewed every day. They served neighbouring Islands as well as their own people, so this work never stopped. Things were merely left on hold at night.

"Now what can I do for you?" she asked. "I have heard your news Sonny and I am delighted. You must have a lot of questions though."

"Yes I have Mother Fulati, but right now I wondered if you could tell me a bit more about the potions you have sent for my parents. What actually will they do?"

"Of course," she said. "You are a good sensible boy not to want to treat your parents with medicines you don't understand. We can't just call a thing magic without understanding what that means. You know that people flying in airplanes from you world never encounter these Islands. The reason is, as probably you have been told, that they exist in higher dimension."

"Yes," said Sonny, "and I have heard about people and planes apparently disappearing into another dimension."

"That may or not be true," said Mother Fulati, "but everything vibrates, you see. Everything in creation vibrates, but at different speeds. You can't see a level of creation which vibrates at a different speed from yours. Our Islands exist on a slightly higher plane from yours."

"I see," said Sonny, and he did, "but I must vibrate at the speed if my own world, and Gogo and Tobo, and even Murgo once, visit my world without disappearing."

"Yes," said Mother Fulati. "They belong to the family of Murgo Pongo and going back into our most ancient history they, and the King, have always had the ability to cross dimensions. They have the ability to slow down or speed up at will. No-one else can do that unless conducted by one of his family. One day Gogo, as a young child, wandered across dimensions into your world and met you. Instinctively he knew how to transmit the energy necessary for you to become his height, and bring you here. You were also a young child living still in the imagination. Alice in Wonderland changed sizes, so there you were, doing the same. You thought nothing of climbing on to Goggles' back. It was that child's faith which enabled you to return here with Gogo. Normally no-one from another dimension is allowed here, but the King recognized that unique faith in you and didn't want to stifle your gift. You proved discreet and an excellent friend. At any moment the King could have asked Murgo's family not to return to your house, but he never did."

"Right. OK," said Sonny.

"My Dad taught me about crossing dimensions when I was quite small. Tobo was also taught. We had to know how to get back, you see, if we drifted, and it was easy for us to drift. Normally I see a place in my mind's eye, and fix it with an intention to get there, and I do. My first trip to your world was accidental somehow."

"How do you make me small?" asked Sonny.

"It's also done in the mind. In your world you can enlarge or contract photos very easily. It's the same process. Big Sonny, little Sonny."

"I get that but I don't think I'll ever grasp how," said Sonny. "But these potions, Mother Fulati. They are to confuse reality and fantasy in my parents' minds. Is that so?"

"They speed up the vibrational rate just a little to bring into focus things which otherwise would be beyond the person's imagination and rejected. The result is that when you describe Pongoland to them they will be able to see it in their mind's eye in the same they would be able to visualise a place in your own world. The vapour from the liquid in the larger bottle for the journey is a bit stronger to lift them into Pongoland comfortably. The effect will wear off soon but by then they will have seen that Pongoland is real. The effects from both preparations are very short-lived."

"Alright, thanks," said Sonny. "The other thing is that they will arrive in Pongoland in nightie and pyjamas! Never mind Pongoland my parents would be dismayed!"

"You are so compassionate, my child," said Mother Fulati, smiling, "understanding their mortification, but the King and Queen will be in the meadow to meet them, and will have beautiful clothes for them to put on immediately. They will take them home with them as keepsakes, and asa proofs later that they really did come here."

By Saturday morning Sonny felt sick with nerves, but there was no going back. Soon before he was due to go to bed he said brightly,

"I've been thinking about what I want to do when I grow up."

"Oh?" said his mother.

"Yes. I want to be a King," he said firmly. His father laughed.

"Seriously," Sonny persevered. "Imagine being King of a country where people live in peace and harmony, where there is no traffic, no pollution, and where everyone has enough to eat and a house to live in."

"If you become King of a country like that, I shall come and live there," his father joked.

"Ah, but no traffic?" said his mother. "Presumably you would have electricity?" she asked, playing along.

"Electricity yes, but no TV or radio Mum. Lots of sunshine to do things outside. Everything hand-made, and an economy based on a barter system. Beautiful countryside. Lots of music, art, and literature, but no money."

"Well," said his father, smiling, "you've certainly got it worked out. You must write a novel about that. However societies like that no longer exist, probably never did. There has always been exploitation."

"Not with a good King in charge," persisted Sonny. He looked so earnest his parents began to look at him seriously. This was the moment to produce the ship!

"See what a friend gave me!" he said proudly, giving it to his father. Both his parents exclaimed. The workmanship was so perfect!

"You can take out the cork to get a closer look," said Sonny. His father took removed the cork stopper and peered into the bottle to see the details of the ship. Then he handed it to his mother, and she too had a close look. They discussed the minute carving of the hull and the tiny details of the deck, but his father said,

"I don't think you can keep this Sonny. Do your friend's parents know he has given it away? I'm sure he was not meant to do that."

"No. It's alright Dad. But I will give it back. I just wanted you to see it first."

"It's perfect," said his mother." It must have been very expensive."

This was his moment.

"No Mum. It was bartered for some medicines. Mother Fulati exchanged herbal medicines in exchange for the ship."

"Wh….what?" said his father.

"In the kingdom I was telling you about, Pongoland." His parents gaped, but the vapour was beginning to have its' effect.

"Pongoland is an Island in the sky. It's one of an archipelago of islands which exist in the sky about half an hour from Earth, owl-time."

"Islands in the sky?" said his mother. "But planes fly in and out of airports all the time. No-one has noticed any islands."

"We have a moon circling the Earth and there's a space-station," said his father. "We are observing the universe all the time, and no-one has seen them."

"No," said Sonny, and going the whole hog while the vapour lasted. "They exist in a different dimension from ours of course, so they are invisible from our dimension. Each Island has a King, and the Islands live as I have been describing. Pongoland's First Minister is Murgo Pongo. Members of his family have inherited the gift of being able to cross dimensions, so one day four years ago, Murgo's son Gogo came to

152

visit Earth and met me. He came here. The islanders fly on birds to visit each other, and Gogo came on his family's bird, an owl called Goggles."

His parents just stared at him.

"So one night," he pressed on, "Gogo took me back to his home in Pongoland. When Gogo holds my hand he transmits some energy, light energy I think, to me and reduces me to his height, which is small. We climb on Goggles' back and off we go!"

"When?" asked his mother.

"In the night, Mum. I come back before morning. We have had so many wonderful adventures in Pongoland. It's a lovely place."

"Every night?" asked his father.

"No. Just at the weekends. That's why I take an afternoon nap."

"So Gogo comes for you on Goggles' back," said his mother.

"Yes, that's right, but a lot of the time Gogo stays here with me during our day. Daytime here is night-time there, so he sleeps on my bed. He's that puppet-doll, except he's not a puppet. He keeps still while you're around so as not to frighten you."

"But he's what? Fifteen inches tall!" said his father.

"Sixteen inches now to be exact. He has been growing, but so slowly you wouldn't notice. And so am I when he takes my hand. He contracts me like we can contract photographs. It's some light process Dad."

He left his account at that, feeling he had better just let it sink in while they were under the influence of the vapour. Gogo and he were to take them to Pongoland tonight, and they would see for themselves. At present they were in a state of suspended disbelief. He hoped they wouldn't be frightened, but Pongoland would be like some perfect holiday resort in their eyes, and he thought they would love it!

Gogo was waiting anxiously in his bedroom, and listened to Sonny's report.

"So, not too bad so far?" he said.

"No," said Sonny. "That medicine helped enormously. It meant they listened quietly and asked sensible questions. They are feeling sleepy now, so hopefully will soon go to bed."

They did indeed. Sonny went to check after some time, and reported to Gogo that they were asleep. Gogo signalled to Goggles who was waiting on the nearby tree along with eight more Pongoland owls. Tobo had brought them through and was directing them. He came to Sonny's windowsill on Goggles back carrying two large sheets. Gogo took them from him and all the boys went into Sonny's parents' room. Gogo took

Sonny's father's hand, and Tobo took his mother's hand, and they were reduced to the size of Pongo adults, in the region of two feet tall, his mother a bit less. The boys then gently lifted them on to a sheet each. Tobo sat beside his mother on her sheet. Goggles brought the other owls, and they lifted the sheets, an owl to each corner. They held the corners firmly and carried them out through their window. The owls were well accustomed to carrying both people and merchandise in this manner. Sonny and Gogo climbed on to Goggles' back and off they all flew, over the tree-tops and under the stars. Tobo spent some time allowing Sonny's mother to breathe the vapour from the larger bottle. Then he signaled to Sonny's father's owls, and climbed on to his sheet. He then allowed him to breathe the vapour for a while too. Sonny felt he needed a whiff of the vapour himself, so extraordinary were the events of the night!

As they approached Pongoland the early morning sun was shining down on the green meadow. It was a beautiful day with the scents of many blossoms in the air, and the greens of the hills and the forest all around. The Palace at the top of the nearest hill shone pale gold in the sunlight, and all the little houses on the hillside looked bright and homely. Each tiny garden was in bloom, and a lot of people were out already doing their early morning chores.

The owls laid the two sheets gently on the grass. Murgo and his wife were waiting for them. They had a jug of fresh juice to revive Sonny's parents, and a set of clothes for each, as well as Sonny's own blue and cream suit kept at Gogo's house. Sonny quietly changed into his clothes and knelt by his parents to wake them. They felt the ground beneath them and awoke startled. They felt the soft breeze and wondered for a moment if they were on holiday. They sat up and Mrs Murgo stepped forward with a large glass of juice for each. They were thirsty from the effects of the vapour and drank it all. They took in the sight of Sonny in his blue tunic and cream trousers, and recognized Gogo as the "doll" Sonny had had on his bed for so long. He smiled at them.

"So….where are we?" asked Sonny's father.

"In Pongoland Dad," said Sonny."We thought you would like to come and see for yourselves. It's nice isn't it?"

Murgo and Mrs Murgo introduced themselves, and Sonny's parents, apart from a greeting, remained quiet. Sonny said,

"Look Mum, these are some clothes for you to wear for today. Tonight we will take you home."

"Oh, thankyou, but darling how did we get here? Don't tell me this is your Island in the sky and we have crossed dimensions!"

"Yes it is Mum. Owls brought you here on these sheets. Look there they are having their breakfast." The owls were tucking into bowls of food provided by Murgo.

"They're pretty big," said Sonny's father. "Much bigger than ours."

"Yes they are," said Sonny. "They are the Island's transport." Mrs Murgo said,

" If you would like to dress behind those bushes we'll take you to our home for breakfast. Then we will show you the Island."

Sonny's parents were bereft of speech really, and quietly did as suggested. His father was given maroon and white, and his mother yellow and dark brown. Sonny felt they would not want to wear the hats so just carried them. They set off up the hill to Gogo's house, making polite conversation about the weather and the scenery. They were long past surprise. They found Gogo's house homely and beautiful with polished furniture, decorative wool rugs, and gleaming bronze and silver-ware. The kitchen dresser was like their own with the crockery stacked on it. Breakfast was ready in the kitchen and they sat down to a cereal, egg, and toast and marmalade. They talked about the house, and about Gogo and Tobo's school as compared to Sonny's.

A simple carriage with two horses had been sent down from the Palace to take them up the hill to visit the King and Queen, and then to take them round the Island, so after breakfast they set off to meet the King and Queen. A royal guard met them at the gate, and another official came out to conduct them in to the King's personal sitting-room. There the King and Queen were waiting for them.

"I hope you are adjusting comfortably to this experience," said the King. "You will be back home again this evening, but we hope you will enjoy your day with us here, and take back memories of this world to your own. I think you will notice that our life-style is very simple. I have visited your world so do know something about it. Our civilization is more advanced in some ways. We can make things happen without the machinery you employ, and we are advanced in the uses of herbs and plants for medication. You will see something of that. Sonny tells me you are keen gardeners so I think you would enjoy a visit to Mother Fulati and a walk round her garden. Then our hills here are rich in minerals and you would probably like to see the men at work there fashioning beautiful things. Our women make fine cloths of silk and wool, and are artists in embroidery."

"Thankyou Sir, Ma'am," said Sonny's father. "We look forward to seeing your beautiful Island."

The tour went ahead and Sonny's parents had a truly wonderful day. They had lunch at the Palace and tea back at Murgo's house. As expected they were especially delighted with Mother Fulati's garden and talked with her a lot about her preparations. As they arrived back at Murgo's house, Sonny's father said,

"So what is this about you becoming King here, Sonny?" Murgo heard him.

"After tea John, the King will come to discuss that with you. He wanted you to look round, and meet us first. Now he will put to you his proposition," said Murgo.

The King arrived at five o'clock and was taken into Murgo's sitting-room. There he outlined for Sonny's parents the life and responsibilities Sonny would have on the Island, first as Prince and later succeeding as King."

"But Sonny is a human boy!" cried Sonny's mother. "What does he know about the way you do things here?"

"He knows us very well. Gogo would be his Chief Minister and attend to all the things that might be difficult for Sonny, as Murgo does for me. Sonny's job would be administration. He would look after supplies, and learn about how much of what is needed for imports and how much of what to export. He would mete out justice and he would handle all the diplomatic affairs of the Island. He would be responsible for the well-being of the people and attend to any matters of concern. In all these areas I believe Sonny to be well-qualified. Management is a practical business and he is deeply practical."

"Of course we have always said that he will be free to make his own career choice, but had never dreamt of anything like this," said his father. "Myself I shan't oppose it. But we will need to talk with Sonny a lot about what leaving our world and living here is going to mean."

"In any case he will live with you at home until he has finished his schooling. I wondered if you might tell people then that he has accepted a job abroad? There will be no restrictions about visiting you of course. The only condition I would make is that he marry a girl from one of our Islands."

"What do you think, Jane?" asked Sonny's father.

"I know he has a good mind and a compassionate heart and I think he could do this, but he shouldn't make a hasty decision. He has eight years left yet of education. He must apply himself as well as if he were planning to go to University in our world. If he continues to want to settle here then so be it," she said.

They had heard and seen as much as they take in for the time being, so Goggles was called to come with the other owls to take them home. The visit had been very pleasurable to Sonny's parents in spite of feeling dazed by it all. Their night clothes were folded up and ready for them to take back, and soon they were on their way. Gogo and Sonny travelled with them and Gogo restored them and all the clothes to Earth size. Then Gogo returned to Pongoland with the owls. Very tired by now, Sonny and his parents got back into bed and were asleep in no time.

Chapter Three

The Ring of the Dragon's Hair

During the next week Sonny's parents talked long and hard with Sonny about his future. They remembered every detail of their day in Pongoland clearly, and how normal and happy it had all seemed. They had the gifts from the miners and the cloth mills, enlarged to the correct size for their world, to show for their adventure. But the idea that they had "crossed a dimension", and that Pongoland was as real as this world, was hard to digest once they were back in their own home.

Sonny did not argue. He listened to all they said about the future which lay before him in his own world, and the sacrifices he would have to make to live in Pongoland. He understood all that fully. His only real argument against what his parents said was that he wanted to live in Pongoland. The very idea of not being able to go back there was too scary to contemplate.

Gogo lay in his bed all day and Sonny's parents got used to the idea that he was sleeping, not inanimate. Every evening Sonny and Gogo talked until Sonny fell asleep. Then Gogo went home for the night. On Friday night he took Sonny with him. He did not put any moss powder under the door because his parents would know where he was.

The King was keen that Sonny should go to the Palace so that he and the Queen could discuss the future. Murgo and Gogo and Tobo went with him. They were all exceedingly happy to hear that he would live in Pongoland eventually.

The King raised the subject of the three tests Sonny would undergo.

"The first test is mainly of resourcefulness," he said, "I know of course that you have plenty of that quality, but the test I am going to set you may be beyond your power to fulfil."

"I can only do my best, Sir," said Sonny anxiously.

"I don't suppose you have heard of the Ring of the Dragon's Hair have you?" asked the King.

"No Sir," said Sonny.

"It has belonged to the King of Meridoland for centuries. It is inherited by each succeeding King, and worn on the left hand. Unfortunately the current King has just lost it."

"Oh no!" cried the three boys, horrified.

"Yes," said the King, "and you would do the very greatest favour to the King of Maridoland, his wife, Lord Lannet and Princess Ahoosti if you could restore it to them. Otherwise he will go down in history as the King who lost the Ring of Dragon's Hair. It won't matter what his other achievements are. That is what will be remembered."

"They must have looked for it everywhere themselves. They do seem to keep losing things! It was a coronet last time!" said Sonny. The King smiled.

"Yes, though that wasn't really their own fault. The history of the ring is a great deal more important than the ring. It is indeed a very fine thing, made of gold with a dragon's head breathing fire crafted from ruby, amber, and quartz. It commemorates an event which took place so far back in history no-one can remember it, apart from what the ring signifies. In those very olden times there were dragons. A King had to defend his people against evil monsters, sorcery, and witch-craft. Those were dangerous times before the people of these islands learnt never ever to use magic against each other. It always bounces back on the attacker. Always. It took centuries for people to understand that. Evil as well as good is a boomerang. One day a wise old hermit told the King that in order to render their Dragon powerless he must steal a hair from its' tail. The tail of the Dragon was long and very powerful and the Dragon hardly ever slept."

Sonny, Gogo, and Tobo were listening to the story with eyes like saucers.

"So what did he do?" asked Gogo.

"Well a King has to save and protect his people, and if necessary lay down his life for them. So he knew he had no choice. The wise old hermit gave the King a sword to conquer the Dragon, but the Dragon was thirty feet long, the sword was three feet long, and the King was six feet tall."

"What happened?" asked Tobo.

"It was a long and arduous expedition, and every Island has the Chronicles of the Kings of Maridoland in its' library if you wish to read it. The upshot was that the King found a good witch living in a cave who made powerful magic potions. In return for a promise that she and her female descendents would always hold a high rank in the kingdom as healers, she made him a sleeping draft so strong that it could put to sleep a herd of elephants. Armed with a vial of this brew the King approached the Dragon in the dead of night. He crept up to the Dragon treading very softly. As he grew near to its' nose it reared its' head in alarm. It opened its' mouth to engulf the King in flames, but before it could do so the King tossed the vial straight into its' throat. The Dragon breathed in the fumes and sank into a deep sleep. Immediately the King leapt round to the back of the Dragon, seized a hair in his fist, and pulled it out! The old hermit gave the ring to the King of Meridoland in perpetual memory of the feat of wisdom and courage he had displayed to save his Island. The story has been an inspiration to every King since, and a lesson in what kingship means."

"And what of the wise woman? Meridoland doesn't have a good witch now," said Sonny.

"No but Pongoland does, and we are not so far away. Who knows what happened in all the succeeding centuries? Many people believe that at some stage a descendent of that original good witch migrated to Pongoland and our Mother Fulati is the current wise woman. She does hold an important rank on our Island," said the King. "I never challenge her."

"How interesting," breathed Sonny. "So it is really important that we find this ring!"

"It is," said the King, "and that is your first assignment. You will need to arrange to come here for a few days to fulfil it, if you can. You wouldn't be able to do it in one day. Don't get confused Sonny. I am not sending you into danger! I wouldn't dream of it. You are children. This is an exercise for your wits. The whole of Meridoland has been scouring the Island for that ring. Gogo will of course go with you."

Tobo was a mature little boy by now, and understood he could not take part in these tests. He promised plenty of advice though before they set off! Everyone laughed.

"Any advice you can give us will be greatly appreciated Tobo," said Sonny hugging him.

The King looked on approvingly. It was this unfailing kindness in Sonny that was in the King's eyes his chief qualification to rule his beloved Island.

"Sir, I have a question," said Sonny, "how is it the people of the Islands speak English?"

160

"Ah," said the King, "there is a belief that one of the Knights of King Arthur of England strayed across the dimensions into ours. Theirs is a very mystical story you know, the story of King Arthur, and the twelve Knights, and the Round Table. All those Knights went on missions and had adventures. It is believed one of them came here in a dream and explored our Islands. Originally the peoples of the Islands spoke different languages, but we all learnt English from him. Then we retained English as our common language. It is even rumoured that Mother Fulati's ancestry goes back to that Knight. You know she looks and dresses differently from the rest of us."

"What!!" exclaimed Sonny. "But what about size differences?"

"Oh come Sonny," smiled the King, "where is your sense of magic? Maybe Murgo's ancestry goes back to that time too to give him the 'touch'?" Sonny laughed.

"Yes of course. Who am I to talk about impossibilities?"

"Quite. An open mind here is polite! Our Kings even acknowledge an allegiance to King Arthur. Some even believe the wise old hermit who gave the King of Meridoland the sword was Merlin. Whatever the reality every new King here goes on a pilgrimage to Camelot. I told you I visited your world once. I went to Camelot. The traditions of honour and chivalry taught by King Arthur we also observe."

"So," said the essentially practical Sonny, "your English has been updated regularly because the Kings of the Islands go to Camelot?" The King smiled.

"Yes, and we also have old books from England in our libraries, reduced in size of course. There's a lot for you to study Sonny. These islands have a rich history, and much culture. But go now and enjoy yourselves. Your test can be done when you can arrange to come here for three or four days."

In the end it was agreed that Sonny should come to Pongoland for his half-term holiday. He and Gogo and Tobo were elated, no matter what the reason, though not so elated when the King said Sonny must sleep at the Palace when not away on another Island.

"He needs to become very familiar with the Palace and how things work here," he said when the boys arrived to see him. "I have written to the King of Meridoland to let him know you will be coming today to look for the ring. You and Gogo will stay in his Palace. I have explained that this is one of your tests as heir to my throne."

161

"O.K.," said Sonny feeling very awkward, "I mean thankyou Sir. Shall we ask Goggles to take us?"

"Goggles can indeed take you but escorted by one of my personal owls. This is an official visit."

Sonny had lunch at Mrs Murgo's house and after that he and Gogo went down to the meadow. The King was there with his owl called Ben and he saw them off with good wishes and blessings.

They arrived after about half an hour. Meridoland was a mountainous island with deep valleys, and caverns hollowed out in the hillsides. There were plateaus also where people met each other for parties or other festivities. The King's Palace had been built at the top of the highest mountains, and the owls drew in to land in its' courtyard. Sonny had been to Meridoland twice before and knew the Royal Family. The King and Queen came out to meet them. They enjoyed the idea that one of Sonny's tests was to find their ring!

"This is going to be a really difficult task Sonny," said the King. "We have so many mountains and ravines, so if for instance the ring was dropped down one of them you really have no chance of finding it."

"No I expect not Sir," said Sonny, "but how could that happen? Our King says it is always on your finger." The Queen sighed.

"That is true,' she said, "but when we went to bed one Sunday night it was safe on his finger, I know for sure. When we woke up in the morning it was gone! Someone stole it. We haven't just lost it."

"So say if it was thrown off a mountain-top, that would be as a punishment or out of revenge wouldn't it?" suggested Sonny.

"Yes but this is a very difficult thing someone did, to take it off my finger in the night! There are other ways of punishing me if someone felt badly treated. And I can't for the life of me think who!"

"The ring is so ancient, Sonny," said the Queen, "that it is believed to have magical properties. Some think Merlin gave it to the King's ancestor, and he was a wizard, a seer."

"What sort of properties?" asked Sonny.

"Well," said the King, "someone might think it has healing properties. It is believed to confer energy and grace on the wearer, and the monarch will commune with it before any enterprise of great importance. One King did that long ago before a battle with the Toliks, before we learnt how to negociate agreements fairly. And as it happened Meridoland won, but I think nowadays no-one would like to say that was because of the ring!"

162

"But nowadays also everyone goes to Mother Fulati for healing. That would be far easier and better than stealing a ring off your finger in the night! Who would risk stealing such a famous ring when all they have to do is fly to Pongoland?"

"I know," said the King. "We are clutching at straws here."

"We have wracked our brains as to who might want to steal the ring for what, and have come up with no answers," said the Queen. "Anyway come in and have some refreshments and I will show you your room. Then the two of you can proceed as you like."

"Everyone has been instructed to help you or answer any questions," said the King.

"Thankyou Sir," said Gogo, "how are Lord Lannet and Princess Ahoosti?"

"They are very well and will meet you later," smiled the Queen.

The Meridos were of the same height as the Pongos, but usually had darker curly hair. The Pongos had brown hair and pointed noses. There was a certain amount of inter-marrying between the islanders so racial characteristics were blurred sometimes. The two boys went into the lobby of the Palace and were served lemonade, and after that they were taken up to their room in one of the Palace towers. It had windows all round and magnificent views across the mountains from all of them. Two beds were made up with primrose coloured quilts, and on the floor were two crimson rugs. Sonny and Gogo just had one bag containing a night-shirt each and a change of clothes. A window seat ran all round the room so they went to sit on it and look outside.

"It really is a puzzle," said Gogo. "Where do we start?"

"Well it might be an idea to ask around to find out if anyone is in any sort of trouble, and possibly thinks the ring could help," suggested Sonny. "We need to wander around generally I think and try to spot anything odd."

"You mean any sort of odd?" said Gogo.

"Yes I think we have to find something which is different from usual. People know where the ring is Gogo. It was taken at great risk, and I believe we can assume it is hidden somewhere. It hasn't been thrown away when it is believed to have magical properties."

"You're right!" said Gogo.

"You remember that plateau where we all met together at the time of Lannet and Ahoosti's marriage? Let's start there. It seemed to be a general sort of meeting-place, and we could mooch around there chatting generally and keeping our eyes open."

"And our ears close to the ground," said Gogo.

They went down the winding stairs in the tower which led to their room, and along a corridor. Then down some more stairs to a back door. They crossed a small courtyard, and took a path which led down to the plateau. They were familiar with area because of having been guests at the wedding. It was a fine walk down the mountain-side. They passed the place where Tobo had had a fall, and soon after reached the plateau. Several Merido children were running up and down and playing ball. A group of women occupied a wooden seat overlooking the valley. Some men were approaching by a path which led up the hill. There were farms dotted over the hillside, and these kept sheep and goats mainly, but some cows. Down in the valley there were fields of corn, and a tractor could be seen at work.

Sonny and Gogo took another seat and waited to see if anyone would approach them. The children did immediately, so Sonny and Gogo greeted them in a friendly way asking if this was a school holiday. The children were curious about them. They recognized Gogo as from Pongoland, but asked Sonny where he was from. The boys chatted with them asking where they lived, and if the women close by were their mothers. After a few minutes they remarked that they were looking for the King's ring. Gogo asked if they had any idea where it might be. The children shuffled their feet as if they feared they were being accused of having something to do with its' loss.

"No we don't think that *you* have it of *course*," reassured Sonny. "You would definitely give it back to the King immediately. We just wondered if you have any ideas, that's all."

"There's an old man," offered an older boy wearing a red cap. "He walks funny and he talks to himself."

"Oh," said Gogo, "that does sound odd, but maybe he's just not very well. Only a fit person could have the ring." Sonny and Gogo had agreed not to discuss any of the details about the loss, so that they could guage the truth of what anyone else might say.

"We are all very fit," said a little girl laughing. "We run up and down the mountain all the time!"

"Even right to the top where the Palace is?" said Sonny. "That is very high."

"If we want," said the girl. "We come here to play after school, or at the weekends. Our houses are along that path." She pointed across the hill road to a path which led off round the mountain.

"Where does that path lead?" asked Gogo.

"All the way round the mountain," said another boy aged about ten. "Sometimes we have races round it to see who can do it the fastest!"

"That's for the grown-ups though," said the first boy. "It's too far for children either to walk or run."

"What is there round the other side?" asked Sonny. "Are there caves or streams or what?"

"No caves!" said the little girl laughing again. "There is a stream, and you can climb up or down beside it to a few farms. Sometimes we go for picnics round there with our parents. We can take a pony and cart along the main path and then walk."

"Sounds nice," said Sonny. "Do you go down to the valley much?"

Seeing the children all talking and being friendly with the newcomers, the women came across to meet them, and heard the question.

"Those of us who live up the mountain-side don't go down to the valley very often because it is such a steep climb back. Even the ponies don't like the climb. Sometimes we go."

"What is there down there?" asked Gogo.

"Two or three arable farms, and there is the town. We go into town once a month by pony-trap for shopping."

"We are here to help the King find his lost ring," said Sonny.

"Oh?" said one of the women. They too looked defensive as if afraid someone might accuse them. Perhaps everyone felt suspect until it was found.

"It's alright, honestly, the King doesn't suspect any of you of course. But someone has it you know. Someone close to the Palace." The women relaxed enough to show their own anxiety.

"That ring is very important to all of us on the Island," said one of them.

"I know," said Sonny. "We do hope we can be of help. Are there any clues?"

"No......," said another, "only that the next day, after the ring disappeared there was a weird light in the sky."

"What?" exclaimed Sonny. "What sort of light?"

"As if an angel was going to appear," said the woman, "but then disappeared again."

"Where?" asked Gogo.

"Over the Palace," said the woman, "Merlin himself gave that ring to the King's ancestor, so maybe Merlin was angry."

"No," said Sonny, "surely not angry. The King has not dishonoured the ring."

"But supposing someone else did?" suggested another woman.

"Dishonoured how?" asked Gogo.

"Dishonoured it by using it as it isn't supposed to be used," said an old woman in the group. "It isn't supposed to be used for magic. Merlin warned that. He said if it was needed for good purposes, the King would receive energy from the ring without even having to ask for it. But if a King ever wanted power from it for a bad purpose the ring would punish." The women fell silent. They were uneasy.

"So you wonder if maybe someone has got it for a bad purpose?" asked Sonny.

"Maybe," said the old woman. The women turned to go, calling the children after them as it was time for tea.

"Weird," commented Gogo.

"Yeah. I mean what possible bad purpose could anyone have on Maridoland?"

"No idea. Think of Pongoland. We had Toplo and his ridiculous bonka. He even captured the Spangles, but he was just silly really. He didn't mean anyone any real harm," said Gogo.

"Well what about Lord Lannet. He and the Princess will rule the Island after her parents. Might there be anyone here who minds that?"

Gogo was uneasy.

"These are bad thoughts Sonny," he said.

"I know Gogo, and we won't say a single word of this to anyone else, but maybe between the two of us we should explore the possibility?"

"I think there was another lord who had wanted to marry Princess Ahoosti, but she chose Lord Lannet." They pondered for a moment.

"O.K.," said Sonny, "who was that?"

"Er......Sesko........Sisko. Sisko it was. Lord Sisko. He lives somewhere to the North of here."

"Well, just in *case*, I think we should find out where. Don't let's mention it in the Palace and cause a hullaballoo there, but tomorrow morning let's ask for a pony and trap to take us down to the town. We can ask around there, and find out how to get to his house."

166

"Castle. He lives in a castle. He's quite wealthy I believe. His family is very distantly related to the Royal Family."

"And he expected maybe to marry Ahoosti and become King?" said Sonny.

"Yes, probably," said Gogo.

"So what has changed? Why now? I mean supposing he's got the ring."

"Sonny he might even feel the ring should be his. You know how sometimes there is more than one valid candidate to succeed as King. In that case the Islanders vote. Whoever they choose is crowned."

"Did that happen, say, with Sisko's father at all?"

"Not that I know of, but there might have been bad feeling. Or Sisko just wanted to share the throne by marrying Ahoosti, supposing he's involved, which we don't know."

"No, but let's make that our investigation tomorrow," said Sonny.

"We're always getting involved in these big messes, and we are children," grumbled Gogo.

"All the same we have done O.K. Gogo. Cheer up," grinned Sonny.

The next morning, on their request, a pony and trap arrived for Sonny and Gogo after breakfast. They could ask Goggles to take them, but they wouldn't see anything from his back. Gogo was used to driving one so he took the driver's seat, and they set off down the hill to the town. The King and Queen were not surprised that they should wish to go there, and they told the boys about the town and the routes leading from it. Sonny and Gogo asked the useful questions about the area without betraying that they intended to go to Lord Sisko's Castle. It would have been helpful to learn more about him but not so good to raise suspicions against him.

The day was beautiful as days usually were in the Islands. The journey down the hill took about forty-five minutes, so they would need to allow an hour to return up it. The little town was already quite busy. The shops were opening and people were setting off to work. They took the pony and cart to an Inn the King had told them about. They went inside and found themselves in a large room in which small tables were arranged, each with a coloured cloth. Sonny and Gogo chose one with a green cloth, and a young Merido girl came to ask them what they would like. Gogo asked for two glasses of mixed fruit juice. When she left them to get the drinks Sonny muttered,

"Somehow we have to get into conversation. We need to know more about Sisko without introducing his name if we can."

"We can try to get her to talk about the sights on the Island," said Gogo, so when she returned with two glasses of pink fruit juice on a little tray he said,

"We wondered if you could suggest places for us to visit this morning? I am from Pongoland and this is my friend. We have a pony and trap and would like to visit some of the interesting places in Maridoland."

The girl put down the tray. She wore a blue uniform dress with a white apron. In its' pocket she carried a note-pad and pencil for taking orders.

"O.K.," she said, "would you like to look at the countryside, or are you more interested in historical places?"

"Er.....what historical places could you suggest?" asked Sonny.

"We've got a Wishing-Well," she said with a smile. "People usually like to go there. You drop a pebble into it and make a wish. That is up a hill-side. A little stream trickles down the hill and long ago the Well was built into the hill so that water would run into it. People believe that the wizard Merlin built it and blessed the stream, but I'm not sure that is true!"

"All the same we'ld love to make a wish," said Gogo, laughing. "Is there anything else interesting to see in the same area?"

"Er, well, you can go on up the hill. You will see a grey Castle at the top. It isn't as big or as fine as the Palace, but it is linked to the Well. The story is that long ago Merlin visited the Island. He liked it so much he built this Castle to stay in, and before he left he built the Well as a thankyou gift to the islanders. He blessed the stream and told the Maridos that if they throw a pebble into the stream and make a wish it will come true."

"Wow!" cried Sonny. "That's really interesting. Can we go inside the castle?"

"It belongs to the Sisko family. You can go in but you have to knock on the gate-keeper's door and ask to see round. He will probably ask someone to take you." Gogo asked,

"Are there any other interesting places to see in that area?" The girl took out her note-pad.

"I'll draw a little map," she said. "You take this route out of town and follow the road to Hermit's Hill. The road is a bit steep but not too bad. The Well is on the left at the end of a little path leading off the road about half-way up the hill. It is sign-posted. Travelling by trap it is about ten minutes further up to the Castle."

"Thanks!" said Gogo. "This is really helpful. Who is living in the Castle at the moment?"

"Lord Sisko," said the girl. "It's been the Sisko family home for centuries. The present Lord Sisko is the last of the line."

"The last?" queried Gogo. "You mean he isn't married?"

"No," said the girl, "though a few girls would be willing! He has a cousin who is married with two children and settled on another island so he has family, but no-one here."

"Are we likely to bump into him?" asked Sonny hopefully.

"You might. He's a keen gardener and spends a lot of his time working outside with his gardener. They produce a lot of fruit and vegetables which are brought down to our weekly market in the town square. Otherwise if Lord Sisko is indoors it will be more difficult. You would have to produce a good reason for wishing to meet him to the guard at the gate. He is royalty."

"Well thankyou a lot," said Gogo. "We'll call in here on our way back if we can to tell you what happened!" The girl smiled and wished them luck.

"This is really good," said Sonny as they climbed into the trap. "I thought we would end up wandering around aimlessly looking for hiding-places or guilty-looking islanders."

"I know! At least we've got somewhere to go, and hopefully someone to meet," said Gogo.

The two boys enjoyed the ride up the hillside. They had given the pony a drink of water, and had a bag of seed to give him at lunch-time. The views were magnificent across the mountains, and the sun was shining.

As predicted, they arrived at the Well around an hour later. A notice pointed the way along a little path to the Well.

"Did you know about King Arthur?" asked Gogo.

"Oh yes. He was a great King of England many centuries ago. So many stories and poems are written about him and his Knights that they are famous in English literature. Merlin was a seer or a wizard, and mentor to King Arthur."

"So they really existed," said Gogo.

"In Camelot yes," said Sonny. "All of the stories won't be true, but they sat round a famous Round Table for meetings, and they had ideals about bravoury and honour and chivalry. They called themselves the Knights of the Round Table."

"And the people of Maridoland think that Merlin and one of the Knights somehow visited here," said Gogo. "It's very romantic."

"Well they do seem to know a lot about him," said Sonny. "I wouldn't deny it."

"And they crossed dimensions in their dreams?" said Gogo doubtfully.

"I know. Weird. But there you are. I am no-one to challenge theories about dimensional travel am I?" said Sonny. "In any case that isn't our problem. Our problem is the ring. There is a connection between Merlin and the ring, so let's go and look at his Well."

They didn't have far to walk down the path before they came upon it under an over-hanging rock. A cave had been hollowed out into the side of the hill and you could walk all round the Well. Water dripped down through a hole in the roof of the cave into the Well.

"This is it!" said Gogo. His voice sounded hollow. They gazed down into the Well but could not see the water.

"I wonder how deep is," said Sonny. Gogo dropped a stone into it but the small splash came after a pause.

"Deep," said Gogo. "Let's make our wishes."

"No you can," said Sonny. "I'm going to keep mine in case I need it later. I might not be allowed two!"

"O.K. I'll keep mine as well so we have two wishes in case we need them," said Gogo. They returned to the trap and continued the climb to the top of the hill. By now they could see the Castle, grey, turreted and forbidding.

"Scary place to live!" said Gogo.

"Yeah. Oh look it has a moat and a draw-bridge and a port-cullis like in English castles. So that's another link with King Arthur," said Sonny.

The draw-bridge was down so they drove the pony-trap across it, under the port-cullis, and into the courtyard of the Castle.

"Everything is so still!" exclaimed Sonny, "As if no-one lives here and it is asleep waiting for someone to come and wake it up."

"You could say that," said Gogo, "or you could just say it's sinister waiting to pounce on unwary visitors."

"There's the guard. Let's ask if we can see round the Castle," said Sonny. The guard wore a red and gold tunic with black trousers and a black cap.

"Excuse me Sir," said Sonny bravely, "we wondered if you would let us look round the castle?"

"I don't know about that," said the guard, "who are you?"

"Oh sorry. This is Gogo from Pongoland and I'm Sonny, his friend. We're having two or three days' holiday in Maridoland. Someone in the town told us that this is an interesting place. We have just been to the Wishing Well."

"Alright," said the guard, "there is a boy about your age who works in the kitchen. He can take you round but there is not much to see. It is a small castle. Be careful of the walls. Some of the stone-work is a little loose, and be careful you don't slip on the stone. The steps are polished with age." He called for Danny, the boy from the kitchen. Danny was about the same height as Sonny and Gogo and was very pleased to see the two boys. To take them round the Castle was an unexpected treat.

"Do you like working here?" asked Gogo as they walked away. "I'm from Pongoland and we don't have children working there except as training."

"We don't either but my mother is the cook here, so she often brings me along in the school holidays. I love it up here. I don't mind helping out cleaning the silver and bronze. I get a new suit of clothes in return," he grinned. "My Dad works on the Castle farm down in the valley. I want to be a farmer when I grow up. Shall I take your pony?" They unfastened the pony from the cart and Danny tethered him in the courtyard.

"We've got his lunch here," said Gogo. "Maybe he'ld like it now." Danny took the food and poured it into a feeding-bag and attached it to the pony.

"O.K.," he said, "so let's go!"

"Where is Lord Sisko?" asked Gogo anxiously, "I hope he won't mind?"

"Lord Sisko?" said Danny, "No he's in the garden outside the wall. He won't mind. I often do little jobs for him. He's like my friend even."

That's like us and the King of Pongoland, thought Sonny.

"Does he live here alone?" he asked.

"Yes, by himself," Said Danny. "It's a bit lonely really."

"It must be," said Sonny, "how come he isn't married?" Might as well take the bull by the horns, he thought.

"Oh he wanted to marry Princess Ahoosti," said Danny cheerfully, "but she chose Lord Lannet."

"That was sad," said Gogo.

"Yes they all grew up together and played together, they and a few others in the town. There's a lady, Maria, who loves him, but he won't look at her. She's a teacher in the school now."

"How do you know she loves Lord Sisko?" asked Sonny, amazed that poor Lord Sisko's love-life seemed to be so well known.

"Because of them all playing together. All our parents knew Maria wanted him, but he was determined to marry Ahoosti.

"Goodness," said Gogo, "we don't know all those things about our Royal Family."

"Your Royal Family doesn't have children. It's the children who get to know these things. Ahoosti and Lannet used to be in and out of peoples' houses like Lord Sisko and Maria and others. I can remember them."

"So does Lord Sisko hate them now?" asked Gogo helpfully.

"No he doesn't hate them, but he doesn't go to the Palace," said Danny.

"Not ever?" asked Sonny.

"That is to say he doesn't go often. Sometimes he does diplomatic jobs for the King, so then he goes to discuss business, but he doesn't attend their parties, and he didn't go to the marriage."

"Well he wouldn't would he?" said Gogo.

"No but he was more fed-up than heart-broken," said Danny. "I know because he talks to me. See, be careful going up these steps. Some of the stones are a bit loose."

They had reached the bottom of a spiral staircase leading up a large tower. It was pretty dark inside, though there were a few turret windows.

"Why was he so dead-keen to marry her then?" asked Sonny.

"Oh because of King Arthur," said Danny a bit impatiently

"What?" cried Sonny, and Gogo stopped climbing.

"You mean the King who had the Round Table?" he asked.

"That's the one. Ancient history."

"But why would King Arthur have wanted Sisko to marry Ahoosti?" asked Sonny. Things were definitely weird!

"Sisko was a lonely kid in this old Castle, so he made up stories about himself. People believe Merlin built it and lived here a while, and some believe, anyway Lord Sisko believes, that King Arthur lived here too. In Lord Sisko's imagination King Arthur had a son here by some girl in the village. Lord Sisko studies all these old manuscripts in the Castle library."

"Has he got manuscripts to prove King Arthur lived here?" asked Sonny.

"Listen, the manuscripts aren't *that* old! The oldest is probably no more than five hundred years old. He thinks, or I should say he likes to pretend to think, that they record true history handed down by tradition. He says the records imply that King Arthur was here, but I've seen them. The stories about Merlin and King Arthur are long poems. That means someone made them up but Lord Sisko thinks of them as his history. He has set them to music."

"Oh dear," said Sonny sadly.

"Oh yes," said Danny, "he's got this big idea that he is a descendent of King Arthur. His family has always lived in this Castle you see. I don't try to contradict him, but Merlin was here well over a thousand years ago. I do believe that. This is a seriously strange place. But King Arthur? And a son in Meridoland? No evidence I say. Lord Sisko's problem was being alone here so much as a child, and you know how you imagine things when you are a child. His parents were always busy, and away a lot. No-one to put him straight, and they died before he was grown up."

"It's really sad, isn't it?" said Sonny.

"Yes it is. He tells me because I am a child. He trusts me to take him seriously. He knows, I suppose, no grown-up would. I have been like his playmate sometimes. Not so much now. After playing in the village the other kids went home, but he had to come back here."

"I expect he had to tell himself stories to stop himself from being frightened!" said Sonny. "Does Maria know about his stories?"

"Don't know," said Danny. "He doesn't talk about her. See, this is Lord Sisko's room. We can just peep in." Danny pushed open a heavy wooden door with a large iron ring on it. Inside the room was unexpectedly cheerful! The bed had a colourful patchwork quilt. A fire was laid before a thick red woollen rug. There were gleaming brass fire-irons in the hearth. On the mantle-piece were ornaments and pictures. There was a large book-case with interesting-looking books.

"Very nice!" exclaimed Sonny.

"Yes it is," said Danny. "His Mum set it up for him originally. Come along. I'll show you the library." He closed the door, and they went along the corridor to the next room. This too had a heavy door, very old. The room smelt of old parchment. There was no fire-place but there was a long table with four chairs drawn up to it.

"Come in." said Danny. "He won't mind if I show you the books. These aren't the ordinary readable books," he joked. "This is stuff for scholars, but after all he is a scholar."

"Oh, he's a scholar? So why does he believe in the poems?" asked Sonny.

"Because he wants to," said Danny. "His father never thought he was descended from King Arthur, though he once said he thought the King might be."

"The King of Meridoland descended from King Arthur?" cried Gogo. "That is as fantastic an idea as Lord Sisko being a descendent!"

"Yes it probably is," said Danny, "but look under the surface here and you do find these theories going around. I don't think the King himself thinks so, but that Merlin built the Castle? That is a general belief. And gave us the Well? You bet!"

"Well I think it's awful that Lord Sisko should spend his life here alone because he thinks he should have married Princess Ahoosti, and why? Because he thinks he's descended from King Arthur?" exclaimed Sonny.

"Therefore," pointed out Danny, "he should be next King of Meridoland."

"Oh!!" cried Sonny. "Right!!"

"Yes," said Danny. "His rightful heritage."

There was silence for a moment while Sonny and Gogo digested this bombshell.

"O.K.," said Gogo, "but he didn't marry her. Can't he just get over it and marry someone else?"

"He's fixated," said Danny. "You can't talk sense into him. I've tried."

"Wow," said Sonny, "what a conundrum! Er….you know this ring which the King has lost? That was supposed to have been given to his ancestor by Merlin for slaying a dragon. Do you think that is true?"

"Yes," said Danny. "We believe that. The ring is there after all, and there are records in the Palace of the amazing feats and achievements of all the Kings and Queens."

"Do you have any theories about where the ring went?" asked Gogo. "They have scoured the Palace for the ring."

"No idea," said Danny briefly. Sonny looked at Gogo.

"What properties does it have?" asked Sonny.

"How would I know?" asked Danny. "No-one talks about that. The King just wears it as a memorial. That's all."

"No. I just wondered. If Merlin gave it to the King at that time, don't you think he might have blessed it, as he did the Well, so that each King would receive his blessing?"

Danny stared at him.

"I never thought of that," he said.

"He very well might have Danny. Think about it," said Sonny. "Merlin wouldn't just have said, 'here, take this ring as a keepsake,' would he? These were royal people. There would have been a ceremony, a sacred ceremony, and you can bet anything the ring was blessed, like even wedding-rings are blessed, but if Merlin blesses a thing it jolly well stays blessed!"

"Gosh yes," he breathed.

It's now or never, thought Sonny.

"Danny, has Lord Sisko been to the Palace recently at all?" Danny stared at Sonny.

"You mean………?"

"Yes, and just think of that also. He's alone here in the Castle, fixated on King Arthur, and how he has lost his chances. What might he do?"

"I'ld have to look in his room," said Danny.

"Well would you mind very much just doing that right now please?" asked Sonny. "Meanwhile Gogo and I will search the library."

"Alright, but only if you promise faithfully you will never tell anybody?" said Danny.

"We promise," said Sonny. "It will just be between the three of us. Right Gogo?"

"Agreed," said Gogo.

Danny went back to Lord Sisko's bedroom while Sonny and Gogo studied the walls and books of the library.

"It need not be such a very secret place, after all," reasoned Sonny. "There's only Danny and his Mum work in the Castle from what I can see. They won't be poking around."

"True," said Gogo, "we need some little compartment, or box, or behind some special book?"

"Book!" cried Sonny. "King Arthur?"

They searched the shelves of ancient history. There was a brown leather-covered tome called simply 'Merlin'. Sonny stood on a chair and lifted it down. He opened the front cover, and discovered, rather to his horror until he realized it wasn't a real book, that a hole had been carved out of the blank pages, and in the hole lay a gold ring with a splendid dragon inlaid in it in ruby and amber and quartz.

"Gogo....." he whispered.

Quickley he lifted out the ring, closed and replaced the book, and climbed down from the chair. They examined the ring and marveled at its' workmanship. However there was no time to lose. Gogo put the chair back in its' place and they left the library, closing the door carefully behind them. They met Danny in the corridor, returning from Lord Sisko's bedroom.

"Nothing there," he reported. "What have you got there?" They showed him the ring.

"Oh no!" he cried. "Sisko *stole* it!"

"No," said Sonny firmly. "He borrowed it. He wanted to commune with it somehow and feel close to Merlin. He's been in great distress. He was looking for help."

"You are very nice boys," said Danny. "You'ld better just take it as fast as possible back to the Palace. But you won't tell where you found it, like you promised?"

"We won't," said Gogo. "The main thing is we have found it, and Meridoland will feel at peace again."

They hurried down the steps and climbed into the pony-trap. The pony had finished his food and was ready to go. Danny stood by the trap looking up at them.

"I hope I see you both again," he said, "don't forget me."

"Never," said Gogo, "when all this is over we'll come again to say thankyou."

"What happened here?" asked Sonny. "What made Lord Sisko do this now?"

"Oh! That's easy I think," said Danny. "Princess Ahoosti is expecting a baby. He may have thought it's now or never to make his claim. Desperation really," he added sadly.

"Someone saw a light in the sky," said Sonny. "Might that have been Merlin?"

"Who knows?" said Danny. "Maybe someone will write a song about that one day."

"What *you* need to do," said Sonny to Danny very firmly, "is get Sisko and Maria together. Use your imagination! Do something! Merlin *might* have come in response to a cry from Lord Sisko you know! Who else is there but you to help?" Danny laughed.

"You have given me a mission! I will do my best" he promised.

When Sonny and Gogo returned to the Palace with the ring that evening the King couldn't believe his eyes!

"I'm stunned!" he cried. "Where was it?"

"We are pledged to secrecy," said Gogo. "But Sir, would you mind if we return to Pongoland right away? This has been a wonderful visit. We have really enjoyed ourselves, but I do feel we shouldn't linger."

Goggles was waiting in the courtyard to hear about their progress, so a Palace servant went up to Sonny and Gogo's bedroom to fetch their luggage.

"I hope there aren't going to be any repercussions," said the King doubtfully.

"Whatever might be said, you know nothing about anything," said Gogo. "You can make up a cover story about how the ring was returned if you like. We can guarantee no-one will argue."

"Alright, well many many thanks boys. I do hope one day I can repay you."

With that Sonny and Gogo climbed on to Goggles' back, and in no time away they were flying over the tree-tops and under the stars.

When they arrived back in Pongoland everything seemed to be as usual. Goggles took the boys straight to Gogo's house. Tobo rushed out, overjoyed to see them.

"What happened? Did you find it?" he asked excitedly. His parents were on his heels equally happy, if anxious, to see them.

"Yes!" said Gogo. "Mission accomplished!"

They went indoors, and sat down to a sumptuous tea of salad, fruit trifle, scones, and a sponge cake. Never was such a joyful celebration!

"And you can never tell us where you found it?" said Murgo later.

"That's right. We promised, but we placed the ring back in the hand of the King, so that was all that mattered," said Sonny.

"And all's well that ends well," smiled Gogo.

Chapter Four

The Tower of Tolikland

The King of Pongoland was delighted with the results of the ring of the Dragon's Hair test. Although he had talked to Sonny and Gogo, and they had told him what they could, he had had to allow them their secret as to where they had found it.

"Ah well," he said, "a lot of work among the Islands involves diplomacy, so in this case I have to respect your secret. But very well done, and thankyou boys."

That was all Sonny and Gogo needed. The King's approval was always sufficient reward. He said they needed a rest before their next test, so for some weeks there was no talk of expeditions. The King, however, asked Sonny to stay at the Palace one night a month. He said Sonny must become familiar with the ways of the Palace. He needed to learn who was who, and how each of the Palace staff was to be treated. Each had an individual role, and each needed understanding of his role.

In addition the King had appointed a tutor to teach Sonny the history of the Islands, as well as the geography of the whole archipelago. He needed to learn about the people and the customs of each Island, and about Pongo relations with the different Islands. So during his stay at the Palace he had an hour of history and an hour of geography. Sonny's parents agreed that one Saturday night a month he would sleep at the Pongo Palace. That meant Saturday and Saturday night in this world's terms. He returned home by evening, and went to bed late.

Otherwise he spent time in Gogo's home with Gogo talking to Murgo about his work. They both spent time in the mills and the mines, and visiting the farms on the Island. They talked with the adults, learning about their work and their problems, and they were shown how things were done. They played too in the meadow and practised their athletic skills. Sonny, Gogo, and Tobo all planned to compete in the next Sports Day.

179

After a few weeks the King invited Sonny and Gogo tp come to the Palace to learn about their next test. This was in connection with the mystery of the Tolik tower.

"It is the most amazing thing, boys," said the King. "The owls, and people who have been to Tolikland in recent weeks, describe this tall narrow tower reaching to the sky, and built of some sort of shiny reflecting material. It seems to be black. The Toliks refuse to say a word about it. You know that of the Islands Tolikland does have a reputation, not of criminal activities of course, but sometimes of suspicious activities that make others worry about what is going on. Odd things you know. Everything they do is not always in the best interests of the Islands as a community. So this secrecy is a matter of concern."

"So you would like us to go and find out what it is and what it is for," said Sonny.

"Precisely," said the King, "and that's not going to be easy because if they've got a secret you won't be welcome! And it won't be easy forcing your presence around the Island if they don't want you!"

"Oh dear," said Gogo, "it's going to be really awkward!"

"Yes it is," said the King, "and that is the test. To insinuate yourselves into their confidence, or at least into the Island for a stay in the first place, and then to find out what they have built. I am most eager to know!"

Tolikland was quite a long distance away from Pongoland, but could be reached by making a stop-over in Galipoland. The Galips were friends of the Pongos once the business of a certain incident with Mother Fulati had been sorted out, and Sonny and Gogo were able to get refreshments for themselves and Goggles. They allowed Goggles an hour's rest before setting off again on the second leg of their journey. The boys weren't greatly keen to see the Island. Their only experience with Toliks had been when a Tolik man had come to stay in Pongoland in order supposedly to learn metal-work. It turned out that he had not wanted to learn how to craft gold and silver into beautiful objects, but had come to steal a large quantity. Two other Toliks had arrived to help carry the stuff away. Unfortunately for them Murgo had arranged a family picnic near the spot where the two arrived, and they had been seen. Sonny and Gogo had sat on their birds to prevent them from escaping with their loot. Murgo had called the Palace guards to arrest the Toliks.

As a result Sonny and Gogo were not feeling too friendly as they approached the Island. All the same the dominating feature of the landscape was this very tall, narrow, black tower, and they were amazed!

"What can it be?" exclaimed Gogo.

"It doesn't look like anything except a tall square pole made of something like black glass or steel," said Sonny.

"How tall would you say? Fifty feet?"

"Don't know but this is certainly an interesting investigation," said Sonny.

Goggles landed on some spare land around the pole, and they got off his back to go and take a closer look at the object. A Tolik man was sitting close by it and looked at them suspiciuously.

"Where have you come from? Pongoland?" he asked.

"That's right," said Gogo, "what's this?"

"Have you come all the way from Pongoland just to ask that?" said the man, looking gratified.

"Not entirely," said Sonny vaguely. "Is it yours?"

The man stood up. Toliks were mostly quite tall and thin with brown hair.

"No," he said. "I'm protecting it. I'm on guard."

"Protecting it from whom?" asked Gogo.

"Anybody. It's precious."

"Is it a work of art?" guessed Sonny.

"You could call it that," said the man.

"Or a watch-tower? Does it have a perisciope mirror at the top?"

"No," said the man, enjoying himself now, "it's not a watch-tower, though I expect we could attach a mirror at the top if we wanted."

"Who's 'we'," asked Sonny.

"The King and his staff," said the man.

"Right," said Sonny, "so the King built it?"

"And his staff," said the man.

"What for?" asked Gogo.

"For his own purposes. Wouldn't you like a drink or something?" Clearly the man was flustered now by all the questions.

"Is there anywhere we can stay overnight?" asked Gogo. "Pongoland is too far away to come and return in one day."

"I don't know. I'll have to ask," said the man, "but we've got a tent here with refreshments for the guards. We take shifts. Come along. You can have something to drink, and your owl would like water I expect."

Sonny and Gogo were relieved to find the man quite friendly really. It seemed the Toliks weren't all hostile!

"Thankyou," said Sonny, "that would be really nice."

"You aren't a Pongo," remarked the Tolik.

"No, I'm a friend of Gogo here, and visit quite often. I live somewhere else mostly."

The man led them to a little blue and white tent erected in the shadow of some cliffs. Little seats and tables were arranged outside, and a Tolik girl came out with a tray. She had automatically poured out juice for three. She went back and brought out a bowl of water for Goggles. This was all very hospitable and not at all what Sonny and Gogo had expected.

"How long will you be here guarding the pole," asked Gogo.

"Tower," said the man. "Oh for quite some time. A lot of people want to see it. We have set up this tent partly so visitors can sit and look at it."

Sonny and Gogo looked dubious.

"I'm Sonny," he said, "and this is Gogo."

"I am Flinn and this is Bella," replied Flinn.

"So the tower is like…entertainment?" asked Gogo.

"You might call it that," said Flinn.

"In that case," said Sonny, "you need more things for people to look at when they get here. One narrow tower isn't enough."

"Lots of people love it," said Flinn defensively, "you'ld be surprised how many people we serve in this tent every day."

"So it is a sight for people to come and see," said Sonny.

"You could call it that too," said Flinn.

"But Flinn!" cried Sonny, "you need to develop this place!"

"It doesn't need anything," said Flinn firmly, "it's beautiful as it is. You can see it for miles as you approach on a bird."

"That's true," said Gogo.

"Yes….well……no-one thinks the Toliks can do anything. Then when we do everybody criticizes," grumbled Flinn.

"Who's 'everybody'?" asked Sonny.

"Well you two, and a few others who have been from other Islands. We in Tolikland like it just as it is."

He retired to sit by the tower in a huff.

"Right," said Sonny to Gogo, "it's meant to be a tourist attraction."

"Wow," said Gogo, "you'ld have to be seriously bored to come and look at it."

"Well we've come," said Sonny.

"Yes because the King wanted to know what the Toliks were up to! We wouldn't travel a day to see a possible work of art, but probably not."

"No," said Sonny, "still I feel sorry for Flinn. He seems proud of it."

182

Gogo went over to the table where Bella was arranging plates of sandwiches and buns.

"Hello Bella, is the tower all you've got to show us, or is there anything else around here?"

Bella turned pink, ashamed or embarrassed.

"You shouldn't have made Flinn feel small," she said.

"Feel small?" exclaimed Gogo. "We were just asking what it was."

Well he designed it, and he's very proud of it, and you didn't praise it," said Bella. "That sort of thing makes people feel small."

"Oh sorry," said Gogo.

"Who asked him to design it?" asked Sonny, coming up.

"The King asked for designs for a spectacular attraction," said Bella.

"OK so Flinn certainly succeeded," admitted Sonny. "What did he get? A prize?"

"Yes he did," said Bella defensively.

"What else was produced?" asked Gogo. "Everything ought to be on display here, and that would make an exhibition of Tolik handicrafts."

"I don't know," said Bella. "The King just put the tower up and this tent." She offered sandwiches and buns to the boys, so they went back to their table to eat."

"Something's wrong, isn't it?" said Gogo when they were alone.

"Yeah," said Sonny. "Weird I'ld say. Something is certainly wrong here."

"Looks as if people have nothing to do and nowhere to go, if this place is typical of Tolikland."

"That Tolik who came to Pongoland to learn metal-craft?" said Sonny. "The King had sent him, hadn't he? He wasn't supposed to steal. He was supposed to get some training. The Tolik King was very angry about the robbery wasn't he?"

"He certainly was," said Gogo. "He was livid. He'ld had some idea of building up an industry here."

"You know, we sort of represent our King here," said Sonny. "Not exactly, but he sent us. I think we should go to the Tolik Palace and see if we can find out what's going on. I wonder if the Palace is far from here."

"Good idea, but what shall we say we've come about?"

"We could start with mentioning that thief – what was his name?"

"Kilti."

"Kilti, and that as we were in Tolikland we thought we'ld ask how he's doing," said Sonny.

"Is the King going to want to be reminded about him? It's hardly tactful to mention him."

"O.K. maybe not," said Sonny, "But why are we here? Unless we blow up all this stuff about the tower. Say our King had heard about it and wanted us to see it etc etc? So we wanted to ask about the idea behind it."

"Alright. We'll just have to fudge it along. I'll ask Bella the way to the Palace," said Gogo.

It seemed the distance to the Palace was walkable so they left Goggles to eat and relax, and set off along the road Bella had pointed to. The Tolik scenery was really very attractive with cliffs, and hills covered with thick woodland, and a valley through which a river ran southwards to somewhere. Was there sea on this Island, Sonny wondered. But where would the edge be?

The Palace stood on a rocky promontory, overlooking the river. A path and then steps led up to a high wooden gate.

"More adventures!" whispered Gogo.

"Yes, this is a bit nerve-wracking though. I wonder what the King is like," said Sonny.

There was a long bell-rope, so they pulled it and heard a distant gong. Then a shuffling of feet, and the door was opened by an elderly man in a maroon uniform with a cap. He was very surprised to see two boys, but Gogo told him they had come from the King of Pongoland, so they were invited in. They entered a cobbled court-yard with trees overhanging it, and in the centre there was a little well with a seat all round it. They walked past this and into the Palace itself. The boys found themselves in a large hall with a tiled floor. Above it was a very high glassed dome. Around the walls the boys saw old paintings of bygone Tolik monarchs and their families.

"It's a bit fusty isn't it?" whispered Sonny.

"Yeah. A bit sort of dead," said Gogo. "Everything still."

In a few minutes the man returned to take them to the King. They were invited into a large sitting-room, furnished comfortably, if a little shabbily, with sofas and arm-chairs. The King and Queen were seated in front of a high fire-place. The King was dressed informally in a dark green tunic with black trousers, and the Queen wore a sprigged muslin full-length dress. They asked the boys to join them by the fire.

184

"Well, this is a surprise," said the King. "Have you travelled all this way by yourselves from Pongoland to see me?"

"Our King was very intrigued, Sir, to hear about your amazing new sculpture," said Sonny. "A lot of people have been talking about it, and he wanted to learn more about how it looks and who made it."

You can't get more diplomatic than that, thought Sonny. He caught an admiring glance from Gogo. However the King was not fooled.

"Come, come, young man," said the King, "you can't flannel me. That pole is bizarre!" Sonny and Gogo were stunned.

"Tower," corrected Gogo inadvertently.

"Oh! You've been talking to Flinn? Tower then."

"Don't you like it?" asked Sonny incredulous. "You awarded him a prize."

"I had offered a prize, and his was the only contribution, so he got the prize, that's all. Be honest. What did you feel when you saw it?"

The boys shifted uneasily. This was so embarrassing.

"Curiosity!" Sonny came up with.

"Bravo," said the King, "a quick wit! And when you looked closer?"

"Er, we asked Flinn if it was a work of art, or just a sight to come and look at, or maybe an entertainment," said Gogo. "But he wouldn't commit himself."

"That's because he just built a tower of bricks essentially, slightly expensive ones but that's all they are, and he had to borrow a step-ladder from the Palace. The pole goes up as high as our tallest step-ladder."

Gogo burst out laughing. Sonny looked scandalized at his friend's lapse, but he had set the King and Queen off laughing too. The Queen rang for someone to bring refreshments.

"OK," said the King. "Now I have come clean, I pray you will. You did not travel all this way to look at Flinn's pole!"

"We did Sir, truly," said Sonny, "but that was because our King was worried about it."

"He wondered what we were up to," said the King.

"Something like that," said Sonny. "Well not that quite, but he was curious."

"Yes I see," said the King. "After that attempted theft by Kilti we were deeply mortified. Tolikland has been declining for some years. We do wood-carvings, but no-one wants wooden utensils nowadays. Galipoland produces all that wonderful crockery. We have learnt that we can't compete equally amongst the Islands and have nothing to produce for the

Trade Fair. You have to take enough of your own produce to have something to exchange for other peoples'. We survive here mostly on our own produce. We have become self-subsisting, but our people have grown lethargic. They are bored. I had thought we might buy raw materials from other Islands to make utensils and household items ourselves, so I sent Kilti to learn some skills, but he let us down so badly we could hardly hold our heads up after that. We didn't even attend the last Trade Fair."

"I think you aren't the only Island which has had that problem in competing in a market which is dominated by those who have a lot to offer," said Sonny, remembering another Island which had had a similar problem but which had turned itself around with a bit of initiative and a lot of hard work.

"So you were trying to stimulate some talent when you announced the competition?"

"Exactly right," said the King. "I thought Tolikland can't be entirely without talent. It's just that those who have it haven't been motivated to use it. However, only Flinn responded," he sighed. The Queen shook her head.

"I wanted to get our women into weaving or knitting, but we would have to buy the wool from somewhere." Sonny couldn't believe what he was hearing. All this was pretty pathetic. Those Islands did well where the King and Queen were energetic about organizing production and trade. Things didn't happen without effort. This Island had a surplus of wood, and a big potential for sheep-rearing, just for starters. So OK, plunge in.

"Yes, I see your problem but shouldn't someone be managing your land? If you had a lot of sheep you would have plenty of wool. You could have distinctive Tolik rugs, say, with a local design. If that pole got famous as a local landmark it could even feature as your Tolik trademark for woolen goods! I mean I'm just playing with ideas. Tolik sweaters. You have a lot of wood. You could make ladders, wooden buckets, furnishings. The list is endless."

So why don't you? He thought. The King sighed.

"You make it sound so simple," he said glumly.

"Pongoland has farm-land maintained for sheep and goats, extensive woodland which provides ingredients for Mother Fulati's medicines, and lowland where sheds are built for spinning and weving. The rocky areas are mined for precious minerals, and a lot of the men of the Island sit all day fashioning beautiful things. Everybody works, Sir," said Sonny.

"We seem to have sunk into depression, I suppose," sighed the King. "We think beforehand that we will fail, whatever we do."

"Why not let your young people get busy on something?" suggested Gogo. "Our King had an athletics field set up, and built a swimming-pool, and all the young people train to take part in an Annual Sports Day. The young people of Meridoland are very musical and produce wonderful concerts!"

"Yes all that sounds wonderful," grumbled the King, "but look what happened when I organized a talent contest! I got one tower of bricks."

Sonny and Gogo smiled.

"Well we come from a very energetic Island," said Gogo. "How would it be if we were to wander round Tolikland a bit talking to people, and possibly ferreting out latent ambitions?"

The King waved a hand.

"Do, do," he said, "find all the latent ambition you can! I'll be delighted. But you will discover this is a dull-as-lead Island. Nothing happens."

"Well I've got one idea," said Sonny, "if you don't mind me making suggestions here and there."

"Not at all! Not at all!" said the King who seemed too lethargic even to ask what the idea was. No leadership, thought Sonny. Hopeless. The Queen roused herself to say they must stay at the Palace while they were in Tolikland. She was a kindly woman, and told them to go and come as they wished. Dinner would be at eight, and they would have a room in the Palace.

So that was that sorted, thought Gogo. The boys excused themselves and left the Palace.

"Wow!" said Gogo, "compare them with our King and Queen!"

"I know," said Sonny. "We're going to have to work very hard during our time here if we are going to get anything started. Even Flinn is just sitting by his tower. What's the matter with them all?"

"Well Bella was walking backwards and forwards, and preparing food," said Gogo.

"True. My first idea was for that land by the tower. They could make an amusement park there. I can see it all!" said Sonny, his eyes sparkling. "They could attach a big wheel to the tower. A little restaurant can be built where the tent is. There can be swings and roundabouts and a Big

Dipper. Games. And what do you need to build those things? Wood! We need some musical people to create music there. Just imagine Gogo! A first class amusement park right there where the birds from other Islands land! You could have people arriving in droves with their children for a day out in Tolikland! Good food, skittles, a bowling ally, a shooting range!"

"I can see why the King wants you to succeed him," smiled Gogo. "Some of those things you mention though might not be known in the Islands. You would have to explain them."

"Of course. Glad to help. I can see it all!" he repeated, "Let's go and wake up Tolikland."

"Sonny," said Gogo anxiously, "how would people pay for their turns on the roundabouts and everything?" He had been around enough in Sonny's world to have seen fair-grounds, and knew that there you needed money!

"We'll think about in detail that later. People would have to bring goods from their own Island, and a Tolik could assess the worth. Or better, there could be some sort of catalogue containing lists of items for exchange in return for so many hours in the park. Something like that. Perishables would have to be used by the Toliks, or in the restaurant, but other stuff could be stored to take to the Trade Fair."

Gogo began to feel excited too, but implementing the ideas was another thing.

"We'ld better talk to Bella then. Flinn won't be able to help. Bella was working her socks off, a bit fed up maybe, but not defeated."

"You're right," said Sonny. "Let's start with Bella."

As they walked back to the tower Sonny added,

"What I feel is if we can get them enthusiastic about the amusement park idea and using their wood to make the equipment, carpenters would have to be properly trained for the work and then hopefully persuaded to go on and make other things. There must be carpenters here, so they could train others. Then you'll have them producing things to barter."

"Sometimes I forget we're children," said Gogo.

"We have to forget that if we are going to stir people up!" said Sonny.

When they arrived back at the tent Bella was sitting having a cup of tea herself. With her was another girl.

"Hello," she said, "this is my friend Tania. I've been telling her about your visit."

"Yes," said Tania. "You think that tower is pretty tacky huh?"

"Er…….well……..," mumbled Sonny.

"No. Be frank," said Tania.

"The thing is, I think it's got potential," said Sonny. Bella's ears pricked up.

"Oh do you? Flinn is so depressed. No-one is really coming to view his work. A few drop by for a cup of tea."

"The thing is that by itself it isn't enough to attract crowds," said Gogo. Tania collapsed in giggles. Bella ignored her.

"So what do you think we can do to improve things?"

"Build an Amusement Park," said Sonny firmly. No time to beat about the bush.

"A…a…what?" asked Tania.

"You know…….swings, roundabouts, slide, games, toffee apples, candy floss, the lot!"

"So, where does Flinn's tower fit into it?" asked Tania. Sonny was encouraged that the girls didn't just laugh at him. Instead they were trying to visualize what he was describing.

"That will be really useful," said Sonny to Bella. "We can attach the Big Wheel to it. Of course it will need supports."

"Right," said Bella. "Wow. Who's going to do all that though? You will have noticed how things are here."

"Well there are you two, and we will help. Don't you have friends who would love to get involved in doing something really exciting? We'll need a lot of wood and trained carpenters. You must have them?"

"Yes of course. Who do you think makes all our stuff?" said Tania.

"So could we present our ideas to them, and ask them to take charge of building the equipment? Gogo and I will draw sketches showing what we need. And we will need stalls for games and snacks."

"Do you have anyone who is musical?" asked Gogo. "You can't have an amusement park without lots of music!"

"Yes………," said Bella doubtfully, "we do but they are very angry."

"How so?" asked Sonny. Bella sighed.

"They'll be in the village hall now. There is a good musical group. They call themselves Dark Danger and they are led by the King's son Prince Carlos."

"Heavens!!' exclaimed Sonny. "The King and Queen never mentioned him!"

"No well, there's bad feeling!" said Bella.

189

"Prince Carlos is one of the angry young people?" said Gogo.

"You bet!"

"May we come and meet them now?" asked Sonny. "We don't have too much time really. Everyone will get worried in Pongoland if we delay much."

Bella and Tania led the boys to their pony-trap. The pony had been grazing and lifted its' head expectantly as they approached. He was hitched on to the trap and they all climbed in. It was a short ride to Tolikland's main town centre. There was a central social area with seats and lawn and trees, and round the perimeter of the square there were shops, some houses, and a large building which turned out to be the Community Hal. lt was painted white and had a red tiled roof. Bella drove the trap round and came to a halt in front of it. They all climbed down from the trap and on Bella's bidding, climbed the three steps up to the main entrance. The building had tall windows and two large doors. Inside there was a big hall. The atmosphere was rather dusty, and there was a good deal of noise. At the opposite end to the door there was a low stage, and several young people were practising on their musical instruments. About a couple of dozen other young people thronged the hall shouting to each other and laughing. Someone threw a ball. As the four of them entered the room they all fell quiet, deeply curious and maybe apprehensive. A boy called,

"Hello Bella! Hello Tania!"

"Hi Bailey!" Bella called back. She led Sonny and Gogo down the hall to introduce them.

"These are Sonny and Gogo from Pongoland. They are visiting. They thought Tolikland seemed a bit dull I think, so I brought them here. They wanted to know if we have any music." She turned to Sonny and Gogo. "These are Dark Danger, our scary music group!" she laughed.

A dark-haired, darker-skinned boy perched on the edge of the stage looked up. He had brown eyes, though most of the Toliks seemed to have green eyes. The Royal Families of the Islands inter-married so that their physical characteristics were often different from the Islanders own.

"This is Prince Carlos," said Tania. "He is the leader of the group and plays the guitar. And this is Andrea," she said turning to another boy close by. "He plays the harmonica. When they are all here there are six in the group."

Prince Carlos looked watchful, as if suspicious about their intentions. Andrea was out-going and greeted them in a friendly way.

"Glad to meet you," he said. "How long are you staying?"

"Not long," said Sonny. Might as well tell them….. "Our King sent us to look at your pole and report back about it. What it looks like close up and what it's for and so on."

"Our pole?" said Carlos. "Oh you mean the tower thing. What did you think it was?"

"No-one had any idea. It has created quite a stir!" said Sonny.

"Oh well good. More than any of the rest of us can claim," said Carlos. Have to be blunt, thought Sonny.

"What's going on? You look like a cell of revolutionaries!" he laughed. Immediately Carlos was on his feet, angry.

"What do you mean a 'cell'? Who said that?"

"It's just that you look as if something is going on. A cell means a small number of people dedicated to bringing about change, often through violence." Gogo was looking very uneasy indeed. Sonny was in way over his head here. Prince Carlos stared hard at Sonny for a few long moments.

"You are far too young to be a spy for a counter-revolution!" he remarked, relaxing. "You are very intuitive though. A revolution is indeed in the making, right here, right now."

"At least the tower is a talking-point," said Sonny, "and I've got ideas about how you can develop something really productive and interesting around it."

"So you're not only intuitive! You've got ideas! The King of Pongoland has a right to wonder what we Toliks might be up to, but sadly that tower of bricks is our only claim to fame currently. Not that you can knock it over like a toy. Its' foundation goes down three feet into the ground, and metal supports run all the way up its' four corners. Reflecting polished slates of granite form the sides, and they are glued together with builders' glue. Flinn worked very hard on it. The ladder he borrowed reaches to the roof of the inside of the Palace dome, so that's its' height." He smiled, and Sonny and Gogo suddenly saw his underlying charm.

"Hats off to Flinn, I say," said Carlos. "While others stared at their navels he worked hard, and I shall never forget it." Bella smiled, pink with pleasure, and storing up the Prince's words to tell Flinn later.

So," said Sonny, getting to his point, "we can safely attach the Big Wheel to it."

You could hear a pin drop.

"What!" said Carlos. "What big wheel? For water from the river?"

"No no no," laughed Sonny. "The Big Wheel some of us are planning for the Amusement Park on that site."

"Just a minute! Just a minute! Just four beats to the bar! What Amusement Park is who planning?" said Carlos.

"A few of us. That is Bella, Tania, Gogo, and me. We can draw you the plans if you have time?" said Sonny. "A Fair-Ground? The Big Wheel of course with seats on it all round, several roundabouts, big swings, a Big Dipper, slide, amusement galleries with skittles, a bowling ally, a shooting ally , coconut shies, snacks like candy-floss, toffee apples, ice-cream. AND - lots of music! That was why we wanted to come here and meet you now. Your group could be on a grandstand there, and keep everyone entertained with music. That land is where the birds arrive from other Islands, so you should have lots of visitors coming in with their children for a day out!"Prince Carlos just stared.

"And," pressed on Sonny while he had the advantage, "to build all the equipment you will need to use lots of your wood! Your carpenters can train apprentices up to be master carpenters while they work on the fair-ground. Then they will be qualified to make useful or decorative items to bring to the Trade Fair! Of course there is the issue of the exchange rate of produce people will need to bring for their day in the Amusement Park. We were thinking maybe you could draw up a catalogue listing the value in terms of hours at the Fair of common items of produce used for barter among the Islands. Something on those lines. Of course that needs hammering out, and there is the question of perishables which would have to be consumed by your Islanders, or used in the little restaurant we thought would be good to replace the tent? Balla could run that very well with Tania maybe if they liked."

"WAIT!" bellowed Carlos. "Your ideas are criss-crossing with my ideas, and you aren't even Toliks!" Sonny paused.

"Your ideas? What are you planning?"

"Like we said. A revolution, but you have to swear allegiance before I tell you anything," said Carlos.

"We can't swear allegiance to you Carlos," said Gogo. " We owe allegiance to the King of Pongoland."

"Alright then," said Carlos, "but you have to promise secrecy." Sonny met Gogo's eyes.

"We're good at that," he said.

"Alright. Everyone here is in on this. We are going to lock up the King in part of the Palace, and I'm going to take over as Prince Regent."

"Lock up your father!" exclaimed Gogo.

"You bet. He's had years to turn things around here, and what has he done? Nothing. And when I begged, implored, him to make changes in Tolikland, he announced a competition! And you've seen what that produced. No. Our patience is worn out. I shall send my mother to Rainbowland to her family, and just take over. Then you'll see what Tolikland can do."

"Can't you send your father to Rainbowland too?" asked Gogo.

"No. The birds wouldn't take him. I'll ask my mother nicely to visit her family for a few weeks, and she will go."

"So what are your plans once you are Regent?" asked Sonny eagerly
.

"That's what we have been planning," said Andrea mysteriously.

"And?" asked Sonny.

"You ask too many questions. We haven't finalized those yet. First things first," said Carlos.

"You mean you haven't got any ideas either!" accused Sonny. "What you'll end up doing is take over the Palace and having big parties!"

"No!" said Andrea, annoyed. "The trouble is Tolikland has become like a like a lake in which all the silt has sunk to the bottom, and there isn't even a ripple. It will be difficult to work up a storm."

"Alright," said Sonny, "well call us the storm! We've got plenty of energy."

"Starting with an Amusement Park," said Andrea.

"Yes! Don't you see! That will get people stirred up. Give them each a job. Gogo and I will give you the list of the things you are going to need, and you can present it to your workmen. Gogo and I will draw sketches of the main things, but when I reach Pongoland I will send you proper pictures." (From my world, he thought.) "Get things going! Each person has to be given a responsibility. And after the Fair is built your carpenters then need to do real hard work making things for the next Trade Fair. I'll send you pictures of nice or useful things they could make. A catalogue possibly will have to be written listing all the things people are likely to bring to exchange, and you have to decide how much of each is worth how many hours in the park. You can even post lists in the landing area. Like a plain woolen shawl would mean half a day for a family till one o'clock, and an embroidered shawl would mean a whole day for a family. That sort of idea."

"Then we store up what we receive for the next Trade Fair," said Carlos.

"Yes! The Islanders are constantly exchanging goods after all," said Sonny.

"We can ask our Chief Minister to draw up the catalogue, with one of us at his elbow," said Andrea, "and send round copies to all the nearby Islands!"

"Yes. WHEN YOU ARE READY!" said Sonny firmly. "First the work has to be done. The Fair would run throughout the year, so you will need to keep adding to it to keep people interested. And Andrea you will need to work on your music. Do you have plenty of compositions?"

Andrea looked uneasy.

"OK," said Sonny. "Meridoland has wonderful musicians and a group called the Spangles. Would you like to invite them here for a week or so to work on your repertoire with you?"

"That would be really helpful," said Carlos. "We're keen you know but we may have stagnated."

"So before we leave, would you like to write a letter to the King of Meridoland asking if the Spangles might pay you a visit? I will see he gets the letter."

"Wonderful," said Carlos. "We do need some collaboration."

"You have to make friends with the other Islands. No Island survives well on its' own," said Sonny. "The Fair will help you to make lots of new friends."

"You have an old head on young shoulders, young Sonny," said Carlos.

"Other people have said that," said Gogo smiling.

"I think we need you two to stay with us a while to help us get things started," said Andrea.

"No," said Sonny. "You have to do it for yourselves. Why don't we call a meeting of the islanders tomorrow morning by the tower to discuss the whole project, and alot tasks to everyone?"

Immediately the young people in the hall were talking together excitedly, already making suggestions. Sonny took Carlos on one side.

"Why not postpone locking up your father? Have the meeting and then present the islanders' plans to him. If he still digs his feet in, then OK lock him up – temporarily, in his own rooms."

"How long are you staying?" asked Carlos.

"Three days," said Sonny.

"Counting this the first day, and leaving the day after tomorrow?"

"Yes."

"So tomorrow we hammer out a schedule for the development of the Island. Then the following day we present our ideas to my father. If he is obstructive I lock him up, comfortably of course with people to serve him. If he is interested we invite him to participate."

"That would be really good if he would. Would you like Gogo and me to prepare the way with him for you? Talk around the subject a bit. Mention the idea of an Entertainment Park centred round the tower? And possibly a carpentry industry emerging from the work entailed?"

"Yes good thinking. You seem to be pretty articulate so I'll leave that side of things to you. Don't be afraid to shake them up a bit. I shan't let Dad stop this. Tolikland is going to be as good as any other Island in the Archipelago by the time we have finished. Mother will help in her own way, I know."

That evening Sonny and Gogo didn't say anything to the King and Queen about their meeting with Carlos as it was such a difficult relationship. They went to bed early, and by nine o'clock next morning were down by the pole. They had done their best to draw images of the Big wheel and a roundabout. Swings and slides were commonly seen in the Islands, so the helter-skelter was an easy idea. Otherwise they would send good pictures from Sonny's world, (minus people!), of the things they would need. Carlos arrived with Andrea, and three other friends, Toby, Mandy, and Minny. They studied the drawings and asked about size. Then they all studied the land and made marks where tentatively each ride might be placed.

"If you can send one of your birds with us to Pongoland I can get some proper pictures for you so that they can return with them," said Sonny. "I'll look for things made of wood also that your carpenters might like to make for the Trade Fair."

Andrea had brought paper and pencil for them to draft out an idea of how the Amusement Park would look. Sonny showed them a traditional layout with food-stalls, games and the grandstand for a music group. He also showed them how a little restaurant could replace the blue and white tent where they could serve lunches and snacks. Carlos appointed Bella and Tania in charge of that to their huge gratification.

In due course the two carpenters arrived and Carlos showed them the sketches and the ground lay-out. He asked them to appoint three apprentices to train in carpentry, and employ them for the building of the fair-ground.

"You will also need to employ two painters," he said. "We are all going to learn now how to work really hard for our Island, and make Tolikland one of the most vibrant Islands in the Archipelago! I think you could start with the trees on the hill over-looking the Palace on the other side of the river, so go there and decide which ones to cut. You can carve them up there. We don't want a pile of saw-dust here. Then bring the planks and blocks here to build. But first we need the designs. We'll decide together what we need of what. Andrea and I will direct the construction-work so don't worry about that. Nine o'clock sharp here every morning for those not cutting wood!"

The men looked a bit dazed with this sudden rush of activity, but Carlos was well-liked and they were perfectly happy to join in his enterprise. They even felt excited, perhaps for the first time in their lives. Something was happening, and they were part of it!

"Excellent!" said Andre. "And we don't want just your work. We shall need your ideas. So get thinking!"

"One idea for the carpenters might be toys and children's games," said Tania. "They could be used as prizes, or sold, in the fair, and a lot could be stored for the Trade Fair."

"Very good ideas," said Carlos. "Keep them coming, all of you."

Sonny and Gogo felt content with the day's achievements as they returned to the Palace that evening.

"Looks quite hopeful," said Gogo.

"Yes I do hope his father isn't going to be too much of a drag."

"Well we'll do what we can to help, but in the end this is their revolution. They have to carry it through," said Gogo.

The conversation after dinner was difficult.

"We've had a few ideas for the tower," remarked Sonny.

"Oh yes? You've thought of a use for it?" asked the King.

"Yes, it could be the support for a Giant Wheel," said Sonny.

"Wh....what?"

"Yes. We met your son, Prince Carlos, and his friends in town, and they are planning to build an Amusement Park on that land," said Sonny conversationally.

196

"What!" cried the Queen.

"Yes Ma'am," said Sonny. "Sir," he ploughed on, "you wanted to get some activities going, and the tower won your competition. Well Carlos felt you could develop something really good around it."

"You will have heard of amusement parks and fair-grounds, Sir," said Gogo. "Swings, roundabouts, helter-skelters, that sort of thing? And you organize games like skittles and hoopla for the children, and serve refreshments. People would come a long way to spend a day in Tolikland's Amusement Park, and they would bring produce to exchange for a day's fun!"

If Carlos had wanted his parents stirred up, Sonny and Gogo had certainly done the trick!

"Anyway, if you would excuse us Sir, we have a long day ahead tomorrow, and maybe we should get to bed," said Sonny.

"Wait a minute!!" bellowed the King. "What's all this nonsense you are talking? What in the name of Tolikland is a roundapout?"

"Roundabout," corrected Gogo.

"Whatever. Who's going to build a thing like that? Who's going to manage it?"

"Your carpenters were holding a meeting today. They are getting together a team," reassured Sonny. "They are delighted with the scheme. It will bring revenue to the Island and create jobs, and they will have plenty of time left to produce useful or decorative items for the next Trade Fair. They are quite excited. Prince Carlos is organizing everybody so probably he will manage the Amusement Park."

The King looked faint. The Queen was trying to hide a smile.

"Well done Carlos," she murmured.

"What! Not you as well!" complained her husband.

"You wanted Tolikaland to prosper dear," she said. "It rather looks as if it might! Carlos is a young man now, and perfectly capable of organizing things. He's always had plans but you always tried to squash them," she said reproachfully.

"Squash them! I know what is feasible, and what is fantasy, that's all!"

"The Amusement Park is feasible Sir," said Sonny. "He can do it. And he wants to store up merchandise to take to the Trade Fair."

"The carpenters have all sorts of ideas about what to make," said Gogo.

"When I asked for them, all their combined thought could come up with was a pole," pointed out the King.

"I know but now Prince Carlos has got them enthusiastic," said Sonny. "They are eager to help. Carlos said he would come to see you tomorrow to discuss the plans."

"Oh will he?" said the King drily.

"Yes, he wanted to get them properly thrashed out before presenting them," said Gogo.

"And if I say no?" aid the King.

"Why would you do that Sir?" asked Sonny. "You were saying yourself that the Island needs stirring up. And here is Carlos stirring! And he has loads of support, you'll see!"

"Goodnight Sir, Ma'am," said Gogo, and they softly left the room.

"Wow," breathed Sonny as they went upstairs. "That was hair-raising. We've had a lot of adventures, but I don't recall anything as scary as that."

Meanwhile Carlos had remained near the pole talking to the people of Tolikland. He told them about what he wanted for Tolikland, and how they could become great again. Everyone was to have a skill or industry. He talked about the future and how everyone's suggestions would be welcome. They were going to produce their own wool and weave it. They were going to make clothes. But they needed musicians and artists as well as farmers and craftsmen.

"So you see the sky is the limit, and each of us must think about what we will be able to contribute."

The people cheered and shouted, "Long live Carlos! Long live Carlos!"

The next morning a little delegation arrived at the Palace, to present the plans to the King. Carlos had told those closest to him what he intended to do if the King was seriously obstructive. He would be kept comfortable, but he would not be allowed to interfere with the development of Tolikland. Carlos knew in any case that his Mother would be helpful. He just felt that she might be happier with her own family for a few weeks if things turned out badly in the Palace.

Sonny and Gogo did not join them. They knew their presence would be an embarrassment.

Some time later Carlos led his delegation back down again to the crowd waiting near the pole. Prince Carlos stood on a rock to address them.

"People of Tolikland, my Father is not young now, and it is not always easy for older people to accept change. However I am here to announce that he has told me he will not stand in our way. He says history seems to be racing ahead of him, but since I seem to be at the head of the chase he feels his only choice is to let us carry out our plans for this Island. I am sure you will all want to honour his foresight and wisdom in coming to this decision, and to remember how he has served this Island faithfully all his life. He has agreed graciously to open our Entertainment Park when it is ready, and we will all want him to see what we can do!"

A great cheer went up, and shouts of,

"Long live the King! Long live the Queen! Long live Prince Carlos!"

Sonny and Gogo were watching from the back of the crowd.

"We have a lot to tell our King and Queen," murmured Gogo.

Goggles was waiting for them close by, and it was time for them to leave. They had told the Prince that they preferred to leave quietly, so they just waved as they walked to Goggles. Beside Goggles stood a Tolikland bird, ready to accompany them back in order to collect from Sonny the drawings and pictures he had promised. Carlos gave them a salute, and they grinned.

When they arrived back in Pongoland the King invited them to reprt to the Palace immediately, so Goggles too them to the Palace courtyard. The King and Queen were eager to hear what had happened.

"They call that pole a tower, Sir," said Gogo, "though the King just calls it a tower of bricks. It was a submission for a competition he had announced to stimulate creativity on the Island."

"That was all anyone could come up with," said Sonny. "The place was totally stagnant."

"Until you two arrived?" smiled the King.

"Well not just that," said Sonny. "Prince Carlos, who must be in his twenties, had all sorts of ideas and suggestions, but the King wouldn't listen. So we thought maybe an Amusement Park could be built on the land where the tower is."

"And that in turn would get their carpentry industry going," said Gogo. " They've got loads of woodland."

"Good thinking. But I can't wait to hear what the inert King said to that!"

"Well, Sir," said Sonny, "things are going ahead. But the rest of what happened is confidential." The King stared hard at them.

"Right," he said. "So strictly between the four of us what happened?"

"Prince Carlos was planning to lock up the King, send his Mum to Rainbowland for a while, and take over as Prince Regent."

"Oh," said the King. "Were these your suggestions?"

"Of course not!" exclaimed Sonny. "We persuaded him to cool it a bit. We described a fair-ground, and drew sketches. I have promised to send him some proper pictures which I'll get from home. One of their birds has come with us to take them back to Carlos. He's got the general idea. They've set up a little tent where people can sit and have a cup of tea while they gaze at the pole, tower that is. So where the tent is they will now build a restaurant to serve meals to all the people who come to spend a day in the fair. It's going to be great! There are two carpenters so they are going to get together a team of people who would like to learn carpentary, and they will serve their apprenticeship working on the Amusement Park. There will be games and snacks, and souvenirs to buy – "

"What with?" asked the King.

"Their Chief Minister is going to draw up a catalogue of the things people from other Islands use for barter, along with their value in terms of hours in the Amusement Park. It'll work out at half-days or full day usually to keep it simple. Then he'll send copies of the catalogue to all the neighbouring Islands. All the non-perishable stuff will be stored to take to the next Trade Fair."

"So the King is so excited about all this Carlos won't have to imprison him?"

"That's right," said Sonny. "Though of course he would just have been locked in part of the Palace with people to look after him."

"I wish I could have been a fly on the wall when Carlos broke the news," said the King.

"Oh well Gogo and I broke it," said Sonny. "Carlos wanted us to do the preparation work. Breaking the ground so he could come in the next day with the full scenario."

"Right. So what did he say?"

"He bellowed a bit and we tiptoed off to bed," said Gogo. "But the next day he accepted Carlos's plans. In any case the Queen was supportive. She pointed out to him that he had wanted Tolikland to prosper and here it was, about to prosper."

"We have brought a letter for the King of Meridoland," said Sonny. "Carlos has a musical group and he wants to invite the Spangles to pay a visit to Tolikland soon to help and advise in, I would guess, rebranding his own group. It's probably a bit fusty."

"The King and Queen of Tolikland have no idea how big a hand Sonny and I have had in the rebranding of Tolikland. That's why we need to keep what we have told you confidential, if you don't mind Sir," said Gogo.

"So the second of your great exploits must also go under the mat!" said the King. "How am I to demonstrate to Pongoland that you have proved your worth?"

"I know Sir. I can see that," said Sonny.

"Never mind. I will have to use a bit imagination myself, hinting at secrets too sensitive to divulge, whilst bolstering up what I can say to its' maximum credibility," said the King, "shaking his head. "Well let's hope the events of the third test can be blazoned forth in triumph!"

"Really I doubt it Sir," said Sonny. "We are children."

Chapter Five

The Witch of Beldeena Island

Sonny's third test did not come until into the New Year. One day in January the King invited him into his private sitting-room.

He attended classes every weekend in the Palace on the history and geography of the Islands, and on Saturday night he slept at the Palace. He was comfortable now in his little room, and had some of his own things stored away there in the cupboards, as well as his favourite books on the shelves. He was allowed to borrow whatever he liked from the Palace library, so quite a lot of his time went in reading the famous stories and legends of the Islands. From his window he could see Murgo's house, and Sonny, Gogo, and Tobo had torches to signal goodnight to each other.

When he entered the King's sitting-room on that January day the King said,

"Sonny you must have been wondering about your third test. I didn't want just to make up some test. It needed to be real. Now a real test has come along."

Sonny looked curious.

"Have you heard of Beldeena Island?"

"No Sir," said Sonny.

"Well it's a long way from here, so we hardly ever go there. Three birds and two over-night stays on the way. Anyway they havetheir own Wise Woman, rather like our Mother Fulati. Because of the distance the two don't meet much. It's not just that the birds get tired. The riders get tired too. However Mother Fulati has raised a matter of concern. She fears that this witch, (she calls herself a white witch), is involved in making some preparation which has noxious side-effects."

Sonny was surprised. Mother Fulati's rules were always very strict about what she made. No harm was ever done, and non had unpleasant side-effects. Some had unusual pleasant side-effects, as Sonny himself had seen, but there was a serious purpose for these, and they soon wore off.

"I don't wish to send Mother Fulati all that way, though she asked to go, because we need her here. I can't spare her. And Mother Fulati also feels that if Eleanor, (that's her name), does have a guilty secret she will immediately assume, if Mother Fulati suddenly turns up, that she has come to ferret out the secret. Naturally Eleanor would hide it."

Sonny nodded, seeing where this was going.

"What sort of noxious effects does the preparation have? What is it prescribed for?" he asked.

"It's an ointment for muscular aches and pains. You rub it in and it heats the area. The smell is soothing. It is intended to soothe the patient so that he relaxes and allows the muscle to relax. This helps the active ingredient to be absorbed into the inflamed tissue. The story is though that the 'vapour', as it is being called, causes hallucinations."

"What!"

"Yes. For the next few hours the patient is in cuckoo-land. Often he doesn't know who he is or where he is. He giggles and says inappropriate and silly things."

"Why is Mother Eleanor allowed to use it?"

"Because it is very successful with the muscle cramps. Afterwards the patient is most grateful. The pain is gone and he can live normally. As you can see a person who has been having muscular cramps will be delighted. Never mind the period of silliness which the patient claims to have enjoyed. But Mother Fulati says the hallucinations are a symptom of nerve poisoning. It may not be severe, and the patient may be back to normal in a few hours, but repeated use of it will almost certainly cause real harm. Even the patient's attendant is said to start giggling and behaving foolishly. Or did. I believe attendants are no longer allowed. Mother Fulati is quite worried. So what she needs is for you to go and investigate. What ingredients is Eleanor using? If possible it would be wonderful if you could bring back a sample. Mother Fulati herself will decide what is to be done. I rely on her entirely in all such matters. She is our Wise Woman. It isn't surprising Eleanor likes to be called a witch! She doesn't sound wise."

"Yes of course I'll go," said Sonny. "And Gogo will come with me as usual?"

"Ceratainly. Start as soon as you can. I'll send a message of goodwill to the King of Beldeena, along with a request I have to think up. Once you are there look up Eleanor on Mother Fulati's behalf, and I'll have to leave the rest to you. You and Gogo need to talk to Mother Fulati first, and find out all you can from her. She might be able to suggest a line of approach. She will send you on one of her owls because they know the way, but take Goggles too. He could be very useful."

Gogo was quite excited about the long trip into mysterious territory as far as the Pongos were concerned. But first they went on Goggles' back to visit Mother Fulati. It was always a pleasure drawing in over the trees to land in her garden. Immediately they smelt the wonderful aroma of her plants. There were hundreds of varieties, each with a special property.

Both Mother Fulati and her daughter Selina were learned women. They had their own library full of books, but much, or most, of what they knew had been learnt from their mothers. The daughters of their line automatically started to learn to grow herbs and flowers as soon as they could walk, and along with growing them they learnt about their ingredients, and how they should be prepared and used in healing. Mother Fulati hurried out of her house drying her hands on her apron. Unlike the other Pongo women she always wore a long skirt with a short blouse fitted to the waist. When the weather was cool she wore a woolen shawl. She was not Pongo by ancestry, and her origins were unknown, though the word "Merlin" crossed Sonny's mind for the first time. Her family inter-married with others of their dynasty scattered across the Islands, though few were gifted with healing powers. Mother Fulati opened her arms to hug them both.

"Come along in! Selina has just made some scones, and they are hot from the oven. You would like a glass each of lime-juice wouldn't you?" They certainly would. Selina was a dark-haired light brown-skinned girl. She was wearing a full red skirt with a pink design on it and a pink blouse. They all sat down round the kitchen table while Mother Fulati told them about her worry regarding Eleanor's recent activities.

"I can't understand the woman! She knows it goes against all the rules to allow hallucigens to escape into the atmosphere. Very rarely a hallucigen might be prepared for purposes of allaying excess anxiety, or irrational fear, but the dose would always be tiny and never result in giggling and buffoonery. What she is doing has to be dangerous. And not only that, she is bringing disrepute to our profession. We have authority and respect because we understand our work. Who will trust us if we play about with peoples' minds?"

"How would you like us to approach this?" asked Sonny.

"You will meet the King first. Our King is giving us cover by writing to him to ask him for something. So when you have dealt with that you can show interest in the Island, but you can't waste a lot of time on a guided tour. Get to the point as quickly as you can. You can easily mention me because Eleanor is distantly related in our ancestry. Usually the gift of healing goes down through the direct line, but occasionally it will appear in a girl of another related line. Don't let on I sent you. Keep it general. Get yourselves to her house and after that you will have to play it by ear. What you want to know is the nature of some ointment she has for muscular aches and pains. Some new stuff. But since whatever it is seems to have become famous you can't ask outright, or she'll know why you've come. What you want is a sample to bring me and I will give you a little pot to put some in. Close it tightly to keep the aroma in. I can't say how you'll manage that," she said doubtfully.

"Steal it," said Gogo.

"No........we aren't stealing it exactly. I don't want her ointment for my own work. I just need to check it out. A very small sample will be enough for me to test it for known hallucigens. If it is unknown to me that will mean there is something, possibly dangerous, growing on Beldeena Isand which doesn't grow here. I outrank her in this work so I need to know what goes on."

She gave Gogo a little green pot, and after they had finished their refreshments she took them out into the garden.

"And while you are about it," she muttered, "get a look at Eleanor's son. I hear he is handsome and a good worker." Sonny looked startled.

"Her son? Does he live with her?"

"I think so, but whatever you do make sure you meet him. I want a good match for Selina."

"Oh!" said Sonny.

"Yes! Come on you two. You must know there is gossip on the Island about whom she will marry. He has to be of our lineage, but of course he won't be doing medical work. Could you find out what he does do? And I want to know what you think of him."

"Right," said Gogo.

As they flew off Gogo said the Sonny,

"Which do you believe is our primary task here?" Sonny grinned.

" Well practically speaking I think we need to take both tasks equally seriously if we are not to get a scolding! I did want to ask if her line goes back to Merlin, but with that Merido task being so confidential I daren't mention the subject. In a flash she would have been asking where we heard that!"

The journey to Beldeena involved two overnight stops so it wasn't until the third day that they arrived. As they approached they could see a river and rolling green hills. Sonny had learnt in his geography classes that just as the perimeters of the Islands dissolved into mist so that no-one could venture to the edge of an Island, so any rivers also vanished into the surrounding mist. Not only was visibility down to zero, but also the atmosphere resisted penetration. Nestling in a valley by the river was a town. Their attendant owl from Mother Fulati's home led Goggles to the town, and the two birds landed just outside in a grassy meadow.

The boys left them to rest and ventured into the town. Shops and houses lined both sides of the road, and narrower streets led off from it. Quite a few people were out shopping. They were of medium height and slender. They were brown-skinned of all shades from dark to very light brown. The women wore long wrap-around skirts with shirts, and the men wore trousers with similar shirts. Gogo approached a man coming up the road to ask him the way to the Palace. The man of course saw straight away that they were visitors, and they explained that they were from Pongoland. Sonny had realized few were likely to ask him why he looked different. Either people were too polite to mention it, or assumed some Pongo people looked like him.

"We don't often have visitors from Pongoland!" he exclaimed. "Welcome. You've come to see our King?"

"Yes, mainly, though we hope to see a little of Beldeena Island while we are here," said Gogo.

"Well I live along that road," the man pointed, "if you need any help. I am Petrie." The boys thanked him. "The Palace is near that roundabout you can see ahead. White marble."

They walked along to the roundabout and to their left saw high iron gates guarded by a sentry. The Palace was visible among trees behind. They could see the white pillars of a colonnade, and a high white dome. Sonny took the letter from their King out of his blue cotton satchel, and presented it to the sentry-man. The official lettering and the Pongoland crest on the envelope were sufficient for the gate to be opened to them. The boys were allowed in, and another official came out to meet them. He took them through the main door inside. Everything was built on a vast scale. There was a large hall with tiled floor, and a broad staircase to their left led up to the next floor. The dome above was paned so that the whole area was light and welcoming.

Sonny and Gogo were taken to a reception lobby and asked to sit for a moment. This room had large high windows and curtains which touched the floor. There was a big fire-place with mantel-piece, and the room was made inviting by several warm brightly-coloured rugs. Sonny and Gogo sat nervously.

Eventually a servant arrived and he invited them to go with him. They went along a corridor which led off the hall to a much larger sitting-room. Inside, there were the King and Queen, a boy about twelve and a younger girl. The Queen was reading aloud, but she stopped as they entered. It was approximately tea-time by then and there was a tray of refreshments on a low table in front of the fire-place. Sonny and Gogo were invited to join them. They were given a cup of tea and a slice of sponge-cake each. The King was holding the letter from the King of Pongoland in his hand.

"How are your King and Queen?" he asked. "It is several years since we visited your Island though we hope to be there this Summer for the Trade Fair. We have some very fine glass and crystal-ware to bring, as well as some of our famous rugs."

"Thankyou they are very well," said Sonny. "We look forward to seeing you at the Trade Fair."

"Let me see," said the King, putting on his glasses. "His majesty is interested in cross-breeding some of our sheep with yours? I don't know about that. There are all sorts of risks involved in cross-breeding."

Sonny and Gogo knew that the request was a ploy to introduce them on to the Island, and that he did not mind what the answer was. He could always "re-think" any idea later. How to get the subject of the conversation round to the Witch of Beldeena? Diplomacy was a really tough job, thought Sonny. The pitfalls were great and seemed to be scattered everywhere in the course of an apparently simple chat. Fortunately Gogo had sat through a good many in Pongoland, and knew how to ask a leading question in amongst politenesses about climate and scenery. Sonny was keen to learn a great deal in a very short time.

"We didn't notice any woodland as we came down," Gogo observed. "There is quite a lot in Pongoland."

"Yes, I remember," said the King. "You have that whole hill-side covered with trees, and Mother Fulati lives in the middle of them making medicines! We do have woodland, but it is over the other side. Everybody needs trees."

Sonny was about to ask a direct question but Gogo forestalled him by leading into the subject sideways.

"Of course," he said, "some Islands don't have enough and others have too many!"

"Well it is good that each Island has its' own special assets, and at the Trade Fair we can exchange our produce," said the Queen.

"Yes, things work pretty well," said Gogo." Mother Fulati takes samples of her remedies to the Fair and receives orders. Of course people from the Islands close to us just come over to see her if they need medical care."

"It is the same with our Madame Eleanor," said the King. "She makes medicines for us and heals people from neighbouring Islands."

"Is that so?" said Sonny. "And is she also old and wise?"

"I don't think either lady would like to be called old," laughed the Queen.

"Perhaps we might meet her while we are here, and see her work?" suggested Gogo.

"Of course, if you like," said the King. "Why not tomorrow after breakfast? How long do you expect to be here? I have to consult with our shepherds of course about the advisability of any cross-breeding."

"You will stay here of course," said the Queen, "and we'll arrange a pony-trap for you for tomorrow morning. It will be more interesting to see the Island from ground level, and I expect your owls will value a rest."

Things had gone pretty well the first evening, and Sonny and Gogo set off the next morning with high hopes. The King's son, Rick, accompanied them. This could be helpful or it could be awkward, but they had to take things as they unfolded. He was a cheerful boy and proved to be good company. He took the reins and pointed out the various sights. Each hill had a name. Some had sheep grazing on them and some did not. The hills where there were no sheep were partly built on. They could see flat-roofed houses with painted walls and little gardens. It was all very pleasant!

"Do people grow their own vegetables?" asked Sonny.

"Yes they do, quite a lot. The soil is very good, so it would be a waste not to," said Rick.

"I like it here," said Gogo, relaxing back and enjoying himself.

"Yes, we are a happy Island," said Rick. "Everyone helps each other and we have lots of parties and activities together. Of course my father is a good King and a lot depends on that."

"Who does Madame Eleanor live with?" asked Sonny. "Or does she live alone?"

"No she has a grown-up son, Gerard," said Rick. "His father is away quite a lot, but when he is at home he is of course also there."

"What does Gerard do?" asked Gogo.

"He is an artist and sculptor," said Rick.

"Wow!" said Sonny.

"Yes, he's very good. He does art work for the Island to barter, but people commission him to do portraits or whatever they want. He is also very good at room-designing. Décor. So people hire him for that. And he does sculptures for public places. Those of course are commissioned. He gets orders from other Islands."

"A talented family!" commented Gogo. "What does his father do?"

"He is a business-man for both Madame Eleanor and Gerard. He delivers and takes orders, and he advertises."

"Oh?" said Gogo, puzzled. Pongoland didn't have anyone like that because the King handled all exchanges with other Islands. Sonny too was doubtful about this role. The people of Pongoland never had to concern themselves about deliveries and orders.

"Our King does all of that," he felt forced to comment.

"I know," said Rick. "My father isn't happy about it. The Islands are small, and the King makes sure enough is produced of whatever is needed, and not too much of any item. And he monitors how much of what is imported from other Islands. Suddenly we've got Madrico wanting to barter some of his family's products himself with people on other Islands! My father hasn't said anything yet. He's waiting to see what happens. He feels there will be some crisis eventually which will make Madrico decide it would be better for the King to handle things. He's got a bit big for his boots since his son has proved so successful. Maybe he is jealous, I don't know, and wants to be important."

"What did he do before?" asked Gogo.

"He was also an artist, but not a very good one," said Rick. "Gerard is much more popular, and gets all the orders, so basically Madrico is put out!"

"Oh dear," said Sonny.

"Right," said Rick, "so it's a difficult situation, a delicate situation. That's why my father is letting him do his thing for a bit, and see how it pans out."

"And I suppose Madame Eleanor is also very much in demand," said Sonny.

"She certainly is. You don't get many people who understand plants well enough to be able to make medicines, so she is pretty famous too."

"And Dad is squashed between two unusually successful people," said Sonny.

"Yes, that's the situation," said Rick.

"Does he help Madame Eleanor at all in the preparation of the medicines?" asked Sonny. "Our Mother Fulati has a daughter, Selina, who works alongside her. It's a lot for one person to handle alone."

"He dabbles a bit I think," said Rick. "Well he does a lot of the heavy work in the garden, and he helps in gathering leaves or roots or seeds. He knows the plants, and all that would certainly be too much for Madame Eleanor to manage alone. He isn't a lazy man."

"But being a gardener isn't enough for him?" asked Gogo.

"No. He still does paintings, but demand for his work is poor."

By the time they reached Madame Eleanor's house Sonny and Gogo felt they had a good grasp of the general situation there. Madame Eleanor came to the door immediately. She was very surprised to see Prince Rick with two other boys about to knock. She had a low, stone-built house with a red-tiled roof, and like Mother Fulati she had a very large garden. Like Mother Fulati she wore an ankle-length full skirt with a short blouse. Her hair was long and grey and tied into a knot at the nape of her neck.

She smiled a welcome, and Prince Rick introduced Sonny and Gogo. They all went into the house straight into a big kitchen which was warm from an open fire. Things were brewing on an iron stove, and there were interesting aromas. A wooden table was scrubbed clean, and on it was a chocolate cake she had just baked. It was all so reminiscent of Mother Fulati's kitchen. They were invited to sit to the table and she cut three fat slices of cake for the boys. Rick told her they had come from Pongoland and were friends of Mother Fulati.

"She sends you greetings Ma'am," said Gogo, "and hopes you are all well."

"Thankyou," said Madame Eleanor. "Please tell her we are all well. I trust all is well with her. I hear Selina is a great help in her work."

"She is Madame, and is an expert now herself in making medicines," said Sonny.

"She was a promising child I remember," said Eleanor. "We all meet so rarely. We are busy women and haven't leisure to travel so far. What brings you here?"

Gogo said, "Our King wanted us to deliver a letter to your King."

"Well that's very nice," said Eleanor. "My son, Gerard, is out just now, but I expect him back any moment. I hope you can wait?"

"Yes we would love to meet him," said Gogo, looking at Sonny. "Might we look round your garden while we wait? Mother Fulati will be full of all sorts of questions when we get home."

Madame Eleanor was delighted at their interest and took them outside. Some plants were arranged in neat rows, others in square or rectangular patches. Trees lined the pathways, and Sonny could see fruits, and berries, and nuts.

"This is amazing," he said, "and I believe your woods are not far off?"

"No. I have been allotted part of the woods as an extension to my garden, so I have plenty of land for my needs."

"Do you experiment with new preparations as well as producing the regular recipes?" asked Sonny.

"I can see you have spent a lot of time with Mother Fulati! Like her I have many old books and manuscripts. We believe we are related way back somewhere. We have many preparations in common, and we have inherited the same style of dress. I imagine she experiments just as I do. You can't help it. You always try to extend your knowledge. You feel something might work better if you do this, or wonder, suppose I try that? It is always exciting and rewarding work."

"If you prepare a new remedy how do you test it?" asked Sonny.

"I apply it to myself first. I take larger doses than I would give patients, several times. That will show me if there are any unpleasant side-effects. When I am sure it is safe I give it to an appropriate patient, that is someone with the ailment I wish to treat. I warn the first few patients that this is something new, but they never mind because they know I have imbibed generous doses of it already myself. When it works I make careful notes with dates of every new preparation."

"Some of Mother Fulati's remedies have slight mind-altering effects," said Sonny. "They aren't harmful but are used to alleviate anxiety occasionally."

"Yes I too prescribe certain types of sedatives," said Eleanor, looking at Sonny.

"And do you make fruit juices or other things simply to eat or drink?" asked Sonny to change the subject.

"Yes certainly, and I prepare health drinks. Children love them. So do parents. Whenever I visit anybody's house I take along a bottle of one of my health drinks. That helps to maintain a good level of general health on the Island. Here is Gerard now!"

They saw a young man striding up the path. He was tall, brown skinned, dark haired, and handsome! Sonny and Gogo exchanged glances and small grins. He knew Rick of course, and his mother explained who Sonny and Gogo were.

"Let's go inside again," said Eleanor happily, "and I'll give you each a glass of fruit juice right now."

This was all very nice, thought Sonny, but how on earth to get round to the topic of the dodgy medicine? Desperate measures for desperate situations? As they sat down he asked conversationally,

"Mother Fulati heard you have a new ointment for rheumatism. She wondered what the ingredients are." Gogo stared at him hard.

"Rheumatism? Er……"

"You know the one Mum," said Gerard. "You used it on my arm when I sprained it, and it made me laugh."

"You mean it tickled?" asked Gogo interestedly.

"No. I just rolled around laughing," said Gerard, smiling at the memory.

"Goodness!" said Sonny. "What was in it to do that?"

"Gerard is exaggerating," said Eleanor hurriedly. "He was just being silly."

"No I wasn't Mum," he said. "I got a fit of the giggles and you gave me a big drink of water."

Madame Eleanor busied herself at the stove.

"You are exaggerating Gerard," she repeated.

"That could be useful if you need cheering up," said Rick helpfully. "Why don't you put a bit on my arm Ma'am and we'll see if I start laughing!"

Madame Eleanor turned round scarlet with anger.

"Please be quiet, all of you! You have no idea what you are talking about! You are all children, and you don't understand."

"Mum?" said Gerard, surprised.

"It was something I made at the request of your father. A client he had found in Ringoland wanted something to help his daughter. She had had a nasty fall from a tree and couldn't walk. She was very upset and frightened, and he wanted me to send something to help to make her cheerful again. Normally I wouldn't use that ingredient, but your father was desperate because this client had offered him a big commission to do the stage scenery for a play they were putting on in Ringoland. It was all that he could offer in exchange, and it meant so much to your father. I risked making up an ointment with the sap of a certain root added to it. The ointment was to work on her injured back and legs, and the sap was to lift her mood. But I hadn't calculated how much her father was going to apply. He seems to have ladled it on! She ended up in hysterics from an overdose of the sap, and it took a long time to quieten her. Her father was puzzled and very angry. I would have been in serious trouble except that when she woke up from a long sleep she was back to normal again and could walk! To her parents this was a miracle. The thick application of the ointment had seeped into the nerves and muscles of her back and revived them. There had been a miscalculation on my part. There should have been no sap, and a great deal more of the ointment applied than I had prescribed."

Sonny and Gogo listened fascinated. They were all thrilled to hear about the outcome, but realized that in adult work there are risks and chances of things going badly wrong. It is not always happy-ever-after. Madame Eleanor had understood her husband's frustration when his son turned out to be much more successful than he was, even though at the same time he was very proud of his son. So she had acted against her better judgment, hoping to win him the commission. He did get it, but she had been very lucky not have had her reputation ruined.

Sonny thought about this.

"Sometimes you take risks," he said. "You have to sometimes."

"Yes Sonny," said Madame Eleanor. "That is so true. The problem is that if you don't take a risk sometimes you can't learn. That little girl was very seriously injured. I had just needed to know in such a case at least double the normal dose is necessary."

"I have the same sort of fears in my work too," said Gerard. "When I am asked to carve a statue they give me a huge slab of marble or some other stone, and I have to hack away at it, and chip at it, often just hoping for the best. It could end up ludicrous. I have to see the final result in my mind's eye, and then as an image in the stone, and chip away until it emerges for everyone else to see, but that too can be very scary."

Sonny and Gogo felt very sober listening to them revealing the anxieties they experienced in the course of a normal day's work.

"You are very brave," said Sonny. "The Islands are very lucky to have people like you."

Eleanor bent over and kissed him.

"And you have a wise head on young shoulders," she said.

"May we have a look at it? The ointment?" Gogo asked. Eleanor lifted down a large jar from a shelf and took off the lid.

"This is the stuff," she said. They looked at it and sniffed.

"It has a strange smell," said Sonny.

"Yes. Quite a few ingredients go into it, and they don't all smell nice. This has no sap in it. Never again!"

"Can I tell Mother Fulati about this?" asked Sonny. "She would be very interested, and I am sure she would understand about the sap."

"Yes. Tell her. But these things are NOT to be told to other people. Do you understand?"

"Yes Ma'am," said Sonny and Gogo respectfully. "But I wonder, might I tell our King also?"

"Yes. Kings need to know these things. He wouldn't dream of talking about it," she said. "It is such a long time since I met Mother Fulati I do believe we should pay her a visit. Would you tell her we will come to Pongoland in a little while, the three of us? We can't write to each other easily, but tell her April!"

"She will be thrilled!" said Gogo.

"Tell her I will bring her a pot of my ointment," said Madame Eleanor.

"Madame Eleanor," said Sonny, "we heard people call you the Witch of Beldeena. Do you mind being called a witch?"

"Yes I am referred to sometimes as 'the witch'," said Eleanor. "It is meant affectionately by the people of this Island, as much as anything because to say 'Madame Eleanor' is a mouthful! But it isn't incorrect. A white witch works with Nature to perform her healing. She studies to understand Nature, and treats Nature with respect and reverence. In that sense I am a witch. For the white witch the law is 'do no harm'. Any magic I use is the magic hidden within Nature itself. I just harness what is there already for a healing purpose."

"I see yes, thankyou," said Sonny.

The boys returned to the Palace in the late afternoon after a ride around the Island. Sonny and Gogo felt deeply content with their visit to Beldeena, and with their visit to Madame Eleanor.

That evening the King told them that the shepherds did not favour the idea of cross-breeding any of their sheep with Pongoland sheep.

"They say the risk of compromising the purity of both breeds is too great, and this would result in degradation in the quality of their wool," he said.

"That's fine Sir," said Gogo. "We'll take the message back. I hope we will meet you at the Trade Fair."

"Sir," said Sonny tentatively, "we learnt a strange thing today. You know all about it already so we can speak of it. We heard Madame Eleanor's husband is engaged in bartering some of her remedies with people on other Islands, and even taking orders for art-work to be done by Gerard from other Islands. That is very unusual surely?" The King sighed.

"Yes. We are having a problem there. Of course Eleanor's work has always been negociated by me. In return for her services abroad we get vetinary services, for instance, in return. Other things too from different Islands. In return for Gerard's public art works abroad we get construction work done in Beldeena. The negociations there are specific, piece by piece, and I look after it. There are other art exchanges also on a piece by piece basis, individually arranged. All done by me. Then suddenly Madrico starts swapping his wife's remedies for "favours" really. He was distressed because orders for his own art work dropped off as Gerard's work became so popular. So he started trying to promote his own work abroad. He would persuade people to allow him to do a painting where it would be generally visible in return for some general remedies from his wife's cupboard. She, poor lady, didn't want to hurt his feelings even more. He acted on Gerard's behalf too. A portrait done by Gerard if a second portrait was ordered to be done by himself. What could Gerard say? I was waiting a while because I knew what he was doing wouldn't work in the long run. It runs counter to the entire economy of the Islands. In the end he would be sure to realize that himself. It looks as if that moment has come. I will sort it out. I'll try and give him work to do himself. He works very hard in their garden but obviously he needs artistic outlet."

"That's alright then," said Sonny. "I do hope he's soon back on track. We should leave in the morning Sir. We have had a wonderful visit here. Thankyou very much for everything."

The next morning Goggles arrived with Mother Fulati's owl outside the Palace to pick them up. After many goodbyes, and messages of good will to the Royal Family of Pongoland, they finally set off. The King had given them an interesting-looking parcel to deliver to their King and Queen.

The King was over-joyed to hear they were safely home and in good spirits. The boys went first to the Palace to make their report. They told the King and Queen the full story of the ointment laced with a mysterious sap, and the happy outcome. They listened intently, understanding full well the risk Eleanor had taken for her husband. They were very experienced themselves in the snags and pitfalls which lay in the path of all those in places of responsibility. They were the last to judge anyone who tripped on one. They too understood how much was learnt by experience, and sometimes bitter experience. You earned wisdom. It didn't come free. They appreciated also the dilemma faced by the King in handling such a sensitive issue. Such problems were not unusual in the life of a King. The parcel turned out to be a fine painting done by Gerard of a unicorn standing by a forest pool in moonlight. It was breath-takingly beautiful, and the King and Queen gasped with pleasure.

After leaving the Palace they asked Goggles to take them to Mother Fulati's house. Her own owl had gone straight back home so she would know they were coming. She too listened with great interest to the story of the ointment. She was impressed with the cure it had brought about in so severe an injury, and thrilled to be given a jar of it for herself to look at. She said that healing is learnt equally through inherited knowledge, from books, and by experience. Then she took them into the garden to ask,

"And what about her son? What's he like?"

"Amazing! Tall, handsome, and already a renowned artist in their part of the world! Madame Eleanor hints that they will come to Pongoland in April!" said Gogo.

"Ah," said Mother Fulati.

"But where would they live?" asked Sonny. "Gerard is doing so well there. He isn't likely to want to move here. And how would you manage if Selina left you?"

"I would employ somebody good with plants," said Mother Fulati. "We can't arrange other peoples' lives for them. In the future they might choose to make this place their home. Who knows? Things change and you have to let them. After all my own family didn't always live in Pongoland. It is said our remote ancestors lived in Meridoland."

Back in Gogo's house, after registering Mother Fulati's bomb-shell, Sonny and Gogo were happy to relax. The Murgos were just thankful to have them back safe and sound. The long trips, unescorted, had been frightening for them, however much they trusted the owls. No-one had ever forgotten Anton's disappearance. No bird even had ever brought any news. Now, with the three tests successfully completed they too were in a mood to celebrate.

"Goggles needs a day's rest tomorrow," said Murgo, "so you can take Sonny home on Wobbles, Gogo." Wobbles was a deputy to Goggles, to be called on occasionally when needed.

"Now, come along all of you," said Mrs Murgo. "A feast is ready for all you heroes."

Murgo stood up and shook both the boys' hands.

"Well done both of you," he said. "Very well done."

Gogo and Sonny were too embarrassed to speak, but Sonny felt he would remember Murgo's words for the rest of his life, and hoped that for the rest of his life he would be worthy of them.

PART THREE

SONNY FALLS
INTO THE MYSTERY

Chapter One

A Question of One's Wife

Sonny lay in bed early one morning thinking about his life. He was now nearly thirteen years old, and had been in training in Pongoland since his twelfth birthday. He felt strange. Suddenly he was no longer a child. He knew that because he worried about the future.

All he ever used to think about was today, or next week, what he would be doing or where he would be going. Now he realized he had to be somebody, and he had responsibilities. Now he knew a great many people would be affected by his decisions, and he needed them to be wise decisions, good decisions. Now he knew he was alone. His parents could not make his decisions for him. Not even Gogo could do that. Gogo was his best friend. His parents had met Gogo only occasionally, even though Gogo's home in Pongoland was his second home. He belonged there, but he had still several years of schooling to complete, and exams to pass before he could take up his life's work. The King had told him that.

The King of Pongoland, his second father. Sonny rolled over in bed and pulled the duvet over his head. Who was he that he had found himself in this position? Other boys, his friends, had normal lives. They did not think much about the future although they had vague plans about what they wanted to be, an architect, a doctor, a businessman. Normal things.

Sonny had become secretive. His thoughts, his plans, were secrets. You didn't confide, even to your closest friends, that one day you would be a king. Sometimes he wished he could take someone here into his confidence, but he couldn't tell a bit of the truth without betraying the whole story. And no friend could swallow that! His parents knew because they had been there, but they too, outside the home, observed total silence on the subject.

It was Friday morning and tonight Gogo would arrive at his window-sill on the back of Goggles, his owl, and take Sonny back with him to his island in the sky, Pongoland. Sonny's heart lifted at the thought, but at the same time felt heavy. Sometimes he felt he could not endure to live with his thoughts alone. The King had always been a father-figure in his life, but over the last year he had become his mentor and friend. There was nothing he could not say to the King, whereas there were a great many things he could not say to his real father.

He threw back the duvet, at the same time throwing off his mood. His life was this. This was his life, mad and extraordinary as it seemed, and he had to live it. So the first thing on this particular day was to shower. The second thing was breakfast.

He set off at 8.30 as usual to school. His lessons were important. Everyone told him that. He was equipping himself to be the best possible king he could be. Back in Pongoland Gogo and his younger brother Tobo, also went to school, and took their studies very seriously, because they too had responsibilities. Gogo was in training to take over from his father eventually the job of Chief Minister of Pongoland. Tobo was to be a diplomat for the Islands. Toby was still wholly a child, but he understood the part he would play in the life of the Islands. He would travel between the Islands working for good relations between the peoples, and establishing friendships. He would negotiate trade agreements and help to sort out potential disagreements. He must not be found wanting in his knowledge of the history and geography of the Islands and the peoples inhabiting them. His father, Murgo Pongo, trained both his sons in the skills they would need to be in service in Pongoland.

Promptly at 9.00 pm Gogo arrived on Goggles' back, and stepped on to Sonny's window-sill. Unusually for him, Gogo was also a little somber. He stepped over the window-sill into Sonny's room and took him by the hand. Sonny immediately reduced to Gogo's height which was about two feet. Together they climbed on to Goggles back. Sonny's parents did not see him off but they knew he would be going and would return Sunday evening. The two boys rode almost in silence over the tree-tops and under the stars to the archipelago of islands in the sky where Gogo lived. To get there they would pass through from this world's dimension into the dimension of Gogo's world. The Islands could not be seen from this world's dimension, and it was very rare for anyone from the Islands to visit this world. In fact the only people who could come were the King and Murgo's family, and anyone they escorted.

In a little while the Islands came in sight, and the Palace of the King was visible, shining in the rays of the rising sun, at the top of a green hill. Goggles came down to land in the meadow at the foot of the hill. Lots of owls were congregated there having their breakfast, ready to start their day. They were the mode of transport for Pongoland.

Gogo and Sonny slid to the ground and Gogo turned to look at Sonny.

"We have to talk first," he said. "Let's go and sit under the trees for a minute."

The meadow-land merged into forest, and beyond that it was not possible to travel. Gogo led Sonny to a fallen tree to sit on. Sonny was becoming alarmed! Had the King changed his mind? Was he not to succeed as King after All?

"Now don't freak out," said Gogo, "but the King has found you a girl."

"What!" cried Sonny.

"Yes. A girl from Meridoland, a young cousin of Princess Ahoosti, so she is by rank a princess too. You know that there is a very strong tie between Meridoland and Pongoland, and their Kong would really like you to form an alliance with Meridoland. She's a very nice girl though too actually," said Gogo.

"But I'm only twelve! I thought all that would come much later. And I'ld rather pick my own girl!"

"I know. I know. But the King says any moment now you will take a fancy to some girl, and that will be very difficult if she's a girl from your world. I suppose he wants to concentrate your attention."

Sonny sat quietly, grappling with the prospect of this new challenge.

"But what am I supposed to do? Propose?" Sonny boggled.

"No, no, no. Just get to know her. She will spend some time with us and Tobo. Maybe have some adventures with us. That sort of thing," said Gogo.

"And what if I don't take a fancy to her. Or her to me?"

"He'll bring along other girls into your life. This is a start." Gogo in fact looked very awkward.

"But isn't she going to know why she is suddenly thrust upon us? It will be so embarrassing."

"Yes I know. These things are, but that is how relationships tend to be formed here. She's very pretty."

"Right," said Sonny. "Of course she might well not like me. It's a two-way thing after all and I don't have pointy ears. That could really put her off."

"True," said Gogo. "And we can only play it by ear."

"Where is she?" asked Sonny guardedly.

"At the Palace. Anyway you will come home with me for breakfast. We don't have to go straight up there. We will all go together later this morning."

"Suppose she fancies Tobo? He's the most handsome of the three of us," said Sonny.

"Oh I think she would consider Tobo way too young," said Gogo.

The two boys chortled as they climbed up the hill, imagining ridiculous scenarios and enacting Sonny's proposal.

However Mrs. Murgo met them at the gate and Sonny soon realized all this was indeed no joke. She had laid out special clothes for him, and Murgo talked seriously about manners and etiquette. Mrs. Murgo's attitude was more light-hearted, reminding her husband that Saraya was also a child and the children should be left to form their own relationships.

"Saraya," thought Sonny, "pretty name, pretty girl, oh well."

Gogo watched him as he digested the situation, noting that although he was partly horrified about his situation, he was also intrigued. He knew his own turn would come but doubted there would be any girl for him who matched Saraya.

Sonny, always perceptive, noted his sigh.

"Gogo, you know her do you?" he asked.

"Yes, yes I know her. The Merido Royal Family visit here from time to time, and we go there. We've played together quite a lot really."

"O.K."

So that was a factor Sonny realized he would need to handle somehow. In his own world he had held himself aloof from girls, aware that his destiny lay elsewhere. So now, faced with the prospect of meeting a girl who potentially could be his destiny, he had to change gears. Then on top of that he realized that he had to bear in mind secretly that her destiny might well *not* be with him. He too sighed.

"What's the matter?" asked Gogo.

"Gogo, life is about to become much more complicated for us than ever before. Saraya is her own person, and no way shall I assume she's for me, whatever the grown-ups want."

"That is true," said Gogo. "But don't hurt her feelings. She's just a kid. Like you."

"Yeah. Like me," said Sonny wryly, "but do you know what? I don't feel one bit like a kid any longer."

"Nor do I," said Gogo bleakly.

At eleven o'clock the King's carriage arrived to take them all up to the Palace. There was an air of bustle, mixed with a more subtle mood of unease somehow.

The ride up the hillside in the sunshine was charming as always. They passed clay cottages painted in different pastel shades, and higher up past an orchard on their left. Then finally they reached the Palace gates, guarded by two soldiers. How many times they had passed through these gates on one mission or another, or to visit the King and Queen. They had unfortunately no children of their own and for this reason the King had designated Sonny to be his heir. Every Saturday night he stayed at the Palace, and he attended classes in history, geography, and the cultures of the many Islands. They had established a routine now which worked well. Friday night Sonny spent with Gogo who was being trained to be Chief Minister like his father before him.

Today there was an air of formality. The King and Queen stood inside the Palace doors with a Merido lady and gentleman, and their daughter. The Meridos in general had dark curly hair, and the child was indeed pretty. She had been looking down modestly, but glanced up mischievously at Gogo who winked back. Murgo and his wife moved forward to present Sonny, and the child, Saraya, looked at him thoughtfully. He looked back and smiled a bit, but the grown-ups ushered them all into the Palace sitting-room. This was a comfortable informal room off the central hall where visitors met the King or Queen to talk. The four children were given seats together, but were not expected to say much. They were given a fruit-drink each, and then told to go out into the garden.

Outside Gogo, Tobo, and Saraya relaxed. Sonny felt stiff and awkward, and had no idea what to say. Saraya said,

"Why don't we go into the orchard and pick some fruit?" The others agreed and she ran back to beg a basket from the kitchen. Outside the Palace gates they all felt better, and were soon running around looking for fruit which had fallen. Gogo told Saraya about their adventure with the notorious fruit-thieves, the Pelids, whom he and Sonny had scared off with firework. Saraya thought that was very funny, and she remembered the occasion when Ahoosti had lost her coronet. She said she seen Sonny that day. They all fell silent remembering what was really going on here. Sonny, as usual, took control of the situation. He stood up and said,

"Princess Saraya I know what the parents are planning, but I just want to say that all of us children must be clear that in the end we will all make our own choices and decisions. O.K? Don't feel you have to do something so important in your life to please your parents. We will all four of us make our own free choices. Otherwise how could we ever be happy? Agreed?"

The others relaxed, and said, "Agreed!"

Saraya stared at the grass and Gogo glanced at her. Tobo looked at Gogo, and Sonny looked at the Palace.

"The Queen has always been an equal partner with the King," he said. "Good friends. That's how it needs to be if the Island is to be happy."

At that moment Saraya caught sight of a rabbit and ran off after it. It disappeared down one hole while Saraya's foot disappeared down another.

"Ow!" she yelled. The others ran to look at her foot as she sat on the grass.

"I've twisted my ankle," she said. She got up to go but couldn't put much weight on her foot.

"Shall I run and get a stretcher?" asked Tobo.

"No!" cried Saraya. "Let me rest it a bit. It should be alright to walk on in a few minutes. The others sat on the grass beside her while she rubbed her ankle.

"Sorry," she said, "such a nuisance."

Sonny took out his handkerchief and bound it round her ankle firmly to try and prevent any swelling, and she put her foot up on a stone. However in the end Gogo and Tobo supported her back to the Palace. The parents were out looking for them and horrified to see Saraya returning an invalid.

"It was my fault Mummy," she said. "I chased after a rabbit and didn't look where I was putting my feet." The King moved in smoothly with,

"Well I insist you spend the night here to rest your foot." Saraya went crimson. Oh dear. Mrs. Murgo intervened with,

"No, no. Let her come back with us!" She can stay in our house a couple of days, and our owl will take her home on Monday."

The grown-ups' brains were positively zinging as they registered all the possible implications and possibilities. Gogo was also now scarlet with hope, and embarrassment, and Tobo was agitated. Sonny said firmly, having great faith in Mrs. Murgo's tact,

"Yes, surely that is much the better solution. The Palace is too big." Mr. Murgo backed up his wife and Sonny, and so it was arranged. Sonny of course was due to spend the night at the Palace, but the King and Queen, for once disconcerted, were forced to agree.

Gogo shot a surprised look at his friend, but Sonny's face was inscrutable. Tobo flicked a glance at Saraya who smiled faintly. After lunch in the Palace banqueting hall Mr. Murgo's party set off back down the hill in the carriage, while Sonny remained behind in the Palace. Saraya's parents' handsome scarlet and grey birds arrived to take them back to Meridoland, and then the King and Queen and Sonny retired to the sitting-room.

"Well Sonny, what was all that about?" asked the King. When Sonny tried to look puzzled the King said, "You know what I mean."

"I just felt Saraya would be more comfortable there," he said.

"And do you know? I have developed such faith in your instincts I am sure that somehow you are right. That's why I didn't argue. But didn't you feel this was a good opportunity to get to know Saraya better?"

"I don't think things should be rushed," he said. "She will be happier at the Murgos' house."

The King stared at him hard.

"Alright," he said.

Chapter Two

Sorted!

Monday morning, back at home in his own bed, Sonny woke to the realisation that he was indeed past his childhood. He thought back over the many happy times he had had with his parents and grandparents, the parties, the outings, and he thought of his friends, his playmates really, as he still thought of them. He remembered then the countless visits to Pongoland and the adventures he had shared with Gogo and Tobo. He remembered Tobo as he had been a few years ago, so often getting into messes, and as he was now, mature beyond his years, resourceful, intelligent, and loyal.

What about himself? He and Gogo were so close he had hardly thought of him as a separate person, but he was. He had hopes and ambitions, and his own feelings which he did not necessarily share with Sonny. And he also had, as he well knew, had private thoughts, private fears and worries, and in the last year it had been more with the King that he has shared his hidden self.

This must be what was meant by growing up. You started to take responsibility for yourself. His parents were always there for him, but they could not sort out his life for him, as they used to do. Even the King did not try to do that. He had merely set up a training schedule, and he was always there to listen to him.

Now this. Saraya. He had imagined there would be no talk of marriage until he was about seventeen. He wasn't even quite thirteen yet for goodness sake. Saraya was eleven, he discovered. Now suddenly they had been thrust into a complication he had never dreamed of encountering. There was no doubt about it. Gogo had secretly wanted her to be his wife. The very subject was laughable. Wasn't it? No it wasn't. Gogo was growing up faster than the children of his world. He had always known he would succeed as Chief Minister, and his whole life was a preparation for that responsibility. Naturally his parents would want a suitable and supportive wife for him to share the work. And Gogo liked Saraya.

That meant that whatever the King and Queen, or Murgo and Mrs. Murgo, planned there was no way he was going to marry Saraya. Possibly Mrs. Murgo understood and might be his ally, but that was conjecture. She had stepped in instantly to invite Saraya to her house. It made no difference to Sonny after all. He had never even heard of her till this morning.

Sonny mulled over how he was going to play all this. He would have to of course stone-wall the King until the latter got the message that his answer was no. Then he had to signal somehow to Saraya that she need not worry he was going to put a crown on her head. And he had to signal to Gogo........No, not signal, spell out to Gogo that his answer to the King was no. Hopefully that would clear up his relationship with Gogo.

Beyond this broad plan he would have to play it by ear as things developed.

Time to get up. Now he was Sonny, going to school.

The week passed by quietly. Gogo no longer came for him during the week. They were both in senior school, and needed to study and get regular sleep. So it was not until Friday at 9.00 pm that Sonny met Gogo again. He invited him into his bedroom and Gogo took his hand to reduce him to Pongo height. Instead of immediately climbing through the window on to Goggles' back though, Sonny gestured to Gogo to sit on the bed for a minute for a chat.

"This marriage thing," he said, "came as a complete surprise."

"I know," said Gogo, "sorry. It was a surprise to me too. Otherwise I would have warned you."

"And not a happy surprise," said Sonny flatly. Gogo glanced up quickly.

"Didn't you like her?" he asked.

"That's not the point. She seems a nice kid, but I shan't marry her." A light flashed for a second in Gogo's eyes.

"Why ever not?" he asked.

"Well, all sorts of reasons. I do feel that's a choice I have to make for myself as I get a bit older. In my world we still very much kids at thirteen. Then I would have to be absolutely sure that the girl wasn't going to marry me just because her Mum and Dad told her to! But mainly because I think she would be much happier as Mrs. Chief Minister."

Gogo hung his head.

"You'ld noticed of course."

"Couldn't miss it. So I wanted to say before we get mixed up in Pongo affairs again that I shall make it known to the King that he will need to go on looking around. Obviously I am going to need help in the end. I can't do social calls alone around the Islands to look at girls. But I don't want help yet! Too early."

Gogo jumped light-heartedly on to the window-sill.

"Oh great Sonny, honestly. Somehow Saraya and I have had a connection for a long time, and without ever saying anything. I think we just took it for granted that one day I would ask her to be Mrs. Chief Minister."

The two boys clambered happily on to Goggles' back, relieved and cheerful that the little cloud which had gathered over their heads had been dispersed. Together they could easily handle the King and Mr. Murgo Pongo.

As they approached the Island they could see it shining in the morning sun, and landed in the green meadow in time for Goggles' breakfast with the other owls. The owls could actually speak English with their families, and understood what was said to them, but they never usually initiated conversation. They were domesticated birds but had a strong bond of comradeship with each other and to-wit-to-woo was their language of choice. Sonny had gone straight to bed after school and slept till just before 9.00, so he was ready too for the wonderful breakfast Mrs. Murgo always prepared for the family on Saturday morning. In our world it was night and people were going to bed. Sonny caught up on sleep either in the form of naps or early nights.

As Mrs. Murgo served her special omelette with crispy fried rolls and fresh mushrooms everyone talked happily. Sonny glanced at Mr. Murgo who looked back at him. Mr. Murgo winked. Did he? Had his wife enlightened him? Anyway as long as things with Gogo were alright, he could handle everything else.

"What plans today?" he asked.

"Shall we go to the mines?" suggested Gogo. "They've got a batch of apprentices from Tolikland to learn metal-work. Prince Carlos has an idea to import some gold, silver, and copper to do inlaid metal-work in their wood-carving. He has organized his team of carpenters, and cabinet-makers, and is keen to up-grade their skills and products. They are here for six months to learn the basics, and then a couple of our metal-workers will go back with them to get them started."

"Wow! Impressive!" exclaimed Sonny. "So Tolikland is expected to flourish I guess under Carlos."

"Seems like it," said Mr. Murgo. "And they never forget the events of your visit there last year. Prince Carlos is keen for you to meet his workers. He even hopes you might go back there with the Pongos for a visit."

The Islands depended for their economy on trading amongst themselves. Every year a big trade Fair was held on one of the Islands and everyone took their wares to barter at the Fair. Those Islanders who worked hard did well, but a lot depended on the Kings. The Pongo King had always been an industrious and energetic administrator. Everybody was organized, and everybody trained for the tasks. After the Fair the bulk purchases were stored in the Palace to be disbursed gradually over the next year to the peoples of the Island.

People bought things also on an individual basis for their own use or for exchange in the Island market. Every week the Palace store was opened for anyone to come and stock up for personal use, or for exchange in the little local shops. Tolikland's King had become increasingly indolent, and had allowed his Island to slide into penury. His son Carlos was of a different caliber, and on the occasion of a State visit by Sonny and Gogo to Tolikland they had helped avert a coup. The Prince had been set to lock up his father in the Palace, and take over the reins of running the Island himself. Sonny and Gogo were staying at the Palace and they acted as inter-mediaries. The King had finally understood that he needed his son to take over the government of the Island. Since then all sorts of things seemed to have been happening! Sonny was excited to hear this and keen to meet the workers from Tolikland.

Tobo remarked, "You remember Kilti and his tower?"

"Yes?" said Sonny.

"Well now it is the pivot of the Giant Wheel of their fair-ground. They are still in the process of building it. Carlos wanted to honour Kilti by making his contribution to the King's contest the centre piece of the fair. He was the only contributor after all, the only one in the Island with the intiative to get down and do something!"

Gogo burst out laughing. Indeed the whole family had been diverted by the boys' description of Kilti sitting on the grass by his pole, jealously guarding it, and insisting it was a tower. Two kind girls had even set up a little tea-tent close by to serve refreshments to people who came to view it. Now it supported a Giant Wheel and was clearly visible from above to all who flew in from other Islands! The message to the Island was hard work would be rewarded.

The concept had been Sonny's. The Islands had been rife with rumours about a tall pole which had appeared in Tolikland, and the King mod Pongoland had sent Sonny and Gogo to Tolikland to discover what it was, and what it was for! The pole had indeed been the outstanding feature on view as they arrived with Goggles. Later when they had heard the story Sonny started to visualize a purpose for it, and came up with the idea of building a fair-ground. It was to be a tourist attraction to earn revenue. Carlos had never seen a fair, but he was ready to have a go, so Sonny had made sketches of fair-ground equipment common in his own world. He had promised to send Carlos pictures of working fair-grounds. Carlos obviously was not a man to let a good idea fester, and his fair-ground was under construction!

As soon as breakfast was over Goggles, and Wobbles, the Murgo owl, were sent for to take Sonny, Gogo, and Tobo to the mines. They arrived, travelling cross-country, soon after, and landed on a neighbouring hill outside a large cave. The hill was rich in mineral deposits and one of the trades of Pongoland was mining for, gold, silver, and copper. Others were highly skilled workers in crafting the minerals into fine objects, and jewelery. They even made gold and silver thread to be used in the Island's clothing manufacturing shed in beautiful embroidery. Those who wished to become an apprentice could do so from the age of twelve. Now a group of four boys and two girls had arrived from Tolikland to learn the craft. There was a small hostel close by to house apprentices from other Islands.

The boys first went into the cave to say hello to everyone. Work benches were fashioned out of the rocks inside the caves. Inside each cave burned a furnace, above which an exhaust-pipe allowed the fumes to escape into the open air. The children had always loved the caves. Everyone working there was industrious and happy, and the atmosphere was companionable, that is to say usually. Today the atmosphere was a little fraught. On seeing the boys one of the craftsmen came to greet them.

"How are the apprentices getting along?" asked Gogo. The man grimaced a little.

"Not very well so far. These children have no idea of discipline and hard work. Ten minutes of concentration at a time is their limit."

"Tolikland had become very lax. Teaching them even the meaning of work should be a help. That's what we're trying to do. Get them up and running again, " said Gogo.

"Yes, understood," said the man. I am trying to instill a work-culture. To start with I am insisting on half and hour's solid effort, and then five minutes' relaxation. They will observe I hope that no-one else gets five minutes break twice an hour. I'm hoping to stimulate some self-respect."

"Hopefully when they start to actually shape something they will take more interest," said Sonny.

"We'ld better go outside," said Tobo. "We are distracting them."

This was true. The six Toliks had stopped work to watch them.

"It's amazing they learn anything with such poor attention," said Tobo. "Can they read?"

"Just about," said the man, "but they are way behind the average in our Islands."

"Well let's hope with Carlos at the helm everything will tighten up," said Sonny. "It was extraordinary that when their King announced a competition only one person responded. We would all have been as busy as beavers and very excited."

"It's really sad," said Gogo, "but those teenager we met there were pretty keen about their music."

"Yes, I wonder how that is going," said Sonny.

After the visit to the mine, Sonny went straight up to the Palace on Goggles' back. Gogo and Tobo went home, and Sonny would rejoin them after breakfast the next day. Much as he appreciated his day and night at the Palace, and all that he was learning, Sonny was always happy to be back in Murgo's house. Tomorrow, Sunday, he would spend there, but had to get back to his own world for Monday morning in his own world. Today the King called him to his private study for a chat. Sonny had been expecting this and quaked a bit. He took his usual place in the chair opposite the King in front of the fire. The King studied him.

"So how did things go with Saraya?" he asked. "What did you think of her?"

"She seems to be a very nice girl," he said. "Very young."

"Eleven," said the King. "She knows that by that time she is sixteen she will be betrothed. She is a princess. Marriage usually follows two years later."

"So isn't it a bit early to make a choice at eleven?" asked Sonny.

"Not all that early. Until one or the other is sixteen there is informality and flexibility. All the young people mix together and form their own friendships. It is just that they know they are expected to make choices while they are in their teens. With royalty there is less choice because a great deal of responsibility falls on those in high office. In your case there has to be some adult intervention because whoever you choose will be Queen, and she could wreak havoc if she is immature or unwise. The Queen and I are looking for well-bred sensible girls."

"Right," said Sonny.

"And we both feel Saraya fits the bill. Of course if you don't like her so much there is no hurry yet."

"Right," said Sonny. The King watched him.

"What is it Sonny? I know you have reservations. We have to work together on this, and I want you to be happy."

"May I speak privately Sir?"

"Of course."

"Has it occurred to you that she might be happier as Mrs. Chief Minister?"

The King was silent for a minute while he processed what Sonny was saying.

"I.........see, I think. Gogo likes her?

"Yes but that is private. I don't feel therefore that I can possibly think about her for myself, if that suits you Sir?"

"Or even if it doesn't suit me? Alright. Heard and understood. And I imagine you sense also that that would be Saraya's preference?"

"Yes."

"Alright, well thankyou for being so honest about it. For the time being – they are very young - I will place her with Gogo in my mind. His wife also needs to be up to the job. I'm glad we had this little talk."

The next morning when he reached Gogo's house he muttered to Gogo,

"All sorted re the wife thing."

"You mean?"

"Mrs. Chief Minster."

"Great! There's a problem Father wants us to sort out. One of the Tolik kids is playing up. Won't work. Can't sleep. We are all three to go there and look into it."

"OK. Now?"

"Yes. Goggles and Wobbles are waiting for us."

So with a bye-bye to Mrs. Murgo, and apologies they couldn't do any housework just now, but would be back later, they set off. When they reached the mines they left the owls at some distance from the cave entrance, because the noise and the fumes troubled them. Then they approached the cave to find someone to talk to. A gold-metal specialist saw them and came out wiping his hands on a cloth.

"Oh good," he said. "You've come. It's this girl, Lily. She was crying in the night, and won't get up. She says she wants to go home."

"Would there be any problem sending her home if she doesn't like the work?" asked Sonny.

"Only that it would look bad for the whole scheme! You talk to her and see if you can make out what the problem is."

"She's probably just homesick," muttered Gogo.

"Yeah," said Sonny. "Let's see if she has issues at home though."

Chapter Three

A Career Switch

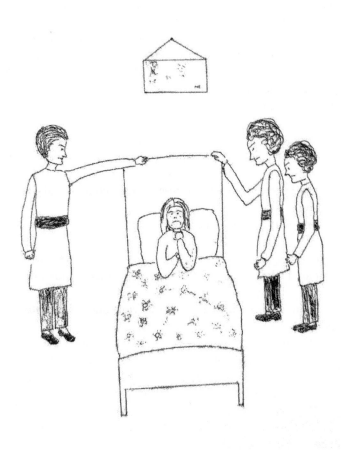

The three boys went further round the hill to where the hostel stood away from the noise and fumes. It was not much more than a large stone cottage with six bedrooms in a row with attached bathroom behind, and a large living-kitchen at one end. A middle-aged couple lived in a cottage close by, and they looked after the apprentices and the hostel.

When Mrs. Macky saw the boys approaching she called them into the kitchen.

"I don't know what is the matter with the lass," she said in despair. "Won't say hardly a word and now won't get out of bed. She wants to go home."

"How does she get on with the other apprentices?" asked Sonny.

"Well she isn't very sociable, but they all seem to be O.K. with each other. And six months isn't a life-time. They are kept busy, as busy as they can be kept, that is to say. They prefer to loaf around. That's Lily's room," she said, pointing to the next to the last room in the row.

They went along to Lily's room, and when she didn't reply, went in anyway. They saw a thin-looking fairish-haired girl lying with her eyes closed, although she peeped as they went in.

"Hello Lily," said Sonny. "What's up?"

"Go away," said Lily.

"In a moment but you are a guest here, and if you aren't happy we are really sorry to hear it," said Sonny. "Has somebody been saying nasty things?"

Lily looked up then to see who they were. She focussed on Sonny and then on Tobo.

"I've seen you before," she said. "You came to Tolikland last year didn't you? You are friends of Prince Carlos."

"Yes that's right," said Sonny. "So naturally we feel responsible to him if you aren't happy here. He would expect us to look after you after all."

"O.K.," she said, sitting up. "I'll tell you, but it's private. Alright?" They nodded.

"Well it's this metal-work training. Carlos wants everyone to pull their weight now in Tolikland, and things are quite exciting. Lots of stuff going on. He asked for six volunteers to come to Pongoland and learn metal-work. My brother really wanted to come but Carlos already had four boys. He wanted another girl and my parents made me offer. They said even if Jem can't come it would be really good for our family if one of us came. So they put my name down and I was selected. I was so

239

angry! Jem is very disappointed, and no way do I want to do metal-work. And Carlos is saying it's all about developing our potential! Look at my fingers!"

She held out her hands to show the scratches she had suffered from the gold wire she had been handling. Sonny, Gogo, and Tobo were all upset.

"This isn't at all what Carlos had in mind!" exclaimed Gogo. "It's ludicrous."

"I know," said Lily. "That's the Toliks all over, excuse my parents. Short cuts."

"Yes," said Sonny, "but all the same the Toliks are making great strides in spite of hiccups. We need to tell someone Lily. This has to stop."

"Yes but who? Your metal-workers are all about commitment and dedication. If I say I don't want to learn their work they will just think me a wuss."

"Prince Carlos of course," said Sonny.

"And how do I tell him?" asked Lily unimpressed.

"Lily would you mind if we talk to our King? The Royal Families have quick access to each other about Island matters. Once our King realizes there has been an error he will send a message to Carlos. We will explain what to say as we were in Tolikland last year and know what is going on there." Lily brightened up.

"Alright then," she said. "He will be cross with my parents, but that's better than both Jem and me failing in the wrong careers."

"What would you *like* to do?" asked Tobo. She looked at Tobo and smiled.

"Do you know, that's the first time anyone has asked me that? I want to be an artist, a painter. I worked hard at school at art and my teacher liked my work, but after I left school that was it. You can't study art in Tolikland."

"Oh I'm really sorry," said Gogo. "We don't have an art school in Pongoland either. Otherwise we would definitely fixed you up."

"You are really nice boys," she smiled. "Thanks. You have cheered men up a lot. I'm sure Prince Carlos will help if he hears what happened."

"I think in the meantime we should ask leave of absence for you for a few days until your hands are better, and perhaps by then we will have news for you from Tolikland."

"Let's ask if she can come to our house," said Tobo. "Mum can put some ointment on her hands and we can show her round Pongoland!"

"Yes!" said Gogo, "and we can take her to talk to the King herself."

"Right," said Sonny, "would you get up and get dressed please Lily while we talk to your manager here? And then we will take you to Gogo's house." Lily was up in a second, suddenly energized and looking hopeful.

"We've taken quite a lot upon ourselves," muttered Gogo as they walked back to the mines. "This training scheme is supposed to be a Pongoland/Tolikland agreement, and our combined ages are what?"

"Yeah," said Sonny, "true. But when has that ever stopped us?"

An hour later at the Murgos' house Mrs. Murgo was bathing Lily's hands and tut-tutting.

"It was my own fault," said Lily. "The other apprentices aren't cut. I suppose I was clumsy because I was so cross."

"Yes," smiled Mrs. Murgo. "Being cross never helps in fine work. Not even in embroidery."

"Mummy works in our embroidery factory," said Tobo. "They also do fine work but with silk or cotton thread."

"Though we also use metal threads from the mines," said Mrs. Murgo. "You can come with me this afternoon if you like and I'll show you while the others talk to the King. We do shift-work according to our own timings as long as we complete our assignments on schedule."

Up at the Palace the King was most concerned to hear about Lily's plight.

"Her parents sound a bit over-bearing don't they? How stupid can you be to send one of your children on the course the other child wanted? Prince Carlos sounds keen to get everyone involved in something. They could have asked him if there was something suitable for Lily." The boys nodded.

"Would you be able to send word to Prince Carlos Sir about Lily?" asked Sonny.

"Yes of course. I will send someone today. Maybe until we get a reply she might like to learn a bit of embroidery, do you think Gogo?'

"Yes I'm sure Mum will be happy to take her along. And that would be another skill to be introduced in Tolikland. They can send a bunch of students to learn that!"

It was in fact a week before the answer came. The boys showed Lily round the Island, and she went to the embroidery factory each afternoon with Mrs. Murgo to be taught a little fine sewing. When news came from

Tolikland the King sent for the three boys and Lily. She was nervous now in case Carlos had been angry, or sent an instruction that she was to complete her metal-work course.

However she need not have worried. As she went into the Palace sitting-room she saw, waiting for her, her brother Jem!

"Jem!" she cried. "You've come! What did Carlos say?"

"He told me to come straight back with the Pongoland messenger! He said Tolikland is trying to develop talent, not force-feed it! He was angry with Mum and Dad though."

"I'm so happy for you Jem," said Lily, hugging him. "This was what you wanted. Am I to go back on our bird now?"

"Wait a minute, wait a minute," said the King. "Let's all sit down and have juice and biscuits, and a talk."

Both the King and Queen were present with Jem and Lily and the boys.

"Now ," said the King. "You remember your visit to Beldeena Island last year Gogo and Sonny? Madame Elaenor?"

"Yes of course Sir," said Gogo. How could we forget?"

"And your remember Gerard her son?"

"Yes Sir," said Gogo.

"Ah," said Sonny. "You mean?"

"Yes I think so don't you?" said the King.

The other young people were puzzled, wondering what the King might be planning.

"Lily," he said, "lastr year Sonny and Gogo had occasion to gp to Beldeena Island. Have you heard of it?"

"Yes Sir," said Lily. "In geography lessons.

"Yes. Well just as we have our wise woman in Pongoland, Mother Fulati, on Beldeena Island they have a similar wise woman called Madame Eleanor. Sonny and Gogo went to meet her, and they also met her son Gerard. Now he is a famous painter in their part of the Archipelago. See that painting?"

The king drew their attention to the wonderful painting on the wall of a unicorn standing by a forest pool in moonlight.

which Gerard had sent to the King and Queen.

"That is an example of his work," said the King.

"It's wonderful," breathed Lily.

"Yes indeed it is. Now the fortunate chance is that Madame Eleanor and her family are due to arrive here next week. The wedding is arranged

242

between Gerard and Mother Fulati's daughter, Selina. Now, if you like the idea Lily, I can introduce you to Gerard, and I will ask if you might go back with the marriage party to Beldeena and be given a course in painting and sculpture."

Lily could hardly believe her ears!

"What? Really? It seems a bit of an imposition doesn't it?

"No, not at all," said the King. "Island relations have been very good for a long time now, but it has come to our notice that in fact all is not well. Some Islands prosper while others are relatively poor. Sometimes the problem is a lack of natural resources. Sometimes the King is incompetent. There are all sorts of factors, but many of us now are trying to initiate a spirit of sharing. The only way this can be done is for flourishing Islands to advise poorer Islands, if they wish, on how to improve their production. Sometimes after sharing an expertise with an Island it can kick-start an industry of its' own, preferably not just like the one of the sharing Island! But complementary to it. We all survive by exchanging produce at the Annual Trade Fair."

"Yes!" exclaimed Lily. "The Spangles from Meridoland are still in Tolikland training our young people in musical skills."

The Spangles were a group of musicians from Meridoland with whom Sonny and Gogo had put Prince Carlos in touch.

"Yes, that sort of thing," said the King. "Beldeena has Gerard who single-handedly boosts their contribution enormously to the Trade Fair every year. In the interests of inter-Island co-operation and development I'm sure he would agree to give you art classes, either himself or one of his apprentices. They have a School of Art now. There was a bit of an upheaval last year, and the upshot was they have this school now, managed by Madame Eleanor's husband Madrico. I'll talk to their King and Gerard, and introduce you."

"Thankyou so much Sir," said Lily."You can't imagine how grateful I am."

"We can take you to meet Mother Fulati," said Tobo. "They have a marvelous house and gardens up in the forests!"

"She'll love to meet you," said the Queen, "but remember she is in the middle of planning a wedding!"

"Yes Ma'am, definitely," said Sonny. "We might be able to help though? Is the banquet to be held in the meadow?"

"Yes, indeed," said the King. "Our Palace caterers are taking care of that."

Goggles and Wobbles and another owl took the three boys and Lily across the hills to the one where Mother Fulati and her daughter Selina lived. The house and gardens were visible from a distance because forest-land had been cleared centuries ago to house the Island's wise woman. The position was hereditary, and no-one could remember the first. Mother Fulato had said once that her family came originally from Meridoland. The clothes worn by her family were different from those worn by the Pongos. Mother Fulati and her daughter wore long full skirts to the ankles with short long-sleeved fitted blouses. Mother Fulati was in the garden as they arrived and when she saw the owls approaching she shaded her eyes and waved. The owls landed as close to the house as they could. The trees were full of small birds, and on one occasion a cat. The arrival of visitors usually caused a commotion which disturbed them.

The four of them were ushered into the kitchen as usual, and as usual Selina had put on the kettle in readiness.

"Shall you have tea or a cold drink?" asked Selina with a smile. She looked very beautiful today in new clothes and with her hair piled up on the back of her head. She wore long dangly ear-rings and gold bangles.

"Hello Selina," said Gogo. "You look smart! We've brought someone to meet you. This is Lily from Tolikland."

The two young women smiled and nodded to each other. Places were laid round the table and one of Mother Fulati's speciality fruit juices was served with scones.

"What brings you to Pongoland Lily?" asked Mother Fulati.

Sonny explained the situation and introduced the subject of possible art classes in Beldeena. Selina looked away, suddenly shy.

"That sounds an excellent idea," said Mother Fulati. "They've got a proper Art School established there now you know? Madrico is the manager and helps out a bit, but they have four student-teachers who are already artists in their own right. Gerard helps and advises and they all produce work for the Island. Gerard himself doesn't teach visiting students because he is busy full-time on his own work. We heard all about it when they came to visit us in the early Winter."

"That's great!" said Gogo. "And Mr. Madrico is now included in the art activity."

"Yes, he is," said Mother Fulati.

"We wondered if the wedding-party from Beldeena might take her back with them to do say a six months course?" said Sonny.

"What about her parents?" asked Mother Fulati.

"Well this is the King's idea. If Madrico is agreeable he will send word to Prince Carlos that Lily is to go straight from here to Beldeena. Carlos will talk to her parents. They are going to be only too pleased!"

"Well it all sounds good to me," said Mother Fulati. "The wedding-party arrives on Wednesday next week. The marriage will be on Saturday. Everyone is invited, it goes without saying. I can speak to Eleanor about it too. They will be thrilled I imagine! A student from Tolikland! All good for the image," she smiled.

Lily was very excited. Mrs. Murgo invited her to stay with them until the wedding, and Lily in the meantime would learn basic embroidery stitches. The King excused Sonny from classes this Saturday so He and Gogo and Tobo walked slowly up the hill behind Murgo's home.

"So we helped with a marriage arrangement!" remarked Sonny. "I never expected ever to do that."

"I know!" said Gogo. "When Gerard came to meet Selina in the Winter they must have clicked!"

"Unlike you and Saraya," said Tobo to Sonny.

"Yes.......well......in my world twelve or thirteen is too young to choose a wife. Usually!" Sonny glanced at Gogo who said nothing.

"Shall we go to the mines to see if Jem is settling in comfortably there?" suggested Tobo They all agreed and Tobo ran back home to call for Goggles and Wobbles.

The owls landed on the grass not far from the largest cave. The boys walked on to the cave opening and peeped in. No-one was there!

"What the.........?" said Sonny as they hurried further inside to look down the passages which led from the cave into the hillside. There wasn't a sound anywhere. The furnace had not been lit.

"Let's ask Mrs. Macky," said Gogo. They went round to the hostel kitchen but no-one was there. The hostel rooms were empty!

"It's Saturday," said Tobo. "Maybe they've all taken a day off?'

"It's possible," said Gogo, "but I don't ever remember them all going on leave together. There are always some workers busy here, sometimes well into the night."

"I don't like it," said Sonny. "Things feel really odd."

They wandered round for a while hoping to see a glimpse of someone somewhere, but everything was very still.

"It's so weird," breathed Gogo.

"Yes," said Sonny. "Do you feel it? It's even sort of difficult to breathe? I feel short of air."

The others agreed.

"I think I'm going to faint!" cried Gogo. He lay down on the grass and closed his eyes, and the next minute the others did the same. Sonny took deep breaths and hoped the strangeness would pass soon, but it didn't and he passed out.

Chapter Four

Sonny, Gogo, and Tobo Fall into Spider 6!

After what seemed to be about five minutes the boys began to wake up. Sonny felt very dizzy and lay still. He heard a moan from Gogo. As soon as he felt steady enough he opened his eyes a little to see what had happened, but all was dark. Was he blind? He called,

"Gogo?"

"Yes?" Gogo mumbled.

"What happened? I can't see!"

"I can't see either but I think somehow it's dark," said Gogo. "We're lying on a stone floor! Where's Tobo?"

"Here," said Tobo. "Were we chloroformed or something? I feel awful. Where are we? I don't recognize this place at all!"

They all peered around in the gloom and as the faintness began to pass off they stood up.

"We must have been brought here wherever we are," said Sonny.

"Daylight is coming from that corner," said Gogo. "Let's see."

They walked cautiously across what they hoped was empty space to the source of the light. The ground was hard and dusty and the air quite stale.

"This looks like maybe a place people have used to hide in," said Sonny. "Obviously it can't be used for storage, but that opening would be easy to defend."

The opening in the corner led through a narrow passage to what looked like outdoors.

"This is a cave then," said Gogo, "but not one used for mining."

"Who could have brought us in her, and why?" exclaimed Sonny. "We were anaesthetized and kidnapped but we aren't locked in!"

"Well I thought I had explored all the caves on our hill, but this is clearly not in use," said Gogo. "Let's go out and find where we are."

"O.K.," said Sonny. "I'll go first."

He slid through the passage, which was about three feet in length, and came out on to the grass. The others followed and they looked around. They were on a hillside at the top of which was an old stone castle.

"We've never been here before," said Gogo, "I don't think. But it's sort of familiar."

"It's like Pongoland," said Tobo.

Sonny just stood, trying to get his bearings. The place was indeed familiar, but it didn't seem to be Pongoland.

"Well let's go up to the castle, and find out where we are. The inhabitants might be hostile since we were brought here unconscious, but we have to find out more. Keep an eye open for anyone."

The castle seemed to have grown out of the earth. The walls were high and thick, and there were slit-windows dotted around. The stone was grey and somber and there were battlements round the top. To their left there was a square tower with a viewing platform about twenty feet above ground level.

"You could see for miles from up there," said Sonny. "Let's see if we can find an entrance."

They walked along the wall towards the tower, and discovered heavy wooden doors with large iron rings nailed into them. Above each ring a large pentagram had been formed from brass studs.

"Shall I knock?" asked Gogo.

"Wait a minute," warned Sonny. "Should we walk round the castle first to see if anyone is around? Whoever put us in that cave might return at any minute."

"Do you think the cave could be linked to the castle, say by a tunnel?" suggested Tobo. "In case of an attack you would expect them to be connected. If so the cave could be used for storage and definitely to hide in. We didn't explore the walls of the cave."

"You're right," said Sonny. "And our captors might be in the castle. Don't you feel all this looks familiar?"

"It might be like a place we have visited for a picnic or something," said Gogo.

They proceeded on round the walls of the castle until the tower appeared again ahead of them.

"O.K.," said Sonny. "So there's just the one entrance. Let's just knock on the door."

They put their ears to a door to listen for signs of activity but could hear nothing Sonny took hold of one of the iron rings and banged it down on the wood a couple of times. They waited for a short while until they heard the sound of a wooden slat being pulled to one side behind the door.

"Who goes there?" boomed a male voice.

"We are three visitors from Pongoland," said Sonny trying to sound authoritative.

"Pongoland?" said the voice. "This is Pongoland!"

"I don't think so Sir," said Sonny bravely. "Are you the person who kidnapped us and brought us here? Pongoland has a palace but no castle."

The door opened wider, and they saw someone who looked like a Pongo but dressed in a red tunic over what looked like chain-mail and loose Pongo trousers. Round his waist was a black sash. He bowed.

"Greetings," he said.

"Greetings," said Sonny. "There seems to be some confusion. We don't know where we are then. We have come from Pongoland definitely, and we are looking for our friends.

"Pray do come inside Sirs," said the guard, if that was what he was. The three of them trooped into the castle, hoping that the inhabitants were not enemies.

"Sir, we are very puzzled. Who lives here?" asked Sonny.

"Why the Knights of the Order of Pongoland," exclaimed the guard. "You must be strangers here."

Sonny, Gogo, and Tobo stared at him speechless.

"Please come this way," said the Knight. "You must be tired from your travels. We are always ready to provide hospitality to those who engaged in pilgrimage."

O.K. There seemed to be nothing else to do but follow him into the large central hall. In the centre was a round table divided by six lines across the diameter into twelve seating places. To the right there was a fire-place piled with logs, and arranged in front of it were four high-backed wooden chairs. The Knight gestured to them to be seated while he brought refreshment. They sat quietly looking meaningfully at each other and presently the man returned with a tray bearing three pewter mugs. They said thankyou and sipped. Mead? In a moment another man appeared from the passage beyond the fire-place. He wore a blue tunic over chain-mail. The boys rose to greet him.

"Well met," said the man. "How may we be of service?"

"Actually Sir, we are looking for our friends, about fifteen of them. They disappeared from the cave where they were working."

"You mean without a trace?" asked the man.

"Yes, without a trace. We thought they might have come up here to the castle," said Sonny.

"No, indeed. You say mines? But they are across the valley on another hill."

"You have mines?" asked Gogo.

"Yes they are quite famous. We produce fine work in copper, lead and silver. Everybody here knows them. Where did you say you come from?"

The man was still courteous but obviously doubtful of their credentials. "You are but children. Where are your parents?"

"At home Sir. In Pongoland," said Sonny, feeling close to tears.

"Now you are mocking me!" said the man, growing angry. "If you were older I would put you in the dungeon until I know more. Someone follows behind you."

"Indeed Sir," said Gogo, "an hour ago we were at home on our own Island of Pongoland. This seems to be another. Somebody drugged us and left us here. When we woke up we found ourselves in the cave down the hill below the castle."

The man rose, said a word to the guard, and left the room. The guard stood watching them. After about ten minutes the Knight returned.

"Please come this way," he said.

The boys rose and followed the Knight down the same passage to a room on the right. Onside there was a golden-yellow carpet with tiny red dragons worked into it. On the right again was a fire-place and a tall-backed arm-chair covered in brown velvet and brocade. A man seated there wore a heavy scarlet embroidered tunic with a black cummerbund and narrow black trousers. He wore no chain-mail. He studied them and asked the Knight to bring forward a sofa standing against the opposite wall. The boys rushed forward to do it themselves. The man by the fire and the Knight watched them.

"They have manners," stated the man by the fire. "Please be seated and explain yourselves."

The Knight withdrew and closed the door behind him.

"Do you know who I am?"

"No Sir," said Sonny. "I'm sorry. We don't even know where we are."

"I am Prince of Pongoland, and I am very interested in your story. You say you were drugged. Who drugged you?"

"We didn't see anyone Sir," said Gogo. "We went to our mines to meet a friend working there, but when we arrived the whole place was empty! There wasn't a soul to be seen! We looked everywhere. The place was deserted. So we sat on the grass for a moment to talk. The next minute we all felt faint and had to lie down. We must have fainted because we passed out. We think now that we had been drugged. When we came to we found ourselves in that cave down your hill. We made our way out through the narrow passage and came up here to your castle. That's all."

"We are lost Sir," said Sonny.

The Prince said nothing for a long while.

"Who is your King?" he asked.

"King Ferdinand Sir," said Sonny.

"Ferdinand!" The Prince began to shake and tears came into his eyes.

"What Century is it?" asked the Prince.

"Why the Century of the Spider Twenty Sir" said Gogo.

"The Century of the Spider Twenty? Here it is the Century of the Spider Six."

They all stared at each other.

"Boys, what are your names please?"

"Sonny, and Tobo, and I am Gogo," said Gogo.

"And what is your lineage?"

"Tobo and I are sons of Murgo Pongo Sir, Chief Minister. This is Sonny from beyond our world. He is heir apparent to King Ferdinand."

"Heir apparent? How is that? Does Ferdinand have no sons?"

"No Sir," said Gogo. "He has adopted Sonny."

"There is a great mystery here," said the Prince. "I will talk with you all later, if I may. Would you do us the honour of dining with us here at six? In the meantime I will ask one of our knights to take you to our mines. You will be interested to see them, and maybe you will get news of your friends. But promise you will not leave this Island before we have talked again."

"Indeed Sir," replied Sonny, smiling to himself inwardly that he was beginning to talk like these people, "we have no power over our journeying. We arrived here by someone else's will. If we return it will be by that same will. We have no power to go of our own volition."

"No. You don't," said the Prince.

The Knight in blue returned to take them to the mines. He said his name was Camlin. When they left the castle he clapped his hands and a flock of four owls appeared. The boys just looked at each other and shook their heads. They were beyond speech. Beyond anything in fact. They climbed on to an owl each and rode cross-country by a journey they recognized to the mines of Pongoland. The owls alighted near the mines and the familiar tap-tapping of small hammers and the crashing of big hammers could be heard. As they entered the largest cave the fire of the furnace was blazing and filling the space with the same smoke, except that the exit shaft was narrower and the atmosphere of the cave more dense. A foreman came forward to greet them.

"These are guests of the Prince," said the Knight. "They would see your work. This is Toplo," the Knight told the boys.

"Toplo!!"

"Yes I expect you have heard of him," said the Knight. "He makes very fine musical instruments. We are very proud of them and we trade them for swords and spears and such things of a heavier metal," said the Knight.

"I think I'm going to faint again," muttered Gogo. Tobo spluttered but managed to change it into a cough.

Now that they had accepted they were somewhere in cuckoo-land, they made the most of it. The work they were shown was indeed fine, but crude in comparison with that of their own mines. The craft had been stream-lined considerably in fourteen centuries The workers responded to their un-feigned interest with pride, and insisted they accept a set of six pewter plates. As they left the cave Sonny said,

"So, we have come back fourteen centuries. Unless of course someone hit us over our heads and we are in three comas."

"I don't have a headache though," said Tobo. "The air was a bit thick in there but that just makes you cough. The Islands are magic Islands after all. We tend to forget that in our daily lives and take things for granted, but the truth is that anything can happen."

"You're right Tobo," said Gogo. "You have put your finger on the truth. Even we have no idea how this can have happened Sonny, but it is to do with the very air of Pongoland."

"So bearing that in mind we should make the most of this and remember all we can. And learn all we can. We are rooted in Pongoland. Or, that is to say, you two are, and our roots will call us back. Not sure about my roots, but if they are anywhere they are here in Pongoland but in the Century of the Spider Twenty."

They climbed on to the backs of the waiting owls and were soon back at the castle. Camlin took the boys back to the Prince's room. He was working on some scrolls on a table near the window.

"Would you like to see these?" he asked. The boys clustered round the scrolls, eager to see the medieval writing first-hand. They were all familiar with the vast collection of scrolls housed in the library of their Palace.

"You will have realized now that you have travelled back in time," said the Prince.

"Yes Sir," said Gogo.

253

"These are what we write on. I am preparing a very special scroll for your King, King Ferdinand. I am making it small so you can keep it tucked it into your waist-band all the time. We don't know when you will disappear from here but I believe you will sooner or later. I believe you are here for a purpose, and I want this scroll to go back with you, and be delivered into the hand of the King. Will you promise me that?"

"Yes Sir," said Gogo. He looked a little tearful, and Sonny thought he must be feeling homesick.

"Now let us dine," said the Prince.

They were taken to the round table in the hall. It was set for eight people. Two more Knights had appeared.

"You will have made the connection here with the stories of King Arthur, known also in your own time," said Camlin. "My name is a derivative of Camelot," he smiled. "The values of the Knights of the Round table we try to emulate. There is no high and low. This table, like the other in Camelot, teaches us that God is eternal and all men are equal. We all sit round the one table."

"Yes Sir," said Gogo.

"Who is your King Sir?" asked Sonny.

"I am Prince Regent Sonny," said the Prince. "I was placed here to rule and establish the ideals of King Arthur, but he is not here."

"That is a very fine concept Sir," said Sonny. "One day I shall have to rule, though that day is far away. The King is training me in kingship, and now I am seeing another example of Arthurian principles in practise."

"And do you have a Lady in readiness?" asked the Prince with a smile. Sonny laughed a bit.

"No, but apparently I am expected to make a choice pretty soon!"

"Not so," said the Prince. "You can not choose your Lady. You have to appear before her as a suitor, one among many. It is for her to make the choice. If she chooses you you will be at her service for the rest of your life."

"Right," said Gogo

"Sir we have a wise woman called Mother Fulati. Last year we paid a visit to Meridoland. Do you have a neighbouring Island called Meridoland?"

The Prince inclined his head.

"The interesting thing was that we were asked to find the Ring of the Dragon's Hair. Their King had lost it. We found it eventually in a Castle in Meridoland owned by Lord Sisko. People there think, and Sisko definitely believes, his castle was built by Merlin. And he thinks he is a descendent of an illegitimate son of King Arthur, by a village woman."

"That is not true," said the Prrince. "King Arthur to our certain knowledge never had a consort in the Islands, and certainly no children. That would have been an event of far-reaching consequences, and could never have been kept secret."

"No, well I think only Sisko believes it," said Gogo. "His gardening boy told us he had been a solitary kid who fantasized a lot."

"But there is another story in Meridoland," said Gogo, "that a Knight of King Arthur visited there and had a daughter by somebody. And she was magic and became the first wise woman. And the story is that her wisdom is passed down through the female line. Once Mother Fulati remarked that her ancestors came originally from Meridoland. So now Sonny and I fantasize that she is a descendent of one of King Arthur's Knights!"

"Well I suppose that could be true," said the Prince.

"But you haven't heard news of it here in the sixth year?" asked Sonny.

"No Sonny I haven't. I have been to Meridoland and have seen the Castle, but the Island is sparsely inhabited as yet. There is an overlord in the Castle, but no King. If there is a young woman living in Meridoland practicing as a wise woman her name is not yet established."

"No of course not," said Gogo.

"You must stay the night here, and if you are still with us in the morning I will show you more of our Pongoland."

"Thankyou Sir," said Sonny.

The boys got up and began to walk towards the door, but Gogo suddenly ran back to the Prince in tears, and started to hug him.

"Lord Anton I remember you!" he cried. "You are from our time! How did you get here?"

Sonny and Tobo watched, transfixed.

"I fell asleep on my owl Gogo, son of Murgo, and I woke up here."

"But you never returned! Why not?"

"I have no means to travel there Gogo. In your time I was to be a diplomat, but here I am establishing good governance. I am to make Pongoland an example for all the Islands. In other words I am civilizing the Islands. As you know in Pongoland the King visits Camelot, the seat of King Arthur. My own teaching comes directly from him. From time to time I go to Tintagel to re-charge my energies. I am taught the precepts of wise government and of good citizenship. I have worked hard to develop industries, and commerce between the Islands, and I have helped newly developing Islands to frame their laws. This is my world."

Gogo clung to him still weeping.

"My parents were devastated by your loss, and the King has never recovered. He too is a good King, the best of all the Kings of the Islands, but he had no son. He lamented that you were not there to a son or daughter to inherit."

"Are we permitted to tell the King about all this?" asked Sonny. "That is to say, if we go back."

"Yes you must tell the King and Queen, and Mr. and Mrs. Murgo, and Mother Fulati and her daughter, but no-one else. If the story is told generally even wilder versions will result!"

Tobo approached him shyly, and took his hand, and Anton bent to kiss him. He buried his face in Anton's tunic.

"You didn't marry anyone here then?" he asked, feeling it was important to return home with a full account of his circumstances.

"No," said Anton, "there was a woman I wanted, but her destiny lies elsewhere."

"O.K." said Gogo doubtfully.

Camlin conducted them upstairs to a bedroom, but not before Anton had given Sonny the scroll for King Ferdinand. He promised to bind it carefully to his waist inside the cummerbund, and keep it there day and night. Then boys were glad to tuck down on their straw mattresses wrapping the blankets they had been given around them warmly. It had indeed been a long hard day!

Chapter Five

And Behold a Mystery

Slowly Sonny opened his eyes. His bed felt hard! What? The sky above him?

"I'm back!" he cried. He looked round and saw that Gogo and Tobo were also back He felt his waist-band. Thank heaven! The scroll was there. What about the metal-workers? He scrambled up and looked towards the cave. The foreman was there and the usual sounds of metal on metal, hammer-hammer, tap-tap. He dare not touch Gogo or Tobo just in case their return was not yet so-to-speak solidified. He ran to the work-shop.

"Where did you all go? We couldn't find you!" he cried.

"What do you mean?" called the man from inside the cave. "We haven't been anywhere. We have a busy work schedule here."

"What time is it?" asked Sonny.

"Just before twelve o'clock. Nearly lunch-time," smiled the foreman.

"Oh it's so good to see you all!" cried Sonny. "Is Jem here?"

"Yes over there," said the man, pointing to a teen-ager hammering lead."

Instead of going to speak to him Sonny went back to find Gogo and Tobo wre waking up. They too were very confused, so Sonny stood watching them quietly.

"Where are we? We're back!" shouted Tobo.

"Oh wow, thank goodness," said Gogo.

"Are the workmen there?" asked Tobo. "Or did they go to ye olde Pongoland too?"

"No they are here and the foreman says they have been working here all morning. I ran to check on them. I didn't argue. We must have had a time-slip? Maybe we couldn't see them when we came because we were already in the slip."

"Whatever, it's good to be back home," said Gogo. "Love it love it." He kissed the grass.

"Me too," said Sonny.

"Have you got the scroll?" asked Tobo.

"Yes, safe and sound," said Sonny patting his tummy.

"We have to go back to the Palace immediately," said Gogo.

They called the owls and scrambled aboard. According to them the boys had just had a sleep. Gogo and Tobo could still ride together on Wobbles. Sonny rode on Goggles. When they reached the Palace they were over-excited but the guard gathered they wanted to see the King and Queen straight away! He showed them into the sitting-room, and asked for fruit-drinks to be served to the disheveled boys.

They had to wait a short while as the King was still in court but eventually he and the Queen arrived concerned and a bit worried.

"What's happened?" cried the King

"Nothing bad Sir. In fact something strange but very good!" said Sonny.

He launched into their story beginning with their intention to call in on Jem. As he continued with the account of their extraordinary journey to a replica Pongoland King Ferdinand looked at them intently. He did not seem unduly incredulous. Did he know about time-slips? All the boys were in agreement about every detail.

"And please prepare yourself Sir for some astonishing news," said Gogo. "The Prince Regent ruling there was your brother Anton! He told us he went back in time just like we did. He fell asleep on his owl and woke up there!"

The King and Queen were speechless. The Queen went and sat on the arm of the King's chair and put her arms round him as he began to weep uncontrollably. The boys waited quietly for the news to sink in, and shed tears of sympathy themselves. The King took out a handkerchief and blew his nose, and wiped his eyes.

"Never in this world could you invent a story like that. Nor would you of course. So I have to realize that my brother is alive and well, but in another dimension. Not this time of space, but of time. Although, having said that, we in the Islands know that everything goes along together at the same time. The theoretical possibility of crossing the circles is always there."

"Prince Anton says he was taken there for a purpose," said Sonny. "His mission was to establish good governance and good citizenship in the Islands. He has developed Pongoland as a sort of template for the other Islands to copy. They travel there on owls as we do, and he visits the other Islands to help them draw up and administer their laws."

"He's not coming back then?" asked the King.

"No. Not as far as he knows Sir. He can't come of his own volition and his own belief is that he belongs there now."

"Has he married?" asked the Queen.

"No Ma'am," said Gogo. "He said there had been a woman he wanted but her destiny lay elsewhere."

"Well, he was always a pilgrim at heart," said the Queen.

"He says King Arthur did *not* have an illegitimate son!" said Gogo, and the others smiled.

"Who was the woman?" asked the King.

"He didn't say Sir, and it wasn't for us to ask him," said Sonny

"Is he happy?" asked the King.

"He seems to be. Lots of work to be done. He goes to Tintagel from time to time, and King Arthur himself has trained him in Arthurian values, and kingship," said Sonny.

"Indeed!" exclaimed the King. "I too have been trained at Camelot, but not directly by King Arthur in this day and age. That must have been wonderful."

"You're quiet Tobo," said the Queen.

"It was a bit upsetting, Ma'am," said Tobo.

"Of *course* darling," she said. "You won't remember Anton here though I imagine?"

"No. I remember the disappearance though, and everyone distraught."

"Yes that was a dreadful time," said the King. "We sent missions everywhere trying to get news of him. He seemed to have vanished into this air, and now we learn that that is precisely what happened. The Islands hold many mysteries, that is to say possess many properties we do not think about in our everyday lives but which can take us by surprise on occasion."

"Sir," said Sonny, taking the scroll out of his belt, " Anton remembers you very much, and asked me to place this in your hands." Sonny gave the King Anton's scroll.

"My heaven," he murmered. "Boys thankyou very much. I would like to look at this alone. Please stay for lunch. It will be in half an hour."

The boys went out into the Palace garden to mooch around for a while. It would be days before they felt normal again.

"That woman," said Gogo, "the one Anton wanted to marry. I think she was the magic woman in Meridoland, the first wise woman of the Islands. Did you notice his face when he spoke of her? And that would have been her "destiny" of course."

"You're leaping in the dark Gogo," said Sonny.

"I don't think so," said Gogo. "They like wise women, those brothers. You must have noticed how the King is about Mother Fulati."

"Gogo! You're making that up!" spluttered Sonny, but Tobo agreed.

"No. It's true Sonny. Mum and Dad know it too," he said.

"Wow," breathed Sonny. "Does the Queen know?"

"She must do," said Gogo. "But they all have serious responsibilities. The Queen is all a Queen should be, kind and wise, and nurturing. Mother Fulati is.........well we know what Mother Fulati is. The point is they each have a different role, and we, the people, come first."

"Supposing the King had said that I must marry Saraya, you mean you would have accepted that, for Pongoland?" asked Sonny.

"Yes of course. I would have been fed up. I'm a child. But I know my duty."

"I think I have aged ten years in the last ten minutes," said Sonny. The brothers laughed.

"You are the kid with the wise head on your shoulders, remember?" teased Tobo. "But you don't know everything."

"That's true. I am the kid here," said Sonny.

"You're human Sonny. We all know you have limitations. What am *I* here for, after all?" said Gogo, puffing out his thin chest as best he could. Sonny landed on top of him, and the next minute the three boys were embroiled in an energetic skirmish on the lawn.

But then the lunch-bell rang and they had to hurry indoors to wash their hands.

The next day, Sunday, the boys decided to go for an early-morning swim in the Island swimming-pool. The pool in the stadium which the King had built was open for children on Sunday with staff around to teach them and watch for their safety. Sonny, Gogo, and Tobo swam and splashed about for a while, and then went to buy ice-creams.

"Yummy yummy," said Tobo.

"Yes all the ordinary things seem so special now don't they," said Gogo. "I don't think they had ice-creams like this in Spider Six. That Pongoland was very bleak. It had nothing! That grim castle was built on the site where our Palace is now. I don't know how Anton can stand it."

"It really was grim wasn't it?" Sonny agreed. "The Island was beautiful of course but there were no comforts or fun things, or not that we could see. It wasn't homey. I'm scared actually that we might get swooped back again." He shivered.

"Let's go and talk to Mother Fulati," said Tobo. "We are allowed to tell her, and she might know something about time travel."

The boys put on their clothes and went down to the meadow to ask Goggles and Wobbles to take them to Mother Fulati's house. How comforted and safe they felt to be in her warm kitchen with glasses of juice.

"What's the matter?" she asked, concerned. She could see something had happened to disturb, and even frighten the boys.

"Sonny started the story and then couldn't stop, pouring it all out in great agitation.

"And now we're frightened we might get sucked back there again!" he cried.

Both Mother Fulati and Selina had listened quietly, taking it all in, and questioning the implications in their minds.

"How could it have happened Mother?" almost wept Gogo.

"I'm not sure," said Mother Fulati, "but there are several portals on this Island, three that is to say. One is up near the caves. It is extremely rare for anything to happen with portals. They are just there. They are like the possibility of a major earthquake in Europe in Sonny's world. There might be rumblings occasionally, but when does the Earth ever crack wide open in France or Germany? In the same way near our portals one can experience odd sensations or intuitions, and tend to avoid them. They feel a bit scary, but I have never known of one actually to open up and taken anyone through. So it seems Anton's owl passed near one the day he disappeared, and yesterday you three. What is very obvious is that these were not random occurrences. They were planned. Anton says himself he was summoned for a task. You went briefly and came back with important news and information."

"Planned?" asked Sonny. "By whom?"

"By the Great Spirit. Who else would have the power?"

"Where are the other portals Mother?" asked Tobo. "We need to keep away from them!"

"I'll tell you Tobo, but I have to say I don't think it will happen again. My guess is that the purpose has been achieved. Anton was summoned to establish a civilization. Ours. You were summoned, and I believe summoned is the word, to go back there and meet him. Anton must have suffered a very great deal, and needed to communicate to his brother and everyone that he is well, and to explain what happened," said Mother Fulati.

"And the energy which does this is the Great Spirit?" asked Sonny. "Who is that?"

"You have been telling me about how Anton received his training from King Arthur. King Arthur's Knights observed a code of chivalry. They had a round table to show that all were equal. All must be trustworthy. They must never murder, never commit treason against their country. Ladies must always be honoured and protected. They must always be merciful. These were teachings Arthur learnt from Merlin who spoke for the Great Spirit. The Great Spirit governs all things even down to the path an ant takes after it leaves its' nest. As long as you understand all things are held together you don't fear. However, of course, that is not to say that what has just happened to you was not terrifying. But do you wish it had not happened?"

"No!" they said together.

"It was a huge experience," said Sonny. "We have learnt so much! I feel I was just a little kid until yesterday. Now I know I am a kid, but the difference is I know it. And above all the King has received a scroll written to him by Anton's own hand. What better thing to have happened than that?"

"So when you feel scared remember the hugely good results which have come about through the trauma. Until the portals have settled down again however it would be wise to avoid them for a few days. I shall visit each one and talk to it," said Mother Fulati.

"Talk to it!" exclaimed Sonny.

"Yes. Each portal has a guardian. I shall communicate with them to find out what has been going on and to ask if we may expect more of the same."

"You can do that?" asked Tobo.

"Yes I shall sit in a trance near each and communicate."

"But supposing one sucked you in?" asked Tobo.

"If I were, there would be a good reason, but I feel I won't," she said with a twinkle.

"You're so brave," breathed Tobo.

"Not brave. You just have to live each day as it is given to you to do, and know there is a plan."

"Where are the other portals Mother?" asked Gogo.

"One is round the other side of the hill from your house Gogo. We don't have occasion to go round there much except for excursions and walks. If you do go you see a little gorge in the hillside. That is one."

"Yes! We go there for picnics sometimes. You've been there Sonny. You remember that family picnic we were on when we caught the thieving Toliks?"

"Oh yes! So we keep away from there. Where is the third Mother?"

"Under the Palace," she said.

"What?"

"Yes you said you found yourselves in a cave near the castle where the Palace is built now. That cave is still there underground and is connected to the Palace by a tunnel to the Palace cellars."

"That is frightening," said Sonny.

"Well nothing untoward has ever happened near the cellars has it? They feel odd sometimes, but that's it," said Mother Fulati.

""You know them then?" asked Gogo.

"Of course! I have even used them occasionally to store fruit when we have had particularly good crops. Apples mainly. It will be good for you boys to stay around home for the rest of the day. By the time you are back next weekend I hope to have sorted it out Sonny."

"But, Mother Fulati," said Sonny, "Anton went back to develop the world he would live in later! How does that work? I mean is he going round in perpetual circles?"

Mother Fulati smiled.

"Hardly," she said. "We have to conclude that in our century of the Spider Twenty he had come to see how his work had turned out. He wasn't a visitor there. He was a visitor here, though he didn't know it at the time, and then he was taken back home to his own century. He didn't seem to be uncomfortable there did he?"

"No. He was at home," said Gogo.

"And when he was born here he was a roamer wasn't he? He could never settle. What was he looking for? Where did he want to arrive on his travels?"

"In the century of the Spider Six," said Gogo. "Does he understand it like that do you think?"

"I'm sure he must do now," said Mother Fulati. "Probably when he first returned, no doubt back to the same point from where he left, he must have been disorientated and puzzled, but then he would have been delighted, don't you think, to realize he had seen the results of his labours?

Back at Gogo's home they were a little somber, and Mrs. Murgo wanted to hear what was the matter. They told Mr. and Mrs. Murgo the story, as Anton had told them they might. They too were not as shocked as Sonny would have expected, and they were ecstatic to hear Anton was safe and well in another dimension! Goggles arrived to take Sonny home for early on Monday morning in his own world. How safe it all felt here with his parents. His own mission in life looked a little less rosy he had to admit. He too would have to face dangers, and loss, as Anton and Ferdinand had had to. But even when he considered peoples' lives in his own world how many people had no problems and difficulties to endure? None that he could think of. Illness or disability were major challenges for human beings, and this was a world in which harmony was difficult to find. The thing which had attracted him most to the Islands was the harmony. The smallest disruptions were felt by everybody and immediately dealt with. In the end the King would sort it out!

He rolled over in his bed and groaned. One day he would have to be that calm and authoritative figure at the top of the hill who could be trusted to heal wounds and solve problems, and keep everyone fed, clothed, and housed! He experienced a few moments of a despair he had never known existed before, until he remembered Gogo and Tobo would be there, and other wise and capable people. He would have to provide the leadership, but how many faithful and good people there would be around him to make things happen! On these contented thoughts he dozed off.

Chapter Six

A Wedding

Selina and Gerard's wedding was to take place the following Saturday in the meadow, and the chief guests would stay in the Palace, including also Sonny. Gerard and his family and the Royal Family of Beldeena would arrive on the Wednesday. Sonny and Gogo looked forward to meeting the young Prince Rick again. He was their age and very good company.

There would be ceremonies of welcome and some festivities in Pongoland, but Sonny wouldn't be there until the Saturday morning. He would go to bed immediately after school at home and sleep in his own bed till as late as possible. Gogo would arrive at 10.00 to take him to Pongoland. The marriage itself was to be at one, and after that there would be a banquet in the meadow.

In the old days when Gogo was believed by Sonny's parents to be a toy Gogo used to spend the weekdays sleeping on Sonny's bed, and then go home for the Pongo day. That meant the two boys could chat every evening and Sonny would be kept up with Pongo news. Now his parents knew the truth and Sonny had grown out of soft toys Gogo remained in Pongoland throughout the week.

Gogo arrived as planned at 10.00, not yet dressed for the wedding, and took Sonny's hand to reduce his height. Then off they went over the tree-tops and under the stars. Even from a distance they could see the big marquee, and the flags and the bunting in the meadow. The alighted after a couple of minutes among a great many excited people! Trestle tables had been arranged as usual at the opposite end of the meadow from the marquee.

"Better get home," said Gogo, so Goggles took them up to the Murgos' house.Mrs. Murgo was very busy as usual, but whereas normally each family of the Island contribute a dish for an Island feast, today all the catering was being done in the Palace kitchen. Selina was not royal, but she and her mother were always counted as part of the King's extended family. Indeed Mother Fulati was known to scold him on occasion.

Mrs. Murgo had laid out Sonny's wedding clothes, and she sent Gogo to his room to get ready. Sonny was to wear silver trousers with a scarlet tunic. There would be no traditional cap on the grounds that basically the younger people thought it looked silly. The waist-band was of scarlet and silver worked together. Gogo's suit was a royal blue tunic with turquoise trousers, and Tobo's tunic was emerald green with dark navy trousers. Mrs. Murgo was very pleased with their appearance, and they felt quite proud of themselves. Again under pressure from the younger end of the popluation wanting to look more, as they felt it, fashionable, the legs of the trousers were narrower than they used to be, and the boys liked that.

The family walked down the hill together to the meadow. Sonny would be announced officially as the King's heir on his thirteenth birthday, but till then he remained just Gogo's friend.

Both the bride's and the groom's families belonged to the mystical line of witches and wizards. Madame Eleanor was even referred to as the Witch of Beldeena behind her back. Madrico, Gerard's father, had weak magical powers which he hardly ever used. Gerard's were relatively strong, but the real power came down through the females of the line. Selina was now a white witch in her own right, gifted and trained in healing, with a profound knowledge of the properties of plants. Mother Fulati's house was surrounded by forest, and very many varieties of herbs and other plants could be found growing there, or cultivated in the garden.

The leaves or flowers or stems would be garnered and prepared to brew or grind into ointments, salves, or syrups to heal whatever ailed the Islanders. Usually a bird would bring a patient to Mother Fulatiu's house, but if the patient was too sick to travel she would do a home visit. In her part of nthe Archipelago she was the only witch, so many of her patients arrived from other Islands. Her remedies were bartered to other Islands in exchange forn household needs. At the Trade fair she supplied a table of assorted brews and dressings to be exchanged for goods native to other Islands.

Sonny, Gogo, and Tobo went off by themselves to see all that there was to see. The main point of interest was the wedding bower. This consisted of a magic circle of grass, mown fine. Fruits and vegetables were arranged around the circle to symbolize fertility and growth. Then there was light fencing around the inner circle laden with flower garlands, wreaths of wood and leaves, and strewn with orange blossom cut fresh that morning. The perfumes were intoxicating. An entrance had been left for the bride and groom to enter the inner circle for the ceremony. The family and relatives would stand around outside the fencing, and beyond them all the friends and guests. They would all join in reciting and chanting the words of the ceremony. Vows would be spoken by the bride and groom. This was the first witch-wedding since Madame Fulati's own, and few could remember Selina's father.

The boys walked round examining all the details. The marriage party had arrived and were making their final preparations in the marquee. The Spangles music groupfrom Meridoland had returned from their visit toTolikland where they had been training those interested in musical skills. They were to perform later after the banquet. Amongst the royal guests would be the King and Queen of Meridoland, and also Lord Sisko.

Sonny and Gogo were looking forward greatly to meeting him again, but lamented that his gardening-boy, Danny, would not be present. The boys had helped the King find a very precious ring he had lost the year before. The search had been one of the three heroic deeds Sonny and Gogo had had to perform as part of their initiation and preparation for their future lives as King and Chief Minister.

After a while two girls emerged from the marquee and stood on either side of the entrance. Each held a pipe and they began to play music. The Kings and Queens attending the wedding, and the families of the bride and groom, processed out and took their places around the outside of the fence. Finally the bride and groom emerged. Gerard wore an olive-green belted tunic over dark-brown leggings. Selina wore a long misty dress blending all the colours of Spring flowers. It was tied in at the waist and as she moved the colours in the full skirt combined and changed. In her left hand she carried a small wand. Her right hand rested on Gerard's arm. On her head she wore a light crown made of flowers tucked into a circle of twig.

"She's the most beautiful bride I have ever seen," breathed Sonny. "Not that I've seen many and they were all in plain white!"

"Everything represents the natural world," said Gogo.

The piping music continued until the bride and groom had entered the inner circle. Taking Selina's right hand in his left Gerard led her slowly round the circle three times. Then the music changed and they walked round the circle another three times. A second time the music changed and they continued round another three times. Those present who knew the words chanted three verses of a hymn in a language the rest could not understand. Then the bride and groom came to a halt in the middle of the circle. Gerard took Selina's hands while she continued to hold the wand. The pipes played low back-ground music while they recited their vows in the same language. Then they placed rings on each others' fingers and kissed. After a moment's quiet there was an outbreak of loud applause.

The music changed to a polka and everyone was invited to join in the dance.

"'Will you dance with me?' – I don't think!" said Gogo.

"Well I can't dance the polka in any case," said Sonny, "though it doesn't look difficult. Just jumping around really. I'm going to sit down."

"I'll find Saraya," said Gogo and off he went. Soon they were to be seen leaping around as uninhibited as the rest."

Sonny smiled to himself. Tobo came to join him.

"I haven't anyone to dance with either," he said.

"Never mind. It'll soon be lunch!" said Sonny. "I missed breakfast somehow."

"Yeah, but this will go on for some time yet. Shall we go and meet Sisko? He's standing over there by the marquee."

" Oh great! Let's!"

They hurried round the wedding circle to the marquee and were happy to see his welcoming smile at the sight of them.

"Hello!" he called. "I hoped to see you. Gogo's dancing. I wanted to say thankyou again for what you did for me last year. I was daft really. I see that now. And you and Gogo were so discreet and kind."

"We were just glad to be helpful," said Sonny, "and we really enjoyed our visit to your castle. It was a happy day. How are you doing now?"

"Very well as it happens," he said, peering into the marquee.

"Maria, would you like to come and meet my friends?"

"Maria!" exclaimed Sonny. "The school-teacher from Maridoland?

How do you do," he said. "Tobo, this is Lord Sisko's friend in Meridoland."

"Danny told us about you but we never met," he said to Maria.

"Hello Tobo," she said. "I'm really happy to meet you all, though I'll meet Gogo later."

She was a slender light blond girl with grey eyes, very pretty.

"And may we invite you to another wedding later this year?" asked Lord Sisko. "Maria and I are to be married in the Summer."

"Wow! That's great news. Thanks. We'ld love to be there."

"Maria is humanising me," smiled Sisko. "I grew into a solitary old bear by myself in that Castle. Now you could almost call me a teddy-bear," he joked.

"Oh you can still growl a bit when you want," smiled Maria, "but you are allowed to do that. I don't want a tame bear!"

They laughed, and Sisko said, "Will you mind if the two of us join the frey?"

"No! You go ahead," said Sonny, and after they had they left,

"Well that's great news," to Tobo. "They got themselves sorted out in the end."

"Yes I remember you telling us that story," said Tobo.

They wandered on until the music stopped. Then the King clapped his hands to announce,

"And now to lunch my friends! Please take your places wherever you like around the tables, and let the feast begin!"

Gogo and Saraya returned to Sonny and Tobo.

"Was that what it looked like?" asked Gogo eagerly, "Sisko and Maria?"

"Yup," said Sonny, "fixed up."

"Oh great. Well let's go and eat," said Gogo, "I'm starving!"

The children took places round one end of a table so that they could chatter easily among themselves. On the Palace side of the meadow a long platform had been placed, and musical instruments arranged on it ready for the concert.

The rest of the day went by joyfully. After lunch Sonny went to collect Rick to join them for the music, as he knew Rick would rather be with them. The Spangles gave the Islands three spritely songs about youth and love, sprinkled with topical references to Island events. After the concert the King announced that the newly-weds and their families would be taken up to the Palace, and when they had left the Royal Families would follow. Everyone else was free to party as they liked. As Selina and Gerard left the meadow Sisko joined Sonny and Gogo.

"May we have a quiet word?" he asked, and drew them to one side. "I wondered if you both might accompany me back to Meridoland? There have been a couple of strange happenings in my Castle. The King and Queen would laugh at me but I need someone else's take on it. You two don't seem to be fazed by anything, so I hoped you might come along and see what you think?"

"Yes of course," said Sonny. "It all sounds very mysterious! We would like Tobo to come along too though if that is alright?"

"But will it do next weekend because I have to go home tomorrow?" Sonny glanced at Gogo.

"Er. Yes that will be fine. I'll send my birds for you, shall we say next Saturday morning?"

"It should be alright," said Sonny. "I just have to clear it with the King, but I think he will let me go."

So it was agreed that Sonny, Gogo, and Tobo would go to Meridoland the following weekend. The boys were very curious, but troubling him Sisko said this was not the time or place to discuss what was

troubling him.

The next day the Beldeena party was to return home. The luggage was packed and ready on Sunday morning. Mother Fulati had spent the night at the Palace, and must now say goodbye to her daughter for a long time. She and Selina had hardly ever been parted, so this was terrible wrench, but this was the time for Selina to move on to the next stage of her life, so there was no point in weeping or wailing, even if it had been in the nature of either woman to do so.

Mother Fulati and Madame Eleanor had spent a wonderful couple of day together in the herb-garden and in the woods, discussing preparations and comparing notes. Madame Eleanor had baskets full of cuttings and seeds to take back with her for her own garden. Madrico had visited the mines and been given beautiful ornaments made of gold and copper.

On the Sunday morning Lily had been taken up to the Palace to join Eleanor and Madrico for the journey to Beldeena. Madrico was delighted to hear that a student all the way from Tolikland was to study in their Art School for six months!

The Murgo family and Sonny were present in the Palace garden for the final goodbyes, and the next thing they were away! As the Beldeena birds disappeared in the distance everyone felt very flat. Other guests were packing up and leaving, and cleaners were removing the wedding furniture from the meadow.

"I shall need to go soon now too," said Sonny to Gogo. "The King says it's OK for me to go to Meridoland next Saturday, so the three of us will go from your house on Meridoland birds."

"It would be fun except that I can't imagine what can be happening now in Lord Sisko's Castle! Strange light over the Castle believed to be emanating from Merlin! Now what!"

"Yeah. Meridoland is the most interesting Island in the Archipelago, as far as I've seen," said Sonny. "Ours is great, but Meridoland never ceases to surprise. The Ring of the Hair of the Dragon for goodness sake!!"

Chapter Seven

Unexpected Gifts

The next Saturday Gogo brought Sonny to his house in time for breakfast with them as usual. Before they had finished two handsome scarlet and grey birds with black beaks alighted in the garden outside.

"They're here," said Mrs. Murgo. "I'll tell them you will be out in a minute.

Ten minutes later the three boys had climbed on to the backs of the birds from Meridoland and were off. These were Lord Sisko's own birds and would take them directly to the Castle. The boys were quite excited. Everybody loved going to Meridoland, and here they were, on some mysterious mission of sorts. What could have happened to induce Lord Sisko to ask for help? Weird.

Meridoland was scenic with rugged mountains and green valleys. The King's Palace stood on one mountain, and some distance away on another mountain stood the grey Castle which belonged to Lord Sisko. Legend had it that Merlin had built it, and that King Arthur had even lived there for a while! The Castle had a court-yard, and the gardening boy Danny, and his mother who worked in the Castle, were often to be seeing pottering around on their various chores. Sisko himself was a keen gardener, and put a lot of hard work into the land he had cultivated outside the Castle. He and Danny therefore had a companionable relationship. Most of their vegetable produce they sold in the local market in the valley.

The first thing Sonny did on alighting from his bird was to call Danny. The boy appeared immediately through the kitchen doorway, grinning from ear to ear.

"Great to see you back!"

"And to be back!" said Gogo. "This is my brother Tobo. We've brought him along this time."

"Good to see you Tobo," said Danny.

272

"How are thing?" asked Gogo.

"Oh way better than when you were here last year," said Danny. "You will have heard Sisko and Maria are engaged?"

"Yes, was that your achievement?" asked Gogo. Danny laughed.

"Not quite, but I helped things along as per Sonny's instructions. In fact I had a fall? In the valley. Twisted my ankle? I asked Maria to bring me home in her cart, and then to support me into the court-yard, and wait with me until Sisko could take over. Naturally Mum offered Maria refreshment, and one thing led to another."

"Good work," said Sonny. "They look really happy. In fact today we are here as Sisko's guests. He wants us to look into something odd. We haven't been told what."

"Oh......," said Danny.

"You know about it?" asked Sonny.

"Part of it, but here he is now."

Lord Sisko came running down the steps from the upper rooms.

"Greetings!" he cried, "so glad you are here. Danny would you ask your Mother to bring us tea, after an hour, up in the library please? Come this way boys."

Instead of taking them upstairs he led them to the top of some steps in one of the towers.

"These lead down into the cellars," he said. "Come this way."

The steps of course went down in a spiral, and the boys felt quite dizzy when they reached the bottom. Dizzy? When had they last felt dizzy? Lord Sisko proceeded along a tunnel leading off from the main cellar. He had brought a torch to light the way.

"We don't come along here much," said Sisko, "in fact hardly ever. A week or so ago though, just before Selina's wedding, I was attracted by an odd sound in this passage, like wind. But these tunnels are not ventilated. Now, look at this."

He stopped and directed his torch to a little niche carved out in the tunnel wall. It didn't look as if it had been used in very many years but it was definitely man-made.

"Have people ever worked around here?" asked Sonny.

"Not that I have heard of," said Sisko. "The cellars have been used for storage, especially in centuries long ago when the people of this Island were under siege, but mostly they are too frightened of getting lost in these tunnels to stray far from the cellars. You see though this niche could have been made to hold a candle?"

"Yes," said Gogo, looking around. "It's very old, very historic, isn't it? We would need a good lamp each to explore how far this tunnel goes."

"Oh it goes on for miles!" said Sisko. "There are whole networks in these hills. In the days when we had wars – you will have heard that the Meridos were at war with the Toliks once – these underground passage-ways must have been invaluable."

"So what happened here?" asked Sonny, cutting to the chase.

"Yes. Well I heard this rushing of wind, so I came along here to investigate. I brought my torch of course, and poked around trying to discover what had happened to cause a draught, and, you will think I am imagining it, but I saw a faint light along the tunnel."

"Ohhhh...creepy!" said Tobo.

"Yes it was, but I felt there had to be a good reason, so I continued along the passage slowly, shining my torch in all directions, and the light got brighter! Eventually I say that it shone directly on to a section of the wall on my left. Come along. I will show you."

They followed him for a couple of minutes until Sisko shone his torch on the wall. There was a loosened stone about five feet above floor level. Sisko pulled at it and it turned out to be quite large. He lifted it to the ground and they could see a hollowed-out space behind where the stone had been fixed. The interior had been pebbled over to preserve the space for storage. The space was about twelve inches high and several feet long extending behind the tunnel wall. After the boys had all examined the space thoroughly Sisko replaced the rock and leaned against the wall.

"Boys, inside there, wrapped in a piece of black velvet cloth there was a ring, a gold ring with a ruby in it. The stone could be opened on a tiny hinge. Inside was a scrap of parchment."

Sonny, Gogo, and Tobo listened to his story spell-bound.

"Was anything written on the parchment?" asked Sonny.

"Yes. I hardly dare tell you, but you boys have been so kind, so compassionate towards me in my follies. It said, 'Sisko, Merlin's Knight'. I've got it upstairs. I tell you I trembled and wept when I read it. Has somebody played a cruel trick on me, knowing my weaknesses? That is of course what I fear. I have not told even Maria about it yet because I fear a trick, but it is so precious to me, so sacred...."

Sonny put his hand on Sisko's arm, and Gogo patted his shoulder.

"This isn't weakness or foolishness Sir," said Sonny. "It is an acknowledgement you deserve." Sisko looked at him humbly.

"No I don't deserve it. You and Danny know how I have deceived myself over the years, and just when I had managed to overcome my fantasies and accept reality this happened. I feel so honoured, but so afraid it is not true. I can't confide this to anyone boys. I haven't told Danny. I pray you will keep my secret until I can find out if is this is a mystical experience or a wicked trick. I believe in mystical energies of course, but you have to use very fine discernment to distinguish the real from the not-real. I wondered if you would be so good as to help me discover where it came from? You were so helpful to the King. Now I need your aid."

"Sir of course we will," said Sonny. "We will sit down and discuss it carefully together, the four of us, and decide what is to be done."

"Thankyou. Just to talk about it is a relief. There is more. Behind the ring, also wrapped in black velvet, there was a staff, about two feet long, of polished wood. The stick is spiraled in design up to a cup at the top. Then a carved snake winds round the cup. The head of the snake rises level with a ruby which has been placed in the cup. The whole thing is exquisite. A staff like that can be expected to have magical powers. Carved into the side of the cup is the letter M."

"Have you ever heard of the existence of these things, or anything like them, anywhere at all in the Islands?" asked Gogo.

"No. It is our Island which is so specifically associated with King Arthur. Most of the Islands have no conscious association at all. Pongoland has an association because Mother Fulati lives there, and she is descended from the first wise woman of her line who lived in Meridoland. The magic had passed down several generations before one ancestor moved to live in Pongoland. We don't know why. It could even have been for the very practical reason that Pongoland is very fertile, and the witches need good earth to grow their herbs."

"May we see the ring and the staff now?" asked Sonny.

"Yes I have hidden them in the library. I have installed new locks in the door and window and they are in the in the safe. Not even Danny or his mother have a key to the library now. I don't suspect them of course but I need to be sure no-one can get hold of a key. Eventually I will house the ring and staff properly but I have to know first that they are mine, or if not, whose?"

Sonny, Gogo, and Tobo were deeply touched by the story, but were very fearful of a dreadful hoax. Could someone have heard the story behind the discovery of the King's ring in Sisko's library, and used it to devise an evil prank? Sonny and Gogo had told not a soul."

Upstairs in the library Sisko opened the locked safe and took out two packages. He laid them on the table carefully and unwrapped the two pieces of black velvet cloth. He let the the ring and the staff lie on their cloths under a light. How incredibly beautiful they were!

"Sir," said Sonny, "an obvious point occurs to me that these must be priceless treasures. Who could possibly have had possession of them and no-one know?"

"And beyond the price, if these are genuine they very probably date back to King Arthur's time," said Gogo. "I have lived with very beautiful metal-work and workmanship all my life, and I can see at a glance that these are genuine works of art. And exceedingly old. Anyone in our mines could tell you that."

"No-one, absolutely no-one, would give you these as a hoax Sir," said Sonny. "Anyone possessing these would prize them beyond anything."

"And who could possibly know about that closet in your tunnel? You didn't know if its' existence yourself until the light shined on it," said Gogo.

"Thankyou, yes, you have already set my mind at rest to a considerable extent," said Sisko. "But we do need to know more."

"I think they are real," breathed Tobo. "I think they are ancient and come from Merlin. I really do. You can feel the sanctity."

"And thanks to you Tobo," said Sisko. "I am so happy you sense that because I do too, but I feared to admit it. How good it is to stand round like this talking sensibly and openly. You are blowing away my mists and cobwebs. Too much isolation isn't good for the imagination. You soon have troubles with reality."

"Did you know Anton Lord Sisko?" asked Sonny suddenly.

"Yes of course. You mean Prince Anton who disappeared? I didn't know him well but he visited Meridoland from time to time. He was fascinated by the Arthurian legends, and came to talk with me about them a couple of times. He asked me to repeat my version of the stories to him and give him my opinion on their authenticity. Well of course I believe Merlin built this Castle, but I think probably the rumour that Arthur lived here for a while is not true. I mean he had more important things to do! Common sense is important. Merlin was only partly of this world and so beyond our conjecture. It is certainly possible a Knight might have been installed here to run things for a while? Just speculating."

"Anton talked to you about all that," said Sonny.

"Yes he did. He was fascinated by the Castle, touching the stone-work almost as if it were alive. I took him all round."

"Did he see the cellars and tunnels?" asked Gogo.

"Yes we went down there together with torches to try and make out how far the tunnels extend. It is too dangerous to go far as it is easy to get disorientated, and next thing you are lost."

"Might he have noticed the closet?" asked Sonny.

"I suppose he could have, but he didn't say anything if he did. We were looking for possible exits. We found traces of numbering here and there, as from some ancient calculations, and a few crude drawings. What are you thinking?" asked Sisko.

"So it is just possible he noticed that loosened stone?" said Sonny. "I think it is time we told you about our recent experiences, don't you Gogo? May we sit down please Lord Sisko?"

"Yes of course! Let's bring those chairs across to the table. I am very intrigued!"

The five of them sat round the table looking at the ring and the staff as Sonny began his and Gogo and Tobo's story.

"Tolikland sent six young people to Pongoland to study metal-work in our caves, four boys and two girls. One of the girls was miserable because she is an artist and had been sent against her will. When the King found out he sent a message to Tolikland, and her brother came instead. The week before the wedding we three went to the mines to see how he was settling in, but there was no-one there! The whole place was deserted! We searched everywhere, and finally sat on the grass to think. We had begun to feel dizzy and then we all passed out."

Sisko listened, fascinated.

"When we came to a little later we found ourselves in a dusty cave, lying on the floor. To cut the story short we made our way out through a short narrow passage and found ourselves on another hillside. At the top of the hill was a castle, not yours, another one, grey with battlements and slit windows and a square tower. We walked round the castle to the door and knocked. It was opend by a sort of Pongo Knight! He wore chain-mail under his tunic. He invited us in and we found the castle was occupied by a contingent of Pongo Knights of King Arthur."

"What!" exclaimed Sisko.

"Yeah. It only gets weirder. Now it is your turn to just take it in. Guess who the Master of the castle was? Anton. He told us he was Prince Regent of Pongoland."

"No!" cried Sisko.

"You bet. He spoke rather archaic English. He told us he had fallen asleep on his owl somewhere and when he woke up he was there in Pongoland of The Century of the Spider Six. Right?"

Sonny gave Sisko a moment to digest this idea.

"The Century of the Spider Six," he repeated.

"That's right," said Sonny. "We had slipped back in time. He is happy there, but in any case has no means of travelling forward again. We were there in total about three or four hours, their time. We had dinner there and went to bed, fell asleep, and woke up back in Spider Twenty again on the hillside outside the mines. The workmen were all there and said they had been there all morning."

"I can't believe it! I do believe it of course. You say it, so it happened. Have you told anyone else?"

"Yes. The King and Queen, Murgo's parents, and Mother Fulati and Selina. Those were the people Anton said we could tell. We are telling you now at our own discretion, because we think he would want us to, but apart from Maria no-one else should be told. You will feel I think, as we do, that there is a link between our adventure and your experience here."

"Right," said Sisko.

"Mother Fulati's belief is that Anton's real home is in Spider Six. In her view it was here where he was the visitor, even though he was born here and grew up here. He was always restless, always a roamer. He calls himself Prince Regent. He says King Arthur installed him in the castle there to establish civilized societies in the Islands based on Arthurian values. That is what he is doing. He travels among the Islands developing stable prosperous societies. In Pongoland they already mine and work copper, silver, and lead. No gold yet. The times don't correlate exactly. Anton didn't seem to have lost time in Six after his time in Twenty."

"Did you talk to him about me then?" asked Sisko.

"We did. We didn't tell him your stuff about the King's ring of course, but in general. He was interested to talk about the association of Merlin and King Arthur with your Castle. He said King Arthur definitely did not have a son in Meridoland! In fact he did not live here, though a Knight did."

278

"Your King must have been stunned! Stunned and joyful," said Sisko.

"Yes he was. Anton sent him a personal parchment-letter written in his own hand. I had to tuck it in my waist-band."

"So you are wondering if he caused these things to be delivered to me in the closet in the tunnel?" asked Sisko.

"It's a possibility isn't it?" said Gogo, "though clearly they are from Merlin. Anton would never have presumed to write those words himself, nor send you this staff without authorization. They are royal, to be awarded by Arthur or Merlin only, and he is merely a Regent."

There was a knock on the door; Danny's mother with the tea. Sisko went to the door to take the tray from her. He wrapped up the ring and the staff carefully and put them back in the safe.

"Myself I think Merlin did not "send" you those things. I think he manifested them for you," said Tobo. "I think they came direct."

"Good boy," said Sisko. "You have a feel for the mystical and I think your sense of it is correct."

As they were leaving Sonny remarked that he had experienced a dizziness in Sisko's cellar akin to their experience before they passed out.

"I wonder if you have a portal to other worlds in you cellar?" he suggested. "Mother Fulati says there are three in Pongoland. She has been checking that they are all closed properly again after our trip."

"I don't know," said Sisko. "You could ask Mother Fulati about that. She will probably know."

"May we bring her here Lord Sisko?" asked Gogo. "You could take her down there to check out the tunnel. And she could attend to anything which needs attention."

"Excellent idea!" said Sisko. "Please tell her about the ring and staff. I would love to hear her take on what happened here!"

Chapter Eight

Mother Fulati Pays a Visit

The next day, on Sunday, Sonny and Gogo and Tobo told Mrs. Murgo that they needed to talk to Mother Fulati, and could they go there after breakfast? She gave them a look but said fine. So they set off with Goggles and Wobbles early morning. Mother Fulati was very glad to see them. She had spent a lonely week and admitted she didn't know yet how she would manage without Selina close by. The boys understood her plight. Always before Selina had been there to greet them. It would be a long time before they got used to her absence.

Mother Fulati however could not help but be diverted by Lord Sisko's story. Coming so soon also after the boys' experience she too felt there seemed to be a connection.

"Would you be willing to go with us next Saturday to take a look maybe in Sisko's cellar yourself, and see the ring and staff," asked Sonny. "I got that dizzy feeling in the cellar like we had near the mine just before we fainted. It was only slight but it was the same kind of thing. He is very keen for you to go. We could be there and back here again quite quickly."

"Well you know, I think I might take the whole day off next Saturday, and do a proper visit to Meridoland. It would cheer me up! But aren't you supposed to study on Saturday mornings Sonny?"

"Yeah....I keep missing. There has been so much going on. I'll have to ask the King again, but the three of you can go if he says no."

"Oh I don't think it will come to that," said Mother Fulati. "What is going on just now is seriously important. You can do a bit of book-reading any time. In any case I can't just leave the Island without consulting him, so I will consult for both of us shall I?"

"Yes please, Mother Fulati," said Sonny. "Do you know if there are any portals in Meridoland? Have you closed our three?"

"Yes I went into trance close to all three, and the guardians checked all three were securely closed. No-one wants anyone slipping through inadvertently, so you are quite safe now. As regards Meridoland that is between me and them. If Lord Sisko has one in his cellar I'll need to tell him first! Now have a glass of fruit-juice with me and let's talk about yesterday."

Reluctantly Sonny returned home for Monday morning at school. The study regime in the Palace had cut down his fun time in Pongoland considerably! During the following week he turned things over in his mind. Now he could feel his roots stretching down into the deeper layers of the Island, even down into past times! And Mother Fulati had remarked, as if everybody knew, that of course all times travel together.

To reach another time-band you just crossed over! Who was he to argue after he had just travelled fourteen centuries back during a brief nap! Or would it be 'across'? And in trance Mother Fulati could speak with the guardian of portals to other worlds. I mean, what other worlds? Other worlds, would that be, apart from the past of the current world? Like his own world existed in a different dimension from that of the Archipelago. He had been a little child when he first visited Pongoland and he hadn't questioned Gogo's abilty to take him from one space zone to another space zone. They just went! That was it! Now he was baffled and amazed by the complexity and immensity of it all.

And who *was* Mother Fulati, actually speaking, that she was at home across the dimensions? Could she, he wondered, travel across them at will? He wished, actually, that he could have had someone like her around himself one day when he was King. In these magic lands you needed someone who had a compass. No chance. At a pinch, he supposed, he could make a trip to Beldeena to consult Selina in a crisis!

He wanted, very badly, to believe that Merlin had seen Sisko's devotion and loyalty and had reached across the centuries to acknowledge him. Sonny knew now that this was not impossible, but he realized that although the prevailing energies of the Archipelago were those of affection and good fellowship, there were also darker forces looking for ways in to destroy the harmony. The unrest in Tolikland had been contained because his own King had recognized that there was always work to be done to see that every person's needs were recognized. He was putting a lot of effort right now into addressing the inequality of living conditions which had developed across the Islands. He must continue that work; always vigilant, never complaisant. He waited impatiently for Friday evening.

Gogo arrived promptly at nine.

"Lots to do this week," he said, once they were away on Goggles' back. "The King says you can go to Meridoland. He feels it is part of your training in kingship to participate in all activities which move things towards harmony. He was surprised Mother Fulati has chosen to go there after all these years of going practically nowhere. I mean ha ha! How do we know what she is up to, if all she has to do is go into trance to communicate with other worlds! But we can't tell him right now what is going on, with Sisko so frightened someone is playing a trick on him. I'm frightened of that too frankly."

"So am I," admitted Sonny.

They rode straight to Mother Fulati's house. Tobo was already there with Wobbles, and Mother Fulati had her own owl. Without further ado the four of them set off. Mother Fulati was actually quite excited by this unlooked-for trip! And very keen to visit Sisko's Castle again. They flew straight to the Castle to allow as much time as possible for Mother Fulati to take soundings there, so to speak. She was anxious to discover what sort of disturbances had occurred there recently.

"We can land in the courtyard," said Sonny. As they approached they could see Danny and his mother watching for them. To have a visit by Mother Fulati was no small occasion! Lord Sisko came out to join them to receive her. He greeted her effusively; almost incoherent in his expressing of the honour he felt that she had taken the trouble to visit his Castle!

"Not at all Lord Sisko," she said. "You know and I know that my distant forebears lived here. The first magic woman of the Islands was established right here by Merlin himself. Mine is the honour. She was to work here, and Anton, as we have now learnt, was the Knight appointed to work from another castle, in Pongoland." Sisko bowed.

"But may I ask, Madame, how you are her descendent if your ancestor lived here, without, as it were, a consort?"

"Who says she had no consort?" exclaimed Mother Fulati. "Now we have also learnt that my male ancestor was Anton! So strange isn't it? I hardly like to point that out to Ferdinand!" she chuckled.

"But Mother Fulati," cried Gogo, "Anton told us himself that he and the woman he wanted, (if we are to suppose that she was the wise woman), had separate destinies!"

"Well that was what he thought when you visited him! But if you were to go again several years later than that, I am sure you would encounter the Lady Anton and several children, of whom one would be a little girl...... who was magic?" Mother Fulati chuckled again, very diverted by the whole story. Lord Sisko, also seeing the humour of the story, laughed heartily.

"But, Madame, please come and take tea, and I will tell you what happened only recently."

He had no wish at this stage to take his guest into his cellar, so they all trooped upstairs to the library, and sat round the table. After refreshments had been served Sisko locked the door, and took the ring and staff out of his safe, each wrapped in its' black velvet cloth. He opened out the two parcels reverently on the table under the light for Mother Fulati to see.

"My!" she said, "What beautiful things. These are very ancient."

"Yes, they do seem to be," said Sisko. "My anxiety is how they got into my cellar. Who could have put them there?"

"And you knew nothing about the little compartment? That was the first time you opened it?"

"No Madame I had never seen it before and I have explored the tunnels on several occasions. Danny has been with me. And I took Anton down there to explore the tunnels. We were looking for possible exits. There is a little niche on the left as you go along that tunnel where a candle can be placed, but I never saw that stone before. It isn't pleasant down there. There is no ventilation normally and it is airless. As soon as I discovered the compartment the rush of air stopped."

"And you saw a light," said Mother Fulati.

"Yes, Ma'am, when I entered the tunnel I could see it distinctly in the distance. It was misty to start with, and as I approached the loose stone it shone more brightly directly on to the wall."

"So the draught beckoned you, and the light showed you."

"Yes Ma'am."

"Well now we have had our tea, may we clear the table except for the ring and the staff? I need to place my hands on them to hear what they are saying."

"Yes Ma'am."

Sisko and the boys put the cups back on the tray near the door. Sisko motioned to the boys to stand quietly away from the table. Mother Fulati took a chair directly under the light and placed one hand on each object. She closed her eyes and didn't move. The boys hardly dare breathe. There was happiness in the room and they would remember this day for the rest of their lives.

"Sisko," she whispered. "I dubb thee Sir Knight. Defend the weak."

A ray of bright light shone down on Sisko's right shoulder, and then on his left. Everyone stood silent and motionless, except for Mother Fulati who seemed to be in deep trance. Then the light withdrew and her eyes flickered. She looked across at Lord Sisko.

"Sir Knight," she said. Even then no-one could speak, until Sisko whispered,

"Did that happen?"

"Indeed it did," said Mother Fulati briskly. "Merlin saw your fealty and has acknowledged it. You did not spend those years in solitude in vain. You need to browse your books now and read all they have to say about the duties of a knight, and live accordingly. Maria will be your lady. However these things are not to be spoken of. This was a mystical dubbing, not a physical one, and mystical things are best kept to oneself. I would advise against any mention of it to your King and Queen here. However I do feel you should tell Ferdinand. In this world Anton was his brother and across the centuries, in a sense, remains so. And Ferdinand has always been a knight in spirit. And you need of course also to tell Maria."

Sonny, Gogo, and Tobo didn't move. This occasion was not theirs. They had been very privileged to be present, but they were observers. Mother Fulati looked at them.

"You are most blessed to have witnessed this, and you all have a future in the service of the Islands. I would ask you never to speak of it, except to each other and the King. And now you may put these treasures back in your safe Sisko. Eventually you will know how to honour them, but for now they can be kept safe here. If you wish I will place a binding spell round your safe to prevent unauthorized people touching it."

"Thankyou Ma'am."

"Now please leave the room while I attend to things here," she said. "Remember to keep it holy. Offer a word of devotion whenever you enter here."

Sisko and the boys left the room and closed the door. They walked to the top of the steps and then waited for Mother Fulati to join them. Ten minutes later she did.

"Well this has been something for us all to remember!" she said. "Every place in our Islands is a holy place, but we rarely take time to remember it. Every bush alight with the one Spirit! Remember it boys." Sonny, Gogo, and Tobo nodded.

"And now," she said, "I wonder if I might look around the Island? And pay my respects to the King and Queen." Sonny said,

"We'll take you on the owls Mother."

"That will be wonderful dear," she said. "Lord Sisko I will leave you now as I know you want time for quietness. Whenever you feel you want to come and talk with me about these things I am always available. You are not alone."

Chapter Nine

Flannon in the News again

Mother Fulati, Sonny, Gogo, and Tobo flew first to the Wishing Well down Hermit's Hill. Mother Fulati remembered the story that Merlin had left it for the people of Meridoland in acknowledgment of his time spent on their Island. Then they went on down into the little town centre, and ordered cold drinks in the Inn which Sonny and Gogo had visited the previous year during their search for the King's Ring of the Dragon's Hair. They greeted the young waitress there who had directed them up Hermit's Hill to the Castle.

Then the owls took them across and up to the little plateau where children played and mothers sat knitting. The view from that spot was good, and they remembered Princess Ahousti's wedding. After that they went up to the Palace to present themselves to the King and Queen. They were overcome that Mother Fulati was visiting their Island and scolded the boys for not bringing her to meet them first. Mother Fulati told them no. She had had business with Lord Sisko to attend to before doing anything else. They insisted that they all stay for lunch, and hopefully overnight?

Mother Fulati thanked them but said she must get back to her work before bed-time. The conversation turned to a discussion of Selina and Gerard's marriage, and the Queen commiserated with Mother Fulati on being separated from her daughter.

"Ahoosti is still living on this Island and yet I miss seeing her here around the Palace," said the Queen.

"Yes," said Mother Fulati, "such relationships are too deep-rooted ever to be forgotten even for a moment. But......we have to live our own lives!"

"That is true," nodded the Queen, "and now we have a little grandson! He is a great joy."

"And he will grow up on this enchanted Island! What better outcome than that?" said Mother Fulati.

Later there was almost a banquet prepared in Mother Fulati's honour, and at six o'clock she declared they must leave.

"Gogo," she said as the owls took off, "would you please drop by my house before you go home?"

"Yes of course," he said.

So the three owls flew straight to her house, and she ushered the boys into her kitchen.

"There is so little time and we need to talk over what happened today now I think. What did you see from where you were standing?"

"We saw you sitting under the light with your hands on the ring and staff," said Gogo. "You had your eyes closed, and after a while you whispered, 'Sisko I dubb thee Sir Knight. Defend the weak.' Then a ray of light shone on Sisko's right shoulder, and then on his left, and then the light went."

"Did you understand that?" asked Mother Fulati.

"Yes Mother," said Sonny. "The light represented the sword normally used for dubbing a man a Knight."

"You understood that this was not a worldly accolade don't you? It was a mystical accolade, but it will have implications for Sisko. At some point he will have choices to make and challenges to meet, and he will remember he is a Knight of King Arthur. That will determine his choices."

"I mean do you believe King Arthur himself has actually selected Sisko to fulfill some commitments?" asked Sonny.

"I do indeed. You have seen for yourselves now that there is no past as we normally understand it. All goes along together. Across the barrier of time King Arthur has chosen Sisko to join him on his quest. Why were you taken back to meet Anton if not to reinforce the reality of the bonds across time?"

"But the Knights of King Arthur were seeking the Holy Grail," said Sonny.

"Indeed. But the meaning of the Holy Grail is individual to each of us. We have to discover what our own is. Originally the Holy Grail was understood to be the Blessed Cup used by Our Lord at the Last Supper when Christ initiated his disciples as fellow-travelers in their journey through this world. The disciples were recruited as members of his band. Each experienced a different fate in life, but they knew they were fellow-members of a band of brothers and sisters."

"So Sisko can expect an upshot from his initiation?" asked Tobo.

"Oh yes. Without a doubt. It will be something costly but he will triumph. His accolade was to ensure he knows that he is engaged in fulfilling his share in the greater cause."

"What cause?" asked Gogo.

"The cause of making love and goodness prevail over selfishness and greed," said Mother Fulati. "But that can involve facing particular risks and dangers for some people. I imagine Lord Sisko is one such soul. We shall see."

The boys sat quietly for a while, thinking about their own futures.

"I suppose my particular challenge is to become King here?" asked Sonny. "I can well imagine that that might mean facing some very difficult situations."

"Well your challenge and my challenge will go hand in hand," comforted Gogo. "And you must admit we have already faced all sorts of challenges, and have had a great time!"

Mother Fulati smiled.

"Yes, I predict that you two will march along cheerfully enough, spreading your good cheer around the Islands."

"What about me?" asked Tobo.

"Your destiny is more solitary dear. Sometimes you will find yourself facing very difficult situations all by yourself. But in the end you will have a help-mate." Tobo looked vague.

"A wife," clarified Gogo.

"Oh, OK," said Tobo.

Sonny's mood when he went to bed that night in his own home was somber. He had begun to realize what being grown up was going to mean. However his buoyant personality soon re-asserted itself. As Gogo said, the problems they had faced had always brought tremendous fun, and Mother Fulati said they would spread good cheer. That was not at all a bad future to look forward to!

He gave his attention to his studies and his parents that week, feeling consciously how each person and each thing counted. Gogo returned at nine on Friday night.

"Hi," said Sonny. "How was your week?"

"So so," said Gogo. "School fine. Home fine. No catastrophes. Almost boring until Vinit turned up."

"What? Vinit? That guy from Flannon who just wanted to be a farmer until fellow Flannonders had other ideas and brought him to Pongoland as Anton's son, and therefore heir to half of Pongoland. That Vinit?"

"Yeah. Him."

"What did he want?"

Gogo sighed. "He wants someone to go to Flannon. Rumour has got round ??? that he is Anton's son, heir to the throne of Pongoland, and entitled to, at the very least, a handsome pension from our King."

"But that was sorted out long ago! It's total nonsense," said Sonny. "His mother told us herself that she married a Scafe man. Her husband is still there. His people got so difficult about him marrying a girl in

Flannon, that in the end Anton took it upon himself to rescue her and her baby from their abuse, and brought her back to Flannon. Who knows what Vinit's Dad is doing in all this, but he lives in Scafe."

"Yeah. But those Flannon chaps haven't given up. Vinit is doing well, but there's still that attitude, he says, in Flannon that other people owe them a living. Vinit says they are close to civil war between those who want to build up Flannon and, with trade, make it self-sufficient, and those who want to live off Pongoland. Things have turned nasty. His Mum is frightened because they are trying to brow-beat her into saying Anton was Vinit's father. She couldn't do that even if she wanted. Our King knows her husband is Tom."

Sonny couldn't believe what he was hearing!

"What does your Dad say?" he asked.

"Vinit came to our house so he's taken him to the Palace. There's a tentative plan to extricate his mother from Flannon, and give both of them, possibly, shelter in the Palace, but Vinit has his farm to run. He says he can't leave it unattended, so he is in Pongoland on a flying visit. Dad is to go there."

"What's the King of Flannon doing? Nothing?"

"Stuck up in his Palace. The ring-leaders have locked him up until he supports their cause."

"Good heavens!"

"Yeah. You and I can't sort this one out."

"But what is Tom doing? Where is he in all this?" asked Sonny.

"Don't know. Mysterious unknown factor. Crucial factor."

"Anyway I expect we will soon hear all about it once your Dad is in Flannon. He had better take care!"

When they got to Gogo's house his father of course wasn't there. His mother said,

"Flannon seems to have grown so bone lazy they just don't want to put any effort into anything! Vinit and others are keen to grow things, manufacture things, and put Flannon on the map, but the rebel party say why bother? Pongoland is wealthy and can easily send them a yearly allowance to support them as they are."

"Golly," said Sonny. "And absolutely no-one actually believes Vinit is Anton's son."

"Well apparently they do! Even if only a handful of young men was involved in Vinit's abduction and have been discredited here, they have gone round Flannon spreading their lies."

"Shall you come up with me to the Palace Gogo?" suggested Sonny. "I'm going for my studies but you could mooch around and find out what people are saying."

"Can I Mum?" he asked.

"Yes, do. I'm worried too."

Wobbles took them both up to the Palace, and they found quite a lot of activity going on. They entered the Palace rather cautiously. Sonny went upstairs to where his tutor would meet him, leaving Gogo to hang around downstairs. In fact he went down to the kitchen, always a hot-bed of gossip. He was greeted warmly by the cooks and staff. They had known him all his life and were perfectly happy to let him sit at the table and nibble things and ask questions.

"So what's happening with Vinit then?" he asked. "I thought all that Flannon stuff had settled, and everyone was going to knuckle down and make Flannon great?" He helped himself to a biscuit.

"Oh those Flannonders are a feckless lot," grumbled the senior cook. "I don't how they managed to produce a good boy like Vinit!"

"Well his father's from Scafe," Gogo remarked.

"Yes so they say, and I can believe it with that brown hair, but what's his father doing letting his wife and kid fend for themselves? They needed protection from those scroungers!"

"Well according to what I heard they had to escape from Scafe because of her in-laws. They wouldn't accept a Flannon girl," said Gogo.

"Yeah we heard something like that," said a boy who was washing up, "but the Scafe people are fine. It must have been just been that family."

"I think the next door's girl was jealous," said Gogo, adding a pinch of spice.

"Not to mention the property Gogo," said the cook. "If Tom had married that girl they could have joined the farms."

"It's a pity Vinit isn't working his father's land on Scafe," said Gogo, tossing out a line. "He should be with his father."

"But he's got his own farm on Flannon from what they are saying here," said another cook. "He won't want to abandon that now will he? He's made a good job of it, and he's employing ten people! Why would he want to go to Scafe when his father's family rejected his mother?"

"I wonder what the King and my Dad are planning," said Gogo.

"They'll sort something out," said the cook.

At that point his father popped his head round the kitchen door.

"What are you doing here Gogo?" he asked.

"I just came to see what's happening," said Gogo. "We were quite friendly with Vinit last time he was here."

"Well you rescued him from the clutches of those gangsters," said his father, "so he remembers you boys very kindly. That's why he came to our house in this crisis."

"Maybe so," said Gogo. "Sonny is upstairs."

"I've asked Vinit to wait in the sitting-room," said Mr. Murgo. "Would you like to join him and see what else you can find out?"

"Right!" said Gogo, bouncing up eagerly. When he entered the sitting-room Vinit looked towards the door anxiously, but smiled when he saw Gogo. He was a good deal taller than he had been the day he was abducted and brought to Pongoland, and had gained a great deal in confidence. He was a young man now.

"Oh good," he said.

"How *is* you Mum Vinit? She must be very frightened," said Gogo.

"Not good. Your King and Dad want her to come here for safety. I must stay there of course."

"Who will go to bring her?" asked Gogo.

"He's already sent a couple of owls to bring her here, so that's a weight off my mind. I'm going back now as soon as possible. They are discussing what is best to be done about our gangsters."

"It sounds as if they have managed to round up quite a lot of support," commented Gogo.

"Too right, silly men. My Dad's in Scafe!"

"Can't he be fetched?" asked Gogo.

"That's what they are talking about now here," said Vinit. "We don't really know what his situation is. He's still married to Mum. They never brought her separation papers to sign."

"Well with nearly half of Flannon thinking you are Anton's son the matter seems urgent!" remarked Gogo.

"Too right, but to be fair more than half of Flannon is not supporting the rebels, but they are just trying to get on with their lives peacefully. The ring-leader of the rebels is called Muffin," said Vinit.

"You're joking!" exclaimed Gogo.

"No. That was his nick-name as a child and it stuck. If it weren't all so dangerous it would be farcical."

"And no-one has been able to talk to your King and Queen?"

"No. They are locked up and guarded," said Vinit. "A couple of thugs with pitch-forks guard the door day and night. The people who want to build up Flannon tend to be the older people who remember better days. They know we can do well if we just put our minds to it, but a lot of their children don't see it that way. My supporters on the whole are not the militant type! The rebels don't remember what a day's work is. They want the benefits of wealth without un-necessary, as they feel it, labour. They think annual donations of gold, silver, and copper items from your mines would give us ample bartering power at the Trade Fair each year. We would be able to bring back all we need in terms of cloth and food supplies to live comfortably. We are not a big Island. Why slog when hand-outs from Pongoland would keep us in all the basic necessities? We would produce a few things of our own, such as woolen garments and grain to purchase the luxury extras. They have no self-respect."

"Is it *just* laziness or is it that they don't believe they are able to achieve a good enough productivity level to make it worth the effort, or what?"

"Both. They grew up in a period of depression, and are used to living from hand to mouth. The parents remember the days before the slump, and my example has encouraged them to get back into a proper routine of work. A lot of the youngsters just want to play football or swim and so on. We have a large lake where they can catch fish, which is something. They need leadership."

"What caused the slump," asked Gogo.

"I think it was a gradual process of over-consumption and under-production. In the end there was nothing to barter with at the Fair. Our Island is very fertile. We can grow anything! But somehow we lacked proper organization. Sad really."

At that moment there was a tap on the door, and a footman told Vinit that the King was asking for him. Gogo, left to himself, thought about the situation. So basically the young Flannonders needed to be rounded up and some sense knocked into their heads, but they also needed a plan, a proper scheme, to get Flannon into production again.

He couldn't sit around here in the sitting-room all morning so he went out into the garden. Several gardeners were at work, as usual, weeding and hoeing. He went over to speak to one of them.

"Hi," he said. "Have you seen Vinit is back from Flannon?"

293

"Yes," said the young man. "There's an uprising in Flannon they say, but everybody knows his father is from Scafe! They can't try that one again."

"It seems everyone in Flannon doesn't know!" said Gogo. "Some people still think Pongoland owes Flannon a pension because "Prince Vinit" lives there!"

"What people will do to try and get out of doing a bit of hard work!" exclaimed the young man whose name was Tony. "See this flower-bed? I've spent the morning weeding it, and am proud of how it looks now. That's what work does for you. It makes you proud of yourself, and worth a good meal."

"Yes you are right. And all over Pongoland our people produce the best quality work, and we are proud of our Island. If an Island does not have strong leadership though, the work falls behind."

"Vinit has leadership skills. We have heard he has built up his farm so well, and now has ten employees!" said Tony.

"True," said Gogo, "he probably has, but he's a bit young yet to organize an Island. No-one would listen to him."

"Then he needs to get his Dad over from Scafe!" said Tony.

Gogo thought a bit. "The problem is no-one has heard from him or of him for years now. No-one seems to have any news of him. And he has never made any effort to contact his wife. We don't know what's going on in Scafe."

"Well Vinit is old enough now to go there himself to look him up, and then take him back to Flannon and show him to everyone!" said Tony.

Chapter Ten

The Solution!

Gogo went back into the Palace. What Tony had said did seem to be the answer. Gogo was keen to find his father to find out what the King's thinking was. He found the King and Mr. Murgo and Vinit standing in the sitting-room.

"Oh, there you are. We were looking for you," said the King.

"I just went into the garden. What are you going to do? Tony says Vinit should go and get his father from Scafe."

"Tony is right," said the King. "We have been discussing the possibility. No-one seems to know what is going on there, and no-one has heard a word from Tom."

"I thought that was because his family don't accept Mum and me," said Vinit.

"Well there is that problem," said the King, "but he has abandoned you for years! Didn't he want to see his wife and child, and look after their needs? We here in Pongoland have hardly spared a thought for Flannon I fear since you and Mona went back. I suppose I just assumed you were farming your land and getting on with your lives."

"We are Sir," said Vinit. "You would be very pleased with all that we have done. The farm is a flourishing concern now. Until recently people left us alone because we are some of the few Flannonders who produce things for the Island. Then some of the children grew up to be teen-agers and wanted more."

"So we are agreed we need to find Tom, I take it," said the King, "but Vinit can't go alone. A party needs to go, and since it can't go with the authority of the King of Flannon it must go with mine. We were discussing who should join the party, Gogo. You and Sonny can go, if you like, for the experience. In any case you need to travel and neither of you has been to Scafe. I thought Jem might go. He has direct experience of what happens on an Island without leadership, so he could be helpful.

295

We will make up his time in the mines. We need one or two able-bodied young men. You Vinit, and how about Tony since he seems to favour this venture? And of course Mr. Murgo to handle negociations. How does that sound?"

Vinit was overcome.

"That will be wonderful Sir," he said. "Naturally the idea of going to find my father has been in my mind, but my mother has always forbidden it. Prince Anton rescued her from those people, and she doesn't want me putting myself in danger as she sees it. And we are proud of course. Why should we seek out a man who has shown no interest in us?"

"Quite," said the King. "Understandable. Now your first task of course is to find Tom, find out where he is living and what he is doing. By Islands law he is still married to Mona, but who knows if his family might not have nullified the marriage unilaterally? You will arrive and he will be confronted with his full-grown son. I cannot believe he won't be thrilled and excited. The end-plan is to persuade him to return with Vinit to Flannon. We are not expecting him to settle down and live there. We need him to declare publicly that Vinit is his son, not Anton's. That is the basic plan. Ideally we need him to help Vinit do something about Flannon. When he sees how much Vinit has already done I think he might be persuaded to rally the Island a bit. He is also a farmer. Flannon has farming land. We need him to show them that what Vinit has achieved can be achieved by everyone. OK?"

"Yes," said Vinit doubtfully. "That sounds great, but our people are quite volatile at the moment."

"Mr. Murgo will go with you," said the King. "He will provide the authority. I would go myself but I can hardly start issuing instructions on another King's Island. Mr. Murgo will make it clear though that unless their Royal Family is released immediately I will arrive with my Royal Guard to release them myself. Once Mr. Murgo is in direct contact with them he will know how to stiffen their spines. They need at the very least to make an appearance. Murgo will help them regain the reins and re-establish order. After that you will have to play it by ear. I'm hoping Tom and Vinit can show the way. You, Sonny and Gogo, can talk to the children a bit. They need good role models, and they need inspiration that you can do anything if you set your mind to it. That sort of thing."

"And worst case scenario they will have learnt once and for all that Pongoland owes them nothing!" remarked Murgo.

"Technically no," agreed the King, "but in the interests of inter-Island co-operation this is a case where a helping hand is in order. Who knows when any of us might not fall on hard times? Complaisancy is never wise."

"Sonny should be here now," said Gogo. "He's still upstairs."

"Well he can finish this morning's work while we start organizing the expedition," said the King.

When Sonny came downstairs he was very excited to hear about the plan and to realize he was included! However he had to secure permission for leave of absence from his parents. Gogo said they could go together to talk to them. They had accepted in principle that Sonny was now in training for a role in life they could never have dreamt of if they had not actually been to Pongoland, seen over the Island and met everyone.

It was agreed the expedition would take place the next day, Sunday, with Vinit's Flannon bird, five Pongo birds to carry passengers, and two more to carry supplies. The arrival of eight foreign birds should create a stir in Scafe!

Gogo and Sonny set off to Sonny's home on the Sunday morning, his time, to talk to his parents. Essentially they wanted at least one, or possibly two, days off school. Gogo took Sonny's hand to restore him to his normal height, and he carried Gogo downstairs. His parents had never quite adjusted to the sight in their world of Gogo as a living breathing person, but they knew by experience that he very much was, and for a day they too had been his height. They knew all about strange things. They listened to Sonny and Gogo's story enthralled. It was not easy to take days off school without a good explanation, and they refused to tell a lie, so they said that if necessary they would tell the school that Sonny had gone on a foreign trip and been unavoidably detained. If the worst came to the worst they would pay the fine. They could see this venture was an important part of his training, and were almost envious!

"You have wonderful parents, Sonny," said Gogo as they set off back to Pongoland.

"I know. I really do," he said.

When they got back to Pongoland it was time for bed there. Packing had been done, and a couple of bags were standing ready in the meadow on a sheet for two birds to carry between them. Tony was thrilled to be going with them. He could hardly believe his luck.

Scafe was not too far from Flannon. It was a prosperous Island because it combined good green farming land with a couple of hills rich in copper and tin. They too had mines, and produced mainly utensils, but also fine decorative vases, plates, and cups. Murgo said they should go first to the Palace and talk to the King, so the birds took them straight to the Palace courtyard where they alighted before two astonished sentries. One ran inside to inform the King that a large party had arrived from Pongoland. He was in his office and merely asked that they be brought up to him. He also ordered that refreshments should be served straight away.

As Murgo entered the room first he immediately commanded attention, and the King stood up to greet him. Murgo introduced everyone, and they were invited to sit down. The room was sparsely but elegantly furnished, and they took seats which were set round the table.

"So, to what do we owe the pleasure?" asked the King.

"I think you will begin to understand Sir when I tell you that this is Vinit, son of Tom of your Island, and Mona of Flannon."

Murgo was not prepared for the stupefied expression on the King's face.

"Vinit!" he exclaimed. "But Vinit was lost, along with his mother, years ago! How can this be he?"

"Ah," said Murgo. "So you have never had news from Flannon that they returned back there to live on his mother's Island? You may remember a serious family dispute when Tom brought back a Flannon bride? Tom's family had planned for him to marry the girl next door so that the two properties could be merged. Mona was never accepted, and after Vinit was born they tried to send her away and leave Vinit here. Things got nasty. Mona was very much afraid, and Prince Anton took it upon himself to rescue her. He happened to be here in the course of his travels, so he just picked them up and took them both back to Flannon. There he secured a piece of land for her to set up as a farm. So Vinit grew up there, a successful farmer."

"Really!" exclaimed the King. "How extraordinary! But why were we not told?"

"At the time Mona was afraid of being pursued. I would imagine Anton must have intended to tell Tom where his family was, but Anton himself was lost. He set off on his bird, a Scafe bird he had borrowed I believe, and just disappeared around the same time."

"Yes I remember Anton of course, and we heard of his sad loss, but I never connected him with Mona's disappearance. Her own bird was here! He was always a chivalrous young man. He could not have resisted helping a lady in distress I suppose. So he took Mona and Vinit! Well my my! Good heavens, but Tom thinks they are both dead!"

"That might well be so," said Gogo, "but his parents knew Anton had taken them."

"And let Tom believe his family was dead? How iniquitous is that! But Vinit, do you wish to return here now?" asked the King.

"No Sir. I am well-established in Flannon, and we are doing very well. There is another problem. I was presented by some of our crooks at the Trade Fair, when it was last held in Pongoland, as Prince Anton's son. This was with a view to claiming a pension from their King, including back-pay, since the day Prince Anton disappeared. Without evidence those young men hatched a plot to persuade the King of Pongoland that I was his long lost nephew and heir to his throne. My mother was help prisoner in Flannon in the meanwhile."

"I do remember that incident in Pongoland," said the King of Scape. "We left that evening so I never heard what the upshot was. Of course it was a preposterous story. If Prince Anton had married it would have been to a princess, or someone with royal connections, and the marriage would have been attended by all the royal families. He was the soul of honour. Most people assumed they were a bunch of cranks and the King of Pongoland would deal with them."

"Which he did," said Vinit. "I went home, and Mum and I set to work to build up our farm to be the finest in Flannon, which actually Sir is not saying much in our troubled times. A lot of the Flannonders are seriously indolent these days, and I want to get things going on our Island. What my mother and I have done everyone can do if they are prepared to work. I want everyone to pull his weight so that we can get our economy kick-started, but too many people are used to doing nothing, and prefer to keep it that way. So.....they have resurrected the story that I am Prince Vinit, rightful heir to Pongoland. They have led an uprising demanding that Pongoland pay Flannon our rightful dues. The King and Queen are locked in the Palace under guard, and there is fighting in the streets."

"Oh my heaven!" exclaimed the King. "No news of that had reached us! It must be dealt with immediately!"

"Thankyou Sir," said Vinit, "your aid would be most welcome. My own more humble plan was to find my father and persuade him to come back with me to Flannon. I need him to declare publicly that I am his son. Then I did hope, if he would be willing, that he might stay on there a little while to help me wake up my fellow-islanders. We need them to rise up, not to fight against each other, but to realise they need to work to support themselves. They very much need strong leadership. Our King is a nice man, but quiet and retiring. He has no idea at all how to rally the Island and energize people to do something constructive."

"Yes," said the King. "That is a flaw in our Island system. So much depends on the temperament and personality of the King. I will ask someone to escort you to Tom's farm. I may say he has not re-married. If you need help please send my man back to me to let me know."

They left the Palace and a senior official was deputed to escort them to Tom's farm. The flight was not long, and they descended into a field. After they had dismounted the courtier led them to a wooden-built farm with a cobbled farm. All was very clean and neat and in good repair. The lady in the house saw them through the window and came to the door. She looked at Vinit and opened her mouth to scream. No voice came out so they all stood transfixed.

"Do you recognize this young man Madame?" asked Murgo.

"Is it? He can't be! He's the image of Tom when he was a young man!" she exclaimed. She wore a pink checked blouse and full-length brown skirt. Her hair was brown and tied up in a pony-tail.

"Is Tom around Madame? It is with him that we need to speak," said Gogo.

"Tom!" she called, and rushed back into the house. In a few moments a middle-aged man in working clothes appeared at the door. He wore a thigh-length green shirt over brown trousers. He too had long bown hair tied at the nape of the neck. He saw Vinit immediately and couldn't speak. He just stared.

"Is this?......"

"Yes Sir," said Murgo, "this is Vinit aged eighteen."

"But we thought you were both lost that night somewhere in limbo! Mona fled from the cruelty she had experienced here, taking baby Vinit with her, and they were lost! Anton was lost too about the same time. You were all lost!"

"No Sir. Anton took us to Flannon and left us there. Then possibly on his return journey to Scape his bird went down. No-one knows, but probably he was returning to tell you where we were. Anton had fixed up with the King for us to have some farmland, and we have lived there ever since."

"But why did Mona never send word?"

"Because of the threat from your neighbours Sir," said Vinit. "She believed I needed to be kept safe."

"Threats?"

"Oh yes Sir. They were very nasty because you married her instead of their daughter, and I would have got the farm in the end. I'm sorry, did you re-marry?" he asked, looking at the lady. "The King said not."

"No no. This is Anita, my younger sister, your Aunt." He stepped forward and embraced Vinit long and hard, and Anita wept.

"Please come inside," he said to the waiting group, and they all trouped inside into Anita's large kitchen.

"After Mona left I invited my sister, and her husband Dennis, to join me here," he explained. "You have a young cousin, Bunny, we call her, aged twelve. She is already keen to work on the farm."

They all sat down and Tom went out to call Dennis back to the house. When he returned Vinit said,

"It seems we are all farmers in our hearts. Our own in Flannon is doing well."

"So you have fared well, son," said Tom.

"Very well indeed Sir," said Vinit. "I hope you will be proud. Mother and I have worked together and we have ten employees now!"

At that moment Dennis appeared, followed closely by his daughter, Bunny. She wore a long flowered dress tied at the waist. They stood still at the door, trying to take in the scene. It wasn't every day you saw a King's courtier sitting in your kitchen, apart from everyone else.

"Dennis," said Tom. "Vinit is back. Grown up into a young man can you believe? Anton took them to Flannon and it was in his way back, probably, he disappeared. But he had left Mona and Vinit safe and sound in Flannon with their own farm!"

"Well!" exclaimed Dennis. "This is the best possible news in the whole world! Where is Mona? How is she?" Bunny stared at Vinit curiously.

"She's at home in Flannon. We are very well set up there, and I at least shall remain there. A bit of trouble has brewed up though, so I went to the King of Pongoland to consult him."

"Oh? What trouble?"

"You would hardly believe it, it's so ridiculous," said Vinit. "A section of our great islanders decided that rather than work for their living like respectable folk, they would prefer a pension from Pongoland, what with me being their King's nephew and all, heir to the throne."

"But why on earth would they think that!" exclaimed Dennis. Tom was stupefied.

"If you had been at the Trade Fair in Pongoland you would have seen me all dressed up like a prince and paraded on the stage. Prince Vinit! I was long lost Anton's son, and deserved at least a pension, with back-pay. The King had them arrested and it was soon over. They had held Mum prisoner in Flannon though, to keep her quiet. The good thing was that while they were all sorting things out Sonny and Gogo showed me round Pongoland, and I got to see what a well-run Island looks like. So I was inspired to make our farm like farms in Pongoland. Flannon earth is good. No reason why not."

"I missed that," said Tom. "Most of the people of the Island don't go to Trade Fairs. We send our produce all together. Representatives order in bulk to bring back here. I didn't even remember hearing about that nonsense."

"No, well it was dealt with in Pongoland and your King just treated it as some sort of gangsterism."

"The King of Flannon was very embarrassed," said Murgo.

"So the request is Tom that you come back to Flannon with us and announce loud and clear that Vinit is your son," said Murgo. "Those youngsters, and everybody else, need to see you to put an end to the story. Half the population is trying to copy Vinit's example and make a go of the Island, but there is still this stiff resistance."

"And…….Dad…..," said Vinit, "I need you to help me get them started with good farming practices. They have no leadership, and I can't do it alone. You wouldn't have to stay there long. You have your own farm here to attend to here I know, but say for a few months?"

"Presumably there are farms in existence? That is, proper demarcated farms?" asked Tom.

"Yes Sir," said Vinit, "but the farmers need to be taught the basics again. What to plant, where to plant, how to process. And we have a lot of sheep. That side of it goes much better, but they could use advice."

"Go Tom," said Dennis. "Vinit's and Flannon's need is greater than ours. We can hire someone for a few months.

"Not to mention Mum," said Vinit quietly, "but that is yours and her business."

Chapter Eleven

A New Beginning!

By now tea and cake and scones had been set on the kitchen table, and they all sat round discussing plans and options freely amongst themselves. Sonny did not say much but he felt privileged to be here at hopefully the rebirth of Flannon. In between the serious talk Vinit introduced himself to his young cousin Bunny. She gazed at him, enthralled to discover she had a fine grown-up cousin who was already a farmer!

Eventually Murgo said, "Well thankyou everyone. Your King, Tom, has asked me to take you back to the Palace to tell him what we plan to do, and I think it is time to take our leave now."

"Indeed I will go to the Palace, but would you tell him I will come in a short while please? I can't go in these working clothes, nor go to Flannon in them. You could tell him that if he is agreeable I would like to go along there with your party, and do what I can. Of course my own first wish is to meet my wife. I am grieved to hear about all the sadness and fear she has had to endure, but proud to see how well she has succeeded in bringing up our son single-handedly, and presenting her Island with a fully trained farmer! Of course I shan't interfere in what you are both doing there Vinit. Mona and I will have to sort ourselves out and decide on our future, but that is a different story."

The upshot was that with a modest bag of personal luggage, packed for him by his sister, he joined the party that afternoon on their onward journey to Flannon. Sonny and Gogo were a little apprehensive about this visit. Neither of them was used to violence of any sort. However Vinit asked them to remain at his house with Mona while he went with Murgo, Tom, Jem, and Tony to the Palace. They took along their own pitch-forks, but Murgo warned them against actually using them, unless he directed them to do so. Murgo hoped that the sight of him, with all that that implied from Pongoland, should be enough to make the two guards open the door.

Sonny and Gogo greeted Mona joyfully, and she hurried them into her welcoming house. She said she wanted to hear all their news from Pongoland. She had such happy memories of her visit there. Murgo, Tom, and the three young men continued on to the Palace. As expected the two guards wilted at the sight of them, and ran off home! So much for the Revolution, thought Murgo. In the Palace they had a long talk with the King and Queen. Murgo did not mince words while pointing out to them that it was entirely due to their apathy that the current state of affairs had come about in Flannon. Did they not see that teenagers need something to do? Challenges? Activities? Rewards for effort? They should never have been left wandering around aimless. The King had been profoundly shocked by the uprising and saw he had been very lax.

"I failed them so badly," he lamented.

"Well Sir," said Murgo, "we have a plan, if you are willing. We hoped you might appoint Tom here as temporary Chief Minister, working directly under your authority. Give him charge of restoring law and order in the Island, and authorize him to go round to each farm in turn. He will look round each one and assess the situation. He will advise on overhaul, future management, choice of crops and where to plant them, equipment, and all that pertains to running a modern efficient farm. He will tell you what supplies to order in for the Island. I believe that Pongoland and Scafe will provide you with whatever is lacking to get the Island on its feet again."

"Oh! Indeed I would be most grateful!" said the King.

"Tom has his own farm and life on Scafe," said Murgo, "and he will want to get back to them after he has helped you here, so you will need to consider who to appoint Chief Minister in his place later. Vinit might be a choice. As regards authority and decisions you need only show the Island that Tom is acting on your behalf. Tom will see to the rest. In spite of the rebels a lot of people here love Flannon and really want it to succeed."

The King promised to issue a proclamation that a) Tom was Vinit's father, and, b) he was appointed Chief Minister to re-vitalise the economy of Flannon. Co-operation with his advice was deemed essential to the welfare of the Island, and c) Chief Minister Murgo Pongo himself had been directed by the King of Pongoland to come to their Island and help facilitate their efforts. This was of course a veiled threat against non-cooperation. That seemed to cover all corners.

The King had never said such things in his life, but one look at Tom's formidable expression nerved him to the task. Murgo drafted out his lines for him. It was Tom who actually appeared in the town-centre to read the Proclamation. The news that he had reappeared brought everyone rushing from their houses to see him for themselves. The "rebels" mooched around sulkily, but they did start to brighten up when Tom began to outline his plans for their Island. It actually sounded quite exciting! At last something was happening, and it looked as if everyone was going to be involved! There was even a rumour going round that they were going to build a sports centre like the one in Pongoland! Sonny suggested vaguely that maybe there could be joint Annual Sports Competitions between competitors form the two Islands. He had muttered these speculations rather loudly here and there in the town centre, and hoped fervently that his own King would support such as scheme!

Murgo, Sonny, Gogo, Jem, and Tony stayed overnight at the Palace in Flannon, and the next morning flew back to Pongoland. The owls took them straight to the Palace to give the King their report on all that had happened. He was delighted. He even, in the rush of his enthusiasm, agreed to the Annual Sports Competition with Flannon, to be held, said Sonny, in each Island alternately. Later he scratched his head a bit at the prospect of all the arrangements this would entail, but after all it would only be every other year.......

Murgo, Gogo, and Sonny then retired thankfully to the Murgo home, and the welcome of Mrs. Murgo and an excited Tobo. He was over the moon as he listened to their story! Vinit had prevailed and he had got his Dad back! And Flannon was going to be the latest in all that was modern and innovative! Oh wow!

However they all had to get their feet back on the ground for the new working week. Sonny was back at school the next day without having had to take any leave. He was a little shattered both physically and mentally, but at least his parents had not had to suffer. He was very careful of them these days, appreciating their forbearance and knowing the future would be costly for them. During the week he gave special attention to their comfort and convenience. He did little extras like buying his Mum bunches of flowers out of his pocket money, or offering to do jobs for his Dad. They must not feel they had lost him.

At night he reflected on all that had happened. Gogo and he had actually witnessed first-hand the beginnings of a rebellion erupting directly as a result of bad management. That was a lesson for him to take on board!

When Gogo arrived the next Friday he was eager to hear what had been happening.

"Well not much news yet," said Gogo. "No news at all from Flannon. I expect we will hear in due course. I've been to see Mother Fulati a couple of times to see how she is getting on and to see if she needs anything. She's hired a girl to go there each week-day. She's a good gardener, and seems to have an aptitude for mixing up the brews and things. She's called Sitar. Sisko flew over to meet with her. He is still in awe about his investiture thingy. He needs company to talk about it, and he knows she will like to see friends just now. No news from Selina yet. Anyway let's go."

"Shall we go straight to Mother Fulati's to say hi first?" suggested Sonny.

"Good idea but we can't stay long because Mum is waiting."

Mother Fulati hurried out when she saw them.

"Hello you two! Lovely to see you. Let's walk out here for a minute," she said.

"That's all we can do right now Mother," said Gogo. "Sonny wanted to say hello, but we have to get home. Have you had any news from Selina yet?"

"Just a quick note. She has to write when birds are coming our way. She's finding it all very strange of course, but they have all made her very welcome and comfortable. She has started working with Madame Eleanor."

"Well that's all the news we can expect just yet I suppose. I hope she gets on with Madame Eleanor. You should go and pay them a visit fairly soon Mother," said Sonny.

"Yes," said Mother Fulati, "that will be nice sometime, but the King doesn't really like me going far."

"You are a good friend and support to him Mother," said Sonny.

"Yes. Sometimes there is a person in your life you can never get along without you know," said Mother Fulati.

They all looked at the poppies tossing their red heads.

"Anyway, send me a message any time Mother if there is anything I can do for you," said Sonny. "If need be I can come any night you know."

"You are good boys, you two and Tobo, and you bring me much comfort just now when I am missing Selina. I'll soon get used to it. I just need to know she is happy."

"She will be Mother when she has settled down," said Gogo, "but we had better go now if you will excuse us. We'll come tomorrow."

The Murgos were about to start breakfast when they arrived, and Sonny and Gogo joined them. Hot muffins! Sonny and Gogo exploded with laughter. Murgo joined in heartily.

"Oh dear!" said Sonny, wiping his eyes, "any news yet from Flannon?"

"Not yet," said Murgo. "Vinit promised send news in a week or so. Now think carefully. What did you learn from that experience? Sonny?"

"Er. That a King must shoulder his responsibilities if his Island is to prosper. If he doesn't have all the qualities necessary to govern he must appoint a Chief Minister who can supply them."

"Good," said Murgo, "Gogo?"

"Every single person must put his hand to his own plough, and do the work he is given to do. An Island doesn't run itself. It needs its' citizens to work hard and faithfully if everyone is to enjoy the comforts and security of a well-run country."

"Good Gogo. You weren't there Tobo, but what are your thoughts?"

"That we have to grow up mentally as well as physically, said Tobo. "Children know other people will look after them, but when they are old enough to do things themselves, they should do them and not expect to be looked after for ever."

"Excellent. And if we are to grow in our lives we need learn from the examples around us."

"And," said Mrs. Murgo, "from time to time there is an unexpected reward!"

The boys looked at her respectfully.

"Sometimes even," she said, "we have only to look in the fridge!"

"'Yippee!" cried Tobo, and rushed to the fridge. There, ready on a plate, was the yummiest ice-cream –cake they had ever seen, with layers of chocolate, vanilla, and strawberry, and a mixed fruit topping!

They were soon tucking into very generous servings.

"This is the best way to end an adventure," murmured Sonny contentedly.

Ingram Content Group UK Ltd.
Milton Keynes UK
UKHW020045210623
423745UK00014B/435

9 781916 626362